THE PRIVILEGE OF PEACE

**The finest in Fantasy and Science Fiction
by TANYA HUFF from DAW Books:**

The Peacekeeper Novels:
AN ANCIENT PEACE (#1)
A PEACE DIVIDED (#2)
THE PRIVILEGE OF PEACE (#3)

The Confederation Novels:
A CONFEDERATION OF VALOR
Valor's Choice/The Better Part of Valor
THE HEART OF VALOR (#3)
VALOR'S TRIAL (#4)
THE TRUTH OF VALOR (#5)
❖ ❖ ❖

THE SILVERED
❖ ❖ ❖

THE ENCHANTMENT EMPORIUM (#1)
THE WILD WAYS (#2)
THE FUTURE FALLS (#3)
❖ ❖ ❖

SMOKE AND SHADOWS (#1)
SMOKE AND MIRRORS (#2)
SMOKE AND ASHES (#3)
❖ ❖ ❖

BLOOD PRICE (#1)
BLOOD TRAIL (#2)
BLOOD LINES (#3)
BLOOD PACT (#4)
BLOOD DEBT (#5)
BLOOD BANK (#6)
❖ ❖ ❖

THE COMPLETE KEEPER CHRONICLES
Summon the Keeper/The Second Summoning/Long Hot Summoning
❖ ❖ ❖

THE QUARTERS NOVELS, Volume 1:
Sing the Four Quarters/Fifth Quarter
THE QUARTERS NOVELS, Volume 2:
No Quarter/The Quartered Sea
❖ ❖ ❖

WIZARD OF THE GROVE
Child of the Grove/The Last Wizard
❖ ❖ ❖

OF DARKNESS, LIGHT, AND FIRE
Gate of Darkness, Circle of Light/The Fire's Stone

TANYA HUFF

THE PRIVILEGE OF PEACE

Peacekeeper: Book Three

DAW BOOKS, INC.

DONALD A. WOLLHEIM, FOUNDER

375 Hudson Street, New York, NY 10014

ELIZABETH R. WOLLHEIM
SHEILA E. GILBERT
PUBLISHERS

www.dawbooks.com

First Printing, June 2018
1 2 3 4 5 6 7 8 9

For Sheila Huijbregts, who has the patience of a saint.
And for *her* Torin, who'll take us into the future.

And with thanks to Phil Mills, who helped me sound like I
almost understood my descriptions of coding.

ONE

"**REMIND ME TO TELL** the commander we need more recruits from the Navy," Torin muttered, checking the seals on Binti's HE suit.

"That a comment about my piloting?" Craig asked as he maneuvered the *Promise* into position, carefully avoiding the line of sight from both Mictok Station Trilik and the pirate ship tucked between the station and the gas giant.

"You're the best damn pilot I ever saw," Torin told him, "but a boarding party says Navy to me."

"A *serley* small boarding party," Werst grumbled as Ressk checked his seals. "We need more recruits. Period. I'm not saying we aren't the definition of kickass," he continued, "but there's only the four of us going in."

"There's only six non-Mictok on the station and two on the ship," Alamber pointed out. "I'll be into the system as soon as you're inside, Craig will take the ship, and—given you're facing less than two-to-one odds—I don't understand why Binti and Ressk are going."

Werst's nostril ridges flared. "When you put it like that, it does seem like overkill."

"No one dies," Torin reminded them, using the pressure of her chin against the suit's wide collar to turn the magnetic plates in her boots on, then off again. "Pirates may be a waste of oxygen, but I'm not spending the better part of a tenday filling out paperwork before having my ass hauled before the Rehabilitation Committee so I can explain why social expectations weren't met."

Binti grinned. "By us or by them?"

"Either. Or."

The Hazardous Environment suits were bright orange, di'Taykan danger orange, although the color had been chosen for its visibility rather than any cultural reason. *"The Marines don't leave people behind,"* Staff Sergeant Beyhn had told Torin's group of recruits, as he'd told a hundred groups before and would tell a hundred after. *"If you have one of these on,"* he'd added before the warm fuzzy feeling of belonging had faded, *"we've got a chance of finding your body even if the beacon craps out."*

The suits worn by Strike Team Alpha were Marine Corps suits, or as ex-Marine as Torin, Werst, Ressk, and Binti Mashona. The Warden's insignia on the center chest was less overt than the Justice Department preferred, but as the Strike Teams were considerably more overt than the Justice Department preferred, Torin figured it balanced in the end. The helmet made use of H'san technology and held two different shapes; down the back like an empty bag and snapped up over the head into a rigid polarized sphere. Helmet up, the suit could support the tanks by filtering any combination of external oxygen and nitrogen into something essentially breathable. It recycled all fluids almost indefinitely. Self-contained, the suits were comfortable for six hours, livable for eight, and, if breathing remained an option, became progressively nastier after that.

If all went well, they'd be out of the suits before the plumbing had a chance to recycle the morning's pouch of coffee.

Torin didn't expect it to go well. Precedent aside, the anticipation of all hell breaking loose helped keep her people alive. Suits secured, she checked with Binti and the two Krai, then turned toward the control panel. "Ready when you are."

"We'll be in position in five," Craig told her. "Opening inner airlock door."

The airlock opened into the control room. Back when Craig Ryder had been a Civilian Salvage Operator, the control room had been the *Promise's* single cabin, the greater part of the ship the Susumi drive. Justice had upgraded and expanded the *Promise* when she'd nearly been destroyed by pirates, adding the ability to attach packets as needed, but she remained Craig's ship. The other Strike Team pilots flew decommissioned Navy Corvettes—the smallest Naval vessel with a Susumi drive. The other Strike Team pilots would have shit themselves before ghosting into docking position on a gas giant mining station using momentum and air jets and hard-earned skill.

"We're still a surprise, Boss," Alamber called from the second seat as the inner door opened and Torin led the four suited members of her team into the airlock. "Speed matched to within five point seven kilometers an hour. Exit in seven minutes . . . mark."

The countdown appeared on the lower right curve of her helmet.

The inner door sealed, and the pressure began to equalize.

"You really think we can take back the station with six people, Gunny?"

"How many people do we have?"

Behind the lightly polarized surface of her helmet, Binti's brows rose. "Six."

"Then we'll take back the station with six people."

There'd been a rise in violence in Sector Seven—in MidSector as well as OutSector—spreading the Strike Teams thin, preventing them from doubling up. Torin would have preferred to take more Wardens into the pirate-held station, but as there weren't any available, her preferences were moot.

The six of them, in pre-Strike Team Alpha days, had taken down an entire pirate fleet. A single ship draining the tanks at a Mictok-run mining station should be a walk in the cake. Torin frowned. Maybe not cake. Pie? Not for the first time, she missed the late Sergeant Hollice and his command of oldEarth idiom.

Over the last five tendays, three other mining stations had been hit, quick and quiet, the Wardens informed after the fact. The violence had been minimal by Torin's standards, but two Mictok and a Bril had been killed. The Elder Races hadn't fought back because the Elder Races didn't fight back, which was one of the reasons the strike teams existed—the Younger Races cleaning up the damage done to their three species over the long years of the war. That said, everyone agreed the Bril's death had been accidental. They were a strangely fragile species with some of their important parts in unexpected places. Informed of the previous attacks, the manager of Mictok Station Trilik had adopted the very non-Mictok attitude of assuming the worst and had deployed long-range scanners. The moment the scanners had picked up an unscheduled tanker in-system, they'd sent a message to Berbar Station, the Justice headquarters in Seventh Sector and evacuated all but essential personnel, fully aware that had they waited until the tanker came close enough to identify, it would have been too late. The pirates would have blocked the signal.

Having noticed ships leaving the station en masse, smart pirates would have headed for home. Perhaps the pirates thought the Mictok—who had close to a monopoly on mining the Confederation's gas giants—hadn't shared information about the previous attacks. Perhaps they thought the Mictok would be embarrassed to send for help before they knew for certain they needed it. Perhaps they'd never actually spoken to a Mictok, as Torin didn't think it was possible to embarrass one of the giant spiders. Perhaps, after three successful robberies, they'd gotten cocky. There hadn't been resistance, so there wouldn't be resistance.

Wrong.

Three minutes.

With the pressure equalized, the outer airlock door opened.

One minute.

"Speed matched to within six meters per hour. Five. Four. Three . . ."

"On my word." Torin watched the seconds count down.

"Speed matched."

Three. Two . . .

"Go! Go! Go!"

The *Promise* was one hundred and one meters from the station—one meter closer and the station's docking computers would have taken over, announcing their approach. Craig could have nestled his ship up to the airlock—to any airlock—without help, but the Mictok insisted on safety first, most likely because a good seventy percent of the gas they mined was combustible. Thirty percent of the seventy was highly combustible. The potential for disaster put the docking arm used for the arrival and departure of personnel on the opposite side of the station from the gas giant, the bulk of the station a shield against the planetary storms and the tanks filled with potential explosives. This also put the airlock the Strike Team was heading for on the opposite side from the tanks and the pirates emptying them.

On the one hand, they were less likely to be seen.

On the other, they had the entire width of the station to cross once inside.

Torin unmagged her boots three meters before she hit metal, twisting and allowing the much less powerful magnets in her gloves to make first contact, preventing eighty-six accelerating kilograms from slamming into the station and setting off an impact alarm. The piercing, panic-inducing nature of the alarm meant no one, on any station, wanted the sensors reacting to every passing piece of space debris so only those large enough, fast enough, or solid enough to damage the outer hull set off the klaxons. These large, fast, and solid measurements were consistent across the Confederation and, for all Torin's comments about the Navy, the entire boarding party had done this before. A few meters to the right, Ressk filled her peripheral vision. Werst touched down above them, his head to theirs. Binti's aim had put her close enough to the airlock controls she had to shift to the left when Ressk hand-walked over.

No one expected people to cross vacuum and open the door. No one set alarms for the unexpected.

On the other hand, as no one wanted personnel trapped outside a station should the worst happen, the emergency access codes for the airlocks were also consistent across the Confederation.

Torin believed the definition of *the worst* needed changing.

By the time Ressk had keyed in the access codes and the outer door had begun to open, they'd all moved close enough to quickly slip inside.

The inner door opened automatically when the pressure equalized, reminding Torin of how few Primacy attacks had come this far into the MidSectors.

All life signs still gathered at the tanks, Boss—six Human, two Miktok.

Humans had been the only species positively identified by survivors at the other stripped stations. "Please tell me the two life signs still on the pirate ship aren't Human."

Wish I could, Boss, but the ship has a hard shell up and I can't get more than the basics. The happy making news is that I've got clean air and, even happier, no one's monitoring the station sysop. You're clear to advance.

"You heard him, people." Torin unsealed her helmet, rigidity releasing as it dropped down her back. "Let's go."

Sergeants and above came out of both branches of the military with communication implants set into their jawbone. About two thirds of the Strike Team personnel had arrived with implants, and Justice had offered installations to the rest. Weapons used during the thefts at the earlier stations raised the odds the pirates were ex-military although there'd been no other identifiers. Once they had the stations locked down, they transferred the contents of the storage tanks, and were gone—no images, no sounds, no DNA left behind. If the assumption of a military background was correct, a percentage of the pirates had to have implants, opening a way for the Strike Teams to eavesdrop or jack in and use the technology as a weapon.

This trip out, Alamber had been unable to locate a signal.

With Mictok held hostage, they were left with no option but to put boots on deck and do it the hard way.

Out of the docking arm, the corridors through the station were wide and well lit, the bulkheads covered in the art the Mictok were admired for throughout the Confederation. Considering that a high percentage of Confederate species were mammals and the Mictok most decidedly were not, that either made art a universal language or art critics as a subspecies listened to their hindbrains and refused to piss the Mictok off. Torin glanced over at the thick ridges of color and decided it was likely six of one, half a dozen of the other.

Excluding the tanks and the docking arms, the station was round; eight main corridors headed diagonally from the rim into a central space. Their path took them in, across the center, and out. Fast and easy. Except that the central space had been filled with webbing. Going around meant backtracking and making their way through side corridors that hadn't been designed for the convenience of bipedal visitors.

"Fuk me," Werst muttered.

As they approached, Torin studied the thick white cables laid out in an obvious path through the middle of the web and knew if she stopped on the edge, she might not get going again. Knew that if she kept running, so would her team.

"You know, without boots," Ressk began just behind her left hip.

"No." Krai feet were almost as flexible as their hands, and Ressk wasn't wrong; without their boots they could cross the webbing as quickly as a Mictok, but no one skimmed out of an HE suit. If they'd had that kind of time, they could've gone around.

The web flexed as Torin landed on it, one boot on one cable, the other on an identical cable fifteen centimeters away. A continuation of the main corridor design for visiting bipeds, the cables had been connected by a thinner cable in a pattern woven too closely to slip through. Slipping *off* didn't appear to have been considered. Mictok didn't slip. The cables rose and fell under Torin's boots, the undulations rhythmic enough she could keep her balance.

Until Ressk joined her. Just over a meter high, he was heavier than he looked, and his shorter stride on the cables set up a competing rhythm. When Binti joined them, the cable went up where a stride before it had gone down. Torin's right leg sank knee-deep into the interior webbing before springing back up again with enough force her knee nearly smacked her in the chin. She'd have fallen had the gravity not been a third less than she was used to and had Ressk not grabbed the loop of strapping at her hip and thrown his weight against it.

The whole web rippled.

"Werst . . ." She swayed, but regained her balance. ". . . implant cadence. Double-time."

From the back of the march—historically, pre-implant, the position most likely to be heard, codified over the centuries by the militaries of all three Younger Races—Werst began a mouth-closed hum, laying down a rhythm they'd all been trained to follow. A rhythm that let their feet move without any interference from their brains.

It's too narrow.

It's wobbling.

It's a web!

Which was not to say Torin's brain, at least, didn't try.

"That was fun," Binti forced out through clenched teeth as she reached the other side. "I vote we strip to our skivvies and travel through the cold, merciless vacuum of space on the way back."

"Be a lot easier without boots," Ressk agreed.

"Missing my point," Binti told him. "It's a spider thing."

"Human spider thing," Werst grunted, jumping up onto the deck beside his bonded.

I saw that vid. I didn't get how they could have missed the obvious thing to do with eight arms.

"Alamber . . ." A di'Taykan could turn anything to innuendo. And, if given the chance, usually did. That said, he had a point about the eight arms.

Still a clear run to the tanks, Boss.

"Let's go, people."

The control room for the mining operation took up about a third of the arc facing the gas giant and overlooked the two docking positions on either side of the stacked tanks. The pirates, plus the Mictok hostages, were currently in the control room. It being unlikely they'd surrender without a fight, Torin wanted the pirates in one of the docking arms, an area designed to deal with explosive decompression.

On this mission, Strike Team Alpha carried bennies. Made up of a molecular disruption charge and a cutting laser, they were designed for use on ships and stations. The MDC exploded the cellular structure of organics, the amount of damage dependent on a combination of power level and length of contact. The cutting laser, while not originally intended to be a weapon, had certainly been used as one, but both options lessened the danger of random holes in the hull. This trip out, in their continuing effort to keep the Strike Teams from shooting people, R&D had also equipped each of them with species-specific gas grenades—three grenades per Warden, one grenade for each of the Younger Races.

In their previous attacks on the mining stations, the pirates had carried KC-7s, the standard Marine weapon that fired explosively propelled solids and was immune to enemy EMPs. Or, on occasion, badly aimed friendly EMPs.

I have control of the station, Boss. You're about a minute thirty to the hatch.

"Craig?"

Ready when you are, Torin.

"Go."

The klaxon blaring from multiple speakers was a sound specific to mining stations; fragile habitats attached to enormous tanks of volatile gasses. Torin knew there were no leaks, no possibility of immediate explosion, but her pulse still pounded at her temples, subharmonics screaming at her hindbrain to run. Run far. Run fast.

They're running.

"Codes?"

Have been changed.

The stream of profanity spilling through the open hatch between the boarding party and the port docking arm suggested the pirates had discovered their airlock codes were no longer functional and they couldn't get to their ship.

Control room access locked down.

Nor could they retreat to the control room.

Torin paused, waited for the team to fall into position, then stepped through the hatch. Clustered around the airlock connecting the station to their ship, were six pretty standard Humans. Two were paler than Torin, their skin the near translucence of those who never saw natural light. One them, a female a good two meters tall, had veins and arteries tattooed on the visible skin of her arms and face. Torin had seen more Human circulatory systems than she'd ever wanted to—including bits of her own—and she found it disconcerting as decoration. The other four were various shades of beige and brown although none of the six came close to matching the deep, rich tones of Binti Mashona. Five of them were yelling.

The sixth . . .

Hey, Boss! There's only one Mictok registering in the control room. The docking arm's too well shielded for me to get a clear signal, but our hostage situation might be ongoing.

"Acknowledged."

You knew that already, didn't you?

"I did."

The sixth pirate held a Mictok up against her body by an eyestalk. The Mictok could have gotten away; the grip allowed her enough lateral movement to bring her mandibles up to soft tissue, but the Mictok were one of the Elder Races. Socially evolved above violence, The Elder Races had formed the Confederation out of likewise evolved species, those who'd reached the ability to destroy themselves and moved past it. Great in theory, less great in actuality when the Primacy had attacked and the Confederation was unable to defend itself. Their solution had been to grant the Younger Races—Humans, Krai, and Taykan—an early membership in exchange for their agreement to fight in an intergalactic war. Torin didn't know about the Krai and the Taykan, but Human history said they'd taken one look at the advantages, signed on the dotted line, and chambered a round. The end of the war had flooded the Confederation with a large number of all three Younger Races trained to violence, a significant portion of them unwilling to play nicely with others.

The Elder Races were having trouble dealing. Ethically. Politically. Occasionally, one on one.

The Mictok stood on her four rear legs, high enough to take the pressure off her eyestalk. The four legs in the air waved ineffectually. Torin could see the reflection of her HE suit as a line of orange across the smooth black surface of the Mictok's eyes, but she could see no way to get the hostage clear without damage. Or death. Not the death of the Mictok, granted, but coldly killing the pirate had to be a last resort.

"They're all Human, Gunny."

As they so often were these days. "Prep grenades. Deploy on my word. Alamber, turn off the alarm."

The shouting carried on for a moment in the sudden silence then, voice by voice, stopped until the only voice came through the speaker by the access hatch. *What the hell is going on in there?*

"Wardens," Torin answered. "You're under arrest. You, on the ship, power down. You lot . . ." She swept her gaze around the pirates gathered by the hatch, three of the captive Mictok's eyes following the sweep. ". . . drop your weapons."

"Fuk you, Warden!" The speaker was the eldest by a visible margin, his skin wrapped loosely around muscle and bone, the lines around eyes and mouth scored deep.

I have control of exteriors, Boss. They're locked on the nipple.

"We have your ship secured," Torin told them, her tone slipping from Warden to gunnery sergeant, leaving no room for disbelief. "You have nowhere to go. Drop your weapons, surrender, and I'll ask the Dornagain to go easy on you."

"What are they going to do?" the tattooed woman sneered, even as the barrel of her KC had begun to dip toward the floor. "Bureaucracy us to death?"

"Stacks of forms in triplicate," Torin acknowledged. "It's terrifying to watch."

One smile. One dawning realization. Four cornered rats. Tough room.

"We could shoot our way out!" one of the rats snarled, waving his weapon in a way that made Torin think of recruits who wanted to hit back after a lifetime of being bullied. They seldom made it through basic.

"Don't be an idiot," the eldest snapped before Torin could respond. "They've only got bennies!"

"Because *they're* not idiots. You don't carry projective weapons in a station, for fuksake." Odds were high that muttered observation had come from one of the two who were spacer pale. Torin suspected it was the weight of that knowledge, pounded into thick heads by Marine and Navy DI's, that had kept them from firing the moment they'd realized they were trapped.

"So we trash the station! Who cares?"

Torin met the tattooed woman's eyes and raised a brow. Got a silent *What can you do?* in return. Ex-Navy. Petty officer at least.

"You want us, Warden?"

Torin snapped her gaze back to the woman holding the Mictok. She was a good half meter shorter than Torin, with the kind of wiry build and ropy muscle that told of poor nutrition through puberty. Not everyone chose to accept the Confederation's guarantee of a healthy standard of living. Enclaves of Humans insisted on living the way they believed Humans should live—back to the land, happily ignoring that the land was on a planet very different from the planet they'd evolved on making *back* irrelevant. Torin had served with a few and every one of them had resented the hell out of the way they'd been forced to grow up. She could see that same resentment in this woman's pale eyes, along with a good dose of crazy.

"You want us?" she snarled again, lips drawn back off her teeth, the cords in her neck prominent, a shimmer across the lower third of her face. She shifted her grip on the Mictok's eyestalk and placed her other hand flat against the gleaming curve of exoskeleton. "Fine. But we're not going down without a fight."

The Mictok howled.

The hair lifted off the back of Torin's neck. She saw the muzzle of a KC rise and flipped her helmet up. "Gas!"

The Mictok tucked her legs in and keened.

Torn ducked the thrown eyestalk, leapt the arc of glossy black carapace . . .

The pirate collapsed, screaming as Torin's right heel shattered her leg and Torin's left hand ripped the filter off her face. Her eyes widened as she sucked in air, then rolled back, then closed.

"Gunny! They're all down."

Blood roared in Torin's ears.

"Torin! The ship's doing a runner!"

Not blood. Engines powering up way too close to the station. "How'd they get off the nipple?"

"They haven't. Yet!"

Translation: They were about to rip their way free. The clamps on military stations had been designed with a breakaway option, in case the station took damage and ships had to be launched. Civilian stations were missing this helpful feature. When the ship ripped away, a chunk of the station would rip away with it.

"Alpha Team!" The deck plates buckled. Boots unmagged, she rode it out. "Grab a body! Get out of the docking arm and secure the hatch!" She closed her fist around a handful of overalls, turned, rocked in place, and realized the injured Mictok had begun to spew webbing. When stressed, they webbed themselves into small spaces. Seemed they considered the potential for explosive decompression stressful.

They weren't wrong.

"Mashona!" Torin swung the pirate up and over the Mictok. "Get her out!"

Metal screamed. Alarms screamed back.

Had the webbing been as thick as the webbing across the station's center, it would've been faster to pry up the deck plates. Fortunately, propelled by pain and panic, these strands had been extruded in fits and starts, only a few actually connecting to bulkheads or deck, and none of them had completely solidified.

The docking arm tipped thirty degrees.

Torin dropped one knee to the deck and slashed at the sticky white strands holding the Mictok in place.

"Torin! Move!"

"Working on it!" The last strand cut, she flipped the Mictok over and shoved her toward the inner hatch, legs curled into her belly, curve of her carapace providing almost no friction, dignity sacrificed to survival. "Mashona! Incoming!"

Binti's answer was lost in the crack of a weld separating and the roar of air leaving the station. Torin caught a quick glimpse of the Mictok in Binti's arms, or more precisely, Binti wrapped in the Mictok's legs, before the inner hatch slammed shut and sealed.

"Gunny!"

"Not my first blowout." Staying low, she pivoted and let the escaping air press her against the inside of the outer hatch. "I'm suited, I'm fine." Any injury she could survive counted as fine. The trick would be keeping her suit in one piece as decompression pulled debris toward her. An abandoned KC hit the hatch a centimeter from her elbow and she looped her arm through the strap. It never hurt to pick up another weapon. The hatch buckled, the crack along one edge widening as escaping air shredded the seal. Bottom line, hatches were holes in the hull, and holes in the hull, however functional, would always be the weakest point.

She felt the vibration in her bones when the hatch broke free. Boots and gloves magged full, Torin rode the slab of metal out into open space.

Proximity readouts along the lower edge of her helmet spiked.

Open, like empty, being a relative word.

Shards of the nipple. Shards of the clamps. Shards of the arm. Torin felt multiple impacts against the hatch. And if that wasn't enough fun, the pirate's engines had baked the area immediately around the station. The hatch offered her some small amount of protection and while she had a full RAT in her future, as long as the pirates didn't try for a Susumi jump, she'd survive.

As long as she didn't pass directly through the energy trail.

As long as she hadn't been thrown far enough to be caught by the gas giant's gravity well.

As long as she didn't hit something solid and end up crushed between that and the hatch.

She had no idea what would happen should the tanks, on either the ship or the station, rupture. Nor did she want to find out.

Stars whirled around her. She closed her eyes and rode out the spin, teeth clenched. It was common knowledge that the Krai, as a species, never suffered from any kind of motion sickness. Lucky fukking Krai.

Torin!

"I'm fine."

I can't get a line on you until you clear their ship!

Craig had begun to sound a bit frayed. She needed to get on top of that. "Sitrep?"

Like that, then? Fine. I've grapples on the ship. The bastards aren't moving. Their shielding thinned over the bow when they surged ahead; Alamber was on the knocker and took control.

Microsecond window, Boss, but I'm just that good.

"Werst?"

Station lost some pressure, but emergency seals are holding. Bad guys have been restrained. Hostage seems to have a little trouble telling the good guys from the bad guys and won't shut the fuk up. I haven't shot her.

"I'll make a note of your restraint on the . . ." The hatch hit something big. Torin's teeth snapped together. She swallowed a mouthful of blood, realized she'd stopped moving, and unmagged her gloves to have a look.

She'd impacted with the pirates' ship, high on the port side. The hatch had either picked up some free-floating magnetism from the explosion, or emergency protocols had magnetized it for easier recovery, or the ship's hull had been magnetized by passing space pixies— Torin neither knew nor cared. There'd been no equal and opposite reaction flinging her out into space on a new trajectory, and that was all that mattered. Off the hatch and onto the ship, she clumped up to the clear arc that allowed the persons in the control room to look out at space. The members of the Confederation were split eighty/twenty on the need for a visual backup, if only in the control room. Humans acknowledged windows were an unnecessary affectation, that if their instruments went dead, they were in a lot more trouble than eyeballs alone could rectify, and remained firmly in the twenty percent. Structural integrity be damned, they wanted a window.

"Alamber. Patch me through to their control room."

You're in, Boss.

She could see a Human male scurrying from station to station, blood dribbling down his face from a split high on his cheek. With her boots and one glove attached to the ship, she slammed the butt of her rescued KC against the clear ceramic three times.

BOOM!

BOOM!

BOOM!

She couldn't hear the impact, but the man in the control room could. He leapt back, tripped over his own feet, and stared up at her from his sprawl on the deck.

Torin depolarized her helmet and smiled. "You're under arrest, asshole."

"C&C will be here in two hours and twelve minutes." The Clean-up Crew—predominantly of Dornagain, Rakva, and Niln—never arrived until after all possibility of shooting had ended. Unfortunately, as the C&C ship contained the brig as well as a full medical suite, the Strike Teams were stuck making small talk until they arrived. First aid could only be applied to prisoners for so long before it became unnecessary touching and had, as expected, been applied to these particular prisoners while Torin took the scenic route back from her unscheduled EVA. She swept a measuring gaze over her people as she stepped into the station control room. With the plumbing hooked in, stripping out of the suit became not only a more complicated procedure, but one that required a minimum of privacy. In a room with both the Mictok and the prisoners as an audience, the other three members of the team had remained suited. Torin had stripped out of hers on her way through the *Promise*. Stripped, dressed, took the first course of radiation meds, and reassured both Craig and Alamber that she was fine. The Corps considered multitasking a promotion requirement for a third hook, two further promotions and five years out hadn't diminished her ability. "Mashona, sitrep."

Binti nodded toward the line of zip-tied Humans sitting against the curve of the inner wall, prudently away from any live equipment. "No injuries on the side of right. The bad guys have been bagged and tagged. They shook off the gas over thirty to forty-seven minutes depending on mass, and are all reporting headaches. Unanimous description: the back of my fukking head feels like it's in a vise."

"Poor sweet babies." Torin saw another discussion with R&D in her future. Thirty to forty-seven minutes wasn't long enough. Their desire to do no damage to a sentient species might be admirable, but they needed to stop trying to reinvent the wheel and talk to planetary law enforcement.

"Yeoman Fredrick Solomon had a nose bleed, which is why he looks like a slaughterhouse."

"I have sensitive sinuses," the eldest pirate muttered, cracking the dried blood on his upper lip.

"He does," Binti agreed. "We used his spray to stop the bleeding. And you seem to have broken Private Marie Neems' leg."

The woman who'd ripped the eyestalk off her captive sat with her right leg immobilized, her left ankle zip-tied to the inflated sleeve, her expression the slack muscled, not-quite-there that came with the good drugs.

"Fuk you," Neems slurred. "Fuk both of you. I'm nobody's private."

"The happy drugs have not made her happy," Binti added, grinning.

"My bet, anger's the biggest part of her core programming." Ressk moved closer and lowered his voice. "We couldn't retrieve the eyestalk. I don't suppose you grabbed it during your exit?"

The emphasis on exit made it sound as though she'd been skiving off. Because none of them were the type to overreact to explosive decompression. "I did not."

"Pity." He frowned. "Do they regrow? Eyestalks?"

"No idea. You and Mashona go get out of your suits. Werst and I will stay here. You go when they get back," she added as Werst began a protest. "No one stays alone with the prisoners. We're doing this by the book. Go." She layered a few silent consequences for delay onto the command.

Werst and Ressk exchanged a speaking glance that Torin chose to ignore, then Ressk followed Binti out the hatch.

"By the book." Folded hands resting on his weapon, Werst stared up at her. "How pissed is Ryder about your unplanned exit?"

As a Civilian Salvage Operator, Craig had spent years in and out of vacuum, enough time his HE suit had left permanent divots in his skin. A good fifty percent of the battle debris CSOs dealt in couldn't be tagged from the ship and, working alone, Craig had done all the up close and personal inspections himself. He understood what it took to survive in vacuum and, although he trusted Torin's ability to keep herself alive, he hadn't been happy when she'd been flung from the station.

Too many variables," he'd growled, slotting her suit into the charge station. "*And nothing you could do about half of them.*"

"*Don't let that get out. I have a reputation to uphold.*"

"A reputation won't keep you alive."

She'd sealed her uniform tunic, leaned forward, and kissed him. He was right.

Werst couldn't react to her being flung out into space, but Craig could. The job couldn't acknowledge how many ways there were to die while dealing with the lingering violence of a centuries-old war, but the relationship could. Craig could say, *"You scared the crap out of me, don't do that again."* Werst said it by asking about Craig.

It was emotionally constipated, but it worked for them.

"Didn't answer my question, Gunny."

"No, I didn't," she acknowledged.

"All right, then." Gloves retracted into his sleeves, Werst scratched under the edge of the suit's collar. "What happened to their pilot?"

"He's locked on their ship. He's armed himself and set up to take us out as we come through the airlock, but I expect he'll get bored eventually. Oh, and Alamber's running Taykan opera through the sound system."

Werst snickered. "Kid's got a mean streak."

Humans found Taykan music half a tone sharp. "How are the Mictok?"

He shrugged. The Krai had never quite gotten the hang of the Human gesture, but had enthusiastically adopted it regardless. "Told us not to bother them, that they were keeping the station from exploding."

Torin glanced over at the corner where the injured Mictok sat, damaged eyestalk covered in webbing, the other Mictok, the one who'd been left in the control room, had webbed her into place with several thick strands. Pulled out of her ass. Or close enough to make little difference. *Get it off me. Get it off me.* "Seems like we're out of danger. Go get out of your suit as soon as one of the others returns." She headed toward the corner. "Keep an eye on the prisoners."

Werst acknowledged the order, then added, lip curled, "They're being stoically silent."

"Our lucky day." The background clatter of two pairs of mandibles beating out one of the Mictok languages stopped as Torin drew close enough for conversation. "If you need medical," she said, meeting two of the injured Mictok's remaining eyes, "we can secure the control room."

"And who are you?"

It was almost refreshing to run into someone unfamiliar with the vid of Torin confronting the plastic aliens. "Warden Torin Kerr. I'm the leader of this Justice Department Strike Team."

"Oh, you are, are you? The leader?" A slender arm waved dismissively. "You're Human. They're Human. And yet you needed Krai to help you take out your trash."

The Mictok spoke Federate. Torin couldn't blame the staccato sentences on a bad translation. "I beg your pardon?"

"We should never have allowed such an inferior species into the Confederation! You have no respect for life. You brought nothing with you but violence!"

"We were invited into the Confederation to fight a war the Elder Races were losing," Torin pointed out.

"You don't know that! You're barely sentient! You're repeating what you were told!"

"How do we know you didn't bring the war with you?" All eight of the uninjured Mictok's eyestalks turned to Torin. "How do we know you didn't start the war? You wanted Confederation technology, so you lied to make us think we needed you!"

"We never saw a war!" the injured Mictok snapped.

Torin raised her hand and touched the place where, had she been wearing her combat vest, the cylinders holding the remains of dead Marines would rest, ready to be carried home. No Marine left behind.

"Humans attacked the station and took our harvest, too violent to work for what they want!" The uninjured Mictok jabbed a digit at Torin. "Humans, Taykan, Krai; the Younger Races should go back where they came from. You should all go back where you came from. We are lesser because of you!"

"You should shut the fuk up, bug!"

For a moment, just a moment, Torin thought the words had been hers. Then she realized Neems had taken an interest in the conversation.

"We died for you, you creepy crawly bigot!" Voice slurred by the painkiller, she still achieved impressive volume.

"Yeah? Says who? You? Why should we believe you? Why should we take your word for it?"

Neems squirmed into a more upright position, lips curled back from her teeth. "You don't have to take my fukking word for it, there's vids . . ."

"Fake."

Torin, who'd faced down generals and giant lizards in her time, maintained a neutral reaction to the Mictok's declaration.

Neems did not. "Fuk you, bug!"

"So easy for you to fake," the uninjured Mictok mocked. "None of the Elder Races were there to prevent the lie."

"Gunny . . ."

Torin's hands had curled into fists. She straightened her fingers and returned to Werst's side.

"Are all Mictok assholes?" he muttered under the sound of Neems listing increasingly creative ways the present Mictok could messily die.

"Statistically unlikely." But the only Mictok she'd known had been diplomats, and diplomats were by trade opaque. On Silsviss, they'd painted red crosses on their backs and carried the injured off the battlefield—that had been truth. But could she believe anything they'd said?

The other prisoners had begun egging Neems on.

"Stoically silent?" Torin asked.

"Provoked." Werst turned toward the corner as the injured Mictok shouted something about Krai chewing up the other races and spitting them out. "We swallow," he growled. "We don't waste food." He turned back to face Torin as the prisoners cheered and said, "Can we shut them up, Gunny?"

"The prisoners, probably. But since we can't quiet the Mictok, might as well let them respond."

"We should lock you in the bottom of your gravity wells and let you kill each other!" Consonants had devolved to a snap of mandibles.

"Think you can keep us there?" A fine spray of spit from Neems' mouth glistened under the artificial light.

"We'll take you back to mud and sticks where you savages belong!"

Werst's nostril ridges half closed. "On the other hand, we have gas grenades left. Mixing them together might take the Mictok out."

"The Younger Races are all too stupid to know how close to non-sentient you are!"

"Tempting." Torin acknowledged. "Very tempting."

She could understand the Mictok who'd been taken hostage harboring some resentment. A Human had ripped her eyestalk off. From where she stood, all Humans were violent, unpredictable, dangerous animals. Extending that opinion to the Krai and Taykan indicated more deeply held beliefs, likely influenced by the current political discussions of what to do with the Younger Races now the war was over, the least of which was patronizing, the worse bordering on genocidal. Not that the Elder Races would ever do anything so violent, but an angry Mictok gas tech wasn't the first to suggest confining the Younger Races to specific planets for the safety of the rest.

It wouldn't happen, but the political rhetoric had clearly found adherents who bought in.

None of the planets where the Younger Races would be quarantined had a single species population and every so-called solution ended in massive population displacement. Even on oldEarth, the needs of the embassies had created multispecies communities, some of the residents there for generations with more right to stay than Torin who'd never been closer to her species' home planet than a four-day Susumi jump.

"You want to see violence?" Neems spat. "The people you want to lock away have all the weapons! And know how to use them!"

She wasn't wrong.

TWO

"**DEFO HUMANS FIRST**," Craig muttered as the pressure equalized and the airlock opened at Berbar Station. "We get in a bingle with a Human crew these days and they're always Humans First. Can't just be violent criminals, can they? They've got to be deranged revolutionaries."

"They've been busy little bipeds," Torin agreed and counted the demo charges before handing Werst the case. She had no problem with him building an emergency pack—she had one of her own—but he could do it on his time and with gear she wasn't ultimately responsible for. "SOP, people: armory, debriefing . . ."

"Armory, medical," Craig amended as the Strike Team headed down the docking arm. "You went through thirty meters of dirty radiation," he added before Torin could object. "You need to be checked by something more comprehensive than our autodoc."

"I'm . . ."

"You wouldn't let one of us skive off," Ressk said from behind them.

"Fine. Armory, medical, team debrief. I'll let Commander Ng know . . ."

"Told him when we came out of Susumi, Boss."

Torin sighed. "You want to chime in on this, Werst?"

Werst snorted. "Can't see the need."

"Binti?"

"Planned on escorting you, Gunny."

Alamber gave an interested hum and, without turning, Torin knew his pale blue hair had flicked up. "Doc Collins covering this shift?"

"That's what the schedule says." Torin could hear the broad grin in Binti's voice. "And Doc Collins is one fine piece of . . ." Binti paused. ". . . medical practitioner."

"Thank you for not objectifying the support staff," Torin said dryly. There'd been memos. With the number of di'Taykan now on station and the growing number of civilians who'd never previously worked with the di'Taykan, they needed to pay more attention to interspecies compatibility. Military culture had accepted that the Taykan in their di' phase were the most sexually indiscriminating species in known space, tried to keep up, and finally surrendered in exhaustion, cheering from the sidelines. Civilians were . . . complicated.

She paused at the hatch and looked back down the docking arm, her team the only people in sight. Painted a soft gray and illuminated by two strips of pale pink, a color determined by the supplier of said paint to soothe the aggressive tendencies of all three Younger Races, the far end appeared impossibly farther away than Torin knew it to be. She couldn't remember ever seeing the docking arm so empty. It wasn't unusual to have no one between them and the exit, Strike Team Alpha had the closest berth to the station, but it was strange to see the arm empty of mechanics, engineers, or pilots on their way to, or from, the other five ships. At the very least, she'd expect to see someone from the newly formed quartermaster's unit restocking supplies. "Craig, how many ships in?" She hadn't bothered to check as they docked.

"Just us."

"Just us?" Things hadn't been that busy when they'd left.

"You want me to check where the other teams are, Boss?" Alamber had his slate in his hand.

"Please." She could look it up herself, but part of her job involved keeping Alamber from being bored. A bored Alamber liked to prove he could crack security systems like *sainit* shells.

Commander Ng had pointed out to his superiors that Alamber provided an essential service, and the end result wasn't so much official approval as an inability among the senior staff, Elder Races all, to come to a decision. As the only ranking Human Warden available when Torin had suggested armed response teams be part of the Justice Department rather than private contractors, Ng had been given command by default. He'd been a Justice lawyer when duty had called him to the tribunal examining culpability for the destruction of Vrijheid Station, his rank was a title without substance, and Torin had expected him to hand the Strike Teams over to a replacement with military training at the first opportunity.

His reason for remaining in charge had been succinct. *"This is not, nor must it ever become a military operation."*

Torin had come to agree with him and, shortly thereafter, had come to respect him. She'd definitely had worse COs.

"Sent the duty list to your slate, Boss. Delta and Beta are out together, but the rest are one on one."

"So not one hefty, all in incident," Craig added. When Torin glanced over at him, he grinned. "Tell me that wasn't what had your knickers in a knot."

Torin grinned back as she unclipped her slate. "I may have wondered why we weren't invited to the party." Alamber's version of the duty list included the full briefing packets each team had received before leaving, technically not something he should've been able to access. She quickly flipped through the files, separating out enough information to settle immediate concerns, then buried them in with the C&C report Alamber had pulled the moment *Promise* came in range of the station. The Strike Teams had access to C&C at the full debrief, not before, but Torin liked to be forewarned.

Finds Truth Through Inquiry had pulled confessions from the prisoners on Mictok Station Trilik with impressive speed in spite of the Dornagain's preference for paper and their belief that slow and ancient ways of communicating helped the prisoners consider their position. Most of the Strike Teams assumed it was a form of punishment. According to the time stamp, Truth had sent the first files on their way to Justice even before *Promise* had reached the traffic buoy and jumped.

The Humans First manifesto had been scribbled over Marie Neems' prisoner identification form.

"We shall take what is our due. We shall fight to take our rightful place. We have bled for the Confederation, and that makes it ours. I'm not filling this shit out!"

The first three declarations were obviously a regurgitation of the party line. Torin doubted Neems would spontaneously use *shall*.

The passageway outside the docking arm was also emptier than usual. Not surprising; fewer people to support, fewer support personnel. Torin nodded at two Niln engineers as they passed and turned her team toward the armory—situated far enough from the DA that it shouldn't go up if the arm was destroyed, far enough from the rest of the station to be jettisoned by emergency protocols if the engineers had miscalculated. They were no longer at war, but live ordnance was as unforgiving to accident as it was to aggression.

The Strike Teams' entire habitat could be jettisoned if needed, in whole or in part.

On the one hand, Torin wondered what the hell Justice thought was going to happen. On the other, she appreciated that level of paranoia.

Craig leaned in and bumped Torin's shoulder with his. "There's been a lot more of the Humans First shite in the air lately. You think they're up to something?"

"Other than what they say they're up to?" Ressk asked from behind them. "Can't get away from them mouthing off about how they're going to take over the Confederation."

"All mouth, no action," Werst scoffed.

"Yeah?" Ressk turned to his bondmate. "Look at what they're stealing; it's been eighty percent raw materials for the last ten tendays. They're building an infrastructure, and if Anthony Marteau is with them, it's going to be a well-armed infrastructure."

While Marteau had hidden his illegal weapon deals less completely than he'd assumed, unable to anticipate Alamber's familiarity with blackmarket record keeping, he'd been able to hide himself from the Wardens for over a year even though Humans First hadn't been exactly covert of late. Had Torin been able to take the Strike Teams out to kick in a few doors, she knew she could find him. Unfortunately, she also knew that would make them part of the problem they'd been formed to solve. Or contain, at least. Generations of Humans, di'Taykan, and Krai trained to violence and then cut loose wasn't a problem that could be *solved* at the Strike Team level. Using her small celebrity to speak up about the need for expanded veterans services had forced a few people to acknowledge the effects of war, but she doubted she'd accomplished much more than inspiring yet another round of Parliamentary committees.

"If Marteau's making more pistols, we're fukked," Binti declared.

"We can't defend ourselves, let alone anyone else, against a weapon we can't see."

"Pistols could be the least of our problems." Alamber sounded as though he'd given it some thought. "Marteau grew up on the floor at MI, teethed on a KC-7. He's got carbon steel bones and propellant in his blood. I started doing what I do young, and that's made me great . . ."

"And modest," Werst muttered.

Alamber ignored him. "Marteau started younger. Think what kind of weapons he could develop without Parliament peering over his shoulder."

Torin heard the distinct snap of Krai teeth coming together, and Ressk said, "Parliament can shove their constraints up their *gren*."

"Yeah," Binti agreed. "Why send us out with the best when they can send us out with gear approved by committee."

"You didn't think your body count was high enough, then?" Sometimes Craig poked for the sake of poking. This time, he sounded serious.

Binti thought so, too, and answered using the same low growl. "Our body count was too damned high. End the war sooner, though, lower body count."

"The war went on as long as the plastic wanted it to go on," Torin pointed out, keeping her hands at her sides.

"It takes time to collect sufficient data on a new species." The vaguely humanoid plastic alien cocked its head. "Creating extreme situations erases all but essential behaviors and shortens the duration of the study. We began the conflict to shorten the duration of the study, we continued the conflict until we had sufficient data."

"The war was a social science experiment." Torin spat out the words. "It wouldn't have mattered if we'd been using rocks and pointed sticks."

"Might have caught on to them sooner if they'd held us to that," Binti muttered as they entered the armory, then raised her voice, "Hey, Sarge, can you have a look at my bennie? I'm feeling trigger resistance, and I can't find the cause."

Sergeant Urrest was the oldest Krai Torin had ever met. Fine bristles completely covered her head, paler than the lightest of her gray-on-gray mottling, almost white in the bright light behind the armory counter, and her nostril ridges had begun to smooth out. She'd been a lifer, retired only when the Corps had forced her, and had moved immediately from the armory serving 2nd Recar'ta, 1st Battalion to the armory serving the Justice Department's Strike Teams.

"Did you want us keeping our weapons in our quarters?" Torin had asked when the question of hiring Urrest had come up.

Commander Ng's face had blanched.

Sergeant Urrest had helped hire a staff of eight, all of whom seemed happy to concentrate on the Strike Teams' basic weaponry—the KC-7s and the sniper's KC-9, with a significantly smaller variety of ammo than the Corps enjoyed. But then, they had a significantly smaller variety of enemy. There were none of the big KC-12s the heavies carried because there were no heavies. The Humans who became part of the Corps' heavy armor had no trouble finding work. The rare ability to jack into a machine had civilian applications—more civilian than military if truth be told. Torin hoped that the extensive psych evaluations required to become a heavy had weeded out sympathies toward the speciesist rantings of Humans First, but she wasn't counting on it. Every interaction the Strike Teams had with Humans First assumed heavy gunners until proven differently. Better to prep to deal with a problem they'd never face than to have it blow up in their collective faces. Literally, blow up.

Under Urrest, the Strike Teams had personal storage in the armory, but were no longer allowed to walk in and out at will. Weapons were signed for, both arriving and departing. By everyone. When it turned out the definition of *weapons* included personal knives, Urrest had closed her nostril ridges, folded her arms, and stood her ground. They didn't need knives on the station.

Torin knew that. Craig didn't carry a knife. Nor did Alamber. Commander Ng didn't. Their ex-Naval personnel were happy to sign their knives in. The Marines who'd seen combat were not. They followed orders, but they weren't happy about it. Torin's therapist called her blade a crutch. Torin called her therapist a few names in return and skipped the next session for perfectly valid reasons.

Anyone who thought the Marines had completely disarmed were delusional.

"Give it here." Urrest wrapped a hand with prominent knuckles around Binti's weapon and glared down at the energy read. "You recharged on the ship."

"I was trying to isolate the problem."

"Well, stop. It's a bennie, not a KC. What do you know about it, eh?" Urrest swept a narrow-eyed gaze over the rest of them while callused fingertips ran lightly over the stock and barrel. "Anyone else decide to mess with equipment they don't understand? No? Hand them over, then." She nodded down at the live screen on the front of the rack. "And don't skip the thumbprints. I've got more things to do than hunt you lot down."

Torin felt Werst shudder. After Strike Team Alpha's first mission with Urrest in charge of the armory, Urrest had cornered Werst in Musselman's. No she didn't want a beer, damn it, she wanted what she thought were intelligent adults to take responsibility for the safe stowage of dangerous and expensive equipment. Members of the other off-duty Strike Teams in the bar had thought Werst's dressing down and his wide-eyed reaction hysterically funny—mostly because the stream of edged words hadn't been aimed at them. Closed communities ran on gossip and the tale had grown in the telling, resulting in one hundred percent compliance with Urrest's requirements, a better result than any number of less overt reminders. A result the sergeant had been fully aware would occur, given the slight nostril flare she'd flashed at Torin on her way out of the bar.

Snapping her bennie onto the rack, Torin checked that both ID numbers—hers and the weapon's—had registered correctly and carefully pressed her thumbprint onto the screen.

"Nalvon, front and center!" Urrest had a sergeant's ability to fill all available space with her voice. A young di'Taykan emerged from the depths of the armory in answer to her call. "Soon as they're all racked, run these weapons through diagnostics."

His hair flipped back. "Rack says they're fine, Sarge."

Urrest's lip curled. "Rack's not responsible for lives lost if a weapon misfires in the field. We are."

"He's new," Torin said as Nalvon waited for Ressk to finish racking his bennie. Nalvon's hair and eyes were an unforgettable bright orange, his eyes nearly fluorescent with most of his light receptors closed in the shadowless illumination Urrest preferred.

"Served with me at battalion. Wasn't entirely useless," she added, "so when I heard he'd run out his contract, I scooped him up. So far, he's proven to be almost teachable."

While Nalvon's right hand continued moving over the pressure pad, he lifted the left and genially flipped her off.

"I can still kick your ass, boy." Eyes narrowed, she studied Torin's face, glanced over at Nalvon, and focused her attention back on Torin. "Going to be a time when you don't know everyone on the sticks-and-stones part of the station, Gunny, and it's going to happen sooner than you think."

"You know something I don't?" Torin watched Alamber slide in beside the rack, close enough to Nalvon his pale blue hair mixed with the orange.

"I know the oil you prefer on your whetstone's come in. I sent it to your quarters."

Both di'Taykan snickered.

Urrest sighed. "That gets tiresome, boys."

Leaving the armory, Torin made one more attempt to avoid medical. "The autodoc . . ."

Craig cut her off. "I don't give a rat's ass about the autodoc. I want training not programming to have a look. Trained professionals," he amended before she could point out he was the team's medic. "Not talented amateurs. You went through a ship's exhaust."

"I went through quickly."

"Torin."

"You went through a ship's exhaust?" Dr. Tyrub's tongue flicked out, and he glanced up from the diagnostic strip pressed to Torin's chest. "Do ships have exhaust? Doesn't that imply burning fuel?"

"It's an energy trail," Craig explained.

The doctor sighed. "I'm aware. I'm making conversation."

"Torin went through the energy trail."

"So I understand. Intentionally?"

"Explosive decompression," Torin explained in turn. "I was ejected from the station."

"Good thing you were in your suit, then. Or you'd be dead."

"You think?" Craig muttered.

"I think it's a good thing she was in her suit, yes. I also think the autodoc's response is a basic albeit effective treatment. Given the level of exposure, fecal elimination . . ." He paused, inner eyelids flicking over round, protruding eyes. "Of course fecal matter is always eliminated, so I suppose it would be more precise to say radioactive matter excreted in feces." He paused again, small domed head swaying back and forth on a half meter of neck. The Slaink brain was centrally located in the oval bulk of the body, and, if they avoided bleeding out, they could survive decapitation, but other than that, they were essentially bipedal lizards, larger than the Niln, less dangerous than the Silsviss. The Slaink, like the Mictok, were among the elder of the Elder Races, and no one knew why Dr. Tyrub had agreed to become the Justice Department's radiation specialist, bringing his entire extended, multigenerational family to Berbar Station. Torin trusted Alamber to find out if it became relevant. "Never mind." Hooking a claw under the diagnostic strip, he pulled it free. "The point is, your current medication is doing its job, neutralizing and eliminating, but I'd feel better if we sped things up, using the treatment I believe Dr. Je'lip used after you returned Captain Ryder's ship to Hinare Station. It'll straighten out the DNA damage."

"Potential DNA damage?" Torin asked.

Dr. Tyrub's smile exposed the bony ridges that lined the inside of his mouth. "Actual."

Torin could hear *I told you so* in every breath Craig took.

"Would I be correct in assuming you have ova banked? An excellent idea," he continued before Torin could respond. "As I understand it, the genetic material in Human ova can be interestingly fragile and if you ever want to have offspring, this would have . . . Actually, the incident on Hinare Station would previously have . . ." He glanced down at her chart, flipped through a few screens, and frowned. "Never mind."

"So, children."

"I'm not against the idea," Torin acknowledged.

"There's a lot of kids on a salvage station. I'd always thought I'd have a few of my own someday."

"Define a few."

"Torin."

She licked Craig's bare shoulder, the skin warm and salty, then said, "I could eventually be convinced."

"When you're through saving the universe?"

"When *we're* through. Although, I was thinking, more specifically, of when the mammals of the Confederation point out that the Primacy has been using artificial wombs for centuries and the children produced in them are still capable of forming deep interpersonal bonds with their parents." She frowned. "Or the equivalent."

Craig made a soft, speculative sound. "We were at war with the Primacy for centuries."

"And now we're not."

"Parliament may not consider them the best example."

"Then Parliament can push a missile out the barrel of a KC-7," Torin muttered. "Besides, there's enough new people around the station now. Younger Races. Elder Races. Those who mistakenly think the Strike Teams are just as dangerous as the people we bring in."

"Instead of more dangerous?"

"My point is that we don't need to add another small, screaming, pooping body to the mix."

"You're enchantingly maternal."

"Bite me." She threw an arm across his chest, tucked her right leg under his, and went to sleep.

Five of the seven people in Interview Room Three held coffees, two held cups of *sah*, a Krai stimulant illegal for Humans to consume. Two Krai, three di'Taykan, two Humans, their brand-new Justice Department Strike Team uniforms still showing shipping creases. From where Torin stood outside the hatch, her slate slaved to the security cameras, she could see three knives and two Taykan *ven* blades. They'd have to be better than that. She made a mental note to have Werst speak with them. For all he was a meter high, never in his boots, and essentially hairless, Werst hid an impressive number of weapons on his person.

Torin's slate held copies of every recorded detail about the members of the newest Strike Team—from their first childhood civil evaluations before they began school to the final report that accompanied their discharge papers. She'd read about their specialties, their recorded strengths and weaknesses, and their psych profiles individually and interlinked. Death and the Corps threw Marines into fireteams with little concern about how well they'd work together. The Corps expected that their identities as Marines would overrule their differences; if that didn't work, there was always fighting or fucking those differences out. In Torin's experience, Death cared even less than the Corps. The Justice Department, still uncomfortable employing violence, formed teams around minimal personal conflicts. Torin, and the other Strike Team leaders, had analyzed hundreds of applications, sent their preferred choices up to the brass, revisited what remained after legal paranoia, Elder guilt, and psych had finished with them, created teams with as many combinations as possible, and reshuffled again after psych finished face-to-face interviews. All applicants under consideration had served in the military, but not all who'd served could do the job. The extended process took forever, but Justice insisted on being obsessively comprehensive about their choices when those choices would receive a personal locker in the armory and then be sent out to police the civilian population.

"Very specific members of the civilian population," Torin had pointed out. *"Armed members of the civilian population,"* she'd added in case there'd been any misunderstandings.

It hadn't expedited the process.

Torin had presented her team to Justice fully formed, but those carefree days of Gunny-knows-best were long gone. They were building something here and the base had to be strong if it was going to last.

The seven people in IR3 were the last full Strike Team Justice would fund for Berbar Station. From now on, they'd fill Strike Team losses from the distilled list of approved applicants—those who hadn't moved on to other teams in other sectors. Seven teams should be enough. For all violent crime caught the headlines, it remained the exception and not the rule on an interstellar scale. Some ex-military shrugged their service off. Some struggled not to collapse under the burden of memory. Most figured out a way to apply their training to civilian life, went to their therapy sessions, maintained contact with people who'd served with them, and were glad to have gotten out alive. Only a very few took the violence they'd learned and applied it.

Fewer still applied the violence they'd learned to keeping the peace.

Slate back on her belt, Torin twitched her uniform tunic into place. In her opinion, a copy of *every recorded detail* wasn't worth as much as observing candidates for ten minutes under fire, but Commander Ng had refused her request to shoot at them.

She opened the hatch and stepped into the room.

Three Navy, four Marines. Still easy to tell them apart, but then Torin would probably always find it easy. Lorkin, one of the Krai, was visibly young, the rest that indeterminate age where experience and ability still marched in step. Elisk, the elder of the two Krai was a Naval lieutenant, Marie Bilodeau, the young Human, a Marine lieutenant who left the Corps before her second promotion by way of her knee to a major's balls. The major had been given a dishonorable, Lieutenant Bilodeau had taken an escape clause. Captain Ranjit Kaur, the Strike Team Ch'ore Lead, had served with the major and argued for the lieutenant's inclusion on the teams. Two officers, one noncom, four enlisted; the seven had been training together for a tenday now and stood like a team—talking, listening, aware. No one sat in the half circle of uncomfortable chairs. When Torin stepped into the room, a di'Taykan female—SN di'Numanja Tylen—and a human male— Master Corporal Harris Zhou—shifted to opposite edges of the group. Not overtly, but far enough to provide cover if required. Torin hid a smile. Technical Sergeant di'Ahaski Yahsamus didn't bother to hide hers.

Pilot, sniper, tech, leader, and three highly trained and motivated utility players.

Strike Team Alpha had two, not three utility players, but one of them was Werst, so Torin considered the odds remained in their favor.

She'd seen Zhou before, back when he'd arrived at Ventris Station for basic training, hiding how much his step into a new life mattered behind a frown and a slouch. He'd reminded her of herself—she'd discovered from his application he'd also been from Paradise, although that hadn't been a factor at the time—and she'd bet Major Svensson he'd be a lifer. He'd had two accelerated promotions, completed sniper training, and had planned on staying in for his full thirty. After the plastic's manipulations had been exposed, he hadn't been able to reconcile providing data for a social experiment run by polynumerous molecular polyhydroxide alcoholydes with what he'd believed he'd been fighting for. He'd tried, but when his contract ran out, he'd walked away. When Zhou met her eyes, Torin could see the betrayal still lurking behind the calm assessment and he still reminded her of herself.

The team didn't immediately acknowledge her presence, well aware overt enthusiasm was more likely to be ridiculed than appreciated, also aware that waiting too long would be disrespectful. Torin was pleased to see that, as a group, they'd mastered the tricky timing—if only because it was a good indication of their cohesion as a group. When she saw she had their attention, she nodded, once, the motion an echo of DI Beyhn, Zhou's presence reminding her of the staff sergeant long since turned qui and out of the Corps. "Welcome to Berbar Station, Strike Team U'yun." Like the military they came from, the Strike Teams alternated Human, Taykan, and Krai designations. "You have your uniforms, you've had your quarters and ship assigned, you've spoken to Commander Ng; I'm here as the Strike Team Lead who drew the short straw to remind you that you are no longer in the military."

Zhou rolled his eyes.

"That, and I'm currently the only Strike Team Lead on station," Torin continued. "This is your last reminder that the rules you operate under have changed. Our job is not to protect the Confederation from an external threat, but to uphold the law. You think a law needs to be changed? Go into politics."

Elisk shook his head. "We know we're still following orders, Warden Kerr."

"And you all know how to deal with orders you disagree with." Torin and the other Strike Team Leads had made sure of that while sorting the applications. Bilodeau's application of force to testes had only been the most overt incident. "But there's a difference between you doing what you have to in order to get the job done, and you doing what you have to in order to get the job done within the confines of the law. You don't shoot to kill unless there's absolutely no choice, and you'll defend that choice in front of a tribunal after having filled out an astounding amount of paperwork. Some of it on actual paper."

Tylen grinned, enough light receptors open her eyes were at least three shades brighter orange than her hair. "So you're saying we can't call in an artillery strike?"

"I'm saying we don't have artillery. With any luck we can make the job redundant before we need the heavy hitters."

"And then what?"

"Up to you. That's my point. In the military, you followed orders. Here, you make decisions. Each Strike Team contains no more than seven people because if the teams are any larger, decisions don't get made. I don't know," she said before Zhou could ask. "They did studies. Not our problem. Superficially, the Strike Teams look military and remembering they aren't is the hardest thing you'll have to do while taking fire during an advance on an entrenched position. There's a team lead because the buck has to stop somewhere." The occasional piece of oldEarth idiom had made the change into Federate intact although doubt remained over what a buck might have been. "Any questions."

"Warden Kerr?" Bilodeau stepped forward. "Humans First?"

"What about them?"

"They've increased their activities to the point where the news refers to them by name."

"Gleefully in a few instances where the broadcasters weren't Human," Zhou muttered, brown eyes narrowed.

"They've been mentioned in every political broadcast in the last three tendays," Bilodeau continued, "Wouldn't it be easier if, instead of reacting to what they do . . ." She leaned forward, weight on the balls of her feet. ". . . we proactively took them out?"

It wasn't the first time she'd asked the question; she'd asked it during her initial interview, during her psych evaluation, and twice Torin knew of during training. It appeared she was going to keep asking until she got an answer she approved of.

"Yes. It'd be easier," Torin admitted. "But we don't proactively keep people from breaking the law. We assume sentient beings can manage that on their own. We clean up the mess when they don't."

"But Humans First has already broken the law."

"Laws," Torin allowed. "Plural. But you can't arrest an organization, and the kind of social engineering it would require to effectively shut it down isn't our job."

"You infiltrated the organization and made mass arrests."

"Yes, we did. We were contractors then, different rules. We operated . . ."

"Outside the law?" Yahsamus suggested.

"Beside the law. If you—any of you—can get the Justice Department to send us out again, I'll want to know how you managed it because they're not listening to the rest of us. That said, keep two things in mind. First, this is a job, not a profession, you can be fired for being a pain in the ass above and beyond. Second, the suggestion has already been made multiple times, so if you're going to double down, talk to the other teams first and we'll let you know if you're covering old ground."

"Why become a Warden if you got more done beside the law?" Zhou wondered, dropping one butt cheek onto the corner of the refreshment table. He rose in sync with Torin's eyebrow and tried to look as though he'd intended to stand back up.

There'd been a lot of reasons, chief among them Torin's need to belong to something bigger than she was. To belong to something that would take care of her people if she couldn't. As it happened, her first reason was the first reason Zhou had given when asked why he was applying to become a Warden—although she had no intention of sharing that information. "As contractors, we blurred the lines between what was right for the Confederation as a whole and what was right for us. In time, we'd have become part of the problem." Entropy always won. Torin refused to help. "Besides, if it was easy, anyone could do it and you lot would've been here two tendays ago instead of enjoying yet another round of testing."

"So you're saying we're the best?" Elisk asked, nostril ridges open.

"Out of a sorry lot," she agreed.

Corporal di'Burlut Nicholin barked out a laugh, umber hair lifting. Tylen punched him in the shoulder and the other five grinned. They knew they were the best; no one needed to tell them.

"You're off duty until 0800 tomorrow when there'll be an all teams meeting. Unless a team returns in the next eighteen hours, that means U'yun and Alpha—and there's always a chance one or both of us will be deployed before then. My niece's environmental corps has military similarities," she added and Zhou closed his mouth again. "That doesn't make them the military. Your quarters have been stocked with the basics, and your accounts are active. The station will allow you to go one pay period into debt, no more, but if it happens you'll get a visit from What Part of Budget Do You Not Understand—actual name," she added before they could ask. "He changed it recently. You don't want him dropping by. We drink at Musselman's. You need bail, you contact your team leader first, then me, then your mother. If Commander Ng has to get involved, he won't be happy, and if he's not happy, he'll make sure I'm not happy. Technically, I'm not your superior in anything but seniority, we're still working out how much rank structure we want to maintain. That said, you don't want to make me unhappy."

Elisk raised his mug in salute. "Understood, Gunny."

"Who'll arrest us?" Lorkin spread his arms. "We're Wardens."

Giving him the benefit of the doubt, Torin answered the question. "The Strike Teams are specialists, and we're a minority among the Wardens—there are currently two hundred and eleven active Wardens working out of this station who'd happily arrest you in the name of the greater good. Many of the old school Wardens are . . ." She paused and flattened her voice. ". . . adorably idealistic. If you're very lucky, you'll never be lectured by a Dornagain who's just stepped in a puddle of vomit."

"If that's the worst this place has to offer, I can cope." Zhou had been with 1st Recar'ta, 2nd Battalion on Avonbye, the last, large ground offensive in Sector Seven. Both sides had brought along an extra artillery company and while casualties had been below average, the amount of destruction had been excessive. Even for the Corps.

Torin allowed herself a small smile. "Get back to me on that. Settle into your quarters. Explore the station. The range and the gym are both open twenty-eight/ten, decontaminated between twenty-eight hundred and zero one hundred. If you get lost, your implants have been logged with the station sysop." The four enlisted touched their jaws in unison. "Some of you can use the subvocalizing practice and you can't ask a question too stupid to be answered. We have politicians here."

Everyone glanced at Elisk, the team leader. He looked at her.

She let a little gunnery sergeant weight her voice. "Go."

They went.

Technical Sergeant Yahsamus waited for her at the door, dark green hair flipping slowly back and forth.

Torin raised a brow.

"Wondered if you'd heard there's been scuffles on the border with the Primacy."

The Primacy was a six-day Susumi jump from the nearest coordinates the Confederation claimed as its border, but Torin, who'd spent twelve years in the fight, knew what the sergeant meant. "I hadn't heard."

"Could be malcontents, could be probing for weakness . . . the Primacy being an entire galactic civilization of the socially unevolved and all. Three ships, a few shots exchanged, a gas giant mining station destabilized during construction. Brass is keeping it need to know. More than usual." Her eyes lightened as Torin shot her a silent question, and she touched the pheromone masker at her throat, not needing to point out that some people talked during sex. Had interaction with the Primacy involved more than plastic alien-encouraged invasion, the di'Taykan would have made invaluable spies. "Thing is," she continued, "seems like only those actually involved in the interactions know anything about them. There's nothing on the channels I've checked."

Both Parliament and the people required full transparency from institutions paid for by the people. Not all information would be widely shared, but if the particularly pedantic wanted to know how the Corps wiped their asses in the field, they could find out. New interactions with the Primacy should have been top of the news stream twenty-eight/ten.

It took Torin a moment to understand the expectant silence. "What is it you think I should do, Tech?"

Her hair lifted. "You have other channels."

"Hey, Sarge! You coming with?"

She waved at the other two di'Taykan in her team, waiting at the next hatch. "I should if we all pay attention. Gunny."

"Tech."

The Primacy was no longer Torin's concern. The Confederation military was no longer Torin's concern.

But why keep the details of new Primacy aggressions quiet? With Parliament discussing a vote on the unfortunate necessity of locking the Younger Races dirtside, lest their violent ways spread, Torin would have expected the military to shout about the potential of further hostilities. If the Confederation needed a military, then they needed the Younger Races, negating the need for the vote. It seemed obvious to Torin, but she wasn't a politician and forcing herself to think in

circles made her want to fulfill at least a few of the violent fears suggested by Parliament's more alarmist members.

The Strike Teams had been consulted about training facilities when
Justice had added onto the station—the range was a replica of the
most popular range on Ventris—but their quarters were identical to
those housing the station's civilian population. For Humans, a kitchen/
living room, bedroom, and bathroom. Couples had more space than
singles and Justice had made it clear that quarters would be expanded
should any of their new employees decide to start a family now they
were out of the military. The quarters were larger than Torin's NCO
quarters on Fourth, significantly larger than the space she and Craig
had shared on the *Promise* during Torin's short career as a civilian
salvage operator, large enough to be a relief after spending travel time
in *Promise*'s current configuration with five other people.

There was nothing wrong with their quarters. The furniture was
sturdy, the bed comfortable, the tech up to date.

Torin found them isolating.

As she'd told U'yun, this was a job. At the end of the shift, they
went home.

Craig had flown alone before Torin and turned the isolation on
board ship into a phobia, but he'd returned after every trip to the
crowded, unstructured life of the Salvage Stations.

The first time he'd left the hatch to their quarters open, Torin had
closed it.

The second time, she'd realized they had no immediate need for
privacy, two other rooms to be private in if the need arose, and left it
open.

At any given time, at least half the hatches leading to the quarters
of Strike Teams on station were open and life spilled out into the
passageway, making and maintaining connections. Building trust.

When Commander Ng, who continued to live in his pre-Strike
Team quarters, pointed out that decompression hatches were meant
to be left closed, Torin pointed out that no one on the Strike Teams
would remain in their quarters should the station be hit, so the point
was moot.

That evening, while waiting for Presit to return her call, Torin
closed the hatch.

Craig twisted the collar off a capacitor and set it carefully down on their small table. "You need me to rack off?"

Torin took a moment to enjoy the muscles moving in his bare arms. "No, you're good."

He grinned. "That's what I hear."

She checked the buffer on her slate and paced the length of the room. It'd be faster to use the station's communications array, but Alamber had installed some not exactly illegal protections on her slate to prevent the station sysop eavesdropping.

She paced the length of the room again. "Why am I getting involved? I'm not a politician. I hate politics."

"You're essentially the commander's XO."

"I'm essentially the commander's first sergeant, not the same thing."

"You convinced the Silsviss to join the Confederation, you outsmarted the plastic not once, not twice, but three times. You exposed their machinations and ended the war, then you created a new department within the Wardens and armed them."

"None of that involved politics." She frowned. "A couple could be called impolitic."

Craig shrugged. "You get things done."

"I get the job done."

"That's what I said."

"I are assuming this are not a social call?"

Torin whirled to face the slate. Presit a Tur durValintrisy hadn't changed physically since the first time Torin had met her on the *Berganitan*. Her silver-tipped fur was as beautifully thick, the black vee still running up her collarbone and over both shoulders to spread in a dark cape down her back. Her hands still looked like she wore black latex gloves and her claws had, as always, been professionally enameled. Expressions were often hard to identify on the fur-bearing members of the Confederation, but Presit had worn annoyed impatience often enough Torin couldn't mistake it. "I have information for you," Torin began.

Presit's small round ears flicked as she listened. When Torin finished repeating the information Technical Sergeant Yahsamus had shared, she waved a dismissive hand. "No, I are not having heard about violent activity on the border. Probably because the *border* are being a ridiculous construct when anyone who are having a brain are considering the three-dimensional vastness of space."

"Presit." The Katrien reporter and furry pain in Torin's ass had just repeated one of the responses Torin had given during a live interview.

"That are being my name." When she tossed her head, silver highlights rippled through the thick fur of her ruff. "Don't be wearing it out."

Obnoxious was better. Obnoxious meant Presit was paying attention.

On the one hand, decisions, even stupid ones, made by the officers involved in the skirmishes were none of Torin's business. On the other hand, a vote to demote the Younger Races to a secondary status within the Confederation would lead to civil war. Stupid decisions could influence undecided members of Parliament. And, one way or another, if it came to war, people Torin cared about would be involved. That made it Torin's business. Her popularity having grown beyond Sector Central News, Presit, as an independent investigative journalist, had, or could, gain access to everyone in this sector. The Confederation ran on accountability, and the Confederation worked. Torin wanted it to keep working.

For all her faults, Presit held everyone equally accountable.

Everyone except herself.

And Torin.

It was never Presit's fault.

It was often Torin's.

"However . . ." Presit combed her claws through her whiskers, right side, then left, red enamel glittering in even the low lights the Katrien required. ". . . if violent activity are happening on the border, then why are I not hearing about it? That are being the question. I are having broken the top stories in the last decade of the war. I are having been there on Big Yellow."

Out of sight of the camera, Torin pressed her hand flat against the inert surface of the desk. Usually her nightmares involved failing to bring her people home, but—sometimes—her dreams took her back to the ship they called Big Yellow, to sinking slowly into the deck. Losing sight and sound and air. Plastic aliens slipping into her head through eyes and ears and mouth until it became their brain, not hers. Until she watched herself direct the war like it was a H'san opera, only the blood spilled and the lives lost were real.

"I are having been there on the prison planet."

Although Presit hadn't been imprisoned, starved, or drugged, she'd also carried a piece of the plastic aliens in her brain. Torin's fingers curled into a fist.

"I are having announced the end of the war."

With Presit's equipment hooked into *Promise's* distress beacon, they'd been able to spread the news far and fast to both sides of the fight. Too far and too fast to be denied.

"I are not approving of secrets." She picked up a small glass cup and took a sip of the pale green liquid. "Particularly secrets that are being kept from me." Small white teeth showed points against black lips as she lowered the cup. "I are going to be asking around."

"Can you find out if the H'san know?"

"I can." That she could find out anything was heavily implied. Her dark eyes narrowed, the mirrored glasses she wore in non-Katrien light levels beside her cup on the desk. "Why are I wanting to?"

"I don't trust the H'san."

"Everyone are trusting the H'san."

The H'san were the Eldest of the Elder Races. The H'san had formed the Confederation. The H'san sang to welcome the dawn. The H'san loved cheese.

Torin thought of hidden weapons. Of a bio-contaminant almost broken. "I'm not everyone."

"Oh, that are being very definitely true ex-Gunnery Sergeant Strike Team Leader Warden Kerr. And, while you are being undeniably and unfortunately you, you are also being part of a distinct subset, one that are having served the Confederation valiantly, but that are being unfortunately disregarded when other, presumably more socially evolved species are being driven by what are being an irrational fear of the unfamiliarity of peace."

Even with years of practice at deciphering the Katrien's idiosyncratic speech patterns, it took Torin a moment to parse the sentence. "You're against the vote?"

"I are standing beside the Younger Races who are having stood beside us when we were needing them."

Torin considered that declaration for a moment. "Presit, are you running for office?"

"I are thinking of using my influence in a broader capacity, yes. You are having given me a way to be starting the conversation. I are expecting your support." Her muzzle wrinkled. "Be telling Craig that I are still thinking he can do better."

The screen went black for a moment, then Sector Central News began to scroll. Presit no longer worked for the company, but she didn't believe in burning bridges.

Torin thumbed her slate off.

"What is it you want Presit to find out?" Craig asked, separating the final two pieces of the capacitor. "Or do you want her out there shit disturbing?"

"Six of one," Torin admitted. "The military is required to provide full transparency to the press." There were times during the war when the press arrived at the battle site before the military. In a just universe, the Primacy would have used them to range artillery weapons. "What are they hiding? Why are they hiding it?"

Craig dripped what Torin assumed was oil between two tiny pieces, then fitted them back together, large callused hands moving deftly, almost delicately. "You were less than specific."

"When talking to Presit? I didn't need to be specific, Presit's point and shoot. And, if I tell her I want her to do something specific, she'll do the opposite."

Craig grinned. "No lie. Why hide the possibility shooting could start up again, then? That news would shift the go-home-children vote in our favor, and we can all keep playing silly buggers with the grownups."

"Could be they're worried about another round of being lab rats for the plastic aliens."

"Then they should say that."

Torin flicked a corner of her slate, spinning it around on the small desk she seldom powered up, preferring to use the larger desk at work. "Could be the plastic aliens aren't involved. The war went on for generations; it gets to be a habit."

"Some people are assholes," Craig agreed.

Bottom line, she was point and shoot herself. "I hate politics."

"So you say."

"Presit still thinks you can do better."

"So I heard. She's wrong."

Torin stood and crossed toward him. "You couldn't survive anyone better than me."

"Probably not . . ."

"What part of subdue do you not understand?" Arms loose at her sides, weight up on the balls of her feet, Torin glared at the members of three Strike Teams scattered around the gym, most of them breathing heavily. "A nonlethal takedown ends with the criminal unable to either fight or flee, but still able to breathe."

di'Numanja Tylen swiped at the blood dribbling from her nose. "I can breathe, Gunny. And I heard R&D will have the tranq guns working any day now."

"From who?"

"I think she's in R&D . . ."

"R&D tries hard," Torin said flatly and cut the snickers off with a sharp, "Outer reaping takedown. Set." She walked the perimeter as they squared off again. "The Warden moves into a mutual grab situation forcing their opponent's head and upper body back—right hand on left shoulder." This wasn't a situation where the di'Taykan were free to make alternate suggestions and they all knew it. "The Warden sweeps the left foot away from the opponent's body and uses their grip on the left shoulder to force the opponent down to the right. The Warden follows the opponent to the ground, right knee on their chest, their hands secured. No crushing sternums, throats, or noses although all three would be options in a real-world scenario." She frowned. "Options that would result in a shit-ton of paperwork." Back at the front of the gym, she folded her arms. "Opponents, this time try and remember we're practicing form, we're not sparring. No applying knees to groins, teeth to flesh . . ." She nodded at Tylen. ". . . foreheads to noses. Go."

Strike Team Wardens who hadn't been close combat specialists during their time in were required to achieve competence if not proficiency in hand-to-hand fighting. Torin allowed the pilots mere competence as they were rarely in the thick of the fighting, but everyone else put in time having their asses regularly pounded into the mats under the supervision of Werst, di'Tagawa Gamar, or Torin herself. Over the last year they'd gone through a close-combat instructor who'd had twenty in the Corps as well as two ex-Corps pulled from planetary law enforcement. Even Commander Ng agreed that if the patronizing fukkers hadn't wanted bones broken, they shouldn't have smiled and told Torin not to hold back.

A di'Taykan instructor from Ventris would arrive in three tendays. In the meantime, they made do.

Torin saw Alamber reach for his masker and smiled. Increasing the pheromone that made the di'Taykan all but irresistible to almost every non-insectoid species they'd come in contact with gave them a valid advantage in a fight and one time or another every single di'Taykan forgot the training maskers were nonadjustable. While Alamber was distracted, Zhou swept his foot out from under him and took him slowly to the mat. New personnel started out careful of her civilian, but while Alamber had usually wielded wits and words to get out of trouble, his background had eased the physical inhibitions most sentient beings labored under when it came to damaging another sentient being— *nontraditional* substituted for *criminal* on official documentation. That, added to the one-on-one training Torin and Werst continued to give him during the long hours in Susumi space, allowed him to surprise most of his opponents. To his credit, Torin acknowledged as Alamber braced his leg on Zhou's shoulder, flipped them both, and landed straddling his opponent's chest, he'd never accidentally broken anyone's nose.

"Alamber."

"Right. Form." He offered Zhou a hand up. "Sorry, Boss."

Strike Team U'yun would have to attend another nine sessions on form before they could join the significantly more popular *do what you have to in order to win.*

The gym, like the range, originally had a gallery accessible to everyone with station ID. It had taken less than a full tenday for that to change. Officially, Justice expressed concern about the safety of untrained personnel in an unfamiliar, and potentially deadly, situation. Unofficially, the Strike Teams had objected to being stared at like they were a cross between a horror vid and animals in a learning enclosure. Torin had pointed out to Commander Ng that those members of the Elder Races who watched wide-eyed—in cases where physiognomy allowed—clearly appalled by what they saw, were also on the government's payroll operating under full access agreements. The Strike Teams could therefore drop by to stare at *them* working.

"And make fukking comments about how they fill out their fukking forms," Werst had muttered.

Commander Ng had cleaned up the language, repeated the observation in the right ears, and clearances had been revoked before he'd returned to his office. Getting the Strike Team program fully operational had been a learning experience for all concerned.

"Torin!" Craig stood just inside the hatch, beckoning her over.

"Switch sides and do it again," Torin called out, crossing toward him. She ignored the protests rising behind her. "Problem?"

"Presit called. We're invited to a press conference."

A grunt pulled Torin around in time to see Elisk take Ranjit to the mat. The height difference between Human and Krai decided the match in Human favor a lot less often than expected and, for ex-Navy, Elisk's form wasn't bad. He also had no inhibitions about dropping an ex-officer on her ass. She turned her attention back to Craig. "A press conference? About the skirmishes?"

"No. Word is they'll be flashing the plastic sheet from Threxie. Finally give the public an eyeful before the squints lock it away in a lab."

"*Before* they lock it away? Where's it been since we brought it back?"

"Bit iffy, but they didn't put that information on the invite. Point is, we were there when it was found, and Presit wants us there when it's displayed. Says we'll improve the optics." He grinned and scratched his chin through the dark scruff of his short beard. "And it seems Presit has dirt on Representative Hurring because the invitation originated in his office.

"Hurring will never leave the Core." Not once during zir six years in office, had the Justice Minister graced any of the MidSector stations with zir presence. The only Trun Torin had ever seen had been on the Trun home-world, giving weight to the rumor that it wasn't only the politicians but the entire species who refused to leave the Core.

Craig shrugged. "It's not happening in the Core. It's happening on Nuh Ner, at Sector Parliament. Seems we're more important to the planned spectacle than the Minister."

"And they don't want us in the Core." Torin didn't elaborate on who she meant when she said *they*. Craig knew.

"Presit seems to think they don't want *you* in the Core. Where you go, trouble follows."

"She's got that backward."

He smiled, the outside corners of his eyes crinkling. "That's what I told her."

Torin had never been to the Sector Parliament although she'd seen both the exterior and interior of the buildings a thousand times. Multiple vid channels covered political procedure twenty-eight/ten and Torin found it better than meds on nights she couldn't sleep. "A press conference," she repeated. It didn't sound any more believable. "I'd rather be shot. And I've been to press conferences and I've been shot, so that's not a hypothetical observation."

No point in asking if they could refuse. An invitation from the desk of Representative Hurring was as good as an order. "All right, Presit wrangled me an invitation because she thinks I'm a catalyst for disaster, and disaster attracts attention." Presit enjoyed attention. "Why does she want you there?"

"She likes me."

"Fair enough."

"We're leaving on the twenty-six hundred shuttle."

"Tonight?"

"Tonight."

"*Ablin gon savit.*" Like most Marines, Torin had learned to swear fluently in all three languages of the Younger Races by the end of her first year in the Corps. "Have they given the rest of the team leave?"

"No idea, but the commander wants to bend our ears before we go."

Torin pivoted back toward the gym and caught Werst's eye. "They're all yours. Run them through the two-point takedown a few times while I see a man about a dumbass idea."

Commander Ng seemed less thrilled about the invitation than Torin. "I have no doubt the proverbial shit will hit the fan while we're short-handed." After a moment's silence, he sighed. "Still, it'll make Representative Hurring happy. That may help at budget time."

"And if the proverbial shit does hit the fan?" Torin tried not to sound hopeful.

"You'll receive priority boarding on a ship home. But, hard as it is to believe, we can manage without you. For a while."

The rest of the team had been assigned station duties while they were gone. Alamber had been granted permission to help out in the labs.

"Squints were impressed at how he took apart Marteau Industries," Craig said as they packed.

"He's got mad skills he seldom gets to use." She carefully folded her dress uniform along the creases.

"And you'd prefer civilians out of the line of fire."

"Seems reasonable; they're civilians." Tunic squared up on her trousers, she closed the case. "Alamber's a civilian."

"We're all civvies, Torin."

"You know what I mean." She'd never intended Alamber to carry a weapon, never intended the death and destruction that had shadowed his past to shift to the forefront of his present. What was it Hollice used to say about the road to hell and good intentions?

"And me?"

And him, indeed. She leaned against the wall and watched him shove his boots in along the outer edge of his case, fighting the years of experience that wanted her to tell him to start over and get it right. "The other pilots rave about the training simulation you designed."

"They rave?" Craig glanced up, brows raised. "You heard them rave? I heard it wasn't bad, and Pirrtirr grunted that it would do."

"That's raving for a pilot." She smirked. "It's how you rave."

His expression matched hers for a moment, then it disappeared. "Torin." He reached out and wrapped his fingers lightly around her wrist. "I'm not sitting on station running training simulations while you risk your life."

She twisted free of his grip and caught his hand, thumb against the pulse point on his wrist. "I know."

The trip to Nuh Ner was uneventful. Torin noted both the position of the escape pods and who, among the government employees sharing the ship, would need help getting to one. After determining which of the two common areas had better coffee, she settled in to read reports, trying to find a pattern in the recent Humans First activity.

Craig won a week's pay in an illegal poker game; the loser a Justice official on the way to take part in a Parliamentary committee on language drift and adaptation.

"Don't trouble about it, mate." He held out his slate for the transfer. "I'm a Warden."

Nuh Ner had three large land masses and four smaller ones, one moon large enough to influence the tides and a second, smaller moon farther out. The gravity was marginally stronger than Paradise. Not strong enough for Torin to notice given the length of their stay, but strong enough Craig changed his mind about extending their time dirtside. Radiation levels were surprisingly low considering Nuh Ner's position on the edge of the Core.

"Weird that every Sector Parliament is tucked up against the Core," Torin muttered disdainfully as they crossed the Port's open courtyard between Arrivals and City Links, the sky filled with stars enough to light their way.

"Why's that?"

"You'd think politicians would prefer the abyss."

"She's not exactly stoked about politics," Craig explained to a staring Niln.

Inner lids slid over dark eyes and slender fingers tightened around the handle of a metallic case. The Niln's reaction might have been caused by the close proximity of the dangerous Younger Races, it might have been specifically them—Torin had no way of knowing although she hoped it was the latter. Hoped that Parliamentary concern about innate violent natures hadn't spread to the general public. Wondered when she'd become such an optimist.

THREE

THE PUBLIC UNVEILING of the plastic data sheet had been scheduled for the next morning, and Presit collected them from their hotel herself. "So I are being sure you are actually showing up," she explained.

"I'm looking forward to it."

She patted the back of Craig's hand. "I are not talking to you." Head cocked, she looked them both up and down. "Those are being your dress uniforms?"

"No," Torin told her. "We like to dress identically. It's a couple thing."

"You are not being funny."

The Wardens' dress uniforms varied according to species, but the Younger Races, on and off the Strike Teams, wore a variation on their military Class A—Torin having pointed out there'd be a cost savings if the manufacturers could use fabrication parameters already in place. It had been the selling point when it came to outfitting the teams in combat gear as well. Pale gray hadn't been her first or even her second choice, but serving di'Taykan required neutral clothing or a higher tolerance for clashing colors than most species possessed. The Marines had claimed black and the Navy dark gray, and Parliament had been adamant there'd be no confusion between civilian and military actions. No one had pointed out that all three sets of combats had an identical camouflage function, but then no one expected a member of Parliament to be anywhere near the action. The Justice Department crest took up most of the tunic front—Human eyes unable to see the two brightest colors. Torin had been overruled on a distinct designation for the Strike Teams, but won the argument about wings tabs for the pilots and crossed KC7s for the snipers.

"For hairless mammals, you are not looking bad," Presit allowed after a long, critical moment. "And I are happy to report you are both smelling quite pleasant." A number of other species assumed Humans had no sense of smell. Presit knew better, but that didn't stop her from expressing an opinion. Nothing stopped her, as far as Torin knew. She lowered the room's one adjustable chair, sat, and said, "They are not wanting you here, but I are having insisted."

Torin wanted to point out that she hadn't wanted to be there either, but asked instead, "Who are they?"

Her *they* were not necessarily Presit's *they*.

Presit waved it off. "Most are being politicians, some are being military. The reasons for not wanting you here are being the same reasons they are having for you being present while the data sheet are being tested. Politicians are not wanting you being involved because they are not being able to predict what you are going to be doing and the military are not wanting you being involved because you are no longer being military and are being no longer under their control."

Craig snorted.

"Yes. Yes. You and I are knowing they are always having been delusional about that even if ex-Gunnery Sergeant Kerr are not agreeing."

Torin didn't agree, but she knew better than to argue military culture with those who hadn't served. "If that's the case, I can't imagine being seen with us is going to do your future campaign any good."

"Please, you are understanding nothing about influencing public opinion." She combed claws enameled in green ombre through her whiskers, first right side, then left. "Desires of politicians and the military being put aside, I are curious why the scientists are not having the three of us interact with the plastic during the identification process. As far as we are knowing, only the three of us are carrying markers that are being placed by the plastic and we are already having proven the plastic are sometimes requiring the encouragement of numbers to be communicating."

"And sometimes it doesn't," Craig pointed out.

"That are being no reason not to be making the attempt. Politicians and the military should be having no authority over science."

"Not even science involving an ex-enemy of the Confederation?" Torin asked. "Parliament could limit experimentation for security reasons."

"But Parliament hasn't. I would be knowing if it had." Presit's ears flicked. "And I are curious as to why an avenue of investigation are having been closed."

"And who closed it." Torin sat on the side of the bed, reducing the angle between them.

Presit smiled, showing sharp, white teeth. "Yes, and who are having closed it."

The *marker* the plastic had placed in their heads during their absorption by Big Yellow had turned out not to be a marker at all, but a piece of itself. Themselves. Several thousand pieces given the whole molecular polyhydroxide descriptor, but that wasn't the point. They provided context, it had told them, for the war. Had the plastic not disappeared immediately after that statement, Torin would have enjoyed giving them a different kind of context—more personal than mass troop deployment, but as violent. Her therapist had suggested they should perhaps try diplomacy if the plastic returned. Torin had diplomatically suggested her therapist stuff a few pieces of plastic into his head before he opened his mouth again. She liked to believe she'd made progress on her anger issues since then.

"I are having been trying to get the three of us together in the presence of the data sheet for some time now," Presit continued. "I are having no success, but I are unable to be determining why. The latter point are being the larger matter."

"You're good at determining why," Torin admitted.

"I are. I are preferring our interacting with the data sheet to be happening in a more controlled environment, but I are taking what I can get. It are being strange to me that they are not having been exposing us to it first thing."

"So they could cross the obvious off the list," Craig agreed, dropping onto the bed beside Torin.

"Now, there are always being the chance you are having been asked and you are having refused . . ." her voice trailed off and she looked pointedly at Torin.

"Didn't happen."

"And even if you two are having touched it while you are

transporting it—and I are not saying you did." She raised both hands. "Even if, I are not being there, so there are still a variable out of play."

"So why didn't they get the three of us together?"

Torin could hear the frown in Craig's voice. "My guess, they don't want to be dependent on the Younger Races. Not in the current political climate. Not if they want funding."

"Too damn many theys," Craig muttered.

"Today, I are having an audience and you are definitely being Younger Races and we are going to be seen. By everyone." She flicked her ears, and curled her lip. "This vote are having the potential to tear the Confederation apart, and there are those who are being blind to it. We cannot be going backward, we can only be going forward, and today, I are making that point from the podium."

Craig leaned against Torin, hard enough she had to brace herself to keep from falling over. "I'd vote for her."

Torin made a noncommittal sound, and said, "Did the H'san know about the skirmishes on the border?"

"I are still looking into that. Now, be asking me how the H'san feel about you being here."

"How," Craig began.

"Not you." Presit cut him off. "I are wanting ex-Gunnery Sergeant Warden Kerr to ask." When Torin remained silent and raised a brow, Presit rolled her eyes. "Fine. When I are arranging the invitations, it are being the H'san who are being most recalcitrant. They are not being obvious, but to anyone who are having a brain, they are clearly trying to delay a decision until it are being too late."

"Torin makes the H'san uncomfortable."

Torin lifted her lip off her upper teeth in an expression any Krai would recognize. "I'm good with that." The H'san were the Eldest of the Elder Races. They sang to the dawn. They loved cheese. For most of the Confederation, that was enough. Most of the Confederation were unaware the H'san maintained a storage facility of ancient weapons hidden within a planet of their dead.

"I are just happy someone are agitating entrenched opinions," Presit huffed. "I cannot be doing it all."

Under Presit's annoying outer layers was a highly intelligent, dangerously curious inner core. Torin reminded herself, not for the first time, to remember that.

"Because this are being a public unveiling and because you are having been instrumental in discovering the plastic, I are able to finally convince the right people you should be attending. Enough of the right people that the H'san are having to withdraw their ever so very discreet objections. So . . ." She stood and smoothed down her fur. ". . . it are being time to stop talking and to start doing."

Presit had insisted they walk to the Parliament buildings. "We are being three among a multitude, all who are heading in the same direction."

It wasn't exactly a multitude, but all three Younger Races and more than a few Elder were represented in the crowd. Talking, laughing—most of them acted as though they were enjoying a pleasant break in their usual routine. As far as Torin could tell, no one seemed anxious about being exposed to an artifact left behind by a species who'd manipulated two galactic civilizations into war. Or possibly an artifact made up of a species who'd manipulated two galactic civilizations into war. With the artifact still apparently a data sheet almost a year after it had been found, Torin assumed the former. On the other hand, everything they knew about the plastic indicated it excelled at playing the long game, so she could be wrong.

As Presit nodded and waved to fans, she wondered if their visibility was intended to safeguard them against a sudden disappearance. Then she told herself even righteous paranoia had limits and Presit's reasons for visibility were more likely to be ego driven.

The plaza in front of the Sector Parliament Building was about two-thirds full when they arrived. The sound of so many sentients gathered together hung over the crowd like smoke—what would be unbearable noise on a station, reduced to a dull background roar by the open air. Some had brought folding chairs, some sat on benches covered in patterned tile, some were in constant movement greeting friends. Presit circled wide, then adjusted trajectory toward the dais and bleachers set up outside the building's large, double doors.

"Those doors brass?" Craig asked, raising a hand to shade his eyes. "Decent salvage."

"That you are to be leaving right where they are being. The building are being called *Tev Arack Sant,* meaning The Nest Secure. The Niln are having named the planet, the Rakva are having named the Parliament building. The Katrien are having named the city, *Urhayvan*."

"Sectional?" Craig translated. "For the Sector Parliament? Not exactly poets, the Katrien."

Presit waved off the observation, claws glittering in the sunlight. "Not in Federate," she agreed. "It are being a dull compromise of a language."

A Katrien conversation sounded like a cat fight, neither dull nor compromising.

The pointing and whispering increased among Presit's fans in the crowd, and Torin, who could see the potential for trouble, had to admire the way she walked the fine line between acknowledging the attention and encouraging it. With Presit in the spotlight, no one had spared a glance at the Wardens accompanying her.

Were there to be trouble, the planetary law enforcement officers would be little help. A pair stood in the shade on the far edge of the plaza directly opposite the dais, a pair struggled through packed bodies toward a shrieking child, and one stood to either side of the Parliamentary doors, additional trim on their uniforms identifying their positions as primarily ceremonial. Six. Six in case of trouble with . . . Torin broke the crowd into platoons and companies. With roughly twenty thousand civilians. Granted there could be additional PLE she hadn't spotted, threaded through the crowd or stationed out of sight but . . . six? A cursory inspection of the site showed four positions up high with full coverage of the dais and most of the crowd, and another three with partial coverage. Did the PLE have control of all seven?

They should have brought Binti with them.

"Stop it." Craig nudged her with an elbow.

Torin scanned the narrow open area in front of the dais for the faint shimmer of a security screen and didn't find it. "Stop what?"

"Stop assuming the worst is going to happen and that the locals'll be buggered if it does."

Six PLE, twenty thousand civilians. "They will."

"How often does the worst happen?"

"I could work it out."

"Torin . . ."

"Humans First wants the data sheet." Torin thought of the damage a pistol could do, and her hands twitched toward the KC-7 she wasn't wearing. How many more pistols had Marteau printed since he'd been driven into hiding? How easily could he have seeded weapons throughout the crowd?

Realistically, not easily. Nuh Ner was the location of the Sector Parliament and, even after the war, the security protecting the representatives from each of the Planetary Parliaments in MidSector Seven was adequate by Torin's standards. Both shuttle ports and elevator stations scanned everyone heading dirtside. Full, comprehensive scans right down to the identification of stomach and bowel contents. Unfortunately, those scans weren't infallible; they'd missed the presence of the polyhydroxide alcoholydes for centuries.

"Do you honestly think Humans First is going to roar in here, shout we are number one, and roar off with the data sheet? No," Craig answered his own question. "Too in your face for that lot, no matter how up themselves they are. Besides, if they do show up, well, we're here."

"My experience with crowd control involves weapons' fire or a crowd predisposed to do what I tell them and, until recently, your idea of a crowd was me."

"So leave crowd control to the locals, then. You and I, we'll deal with Humans First."

She stopped. "You and I?"

Craig took one more stride, then turned to face her. "You and I."

"Unarmed?"

"Think you can't take them? Because I've heard stories . . ." He smiled when she laughed, the corners of his eyes crinkling. "That's better. Get out of your own way, Torin. You can't keep the assholes in Parliament from being assholes. You can't keep certain groups of Humans from acting like entitled shites. You do what you do."

With the amount of pink in the sky, the blue of his eyes looked purple. "We do what *we* do."

"Here?" He waggled both brows and spread his hands. "Never pegged you for an exhibitionist, but I'm game."

"I are going to be pretending you are both too tall for me to be hearing that," Presit huffed. "Be keeping up. After what I are going through to be getting you here, I are not arriving without you." She waited pointedly until they fell back in beside her, then continued leading them toward the dais.

The data sheet had been hung from a frame on the left of the dais, and the shimmer of a screen surrounding it reassured Torin that not everyone involved in securing the site was an idiot. At this distance, the orange-on-orange symbols scattered over the exposed side couldn't be made out. Earlier, however, Presit had told them that after every time they changed, they returned to the first configuration they'd shown when they were found. The podium to the right of the data sheet broadcast a repeat of the documentary about the sheet's discovery, cutting in scenes Dalan, Presit's camera operator, had shot on Threxie, but primarily using footage taken by government teams who'd arrived after the high-caliber shooting had ended. Torin had always been in favor of noncombatants arriving after the shooting ended. It made her job easier. Not many of the crowd watched the thirty-by-forty–meter projection hanging over their heads, but most had probably seen it before.

Bleachers rose up six levels to the right of the dais. Inelegant but effective, they'd hold twenty to a row, averaging out the sizes of the attending species and allowing for the spreading asses of politicians and upper level brass. Presit had led them to within ten meters of the bleachers when the doors opened and they began to fill, the crowd containing all three Younger Races as well as Niln, Katrien, Rakva, Trun, Mictok, Dornagain, and a single H'san. Every Sector Parliament had at least one H'san as a voting member whether or not there were H'san-controlled planets in the sector. According to the H'san, the placement was used to teach their young responsibility. As they had one of the longest life spans in the Confederation and assumed the greatest responsibility for its continued prosperity, this Confederation-wide training of their young was not so much accepted as welcomed.

And no one questioned the H'san, Torin added silently as this particular H'san, not built for the kind of seat used by the bipedal and unable to fake it like the Mictok, squatted by the end of the bleachers nearest the data sheet, neck compressed, head resting on what served them for shoulders. Torin used to think the H'san presence was at worst paternal. These days, she thought they were at best paternal. She hadn't yet set a new parameter for worst.

A Marine officer wearing a fair bit of brass on his black Class A's glared from the top tier.

"I see General Morris are having spotted you." Presit waved at a Katrien who'd shrieked . . . something. Given Presit's reaction, Torin assumed it was complimentary. "He are having personal opinions on your being present."

"I'll bet he is."

General Morris had sent Torin to Silsviss on a diplomatic mission, fully aware it would end in dead Marines. General Morris had tapped her for the trip to Big Yellow and then tried to use her experience as a boost to his career. Turned out General Morris had been unaware he'd been hosting a colony of plastic aliens in his office, so there was a chance he hadn't sent her anywhere at all. It had been years since she'd seen him. She thought she'd shaken him.

"Is this being a problem, ex-Gunnery Sergeant Strike Team Leader Warden Kerr?" Presit asked archly.

"Not if the general doesn't make it one."

"I'm sure he are having more important things to be doing than to be poking you with sharp objects."

"Let's hope so." Torin could see the general's mouth moving, and the lieutenant at his side had both thumbs working his slate. "I'm a civilian now. He pokes me, I'm poking him back."

Presit flashed teeth. "I are looking forward to it."

Craig leaned in until Torin could feel his breath against her ear. "No worries," he murmured, "he doesn't like me either."

"The man has no taste."

"That's what I'm saying."

"You are to be sitting there." Presit nodded toward two empty spaces on the first row of the bleachers, at the end farthest from the podium and the data sheet.

"And you?" Craig asked.

"I are having work to do." She patted his hand and walked toward the podium.

"She might've mentioned that," Craig murmured.

"She might've," Torin agreed. Hosting this assembly explained how a reporter—however popular—had enough pull to overrule both General Morris and the H'san. At a sudden sound from the crowd, accompanied by a number of pointing fingers, Torin glanced up and counted thirty-seven camera drones maneuvering into position overhead. Cameras, by law, had to be large enough to prevent any chance of recording without the consent of all parties involved. In this instance, entering the plaza for an official government function, counted as consent. Presit usually traveled with an operator, and Torin couldn't recall her ever using a drone. From her expression, fifteen meters high now she was on camera, Presit had strong artistic opinions on their use.

Although the Corps used drones on Crucible during the final two tendays of basic, they'd been of little use during actual combat when both sides used orbital EMPs to keep the war at a flesh-and-blood level. The plastic had wanted to learn about the *people* of the Confederation and the Primacy, and nothing stripped things to a base level like holding a companion's guts in with bare hands. Torin had strong opinions on people who killed by remote control.

By the time Presit finished her opening statements, the crowd was hanging on her every word, an awed rumble rising like distant thunder. Torin had to admit, she was impressed by the way Presit played the crowd, adapting her prepared text to their reactions. When she sketched out the data sheet's discovery, Torin and Craig's faces were superimposed over the Threxie images to loud applause from the plaza and polite applause from the bleachers. The Mictok seated next to Craig, extended her eyestalks out far enough she could look around him at Torin. When Torin raised a brow, the eyestalks snapped back.

"You're wearing your resting murder face," Craig told her quietly. "Not going to help convince the Elder Races we're harmless."

"We're not."

"Fair enough."

Torin noted those in the crowd who looked directly at them rather than at the giant image of them—all Younger Races and the odds were high every one of them had seen combat. That kind of awareness was learned behavior.

The first three speakers were politicians. The drone of their voices washing over her, Torin paid only enough attention to register threat, and, instead of listening, worked out the best way to clear civilians from the plaza in case of attack. Assuming incoming hostiles got past the defense satellites, they'd have to move quickly to achieve their objectives before fighters arrived from the *CF Gartuwan*, currently in orbit. If the hostiles only wanted the data sheet and had half-a-dozen functional brain cells, they'd drop on as steep an angle as their heat shields would allow, scoop, and go. Nuh Ner had nothing on the ground able to stop them, and if they weren't taken out high, their engines would do more damage than most weapons. New game if the hostiles put boots on the ground. She should've brought. . . .

"Binti's running sniper simulations with the new kid." Craig said quietly, voice sliding under the drone. "You were eyeballing the surrounding roof lines again," he added as her brows rose. "Easy enough to figure out why." His thigh pressed against hers, a line of warmth in spite of the environmental controls in their uniforms that made feeling his body heat impossible. She could hear the smile in his voice. "I know you."

He did. He knew all the ways she'd been remade by the war and all the ways she'd been remaking herself after.

"They don't have weapons up there," he continued, "because the Primacy never got this far in."

"The Primacy's not our problem these days," she reminded him. "Humans are."

"Some Humans."

"True." There were Humans on the plaza. A minority among the mixed species, granted, but how many would it take if they were armed with hidden weapons?

"You don't expect an attack."

He wasn't asking. Craig knew where to draw the line between sensible paranoia and monsters under the bed. Within the Confederation, her life had been, and still was, the exception and not the rule. "No."

"But it never hurts to be prepared."

Torin maintained her neutral expression but returned the pressure of his leg. "It's like you know me." When this was over, she'd show him what that meant to her—which, given the current lack of support from up high, gave her a more interesting operation to plan than a planetary defense.

The next four speakers were scientists. Their areas of expertise tripped off Presit's tongue, but Torin had no idea what any of them actually did. Seemed none of the scientists who'd been taken hostage on Threxie, who'd been there when the data sheet had been found, had been asked to speak. Perhaps their trauma had given them the option of refusing *their* invitations. Or, perhaps fieldwork didn't provide the credentials needed for such exalted company; after all, their positions came with clear and understandable functions. After the scientists finished, a cultural historian, a Niln, stepped up to the adjusted podium, tasted the air, and gave a dramatically condensed presentation on the effects of the polyhydroxide on the last three centuries of development within the Confederation. His point seemed to be that the Younger Races had shaken things up.

Torin had to consciously keep her hands relaxed. One of the Krai officers two rows up, snapped his teeth together.

Dr. Lushin, a bicolored Trun linguist, took the podium to point out the most frequent three symbols recorded from the data sheet and what they most likely meant. The symbols were present in three hundred and forty-two images of the data sheet collected on Threxie and seven hundred and twenty images of the data sheet collected since. Torin watched them flick by at a near hypnotic speed after Dr. Lushin warned that nonbiocular species should avert their gaze.

There was only one nonbiocular species present.

"Say Mictok and be done with it," Torin growled.

Craig held out his fist to the Mictok beside him.

She tapped it with her nearer antenna and the two Mictok in the row behind her, clacked their inner mandibles.

The Humans First who'd attacked Mining Station Trilik had been as open about their disdain for other species as the Mictok on the mining station had been about the Younger Races, and Torin preferred that to Dr. Lushin's passive-aggressive commentary as ze sketched soft light representations of what the patterns could mean in the air over the plaza. Cracks in the perfect structure of the Confederation were entirely because of the Younger Races, her firm beige ass.

"What a loud of shite," Craig muttered. "Even I'm hoping for an attack at this point."

"A false alarm wouldn't hurt," Torin agreed. Her ass had begun to go numb. Even as a member of a ground combat unit, she'd been to her fair share of ceremonies; a subset of military personnel clung to pomp and circumstance, bands and speeches and presentations, as though they made up for the blood and the pain and the terror and cylinders of ash carried out after every battle. Maybe for them it did. Everyone coped with the consequences of war in different ways.

When Dr. Lushin finished and returned to zir seat, and Presit launched into the next introduction, Torin realized that every speaker had come from the lowest level of the bleachers. When the Mictok beside Craig unfolded her legs and took her place at the podium, Torin clenched her teeth. Presit had said she wanted the three of them in the presence of the data sheet. Apparently, *in the presence of* in Katrien meant *part of the show.*

Clever. Not even the H'san would want to deal with the fallout of stopping a live broadcast in order to prevent contact that should have happened almost a year ago. Contact that anyone who'd seen the broadcast from the prison planet and who knew about the data sheet, would have assumed had happened.

Torin suspected everyone had seen the broadcast from the prison planet by now. Given the relatively recent acquisition of the data sheet, there might still be a few members of the Confederation who hadn't watched Presit's program on the discovery.

The H'san played with assumptions.

They sang to the dawn. They smelled good. They liked cheese.

They couldn't possibly have a planet of hidden weapons.

They couldn't possibly be preventing basic research on the data sheet.

The Mictok, SciRe Vin'tic, spoke briefly about the search parameters they'd been using in an attempt to find the plastic's home system, one eyestalk bent to keep the bleachers in sight. The math was above Torin's pay grade, but Craig nodded along.

"We have, of course, found nothing as yet." After a brief pause, SciRe Vin'tic dipped both antennae and hurried back to her seat.

As Presit thanked her, scenes from Threxie began playing again behind the podium.

Torin could see anticipation on the faces of the crowd.

Ears forward, Presit gathered that anticipation up and layered it through her voice. "And now, Gentles, we are having a great deal of pleasure in asking ex-Gunnery Sergeant Strike Team Leader Warden Kerr . . ."

"Oh, for fuksake."

A Krai. From a couple of rows up. Torin suspected the Krai officer who'd snapped their teeth earlier, but she didn't turn to look. She agreed with the observation.

". . . and Warden Ryder to approach the podium."

The sound rising from the bleachers had a common theme: This was not on the schedule.

What would happen, Torin wondered, if she stayed where she was? She was almost curious enough about Presit's reaction to try it, but Craig was standing and she wouldn't hang him out to dry.

Two voices rose out of the rumble behind her.

"Are we going to allow this to happen?"

"There's thousands of people in that crowd and they now want what that reporter wants. How do you suggest we stop it?"

Crossing to Craig's side, Torin glanced at the H'san. They hadn't moved since they'd folded their legs and settled into what passed for sitting, neck collapsed into its lowest position. Torin wouldn't blame them if they'd fallen asleep—which was big of her as she blamed them for pretty much everything else. She could feel the weight of General Morris' regard from where he sat amid the military. He wasn't the only disapproving officer up there, but his disapproval felt familiar.

The crowd in the palm of her hand, Presit spoke over silent visuals of Torin confronting the plastic on the prison planet, telling the story as she watched, making old news new again. Torin locked her gaze on the middle distance rather than see the thin, gray line of plastic emerge from her tear duct and run down her cheek. From Craig's tear duct. Down Craig's cheek. Hands behind her back, her feet shoulder width apart, she listened to the flesh-and-blood Craig breathe through his nose. The force of each inhale, each exhale, indicated his dislike of reliving the moment. As far as Torin knew, he'd never watched the vid.

The crowd cheered as Torin-from-then flicked the plastic from Presit's eyes off the end of her finger into the undulating mass. Booed when the alien rose up, gray, bipedal, about a meter tall, its facial features barely formed.

The recording stopped, and the image of the data sheet replaced it—the image larger, brighter, more dangerously alien than the actual item hanging below it.

"No one are arguing that I, as well as Wardens Kerr and Ryder, are having a connection to the plastic. When it are having been in our brains, we are having convinced it to be leaving this part of space!"

Not quite, Torin amended, hands curling into fists.

"It takes time to collect sufficient data on new species." The gray plastic alien's mouth barely moved. *"Creating extreme situations erases all but essential behaviors and shortens the duration of the study. We continued the conflict until we had sufficient data. The data must be analyzed."*

"Today," Presit continued when the noise died down again, "we are going to be telling this piece of plastic we are not wanting *it* around either!"

The roar of approval from the plaza slammed against the dais.

Presit acknowledged the crowd, then left the podium and walked to the data sheet, her image joining its image above the dais. She beckoned to Torin and Craig. "Warden Kerr, you are touching it first and you are maintaining your touch. Then Warden Ryder are to be doing the same. I are touching it last as it are my brain that are bringing it to life on the previous occasion."

"Is it safe?" A di'Taykan from five rows back in the crowd, bright blue hair even more brilliant in the sunlight. Sergeant at least, given the way her voice had carried.

"Is it safe?" Presit spread her hands, claws glittering. "We are standing with ex-Gunnery Sergeant Strike Team Leader Warden Kerr. How much safer are you wanting to be?"

The crowd roared with laughter. Torin caught the gaze of the di'Taykan and raised a brow. Her hair flipped back and she nodded. Good to know there'd be backup if the three of them touching the data sheet ended up in the shitter. The training didn't come off with the uniform.

"Warden Kerr."

The "invitation" from the Justice Minister had only compelled attendance, not the raising of a plastic alien out of an artifact, and a glance at the bleachers showed the occupants split about eighty/twenty between anticipation and unease. While no one had leapt up shouting for them to stop, sometime in the last couple of minutes the H'san had risen to their feet and pulled out a half-circle communicator. They did not look happy.

If the H'san wanted Presit's experiment stopped, then Torin was fine with it going ahead.

She took the final step forward and pressed the first two fingers of her left hand against the sheet. It felt warmer than she remembered, but then it had been hanging in the sun for most of the morning.

The symbols shifted. Paused. Shifted again. Paused.

The crowd cheered although Torin doubted any of them knew what they were cheering for. There was a collective intake of breath from the bleachers, the scientists stared enthralled, and the military personnel fought to remain expressionless.

"Warden Ryder."

Craig pressed his fingers to the plastic six centimeters above hers. As far as she could tell, the symbols responded the exact same way to his touch. Shift. Pause. Shift. Pause. She lifted her fingers; nothing happened, so she put them back down.

"And now, I are applying the final variable." Presit's fingers touched the plastic thirty centimeters below Torin's. Shift. Pause. Shift. Pause.

Torin lifted her fingers again. No response.

Craig lifted his. No response.

Torin put hers back. No response.

No one watching made a sound.

The data sheet remained frozen in the configuration it had taken after Presit's touch.

A thousand people exhaling sounded like the wind through the evergreens on Crucible. On Crucible where the plastic had turned a training exercise into combat and Torin'd had a conversation with Major Svensson's arm.

"Now, we are all to be raising our fingers simultaneously. On three. One, two, three . . ."

A multitude of voices shouted, "Nothing happened!" Presit had made the crowd a part of this and, Younger or Elder, they were no longer content to be passive observers.

"They're one shithead away from being a mob," Craig said under the waves of sound.

"And you wondered why I mapped the exits." If political presentations happened regularly, and the existence of the plaza suggested they did, there was a chance the PLE had just called for reinforcements.

"Shouldn't have doubted you."

"Damned right."

Presit raised her hands and, after a moment, the noise tapered off to a low rumble of conversation. The power of celebrity in action.

"Nothing are having happened, that are being sadly true." She didn't sound sad. She spread her arms, silver highlights rippling through the thick fur, and smiled. "Fortunately, that are not being our only attempt at communication today. When I are being on the prison planet, I are having observed an interaction that are being relevant."

Torin's voice boomed out over the plaza as her image, blistered, starving, and filthy, wearing only boots and underwear, glared down at the plastic alien, and snarled, *"You are one smart-assed comment away from being an entree."*

"The Krai," Presit purred, "are being able to digest the plastic."

The Krai had digested a lot of plastic directly following the reveal, Krai-controlled areas had been stripped of potential enemies with impressive speed. From the expressions on the faces of the scientists, testing that particular data point hadn't occurred to any of them, definitively proving there'd been no Krai among them because it sure as hell would have occurred to one of the Krai.

The young Krai who emerged from behind the bleachers had clearly been waiting to be called. The pattern of mottling on his head identified him as male. The corporate logos all over his clothing said he worked for Sector Central News. He strutted out, lips pulled back off his teeth in a challenge that raised a response from both the crowd and the bleachers. The staccato sound of the hardest substance in known space snapping together split the ambient noise into pieces and it took a moment for less aggressive sounds to recreate the whole.

"It are being common knowledge," Presit said in a tone billions of viewers knew as an introduction to the extraordinary, "that polyhydroxide alcoholyde are meaning organic and if it are being organic, the Krai are being able to be eating it. Are you being ready, Girstin?"

"I am!"

"Then please be applying your teeth."

". . . destroying a priceless artifact!"

Presit peered over the edge of her dark glasses toward the bleachers and pinned the protesting scientist with a patronizing glare. "He are taking a tiny bite, not making a meal."

"Eat! Eat! Eat! Eat!"

Torin could hear half a dozen other languages besides Federate rising from the crowd, but she assumed they meant the same thing. Crowds seldom shouted *have you thought this through?*

The H'san shoved their communicator back . . . somewhere, and their inner eyelids flicked closed, then open. Torin would bet her pension that they'd been told to be ready.

For what?

"Presit . . ."

They stepped toward the plastic.

"Presit!"

She poked a finger into Torin's thigh. "Not now! We are going to be getting answers!"

One way or another seemed to be implied.

Girstin closed his teeth on the edge of the data sheet, the arc in his mouth no more than half a centimeter wide at the deepest point. He straightened, chewing, arms raised, and the crowd roared. Most of the scientists were on their feet, slates in hand. "Tastes like . . ."

"Look!" cried a multitude of voices as fine appendages pointed toward the projection.

The symbols flickered, running left to right, then right to left. Moving faster and faster, until they moved at the speed Dr. Lushin had used in zir presentation.

"Mictok!" Torin's voice was pure gunnery sergeant. "Eyes down!"

The Mictok from the front row of the bleachers scrambled to join the two sitting behind her and they began webbing themselves together. Another group of three higher up in the stands followed their example. The military could take care of themselves—Torin was a Warden now; the civilians were her responsibility. The scientists were on their feet.

"Those are new!"

"They've never . . ."

"Recording this . . ."

"Out of my way!"

". . . my instruments!"

"You're an idiot!"

"Stop right there!" Torin held up a hand, and the advancing scientists rocked to a halt. "No one comes any closer!"

Dr. Lushin's tail lashed and zir ears flattened. "You don't tell us what to do, Warden, we . . ."

The sheet rippled like a Polint dislodging a fly, froze, then the symbols spilled off the bottom. Torin looked down expecting to see an alien forming on the dais, didn't, realized it had been an illusion created by the constant downward movement, and looked up.

A set of six symbols appeared in the center of the sheet.

Disappeared.

Appeared again.

Torin felt her hair lift and the barbed feet of a thousand tiny insects against her skin.

Disappeared.

Appeared again.

Dr. Lushin was shouting at her. Torin ignored him.

Always the same sequence.

Faster.

Torin met Craig's eyes, grabbed Girstin's wrist and swung him away from the plastic as Craig wrapped both arms around Presit and dove behind the podium.

"EVERYONE DOWN! EYES CLOSED!"

Girstin stared up at her in rising panic as they hit the dais, and Torin rolled them so her body sheltered his.

"Close your eyes!" she snapped.

He fought her grip but closed his eyes, and the world went white.

The thousands of insects returned although this time they were the size of the Mictok and they were pissed.

One Dornagain. Torin used to count by H'san. Not anymore. *Two Dornagain. Three Dornagain.*

And it was over.

They'd been slammed against the lower supports of the bleachers with enough force that, had they been standing, they'd have been organic missiles fired into the dignitaries. Girstin had hit the supports first and, given the strength of Krai bone, that had probably saved Torin.

His eyes were open again. Pupils slightly dilated.

She couldn't see any blood. "Are you hurt?"

It took her a heartbeat to realize he couldn't speak because his mouth was full of her arm.

Then the pain hit.

"God fukking damnit, recruit! Teeth!"

Flushing a deep green, he jerked his head back, clanged against the support, and said, "I'm not a recruit."

"Lucky for you."

Her uniform had kept him from breaking the skin, but she wasn't sure about the bone. The Justice Department had saved money by leaving the medical sensors out of their dress uniforms, not that it would have mattered as the sweat dribbling down her sides suggested her environmental controls had been fried. When one set went, the others seldom survived.

"Torin!"

"Alive." She coughed at the bite of chlorine against the back of her throat. Right arm cradled diagonally across her chest, hand tucked into the top of her tunic to hold it there, she got to her knees, rocked back onto her heels, and stood, her eyes beginning to water. The bleachers remained standing, about half their occupants sprawled across the far end, the rest scattered on the ground. The Mictok remained safely secured, webbed in place, and the lower three had been joined by Dr. Lushin, thrown against the webbing before it dried. Torin didn't entirely blame Lushin for the screaming or the frantic lashing of zir orange-and-cream-striped tail. When a Mictok claw slid through the webbing and poked zir in the side, ze fainted.

There was surprisingly little screaming going on, although she could hear moaning, cursing, praying, and someone barking out orders under the bleachers. As she turned, she heard a child shrieking, but couldn't tell the species.

The crowd at the far side of the plaza had panicked and run. The PLE had kept the exits open, and it looked like there'd been a minimal number of bodies taken down in the crush. People closer to the dais were in worse shape, and it was obvious who'd had a trained response to Torin's order and who hadn't. The pulse had gone out at dais level, passing harmlessly over those flat on the ground. The di'Taykan sergeant knelt beside a Niln, one hand applying pressure against a puncture, the other unwinding a diaphanous scarf from around her neck. About a third of the Younger Races in the plaza were tending to the wounded, bullying those closest into helping, but there weren't enough. Then, over the sound of the puking and the sobbing and the denial, Torin heard sirens.

She put her finger and thumb in her mouth and whistled. Heads turned. Pointing toward the only area almost clear enough for an EM vehicle to land, she yelled, "Medical incoming, people! Make a space!"

Then she coughed up drops of blood, the volume having ripped lines in the chlorine-tenderized lining of her throat.

The first of the ships came out of the sun, skimmed in over the surrounding buildings . . .

At least half of the veterans on the ground dropped flat. Torin didn't blame them.

. . . and settled, disgorging medical personnel before it was fully on the ground.

"Props to their emergency response teams," Craig breathed out behind her. "What's wrong with your arm?"

His eyes and nose had run silver trails of moisture into his beard and while she wasn't far enough gone to think he'd never looked better, he looked pretty damned good. "Probably broken."

"We should . . ." He reached for her arm, but she stepped back.

"Krai bite. It's stabilized. No need to look until it can be repaired."

"There's blood on your lips."

"There's snot in your beard. In the words of Hollice," she added as he opened his mouth, "not my first rodeo. Come on."

No one had died, not on the dais, not on the plaza, but that been luck. There were broken bones, lacerations, punctures, and two panic-induced heart attacks. It was probably best Dr. Lushin remained unconscious as the Mictok carried zir to the medics. EM vehicles moved in and out of the plaza, directed by the growing number of PLE on the ground.

Torin did the kind of first aid that required neither an intimate knowledge of the species in question nor two arms. When the last injury on the dais had been taken over by the professionals, she allowed Craig to sit her down in front of a medic. Her arm had swollen to fill the sleeve of her tunic.

"Krai bite," she explained.

"I are giving my compliments to your uniform," the Katrien medic muttered, pulling out a syringe. "Pain?"

"About a seven." Maybe an eight now nothing was distracting her.

"It are going to be an eleven when I are cutting you free. So . . ."

The painkiller spread like a rush of cold down Torin's arm and the sudden absence of pain made her a little light-headed.

"I don't know why you had to wait," Craig growled as the medic sliced through the fabric.

"Because I could."

"There were injures less serious seen sooner."

About to shrug, she reconsidered. "They were on people who were a lot more distressed."

"I hate that you're used to . . . Fukking hell, Torin!"

Blunt force trauma from Krai teeth had detached a chunk of forearm muscle, wobbling loose inside rapidly darkening skin within bands of compacted tissue.

"Luckily, you are having nerve damage."

Torin appreciated the way emergency medical personnel were the same competent take-no-shit miracle workers no matter the uniform. "I thought I might be."

"The absence of screaming are probably giving it away." The medic slid Torin's arm into a medical sleeve, glanced at the display, cycled through the programs, and pressed enter. "This are being enough for now," she said as the sleeve stiffened, "but I are wanting you at the hospital to be exchanging it for a higher functioning version as soon as you can. We are having no more transport, or I'd be sending you myself. It are having been registered," she added, "and they'll be expecting you, so don't be thinking of skipping out."

"Why would . . ."

"I are not having to go to war to be knowing a Marine when I are working on one. Open your mouth."

The spray tasted like fish. Torin considered spitting, but at the medic's glare swallowed instead.

"That are not being so bad, are it? It are all I have left and that are what you are getting when you wait for whiny kits with nothing more than bruising to be seen first." She rolled her shoulders back and, for a moment looked exhausted. A line of fur along her arm had clumped into a row of hard, triangular tufts, the brown darkened to almost black. Then she shook herself, straightened, and continued. "It are made for Katrien, but it are being a surface analgesic that are having broad species parameters to be neutralizing the damage in your throat." Her case closed, she straightened and patted Craig's hand. "Good luck."

"What is it with you and Katrien?" Torin asked as the medic hurried away.

"Damned if I know." He sagged against her uninjured side.

Torin stretched out her legs beside his and stared down at the rust-colored stains on the pale gray.

"One of the reasons the Corps wears black?" he asked.

"Yeah, well, bloodstains are bad for morale."

"And here you are being, back on the bleachers." Presit approached, holding Girstin by the ear, her claws sunk into flesh. She gave him a little shake as they came to a stop. "Be speaking up."

Girstin's nostril ridges were shut tight, but that might have been due to the amount of fur Presit shed with every movement. Eyes locked on the medical sleeve, he mumbled, "I'm sorry I bit you, Warden Kerr."

"There." Presit gave him another shake. "Was that being so hard? Now, go. Be finding out when, exactly, the camera drones are having cut out." She watched him scuttle away, limping slightly, and sighed. "He are trying to tell me, it wasn't having been his fault. It was being his teeth and his jaw, though, wasn't it? I are thinking he are not being cut out for investigative . . ."

"You knew!" The approaching Niln wasn't military or a scientist, so he had to be a politician. He wore a medical sleeve on his tail and an agitated expression. "I was watching you, Warden Ryder, and you knew before the data sheet blew. How did you know?"

Craig sighed. "It was obvious, wasn't it, mate? Sequence kept speeding up—it was revving its engine." He stood and held out a hand. Torin decided that not only was discretion the better part of valor, but the last of the adrenaline had been chased off by the pain mods the medic had given her, and she really didn't want to face-plant in front of Presit who'd never let the universe forget it. Craig all but lifted her to her feet, steadying her as she swayed with a hand in the small of her back. "Come on, let's not keep the hospital waiting."

Tongue tasting the air, the Niln stepped in front of them, blocking their path. "I don't know what revving its engine means."

"Not my problem." Craig scowled down at him. "Now, piss off."

"His *vortees* are being injured, Minister." Presit pushed between them. "Let me be explaining to you his idiom." She tucked her hand in the crook of the Niln's elbow and steered him over toward the entrance to the building, shooting an easily identifiable *you owe me* glare back over her shoulder.

"Let's hope that minister isn't in finance," Torin murmured, leaning on Craig because she wanted to. "The commander won't be happy if I've pooched his budget."

"I don't give a fuk."

"Good for you."

They passed two clumps of scientists bent over their slates, arguing data.

"I thought the slates were dead?"

"Out here. Slates inside the building were unaffected. Those are replacements."

Torin made a noncommittal noise as she watched an argument break out about wavelengths. "They must be pulling data from the satellites."

"Still don't give a fuk."

Without symbols, the hanging data sheet looked like an orange tarp.

"Kerr!"

"Hey." Torin grabbed Craig's arm and hauled him to a stop as General Morris pushed his way through a clump of junior officers standing by the big double doors, resisting the efforts of the PLE to move them inside. "Let him talk. It doesn't mean anything."

General Morris hadn't changed. He was still heavyset, florid, and frowning. He still had two stars on his collar and resentment for the missing third showed in his eyes. "You could have stopped her, Kerr!"

"General Morris." She straightened, squaring her shoulders. "Sir, you remember Craig Ryder?"

He opened his mouth, closed it again, thrown by her response. "Did you not hear me?" he managed at last.

"Yes, sir." Holding his gaze, she waited.

The general cleared his throat. "Warden Ryder."

Craig remained silent, but Torin assumed he'd nodded as General Morris returned his attention to her. "I'm curious how you think I could have stopped Presit a Tur durValintrisy. Confederation law gives the press full access to government procedures, and this was her first opportunity to get close to the plastic. If she'd been given access previously, as the law allows, this wouldn't have happened."

"And you'd know about the law, wouldn't you?" he growled, trying for full bluster and failing.

"Yes, sir, I would."

"You could have refused to touch the data sheet!"

"Touching the data sheet had no effect."

"You could have stopped that Krai!"

"How?"

"You're twice his size, and you've never hesitated getting physical before."

If she hadn't hesitated, he'd be dead, and they both knew that. "Why?"

"What?"

"Why would I stop Per Girstin?"

"So that . . ." He waved a hand at the empty dais. ". . . wouldn't have happened?"

"You knew there'd be an energy discharge if Per Girstin bit the data sheet?" Warden voice wasn't quite the same as gunnery sergeant voice, but it was close.

"What?"

She pulled her slate from her belt and thumbed on the voice recorder. "General Morris, did you know the discharge would happen if Per Gristen bit the data sheet?"

"No!"

"Thank you. If we need more information, we know where to find you."

"That will . . . You don't . . ." Confused, he stepped back. Nodded once and turned to go.

"Oh, General Morris." When he turned back toward her, Torin smiled the smile a gunnery sergeant would give a two-star general. "If you would, please give my regards to Captain Stedrin."

His back straightened. "I'm not your social secretary, Kerr. And Stedrin didn't re-up."

"I'm sorry to hear that, sir." The general's aide had been evolving into the kind of staff officer the Corps needed.

"And if you'd stayed in the Corps, that would matter." Bluster returned, he pivoted on one heel and strode toward the building, a Krai lieutenant hurrying out to meet him.

"He was willing to sacrifice himself to bring the Silsviss into the

Confederation," she replied to Craig's expression. "He misread the situation, and it was a weird last shot at glory thing, but he was willing. I respect that."

"Still want to punch him?"

She thought about it for a moment. About Haysole, and Aylx, and Glicksohn, and the others who'd died on Silsviss because of General Morris' plan. Of hauling Captain Travik's body through the bowels of Big Yellow. "Hell, yes."

"But you don't make gunnery sergeant by punching asshole officers." He steered them past the podium, still smelling of fried technology. "They should make that a recruiting slogan."

"It's covered in basic." The di'Taykan sergeant was with the last cluster of people leaving the plaza. When she turned to face the dais, Torin straightened and nodded. Her hair flipped out and she nodded back. At that moment, they understood each other as well as any two people could. "It's not just violence we learn," Torin said softly and added before Craig could ask what she was talking about, "We need to put together a sitrep for Commander Ng."

"After the hospital."

She froze as she stepped onto the plaza, rocking in place as Craig took another step, his arm around her waist. The bleachers had been mostly empty. The Mictok had been webbed in. Dr. Lushin had been stuck to the lower trio. One by one, she placed the people she remembered in the places she remembered them. "Did you see the H'san after the blow?" she asked as Craig turned toward her, brows up.

"Probably had reports of their own to make. Does it matter?" His distrust of the H'san ran less deep than hers.

Did it? "I don't know."

Torin tapped the medical sleeve against the edge of the table and frowned down at it.

"Stop trying to prove it's not as good as the ones the Corps uses."

"I'm not." She slid the bowl of toasted legumes away from him and threw three into her mouth. "And it's not."

They were on the next shuttle out, but that left them with fourteen hours to kill. The hotel bar had a "host" not a bartender, so they went looking for somewhere they could actually relax and ended up at a bar on the rough edges of town, dropped off by a driver whose nest owned shares in the establishment and who insisted they wouldn't be recognized. If they were, the clientele were more interested in the drinks in front of them and the games being played on both of the big vid screens. It helped that the light levels were Katrien low although there were no Katrien in the bar.

Torin didn't recognize the game, but was impressed by how far a Dornagain could hurl a Rakva and by how graceful the Rakva, who'd lost their wings millennia ago, were in the air. Craig put down a bet on the team holding the goal.

"Do you know what's going on?"

He grinned and drained his glass. "Not a clue."

She drained hers as well and beckoned for a refill. "I don't think that discharge was a defensive move, I think it was a side effect."

"We're talking about this now?"

A gesture took in the main room of the bar, the yelling sports fans, the inattentive staff, and the total lack of visible slates. "This is as close to privacy as we're going to get."

"Susumi . . ."

"Everything said on a government ship is recorded, just in case."

"In case of what, then?"

"Problems. You didn't know?"

"Salvage stations don't have that kind of storage to spare. You don't care?"

"The Confederation was built on transparency and privacy's a limited commodity in the military. No one looks at the recordings unless there's a problem. Or," she added before he could respond, "unless security's bored and they search through bunk shots."

"Seriously?"

She shrugged.

"Then as honored as I am to contribute to security's spank bank, we're talking about this now. Thanks, mate." Craig tapped his card against the server's slate—who rolled his eyes, checked his tip, and set the glasses of beer onto the table. "Gotta love the kind of place where you don't get your drinks until you pay." He took a long swallow and sighed. "Fuk me, that's good. All right, you think the sheet was sending a message? A distress call?"

Torin smiled. All that lovely muscle held up a fully functioning brain.

"Ta, darlin' "

"Did I say that out loud?" While Craig nodded, leaned back, and flexed, the dispensing panel on the hospital sleeve surrendered to a brute force entry. "It's a broken arm," she growled as she disabled the general painkiller and upped the local. "Chewed and broken, but the rest of me's fine." Shoving the shattered circuitry back inside, she reapplied enough brute force to secure the cover. "Okay." She took a deep breath and silently dared Craig to object. He shook his head but kept his mouth shut. Smart man. "Okay," she said again, "I think that was the first time the sheet's physical integrity was disrupted, so yes, I think it was a distress call."

"Space is big." Craig paused as a Rakva spun through the upper goal and the bar went wild. "Space is big," he began again, when he had a better chance of being heard. "What are the odds it'll get a response in our lifetime?"

"What are the odds of *Harveer* Arniz falling in that particular hole? What are the odds of you finding Big Yellow in the first place? What are the odds of us all having bits of plastic in our heads and not having made an independent decision for centuries?"

"You have no idea."

"I have no idea." Torin finished her beer and rode the thrum of pain from her arm. "If the plastic builds tech with plastic, it'd be like us building tech with meat."

Craig choked on a mouthful of beer. "What?"

"Something Vertic said on Threxie." She pressed her foot against his under the table. "I wish I could see the look on the face of Anthony Marteau when he learns about the weapon he paid to retrieve." When *Harveer* Arniz, the soil scientist who'd been part of the original discovery, had been given a chance to properly analyze the contents of the second latrine, she'd discovered it was simply high concentrations of uric acid that had dissolved the plastic. Although she'd admitted she had no way of knowing if the plastic had fallen into the latrine or been pushed. Torin stared into her beer and tried to catch hold of her thoughts. Damned painkillers weren't out of her system yet. "We had a cat when I was kid who'd piss on the stove," she said when the beer offered no answers. "Dissolved the chrome trim." The tiny calico had spent a lot of time riding on her father's shoulder. "Dad loved that cat. My mother kept threatening to make soup."

"I thought your mother didn't cook?"

"She doesn't. She didn't threaten to make *good* soup."

Half the crowd leapt to their feet cheering as the other half yelled insults at the screen, and it took Torin a moment to realize they were reacting to a Dornagain being escorted from the field of play by an official.

"Improper lofting," Craig told her.

One brow rose.

He grinned. "Maybe we should've pissed on the data sheet."

Torin lifted her glass in salute. "Maybe we should've. That would've played well on the news."

· ——◆—— ·

"I understand what you're telling me." Anthony Marteau pressed his fingertips against the workbench and leaned forward. "I don't care."

"Your prerogative, but we had to care about neutralizing the scent. We work with it."

He pinned Kalowski or Kalenski or whatever the hell her name was with a mocking smile. "I put you to work, if you'll recall. Now I want to see results."

Kalowski—or Kanonski—sighed. "The problem, Per Marteau, is that urea at these concentrations is unpleasantly pungent, and we don't exactly have access to laboratory grade samples."

"We smelled like we spent all day being pissed on," Laghari muttered, arms folded.

Her name, Anthony remembered. Tall and thin, she reminded him of a di'Taykan major he'd had to deal with, right down to the brilliant purple hair. Although, on Laghari, the purple covered only the last ten centimeters of her single braid.

He'd had to make a few changes since his precipitous arrival into the bosom of Humans First, although, for the most part, the structure remained the same. Those few who knew his resources had been responsible for most of what the organization had achieved over the years had been given permission to spread the information among the rank and file. And they hadn't merely assigned the credit for ships and arms and the very food they ate, but had made it quite clear that without his awareness of the superiority of Humanity and his willingness to reclaim their rightful place in the universe, there would be no Humans First. He wasn't their leader—he had no interest in dealing with the daily minutiae of revolution—he was their genesis.

No longer their silent benefactor, he took up the mantle of innovation, his position separate and superior to the chain of command.

All of which meant that his request for urea that matched the chemical composition of the urea in the latrines on 33X73 shouldn't be taking so damned long to fulfill. They'd had the information as long as the Confederation government, and he doubted those oppressive marionettes had been sitting around with their thumbs up what passed for their alien asses.

Granted the lack of speed could be at least partially due to the lack of chemists drawn to the cause. Kanonski—Karpanski?—had been a Naval armaments officer and Madeline Laghari, a Marine explosives tech who'd continued to ply her trade after her contract had ended. In a just universe, Laghari would be of more use to him, but in a just universe where Humanity hadn't been driven to the brink of cultural genocide by animals and insects, they wouldn't have had to fight to reclaim their place, so, in that universe, he'd have had no use for her at all. In that universe she could spend a stint in rehabilitation in an effort to keep her from blowing up other people's property without official sanction. Humans weren't perfect—he shut that line of thought down whenever it came up—but they were *Human* and that granted the least of them more leeway with the law. Particularly when the laws had been written by their oppressors.

"I can smell you from here," he told Laghari. "I don't judge, fortunately." Hands in his pockets, he bounced up onto the balls of his feet and smiled. "I also don't intend to allow more Humans to die in alien wars. I can build a weapon to use this new information, because that's what I do, I build weapons. I built the weapons that kept you two alive." He sharpened his smile. "I can't, however build squat until I know the specific corrosive properties of what I have to deliver, properties which can't be precisely determined from ancient molecular samples."

Karpanski—Karnipson?—shook her head. "We have a close estimation . . ."

"I don't work in estimations."

Laghari snorted. "You're building a pressurized tank and a nozzle. How hard can it be?"

Eyes narrowed, he studied her for a long moment. Waited until she began to fidget before he spoke, the edge in his voice the same edge that had cut his way through the volatile mix of weapons manufacturers and politicians; there was never enough war to go around. "I'm building a pressurized tank and a nozzle. I never thought of it like that. Possibly because I have more experience in building weapons than you have outstanding warrants with various PLEs." Technically, his expression remained a smile. "I'd prefer to be told now if you two feel you're incapable of completing your assignment. I'm sure Humans First has other uses for you."

Karnipson—Capaldi?—ran a hand back over pale cropped hair, apparently intelligent enough to recognize a threat. "Distilling gives us the correct concentration, but changes the composition too dramatically for us to match the composition of the samples taken on 33X73." "Shallow pan evaporation . . ."

"Made us smell like we spent all day being pissed on."

"I admire your tenacity, Laghari. I truly do." He cocked his head. "I wonder if you consider applying it to the matter at hand?"

Laghari rolled her eyes. "We're not actually going to piss on the plastic and call it a weapon."

He grinned and enjoyed the way she bristled in response. "I'm thrilled to see you're smarter than you look, but, if we get the chance, we will definitely piss on the plastic."

"It'd help," Capaldi—Canary?—interjected before Laghari could dig herself in deeper, "if the urea donors would eat more meat."

"More meat?"

"Carnivores have more acidic urine."

"I'm appalled that science has devolved to meat, but I'll have a word with the procurement team. I'm sure there's a few savages among us." From the disgusted expression on both faces, Anthony felt safe in assuming that yeast had been the most complex protein either had consumed. "As much as I've enjoyed the banter, we all have things to do. I want results before the end of the tenday."

Laghari opened her mouth, but Kalanowski—he was almost positive it was Kalanowski—jumped in first. "You'll have them, Per Marteau."

"All I wanted to hear." He gave them a two-finger wave, pivoted on one heel, and left the lab. Or what passed for a lab.

The tunnels were empty as he returned to the area he'd claimed, quarters and workshop isolated from the rest of the base when he'd had them carved out and fitted to his specifications some years ago. He'd never intended to use them as he'd never intended to be part of the fighting, his connections and expertise more valuable behind the scenes. When the fighting ended, he'd step in to provide necessary structure. Fortunately, he also believed in planning for every contingency including the one that had him living inside an asteroid where everything but his quarters had been designed by a degenerate civilization.

The Justice Department would never think to look for Humans First on an old Taykan mining station.

He liked to think he was self-aware enough to realize that he was in hiding due, in a small way, to his own enthusiasm. Had he not been so excited about rediscovering a piece of Human history that he'd sent it out to be field tested on a supply run, there'd have been no reason for that di'Taykan Warden to have accessed his data files.

Of course, if that particular di'Taykan had spent his time on indiscriminate sex like the rest of his species instead of learning to crack code in a highly suspicious manner . . .

And if the Berins had stopped the Krai in their crew from gorging and been on time to pick up their supplies . . .

And if those cat things from the Primacy had been as dangerous as advertised . . .

And if it hadn't been for Gunnery Sergeant Torin Fukking Kerr.

What an asset Kerr would have been had she not absorbed the indoctrination she'd been soaked in since childhood. The Elder Races were wise. The Elder Races know best. All members of the Confederation are equal. Bullshit. He'd hoped the discussions in Parliament of locking the Younger Races away now they were no longer needed would have brought her to the Human cause, but she kept fighting for the *ideals* of the Confederation and thwarting the freedom of her own species at every turn. Her Strike Teams—and he, at least, had no doubt they were hers regardless of what the alien-controlled media reported—stood squarely between Humans First and their determination to give Humanity back their rightful place among the stars.

The presence of a H'san at Berbar Station around the time he should have been hearing from the team he'd sent searching for ancient weapons supported Kerr having had a part in shutting that expedition down as well, leaving him with no way to prove the H'san were not the peaceful, cheese-eating Elders they pretended to be.

The lock on his workshop showed two attempts at entry while he was gone. He made a mental note to increase the voltage.

Soft music began to play as he closed the door behind him. He detoured just far enough to lightly touch the small, pink, plastic pre-diaspora pony on its plinth, then crossed to his workbench and picked one of the dozen newly printed pistols. They weren't quite as sturdy as those he'd printed back at MI, the equipment here was a generation older and he'd had to adapt the design to take that into account. Still, they were beautiful. He ran his fingers over the precision molding, and wished for a few more people who could see beyond their indoctrination.

Weapons that could be hidden were wrong.

Weapons used for anything but the war the Elder Races had gotten Humanity into with lies and sparkly temptations were wrong.

Weapons that could be used to redress the wrongs of the universe were wrong.

Every member of the Confederation was taught those beliefs as children and constantly reminded of them as adults. No matter how true a believer in the cause, no matter how willing to stand up against those species who refused to acknowledge Humanity's place, most of Humans First were unable to shake the belief that a pistol was evil incarnate.

A pistol was a tool.

Like a hammer. A hammer could be hidden. A hammer could be used to kill.

A pistol was a specialized tool.

He'd heard his pistols referred to as dishonorable. He couldn't get a decent chemist, but it seemed they had no shortage of philosophers.

"Per Murteau!" The skinny teenager who stumbled into his workshop was unknown to him but there were few enough young people involved in the cause that he allowed the interruption. "Per Marteau! The commander wants to know if you saw what happened on Nuh Ner!"

"On New Brussels."

"Sir?"

"We don't use the alien names."

The boy's eyes widened. "Right. Okay. Did you see?"

He hadn't.

"It could have been protecting itself." Commander Belcerio reached for the bottle to refill his glass.

"I know weapons," Anthony said thoughtfully, staring at the screen in the commander's office as the news report picked up by the closest Susumi buoy ran through the visuals again. "I doubt that's a weapon. Power to area targeted ratio is off."

"It could be a self-destruct, wiping the programming off the sheet."

"Not dispersing like that, it couldn't." He thrust a hand into his pocket and ran his thumb down the back of the pink plastic pony. "It's an emergency beacon. It's been damaged. It called for help."

"It's entirely alien." Belcerio took a long swallow of what smelled like bad whiskey. "You can't know that."

"I have good instincts."

Belcerio had been his personal pick as the new commander of Humans First, his experience in the corporate world of weapons manufacturing balancing his decade in the Corps. He had a tendency to assume more power than he actually had, but it was a minor flaw and nothing Anthony couldn't deal with.

"All right. What do your instincts say we do now?"

The news report had cycled back to the Katrien screeching about the discovery of the data sheet. Anthony turned and faced Belcerio and smiled. "We prepare for the return of the plastic. We prepare to unite every Human in the Confederation as we prove the plastic can be destroyed."

Belcerio emptied his glass. "With urine?"

"I prefer to think of it as uric acid, but yes, with urine. Human urine. Human ingenuity." Anthony didn't regret having Richard Varga killed; his death had been necessary to nudge Humans First in a less rhetorical direction. He did regret having lost Varga's way with words. Varga would have had Laghari and the woman who was probably Kalowski wringing the urine from their clothing without complaint, and had them willingly work day and night to create a weapon that would help unite humanity.

"It's a piss-poor idea, if you ask me."

He smiled, although not at Belcerio's weak attempt at humor. "I didn't ask you."

Back in his workshop, he carefully returned the plastic pony to its pedestal and pulled out the pistol he'd dropped into his other pocket.

Weapons development had been stagnant under the so-called Elder Races. The last thing they wanted was for Humanity to use its creative genius against them.

Somewhere, there was a cache of H'san weapons that should have been his.

The pistol had warmed in his grip.

He slipped his finger past the trigger guard. There were days . . .

FOUR

"**SHOULD'VE TAKEN ME** with you, Gunny. I know how to take a bite of the plastic and make sure it stays down." Werst grabbed a bowl of *hujin* chips with a foot and set it on his lap. "The kid going to get nailed for his part in it?"

"Presit took full responsibility," Torin told him, clearing away the last of the meal debris. Team meals had become tradition after Strike Team Alpha was apart for any length of time. There were one hundred and forty-seven food delivery services on the station and they'd ordered from about half of them. "Girstin is a menial intern at Sector Central News. No one seems to think he could have refused her."

"You do," Ressk pointed out.

"I was just following orders has been a shit excuse for centuries."

By the time they docked at Berbar, the footage from Nuh Ner dominated the commonality hours, the time set aside to ensure everyone in the Confederation received access to the same information. The network of Susumi buoys were a large factor in the position of new colonies, and those destroyed during the war had been replaced first during the rebuilding, the links that maintained Confederation unity reestablished.

"Kind of a terrifyingly blank expression there, Boss."

She glanced over at Alamber as he threw himself down into a chair in a way only a di'Taykan could make look graceful.

"Not your usual remembering the war face," he added, pale blue eyes darkening as more light receptors opened.

"It's her waiting for orders face," Werst said around a mouthful of chips. "Corps teaches it when you get your third chevron. Keeps officers from knowing what the noncoms are really thinking."

"That true?" Craig asked quietly, pitching his voice under Ressk and Werst informing Alamber of the terrifying thought processes of noncommissioned officers.

Torin grinned, temporarily putting aside the realization of how much unity could sound like uniformity. "True enough."

"It's time!" Alamber flicked on the screen.

The news had promised a new analysis.

"Why do they have to show the whole presentation from the beginning every *serley* time?" Ressk thumbed the sound down. "Was it this boring live?"

"Worse," Craig told him. "I'd have given a kidney to have sped things up."

"Whose?" Werst demanded.

The analysis leaned toward ancient tech having broken down, with emphasis on the length of time the data sheet had been forgotten underground.

"What a load." Ressk snorted as on the screen two Dornagain techs removed the blank data sheet from the dais. "Craig's right. I wasn't even there, and the energy buildup was obvious."

"Doesn't mean it didn't break down," Alamber told him. "Symptom, not cause."

The techs looked nervous, cameras picking up shed fur, and there were more PLE around than there had been during the presentation—although Torin had no idea what the hell they were supposed to do if the plastic went off again. From their expressions, neither did they. "It didn't break down. It sent a message."

Ressk shook his head. "The security satellites snagged enough of the beam for them to study the composition. No one who examined the data is willing to say it had content."

"The plastic was here for generations and Confederation scientists had no idea." Craig tossed a new bag of *hujin* chips at Werst. "Not really holding my donger in excitement over their current observations."

"The beam was the message."

Werst paused, a chip halfway to his mouth. "That a Gunny-gut-feeling or a had-the-plastic-in-your-head feeling?"

Torin thought about it for a moment. "Bit of both."

"Got any feelings about what it said?" Ressk wrestled the chip bag away from his *vertras*.

Craig snickered. "It was just in someone's mouth."

"Not always a bad thing," Alamber agreed, grinning.

"Could've been so stoked it sent a party invitation."

"Well . . ." Alamber's hair traced suggestive curves in the air. "If it can take any shape . . ."

Binti stepped through the open hatch and ducked a chip diverted from the steady stream Werst was pelting Alamber with. "That's what I call a pathetic food fight. Don't get that shit in your eyes, Alamber. You'll want to dip your face in yogurt."

Torin raised a hand, and the bombardment ceased. "You're looking good." The deep yellow wrap patterned in green-and-brown geometrics hugged Binti's torso and flowed around her legs. The intricate gold designs on her arms made the color of her skin look even richer and picked up the intermittent flicker of gold light woven into the fabric.

Binti grinned. "I always look good."

"Those the Herish stencils we got on Darmac?" Alamber asked, carefully brushing chips off his lap.

"They are."

"And who did you break them out for?"

"None of your damned business." She held up a multistrand beaded necklace that looked like the wrap remade as jewelry. "Gunny? Little help?"

Werst scowled at the small, flat keeper cleaning chips off the floor. "She blows off a team dinner for a date, I think we should know who it's with," he muttered.

"Taylor in legal," Ressk said.

"Taylor's hot." Alamber nudged the small cleaner buzzing around his feet toward a missed chip.

"Going somewhere fancy?" Craig asked as Torin settled the beads against the elegant lines of Binti's collarbone.

"There's a retro jazz combo in Malan's," Ressk answered before Binti could. "Very upper branch. Very hard to get tickets."

Alamber's hair rose. "Taylor likes you."

"Are you twelve?" Moving only her head, she turned to Ressk. "And why are you paying so much attention to my life?"

"I'm easily bored."

Werst saluted with a chip. "He is."

"There." Torin let her fingers linger for a moment against warm skin, then stepped back. "Surprised you couldn't get it yourself."

"I could." Binti turned, skirt swirling, gold flashing. "But I wanted to show off how fine I looked."

Torin nodded. "Fair enough. You look amazing. Taylor will be knocked on their ass."

"That's the plan. Try to keep all hell from breaking out for the next six to eight hours, would you?"

"I'll do what I can. Binti . . ."

Binti paused at the hatch.

"Taylor's all right for a lawyer."

She rolled her eyes, but looked pleased. "I'll tell them you said so."

Alamber sighed deeply as her footsteps faded down the corridor. "They grow up so fast."

"When do you plan on trying it?"

"You want to see growing . . ."

Craig looped an arm around Torin's waist and pulled her close. "You should get an outfit like that."

"You hate jazz."

"I wasn't thinking of you going out in it." He waggled his eyebrows, and she threaded her fingers into his hair, pulling lightly.

"Yeah, that's adorable." Werst stretched, toes cracking. "Night's young. Musselman's?"

Torin shook her head. "Not me, not tonight. U'yun's due back from their first run, and I want to be there."

The Krai exchanged a look.

"Heard it went okay." Ressk's tone made it almost a question.

"It did. But I want eyes on."

"Commander." Torin fell into step beside Commander Ng as they entered the docking arm and shortened her stride as she would have for a Krai. The commander wasn't much taller.

"Warden. On your way to check on U'yun?"

"Yes, sir."

"Not your job."

"Not technically, no." Although the angle was off, Torin could see purple shadows under his eyes. He'd lost weight, too. "You look tired, sir."

"Thank Humans First for that. This latest round of attacks on the mining platforms has led to complaints from the Mictok Central Council and that's led to me explaining to Justice that we can't anticipate their next target and we don't have the personnel to guard every platform in the sector. *Attempting* to explain to Justice," he clarified wearily after a moment. "They seem to think Susumi capabilities mean we can be everywhere at once."

"If they . . ."

"They won't approve more teams. There's been discussion in Parliament about Justice building a private military."

"By the *send the kids to their room* coalition." Not a question, and she hadn't bothered to dull the edge in her voice.

Ng made a nonverbal agreement—to the words, to the tone, to both—and added, "The minister wants me to address the committee. Again."

In his copious amounts of free time, no doubt. "You need a second."

His exhale was just a bit too vigorous to be called a sigh. "Astute observation, Warden, but no one wants the job. We need a candidate with a military background in order for them to understand exactly what it is the Strike Teams do, but all our military applicants want to be *on* the Strike Teams, and none of your crazy adrenaline junkies are willing to ride a desk."

Torin had never considered herself an adrenaline junkie, but now was not the time to argue semantics. "I know of a possible candidate."

He stopped, turned, and stared up at her. "Do tell."

"Captain di'Rearl Stedrin. He was General Morris' aide back in the day, but he's out now."

"How far from qui?"

"I have no idea, sir." Taykan qui retreated to their family group, not to emerge until their breeding phase ended, and they did not talk about their biology. DI Beyhn had collapsed, his body fighting to throw off illegal suppressants before any Taykan in his 10-12 platoon had been willing to break silence.

"But he'd be a good fit?"

"Yes, sir. Compared to keeping General Morris on track . . ." Which was, Torin acknowledged silently, not entirely fair to the general. Some of his assholery could be blamed on rank not personality. ". . . working for you should be a piece of *clorr.*"

The commander shuddered. "Dornagain food is disgusting."

He wasn't wrong. Even the Krai avoided it. "Bad example."

"Is Stedrin interested?"

"I can make inquiries."

"Do that." He rubbed his palm over his face, fought off most of a yawn, and rolled his shoulders back. "If you're doing the welcome home, glad you survived your first time out meet and greet, there's no reason for me to be there. I've reviewed their reports, had no questions they couldn't answer on their way in from the jump buoy, and I'll see them tomorrow at the all teams debriefing. I'm heading back to . . ."

"Your quarters to get some sleep." It wasn't an order, she didn't give orders to superiors, but it was a statement of fact so definitive there was no room for argument.

Commander Ng stared up at her, dark brows drawn in. Torin maintained a neutral expression and held his gaze. "I assume Captain Stedrin will have more tact?" he asked after a long moment.

"I expect so, sir. He was an officer."

Strike Team U'yun had pulled a good run for their first time out; a Humans First cache of weapons and equipment on one of the larger asteroids in the Idyll Belt, in the same system as Paradise, only 588 million kilometers away. It made sense that they'd attempt to make use of what Paradise symbolized, but Torin had been born there and the thought of them so close to family made her want to break out the heavy ordnance. The mission could've gone to crap had Humans First been dug in.

Ranjit leaned against the wall across from the hatch to the docking nipple. Torin dropped into parade rest beside her; partially a habit when standing next to officers, partially because it was a position she could hold indefinitely. "Cap."

"Gunny."

"I saw Commander Ng on the way down. Sent him to his quarters to get some sleep. He looked like shit."

"If Justice wants him to do his job, they need to get off his back."

"I'm on it."

Ranjit grinned. "Of course you are."

"I know an ex-staff officer who'd be a good fit if he wants the job."

"Let's hope he accepts before they offer it to one of us as a temporary position and we're stuck with it."

"Easier to hire the commander a second than to replace a Strike Team Lead. The commander's second won't be wielding a weapon."

Dark brows rose. "The commander's second will be wielding us."

"Funny how they miss that."

The station sysop informed them that airlock pressure was equalizing, information they could both read off the data pad by the hatch.

"So," Ranjit said after a moment. "Right next door to Paradise. And they sent U'yun." Also from Paradise, Ranjit came from Maharashtra on the other side of the planet, a mere three thousand kilometers from Zhou's home city of Avatari. The first colony world had always had a high enlistment rate.

"Their turn," Torin reminded her.

"I know."

"And Zhou would've been motivated."

"Avatari. Stupid made-up name for a city. No history behind it."

A significant proportion of Maharashtra's original colonists had been Sikh, their beliefs having survived oldEarth's new relationship with the universe better than most, adapting as humanity adapted. Several of Torin's elderly aunties had sniffed haughtily and insisted Buddhism embraced universal expansion on every level. Torin, who believed in pragmatic competence and bringing her people home alive, had been polite.

As the data pad lit up, the station informed them that the lock had equalized.

Ranjit straightened out of her slouch. "If this meeting-the-new-guys is going to be an official thing, we should draw up a schedule."

"Sure, Cap. If we ever get another new team, we can do that." Torin turned to face the hatch.

"You think they'll hold the line? There's not a lot of us."

"There's not a lot of them. Disgruntled citizens trained in violence," she added in response to the silent question. "We have a unique perspective."

"Disgruntled?"

"Seemed less judgy than bugfuk crazy."

"True."

Before leaving, U'yun had scanned the system for any indication

Humans First had a further presence and had left half a dozen drones behind, programmed with known Humans First variables to ping Justice should the terrorists return, but everyone knew it was a symbolic gesture at best. Space hadn't gotten any smaller over the years, and if it was that easy, they'd have had Marteau in custody months ago.

Tylen was first out, a good three strides ahead of the other six. Her hair lifted and she turned, stepping backward over the lip of the hatch. "Hey, there's a welcoming committee. We either did something wrong or something right." She turned again, her hair a bright pink aureole around her head. "You here to pat us on the back, Gunny?"

"I pat you on the back for this, what do I do if you save the universe?"

"You bought me a beer," Ranjit pointed out.

"I don't remember that."

"It's possible I bought myself a beer and put it on your tab. We're here," she continued as the rest of the team stepped into the dockway, "because we were surprised you survived." When Marie flipped her off, Ranjit laughed. "Yeah, you're tough."

They looked rested, calm. Any euphoria at a first mission successfully accomplished had worn off during the three days in Susumi.

"Didn't fire a single round," Lorkin sighed, catching up with Tylen, bare feet slapping against the deck.

"Shorter reports," Torin reminded him.

"Duller reports. I was in more danger last time I went home. *Jernine's* expanding." He shuddered dramatically. "I tried to tell my *jernil* I'd had my DNA scrambled by hard radiation, and she told me she'd served eight years on the *CS Talasin* and I was full of shit. Then she introduced me to seventeen potentials."

"Seventeen? You're not that much of a catch," Marie called from the rear of the group.

"That's what *they* thought," Nicholin said dryly.

"My point is . . ." Lorkin raised his voice enough to be heard over the laughter. ". . . we didn't get to shoot at the bad guys."

"And the bad guys didn't get to shoot at us." Zhou spread his hands as his team turned toward him. "I appreciate not being shot at."

Nicholin's eyes lightened from deep umber to a pale cream. "I'll shoot at you."

Zhou rolled his eyes. "Worst pickup line ever."

"And that's enough of that. Gunny. Cap." Yahsamus nodded at both Torin and Ranjit, then spread her arms and herded her team, minus Elisk, down the dockway. "Come on, kids, move ass to the armory and let the grownups talk."

"Do we get a cookie?"

"You'll get my boot in your butt. Move."

Torin fell in on the right, Ranjit on the left, as Elisk shifted the strap of his KC and headed into the station.

"About half the cache had been shifted," he said after a moment. "And in a fuk of a hurry, too. It was a mess. Weapons were gone, although there were a couple of empty MI cases they'd been using for trash."

"Marteau Industries."

"Well, yeah. They're the merchants of death in this sector, right? Remember that shipyard that got hit, about a year ago? About half the stolen supplies were still there and one of the platform tanks. Assuming they weren't hot racking, there were thirty bodies in house before someone set the tree on fire."

"You think they knew you were coming in?" Torin asked.

Ranjit shook her head, braid bouncing against her back. "Doesn't have to be a conspiracy. If they were building a base, they would've been monitoring the buoys."

"However they found out, they were gone before we were in-system. Weirdest thing, the personnel area, that was right out of the Corps playbook, but the rest? It was like they had a vague idea of what a shipyard needed and had been collecting all the parts, but no one involved had any idea of how to put it together."

"Not a lot of disgruntled Human shipyard designers, then."

"Too bad because at least a shipyard's big enough to find. Bigger than a base anyway." Ranjit amended. "The more coming and going, the more patterns are created patterns and new patterns get noticed."

Torin thought about the compatibility channels.

"And we know they won't drop a shipyard down a gravity well," Ranjit continued, "so we could scratch dirtside searches."

They walked in silence for a few strides, listening to Lorkin try to explain Krai family dynamics to three di'Taykan and two Humans.

"How did the team work out?"

"Like a well-knotted net. A little bitching about the lack of warm bodies to bring in, but . . ." Elisk shrugged. He was no better at the Human gesture than most Krai. "It was good to be doing something useful with our training, and not something for the fukking plastic, but it wasn't very exciting."

Seemed the commander had a valid point about the Strike Teams being made up of adrenaline junkies, Torin acknowledged silently, but it was those similarities that helped them mesh. And considering that neither Corps nor Navy encouraged individualism, it was hypocritical of her to chew at how the Confederation wanted its citizens to have information and beliefs in common. On the other hand, the military needed cohesion to keep its people alive; given that the Confederation consisted of predominantly post-violent civilizations, why work so hard to wipe out differences?

"So, Gunny." Elisk grinned up at her. "Seems you were busy while we were gone. I hear you took a knife to that plastic data sheet and sent a strongly worded message to the rest of the plastic to stay away."

"You heard?"

"People talk, Gunny. People talk."

She glanced over his head at Ranjit who nodded. "The story of you and Ryder taking down the plastic beat you back to the station."

People talking—the weak link in the process of disseminating information.

Berbar's sysop had directed her to a hatch in R&D that opened into a large rectangular compartment with a double line of cluttered workbenches filling the long axis. Five Rakva crowded around a hard-light display at the far end, all talking at once. Unfortunately, they weren't talking in Federate, so even if Torin could parse the spill of words and whistles into sentences, she wouldn't understand them. Given the speed, odds were she wouldn't have understood them even if they'd been talking in Federate. She paused just inside the hatch as feathers literally flew from the force a yellow-and-green Rakva used gesturing at the schematic. It was unlikely the station would have sent her to a sterile room without warning, but she appreciated having that assumption confirmed.

Then a Rakva, almost entirely white with pale pink and gray tinting only the ends of their plumage caught sight of her. They stared down the length of the room. Torin stared back at them. She'd never seen a

Rakva that color—varying shades of yellow, green, blue, and occasionally patches of red, but not white. On the Rakva she was familiar with, the size and shape of the crest would indicate a female, but, all things considered, Torin decided not to make assumptions.

One by one, the other Rakva fell silent and turned to stare.

Torin smiled, keeping her teeth covered. "Dr. Deyell. I hope I'm not interrupting. The station said your hatch was open."

"Warden Kerr." Dr. Deyell stepped away from the group, teal-and-gray feathers ruffled, paused, turned, said/whistled a phrase that sounded impatient, turned again, and began walking toward her. "This one wonders," he said when he was close enough, "why you have brought a weapon into this one's workspace?"

Torin laid the bennie she'd been carrying on a cleared bit of workbench. "I had an idea. You're still working on tranquilizers?"

His rudimentary beak pursed and he sighed. "This one is."

"This should have occurred to me a while ago, but bennies aren't my preferred . . ."

"Boss?"

Torin turned as Alamber stepped into the room. She had no idea where he'd found scarlet combat boots.

"I thought that was your voice. What are you doing in squint land?" He grinned at Dr. Deyell. "Hey, Doc."

"This one wonders why you continue to believe you're funny."

"This one's hurt you think I'm not." One pale long-fingered hand tapped his chest. "Truly hurt."

"Were you looking for me?" Torin asked as Dr. Deyell fluffed his feathers in amusement.

Alamber's eyes darkened. "Always."

"Specifically?"

"No, I'm heading to forensics. They've got the images U'yun sent back, and I wanted to go over them on the big imager to try and figure out what was taken away by the patterns left behind." Alamber nodded toward the weapon. "Sergeant Urrest know you have that?"

Torin raised a brow. "Do I look like I'm asking for a fight?"

"Not currently." He winked, pressed against her side for a moment, then turned to go. "I'm on the range at 1540, Boss, if you want to drop by and check my form. Don't let her shoot you, Doc. Those things hurt. Later."

"He's a very intelligent young male," Dr. Deyell said quietly as Alamber's footsteps faded in the distance. "He's been spending much of his free time in forensics."

"I know."

Dr. Deyell stared at her for a long moment, his crest lifting. "Your idea?"

"His idea."

"But you're not stopping him?"

"Why would I? You're right. He's wasted on a Strike Team."

His crest flattened. "This one didn't say . . ."

Torin waited while his voice trailed off and, when it became clear he wasn't going to continue, she tapped the bennie. "Have you handled one of these before."

"This one does not handle weapons."

"Which is why using it as a base for the nonlethal armaments Justice keeps demanding didn't occur to you either."

"This is nonlethal?"

"It can be. Depends on the species you're firing at and the amount of juice you use. It disrupts cellular structure, so tight beam, full charge, and you can drill through organic matter. You can put it on low at full spread and decontaminate most surfaces, but that's not relevant right now." She frowned and went for full disclosure. "It also has a cutting laser. Also not relevant right now. The Corps uses them on ships or stations where random holes would be a bad idea."

Head cocked, he studied the weapon. "An EMP burst would disable this."

"An EMP burst on a ship or station would disable the environmental controls. As well as the airlocks," she added after a moment.

"What if the enemy were wearing HE suits? Then it wouldn't matter if they also disabled the ship or station."

"HE suits hold a lot of tech. They'll keep you alive without it, but it won't be fun. Also, no one fights in an HE suit if they don't have to."

His crest rose again. "See, this one didn't know that." He leaned forward eagerly, his distaste at being so close to a weapon overcome by new information.

"I was thinking that brains work on electrical signals, so if you adapted the bennie to fire an energy burst that disrupts signals to the brain instead of developing a tranquilizer . . ."

"Which has to be individually calibrated for each species, and this one finds biology annoyingly variable."

". . . you wouldn't have to build the delivery system from scratch."

"This one agrees that would definitely cut development time."

Sergeant Urrest had drained the primary charge to the lowest operative level and locked down the laser, but Torin kept a close eye on Deyell as he bent and lifted the bennie, turning it over and around to check all angles. He couldn't do anything to it, and they'd made it almost impossible for him to do irreparable damage with it, but almost impossible had both won and lost wars.

"Keep your finger outside the trigger guard unless you're ready to shoot."

"This?"

She tapped the lower edge of the curve. "That."

The Rakva voices from the other end of the room rose in volume, one of the whistles growing increasingly shrill. Torin didn't have to check to know they were watching Deyell. One of the Mid Races holding a weapon. Things really had gone to hell since her people were drafted.

"This one doubts the EMP problem could be solved without prohibitive shielding." He set the bennie back on the workbench. "But this one will know better once it's in pieces. That's okay, right?"

He sounded like Alamber, reminding Torin of how young he was. "That's okay."

Straightening, he patted his pockets, didn't find what he searched for, and said, "It sounds like you're thinking of something similar to the item Qurn used on you." He grinned at her raised brow. "This one reads the reports, Strike Team Leader Kerr. This one can't create new equipment if this one has no idea of what you do. We weren't allowed to meet the Primacy team while they were here, but we've petitioned to be included should there be another joint mission."

"We?"

"Yes, fine." He dismissed the question with a wave. "Mostly this one. Although we were all very disappointed not to be given a chance to reverse engineer Qurn's tech. Your medical records, even combined with Commander Yurrisk's and Robert Martin's, gave us nothing definitive we could use."

Qurn, a Druin, who'd turned out to be a Primacy agent within the

Confederation, had used the—Torin hesitated to call it a weapon since it was small enough to conceal, but, realistically, that's what it was—the weapon on two Humans and a Krai. Two very different species, three different body weights. It hadn't been a chemical suppressant, but other than that, the only thing Torin knew was that she'd shaken it off faster than the commander, and it had made her tongue vibrate randomly over the next twenty-seven hours.

"Too bad she took it with her when she was disappeared."

"You mean when she disappeared?"

"No." Qurn hadn't left Berbar Station without high-level government involvement. Torin blamed the H'san. Because she could.

When it became clear Torin wasn't going to expand on her answer, Deyell turned his attention back to the benny. "The range?"

"It's a close-quarters weapon."

"This one doubts we can achieve more range."

The best they'd managed with the prototype tranquilizer guns was accuracy at eighty-five meters. And Binti had taken the shot, skewing the data. "All right." Torin frowned at a bit of teal fluff by the muzzle. "If we need more range, rig one of the KC-9s to fire a contained version of the charge slipped into a modified boomer round. The round would shatter on impact and zap, brain function disrupted, bruised but alive."

"Zap?"

"It's a technical term." It also may have been one of the few words he recognized as it was doubtful he'd be able to identify either a KC-9 or a boomer round. "Large round . . . bullet." Thumb and forefinger curled into the circumference. "In a gun designed to fire variations as long as they're that size." She'd fired a perimeter pin from a nine, more than once, and had fortunately not become an object lesson on why that wasn't a good idea. If the Strike Teams were going to successfully do their jobs, they had to keep lines of communication open with their support staff. Support staff and Strike Teams had to learn to speak each other's language. Coordinate their efforts. Remember this wasn't a military operation, restricted to the Younger Races. Communication remained a work in progress, but at least there was progress.

He considered it for a moment. "No offense, Strike Team Leader, but why didn't the military put the idea into production?"

"My best guess . . . too complicated. War is simple. Peace isn't."

Absently preening the side of his throat, Deyell nodded. "This one will need to research before beginning to make modifications."

"I'll leave you to it, then. Sergeant Urrest is willing to leave the benny in your care on my say-so. Don't shoot anyone unintentionally. If you decide you need to examine a KC, let me know." When she turned toward the hatch, the volume increased in the discussion at the other end of the room. She paused, angled so she could see the white Rakva disdainfully swipe an image out of the air. "Are all of R&D Rakva?"

He glanced over his shoulder. The green-and-yellow Rakva whistled a rude observation. Torin had a specific ear when it came to profanity in other languages.

"No, of course not, but we prefer creating communally and most other species don't. Mictok," he added thoughtfully, "but we won't get Mictok until Justice will unclench enough to hire three. Oh, and this one will need to see precise data on what the weapon in its current configuration actually does to organics."

"The last time you needed precise data . . ."

Deyell smiled. "This time, Strike Team Leader, we'll load you up with a sensor array before you're shot."

Torin remembered drooling. And Craig's reaction. "Joy."

"You think he'll come running?" Craig handed her the mug of coffee and leaned against the inert edge of the desk.

"I think he'll make inquiries." She'd sent the message outlining the job opportunity to the Rearl family. They'd pass it on to Stedrin. "Working here has got to be more interesting than a civilian job."

"This is a civilian job. And you're biased."

"Why would I be biased?"

He tucked a strand of hair behind her ear. "Because you built all this, made a place for your people, and now you're working on stabilizing it."

Torin was tempted to say she didn't know what he was talking about, but she didn't do coy. "The commander needs an aide."

"I need for us to grab a few minutes alone." When she looked up at him, he grinned. "Need. Want. Same same."

A single touch closed the desk. "I'm due at the range in forty-three minutes."

Dimples flashed. "I can work with that."

✤   ✤   ✤

Alamber pulled the lines of code with him as he squatted and peered into the triangular space under the 3D rendering of a pile of fallen metal sheets. Credit where due, U'yun's C&C had done a brilliant job recording on a macro level. The drag marks from the removal of whatever had been supporting the pile were crisp and clean and short enough the dim lights of Humans First had obviously shifted it just enough to wrestle it onto a sled. He scanned it on a micro level, flicked the measurements into his code, adjusted a line, stood, turned, and . . .

"*Ablin gon savit!* Where did you come from?"

"Katryl, where I are attending Win Sar Institute, then Onlin Station, then here. That are being some very clever work." The Katrien leaned in toward the scrolling code, golden-brown muzzle wrinkled as she worked through the progression. "I are never having seen mapping being done this way. You are clearly being smarter than you are looking."

"Yeah, well . . ." Alamber cocked a hip and drew up his smarmiest smile. "More than just another pretty face."

"Back off a bit, Myril." Dr. di'Nakamot Bishami shot Alamber a look about fifty/fifty apology and amusement as she approached. "Myril's a new hire. New team, new C&C, new brains behind the scenes."

"And this new brain are telling you, this mapping are looking like it shouldn't work, but it clearly are working."

"Maybe if you're lucky, he'll show you how he did it. Someday. Not now."

"I are not being able to be doing that." Myril waved both arms, the fine polymer spray the fur-bearing wore in the labs holding her pelt immobile. "It are being wrong."

Alamber held his smarmy smile in place as Bishami took Myril gently by both shoulders and turned her away. "And yet it works."

"It shouldn't be working."

"Go. Your desk has probably stopped running numbers by now." Bashami watched Myril leave the room muttering under her breath, then turned back to Alamber. "She doesn't mean anything by it." Bishami's deep crimson eyes darkened and she moved close enough Alamber could feel the heat along the side of his body. Humans just weren't warm enough.

"It doesn't matter."

"Liar. You stopped wearing that I don't care what you think expression in here over a year ago. You're smart, di'Cikeys Alamber, very smart, and innovative . . ."

He shook his head. "Uneducated."

Bishami shook her head back at him. "Self-taught. And if it means that much to you, get educated. You want letters after your name, I know programs you could test out of in three or four tendays." She spread her arms. "I'd recommend you, Hayate would rec you, Answers Before Questions would rec you. Hell, give her a few days and I'm sure Myril would rec you although you'd find the ceilings in the Institute a little low."

"I don't need letters for what I do." He spread his arms just a little wider. "I'm perfectly suited for the job."

"Are you? I thought you were the team's com guy."

"The boss isn't so much about strict definitions."

"Good for her." Bishami's hands closed around his wrists, circles of warmth. "She's going to get you killed."

About to deny it, Alamber shrugged. "Not on purpose."

"So much better."

He silently pleaded with her to drop it. He wanted to keep working in the labs, he loved working in the labs, but if he had to defend Torin from overprotective scientists, he'd give it up.

Bishami stared at him for a long moment, her eyes darkening. Finally, she sighed and said, "Fine. We could use another set of eyes to clear up some *senak* code in our long-range signals, com guy. Damned sun spots are wreaking havoc."

"Which sun?"

"Exactly."

"I don't know." A glance around the lab showed he was taking up almost all the available space. "Maybe I should leave you lot to actually do your jobs."

"Maybe you should help out because we let you play with our big imager."

He grinned. "I do like a big imager."

Her eyes lightened. "I'll bet."

"So I keep hearing how Justice won't open up the budget." He made himself comfortable leaning against the edge of her desk, thankful they'd gotten through that conversation intact, and waved a hand at the projection of the Humans First base. "How did you manage to pay for it?"

"The PLE I used to work with hired a mine tech, and she got it cheap from her old company. It's an older variation of the program they use for surveys in hostile environments. When the PLE had no use for it, I brought it to Berbar, deleted parameters specific to gas giants, adapted a few other bits, and tah dah."

"I'm all about adapting," Alamber admitted.

Bishami rested her weight against his shoulder, her hair interacting with his. "There's two other di'Taykan in this department and you're alone on your team. We don't do well on our own."

"I do fine," he protested, wondering why Bishami wouldn't let it go. Did all the fussing mean she was headed for qui? He wished he could ask her, but it just wasn't done. "And I'm never alone. Unless I choose to be," he amended. "There's enough di'Taykan on the teams that I can sleep communally if I want to. Or with my team if I want to. Not all my team at the same time." He forced himself to stop talking.

Bishami pressed her forehead to his, her hair lightly stroking his cheeks. "I wasn't talking about sleeping. Or sex. I was talking about day-to-day existing."

"It's not just existing."

"Okay."

"We're like family."

"I'm glad you have that." Leaning back, she smiled. "But working with your family sometimes screws with your perspective."

She sounded like she'd actually been worried about him. Which was ridiculous. "My perspective is fine."

"Okay."

"And the nature of the business means I have plenty of time to hang out in the labs." He pulled away, suddenly afraid that the concern he'd been hearing had been her trying to tell him his access was being cut off. "Unless . . ."

"No unless," she said, her hair adding definitive emphasis. "You're welcome to anything that's not in use as part of an ongoing investigation. The more people we have looking for answers, the sooner we shut down Humans First."

"Then what?"

She laughed and bounced her shoulder off his before moving away from the desk. "Then more of the same. Take it from someone who came from a family of LEOs, there's no shortage of assholes in the universe. If we want the Confederation to be tidy, someone has to take out the trash."

. ——◆—— .

"It's the plan for an Electron Beam welder." Dr. Banard turned the schematic to give Anthony a clearer view. "We used them to build space stations before the Confederation came along with its bag of tricks."

Anthony disliked Dr. Banard. He was surprised at how much. The biophysicist was a verifiable two hundred and two, and although he'd blown past the average human lifespan by almost thirty years, his brain still worked fine. When he used *we*, he meant Humanity. He'd never been in the military, but the military had shut down his laboratory on multiple occasions and sent him to rehabilitation twice. Rehabilitation records were sealed beyond even Anthony's ability to access, but, when asked, Dr. Banard had merely shrugged and muttered, "H'san help us, we should learn anything new about the so-called Elder Races."

Rumor had it that the last time he'd been shut down, he'd had a dozen new specimens on the table. Ignoring how ridiculously large that would make the table, Anthony was more impressed by the total lack of effect rehabilitation had on his interests. He'd never heard of anyone shaking it off once, let alone twice.

Laghari had gone out and retrieved the scientist after they'd been informed their base near Paradise was no longer secure. She'd presented him to Anthony with the not entirely ringing endorsement of, *"He's bugfuk crazy but probably a genius under all that, and he's Human and has ideas about new weapons."*

Given his history, Anthony should have approved of Dr. Banard. He didn't. But he was willing to tolerate him while he determined how much use he'd be to the cause. "And what do you want me to know about your EBW, Dr. Banard?"

"You want a weapon that works in a vacuum; this works better in a vacuum."

"I'm aware." He tapped the screen and read. "*A very precise, clean weld with minimal heating of the material outside the primary area of the weld.* We need heat. High temperatures crystallize the plastic."

"Laser welding . . ."

"I might as well use a benny. The blast the scientists set off on Big Yellow reached just under five thousand degrees—based on the destruction of their instruments." The information was available to the public, but, as he hadn't wanted his name attached to the search, it had taken layers of subcontractors to find it.

"And a welding laser can reach up to twenty-five thousand degrees in the keyhole."

"I'm aware. But not in a vacuum."

Dr. Banard sucked his teeth. "Fair enough."

"And I need broad dispersal. If we don't damage a significant proportion of the plastic with the first shot, it will retaliate."

"Then stop thinking heat."

Anthony showed teeth, about ready to show the old man the door. "Heat is one of only two things we know of that works."

"Madeline told me about your plan to piss on the plastic." He laughed, coughed, and shifted around in his seat until he could drag a piece of cloth out of a trouser pocket. Cloth cupped in both hands, he hacked a mouthful of phlegm into it. "How about we extrapolate from our actual data," he wheezed shoving the damp fabric back where he'd found it. "What holds the plastic together?"

"I don't . . ."

"Of course you don't know, not precisely, but we're talking about a polyhydroxide alcoholyde. It's hardly unique at base. What holds molecules together?"

"Covalent bonds."

"The plastic are a molecular hive mind. If we break the bonds holding them together . . ."

Anthony spread his arms mockingly. "We'll have created a disintegrating ray."

"Yes, because we're in an episode of *Star Wardens*." Banard's eye roll exposed a great deal of yellowed sclera. "There's a symmetrical relationship between the amount of energy released during the formation of a covalent bond and the amount of energy needed to break the bond. So, to break the bond, we need to increase the disassociation energy. Which is what happened during the explosion on Big Yellow. It got very hot, bonds broke, and new substances were formed. Crystalline substances. Very breakable."

"And we're back to heat." Anthony tried to keep his opinion of Banard out of his voice. "I don't think . . ."

"Most people don't. Energy is needed to break the bonds, heat is merely one form of energy, what other forms have you tried? Besides chemical."

"I don't . . ."

"You have the base molecular structure of the plastic, or you wouldn't know you could dissolve it by pissing on it. Which won't work in vacuum, it'll freeze."

"I know, that's . . ."

"You set me up with a large enough system, and I can run simulations until I find the frequency that'll shake the plastic apart. Then I'll adapt an EBW to fire that energy. Pew. Pew. New weapon."

"I don't have . . ."

Dr. Banard waved Anthony's protest off. "Not a problem, I brought an EBW from the shipyard. Which was a balls-up of a shipyard, let me tell you."

"I'm aware." Forearms braced on Belcerio's desk—borrowed to avoid having Banard violate his personal space—Anthony leaned forward. "How long will it take to build this new weapon?"

"After I define these particular covalent bonds, given a halfway decent workshop, shouldn't be long."

"I wonder, then. If it's that easy, why isn't everyone doing it?"

"Because the Confederation's all about creating new weapons." Dr. Banard's sarcasm matched Anthony's. "Besides, how do you know they aren't? What I'm wondering . . ." He blinked rapidly, moisture gathering at the corners of his eyes. ". . . is why you want weapons we can use against the plastic's ships when there are no plastic ships."

Anthony leaned back, absently noted Belcerio's chair was remarkably uncomfortable, and smiled. "There are no plastic ships *now*. I like to cover all possibilities."

"Good for you."

"I want us to do enough damage, should they return, that they'll either run away with their polyhydroxide tails between their legs or open negotiations to prevent us from doing more damage. We'll be heroes. Millions of Humans will turn away from the Confederation and join us. The greater our numbers, the faster we can free our people."

Dr. Banard nodded slowly, although Anthony wasn't certain

whether the lack of speed meant contemplation or a stiff neck. "Seems a sound philosophy. And if the plastic never returns?"

He spread his hands. "I have a new weapon." Banard's genius appellation might still be undetermined, but Humans First very definitely had a use for him.

"Per Marteau?"

"Commander Belcerio . . ." Anthony raised a brow and held Belcerio by the hatch. ". . . excellent timing. Dr. Banard and I were just finishing. Anything you need, Doctor, just ask."

Banard paused after struggling out of the chair, chest heaving. "My di'Taykan?"

"I'm sure they're on the way. It's not like they're hard to get a hold of. I assume you know where your quarters are?"

"Yes, yes." He shuffled to the hatch, glared at the commander as he passed, and announced before moving out of sight, "I'll send you my system requirements."

Standing, Anthony graciously beckoned Belcerio into his own office. Belcerio's dark brows were drawn in and his lips pressed into a thin line. "I strongly suspect that's not your happy face, Commander."

"A Strike Team showed up at Trilik. The team was captured."

And so much for his good mood brought on by the anticipation of a new weapon. "I'd very much like to know how we were caught off guard. I have arrangements to keep us forewarned."

"We didn't get word."

"I see. Spiders can get the word out, but our people can't. I, once again, am at the mercy of the inequalities of the Confederation." He ran both hands back through his hair. "It was Strike Team Alpha, wasn't it?"

"Yes, it was Alpha."

"I knew it. Gunnery Sergeant Torin Kerr?"

"Warden Kerr . . ." Belcerio raised his hands placatingly as Anthony turned on him. "Not important."

"I agree," Anthony spat. "I'd say that what's important here is that Kerr is responsible for our only unsuccessful recovery. That the H'san met with Kerr after the team searching for . . . the H'san homeworld disappeared." Information about hidden H'san weapons was need to know, and Belcerio didn't need to know. "That our operation on XX73X was stopped by Kerr."

"We're better off without Robert Martin." Belcerio dropped into his desk chair, frowned, and made adjustments. "Martin was too fond of using death as motivation."

"I'd like you to remember that Martin was Human and that makes him infinitely more valuable than anything he killed. But he's not the point; Kerr is."

"We can finish outfitting the fleet without those last tanks. Our reserves will be low, but if it becomes necessary, there's more mining platforms out there. The spiders can't get a Strike Team to all of them."

"I repeat, not the point. And, you're right . . ."

Belcerio looked surprised.

". . . we're better off without Martin, given his proven inability to deliver."

"He had Kerr almost to the jump point," Belcerio reminded him unnecessarily. "He couldn't have anticipated Ryder's insane decision to micro jump."

As contact with Dr. Banard left the second chair in need of disinfecting, Anthony leaned back against the bulkhead. "I give Ryder points for Human guts and ingenuity, but Martin should have put a bullet in Kerr's head."

Belcerio's brows drew back in. "You wanted her turned to the cause."

"I wanted. Past tense. Now, I want Kerr in front of a bigger gun." Before Belcerio could respond, a solution occurred. Anthony smiled, shoved his hands into his pockets, and rocked back on his heels. "Or perhaps a smaller gun."

FIVE

TORIN DID A QUICK head count as she slid into her seat for the morning briefing. Five teams on station meant twenty-nine bodies, and although the room could hold fifty, it seemed full. The job attracted a certain size of personality. While no one was being particularly loud or obnoxious, they were very *there*.

The teams sat together, edges fraying out as discussions began, added more viewpoints, and never entirely finished before they became about something else entirely. Torin drank her coffee, answered messages while ignoring Craig's suggestions of what she should tell her mother, and parsed the ambient noise into a small amount of bragging, a few complaints about the cold hands on the new hire in medical, and Alamber's impassioned description of what he could do with the big imager in the labs. She'd only just noticed he hadn't mentioned any of the obvious di'Taykan uses when Commander Ng arrived, took his place at the front of the room, and cleared his throat.

"Good news, people." He almost smiled. "Planetary law enforcement on Seven Sta has offered us the use of their training facility. They've got a thousand hectares in the middle of Sasatoba province, isolated enough that the use of live rounds won't endanger anyone with a functioning brain. No permanent range, but we can install targets and work up a few training scenarios that don't have to take sucking vacuum into account. Warden Kerr's been insisting you lot need training in planetary conditions for a while now, and I've had feelers out." The pause was barely long enough to contain the muttered di'Taykan innuendo. "I suspect Seven Sta's PLE is trying to justify their land grant, but I don't actually care. Two teams will remain on station. With Delta and T'jaam out, that leaves three teams to go . . . planetside."

Torin almost wished he'd said *go down* in a room half-full of bored di'Taykan.

"You'll spend a tenday on the ground. Gravity's ninety-seven percent oldEarth, oxygen mix is a little high and I'd like the di'Taykan among you to remember that before oxygen toxicity occurs rather than after."

"Commander?" Elisk sat up straighter. "Are there trees?"

"Yes, there are trees. I've sent the specifications to your slates. Broadly, Seven Sta is a Younger Races planet. About fifty percent Human, thirty di'Taykan, twenty Krai, although, as usual, the Elder Races have a presence in both port cities. It grew out of colony status just last year, so the population remains around a million. Because the training facility has its own landing platform, you'll take a VTA directly to the site and do little interacting with the resident population."

"You ashamed of us, sir?" Binti called out mournfully.

Ng sighed. "Yes. Yes, I am."

The Strike Teams roared with laughter.

The protesters showed up on their third day at the PLE's training camp.

"Stroppy fukkers." Craig accepted the mug of coffee and stretched his arm along the top of Torin's chair. Up on the big screen dominating one wall of the rectangular canteen, a mix of Younger Races piled out of their filthy crawler. "We're what? Twenty-five hundred klicks from the nearest town?"

Torin lifted her mug in a sarcastic salute. "The determination of the true fanatic."

"They didn't walk," Werst grunted. "That would be a true fanatic."

"That would be insane," Craig amended.

"Yeah, you don't get an opinion. You think the bunks to the canteen is too far to walk."

Marie paused on her way by to nudge Werst's shoulder with her hip. "He's not wrong. Why walk when you can fly?"

"Then why is it no one in the Confederation flies? On their own," Werst expanded. "Without tech."

"Easy answer." Marie held her pie out of his reach and continued on to her own seat at the next table. "Once you've got wings, you're having too much fun to bother with sentience."

Werst nodded thoughtfully. "That explains most of the pilots I know."

The full dozen protesters—eight Humans, two di'Taykan, two Krai—stayed outside the perimeter, setting up camp in full view of a remote security station so obvious, it didn't need the sign identifying it.

"They want us to see them," Ressk noted.

Werst squeezed his thigh with a foot. "No point in them being here if we didn't."

One of the male Humans, pale beige, lighter than both Torin and Craig, with an intricate blue pattern on both cheeks, his hair up in a knot on the back of his head, returned to the crawler. A moment later, the visual jerked then settled with no discernible difference in clarity.

"And fail." Alamber snickered.

When he didn't emerge, they assumed he was continuing his attempt to shut down the system.

"Should Lieutenant Maaren run an ID?" Pie finished, Ranjit dropped her plate in the recycler by the door. "If that decoration's a tattoo, he'll be easy to find."

Maaren half rose from the table where he and the five PLE's "observing" the training exercise sat, but Binti cut him off before he could speak. "Not against the law to protest, Cap." She dropped into her seat with a bowl of . . .

"What the hell is that?" Craig demanded.

"Marilissa . . ."

"Who?"

"The cook. Dark hair, lovely and round. Ex-Navy. Petty Officer Kotas. Marilissa," she stressed the repetition, "called it moo-stah-lev-ree-AH. It's like a grape juice pudding."

Ressk leaned in. "Smells good."

"I once saw you eat a shoe." Binti waved her spoon dismissively. "Marilissa says her family brought the recipe from oldEarth. And, yeah, it smells great, so keep your grubby fingers . . ." Her spoon cracked against Werst's knuckle. ". . . away."

"This is how the Navy eats?"

"Marilissa cooked in the wardroom." Binti closed her eyes and licked pudding off her lips. "This is how officers eat."

"Chiefs and POs eat better," Torin told them.

Half the heads in the canteen turned toward Elisk. Who shrugged. "True," he said. "They were smug about it."

On the screen, the protesters spoke in low murmurs, facing away from the perimeter, hands by their mouths covering conversations, fully aware of exactly where the DL or civilian security equivalent had been mounted. Every few minutes, one of them would turn, face the lens directly, and yell a slogan.

"Violence begets violence!"

"Veterans need help, not harm!"

"End the Violence!"

"We're trying to," Zhou yelled back and accepted high fives from Nicholin and Bilodeau.

The protesters jerked in unison, angry responses spilling into the canteen, too tangled to make sense of.

Nicholin snickered. "I think they heard you, Zhou."

Alamber tapped his slate and the symbol of an open mouth appeared in the bottom right corner of the big screen. "It's a two-way system, guys. They yell at us. We yell at them."

A di'Taykan, who couldn't have been more than a meter and a half tall, the shortest di'Taykan Torin had ever seen, stepped closer to the lens. *"Words can be a weapon!"*

Torin reached for Alamber's slate and tapped the icon closed. "Don't engage."

"Aw, Boss . . ."

"Keep ears on them in case they make plans to advance. We don't need the complication of them wandering into an exercise."

"Stop murdering Confederation civilians!"

Civilians had died on Threxie, and Torin still had no idea how they could have prevented it. Robert Martin had done the killing, but she hadn't stopped him in time. Of course, the military hadn't stopped Martin—hadn't realized how unstable he was when he was discharged—nor had the Confederation as a whole served him well, with less resources than needed going to veterans organizations. Torin wasn't taking all the blame. Only some of it.

"You needn't take some of the blame for everything," her therapist had said. *"They had a bad harvest on Paradise last year. Was that your fault, too?"*

"Only if some asshole armed the corn."

After that conversation, she'd dropped her therapist down to once every four tendays, as required for the Strike Teams. It seemed safer for all concerned.

One of the Human protesters, who seemed absurdly young, crossed her arms and held onto her scowl as she shouted, *"I see no philosophical difference between the Strike Teams and their victims!"*

"Not exactly pithy," Ranjit observed.

"On second thought, shut them up." When the noise of the canteen moved back into the forefront, Torin said, "If they cross the outer perimeter, we'll hear the alarms. We can be at the inner perimeter before they are."

"When we get there, can we shoot at them, Gunny?" Nicholin asked. "I mean not to hit them, just to make them . . ."

"Shit themselves?"

Nicholin pointed at Werst. "What he said."

"It won't. You have to understand the damage a bullet can do before it frightens you." She glanced around the canteen, saw Marilissa watching from the kitchen. "We've all seen the damage. We've done the damage. We've taken the damage. That lot? They've never been closer to the war than a news feed. And that was the whole point of us going out there. If they get to the inner perimeter, we'll go out, and I'll have a word with them."

"Don't you have to understand what a gunnery sergeant can do before one frightens you?" Marie asked.

Torin smiled. "No. And that's lunch." She tapped Craig's thigh, pushed her chair out, and stood. "Let's get back to work."

Little more than empty land and barracks, the training facility could have been automated. Expecting field kitchens, the Strike Teams had been pleasantly surprised to find a cook and four lesser mortals preparing food as well as half a dozen members of the PLE keeping an eye on things. Of the ten, only Petty Officer Miralissa Kotas had served. Torin understood why few veterans joined planetary police forces; it was too similar while simultaneously too different. There were less differences between the military and the Strike Teams and dealing with that disconnect took up most scheduled therapy time.

Humans and di'Taykan started the day with a ten-kilometer run while the Krai worked the nets—although both Humans and di'Taykan enjoyed throwing themselves around the nets, a ridiculous amount of what they did involved running. Running to cut people off. Running to avoid zombie H'san. Running across giant webs.

"Snipers don't run." Zhou and Orrnis, the snipers from U'yun and Ch'tore, stood behind Binti. "We strike from afar."

"And not very far lately," Orrnis muttered.

Torin raised a single brow. "Do I look like I care?"

"Told you it wouldn't work," Zhou grumbled, stripping down to shorts.

"Worth a shot," Binti muttered. "There's bugs down here."

When the PLE's obstacle course proved to be no challenge, they expanded it.

"What would we build a new wall from? And, honestly, do we look like a construction crew? We don't even have heavies to help." Marie turned Lieutenant Maaren toward the cliff rising forty meters up out of a shallow angle of tumbled blocks of rock, a patch of brilliant pink at the ten-meter mark and rising. "Nature provides, and we can't build one of those in a station. I wish we'd brought drop sleeves."

A few meters away, Torin adjusted her harness—she had nothing to prove to Tylen, the four time free-climbing champion of 4th Recarta, 2nd Division, Gamma Company—and enjoyed the juxtaposition of wide-eyed excitement on Marie's face and wide-eyed disbelief on Lieutenant Maaren's.

With their targets at three hundred meters, the long meadow became a range.

"If you oriented in the other direction, you'd avoid the crosswinds," Maaren began. "We can . . ."

Torin cut him off by lifting her KC to her shoulder. "The crosswinds are why we chose this location. No challenge otherwise for the Marines, and the Navy's not going to hit anything regardless."

"I heard that, Gunny," Elisk called.

"It's not a secret, Lieutenant."

Maaren opened the canteen door and stood aside as Surren and Elisk pushed past, hurrying inside. No one got between the Krai and food. "I can't believe you thought that was fun. You people are crazy. You know that right?"

"It's one of the job qualifications," Torin told him.

"It wasn't one of mine." Craig slipped by as well. "You're going to be holding that door until the dogs come home, mate. This lot's got nothing you'd recognize as manners."

"Aren't you one of this lot?"

"Which is why I'm inside and you're still holding the door." He gave him a two-finger salute and headed for the counter.

"He's not wrong," Torin said following. The food waiting in the stasis field was still predominantly a cross-species selection, edible by all three of the Younger Races, and very much like what they'd all eaten while they served, but, unlike at lunch, there was a specific Human, Krai, and Taykan dish as well.

"I made avgolemono," Marilissa explained, nodding at the soup. "It's my way of remembering where my people are from. My staff felt that if there was a Human food . . ." She gestured at the *tomagoras* and the *abquin*. "There's minimal food value for Humans in the filling of the *abquin* and the *kinir* has a lot more fiber than our bodies can comfortably cope with. While you can eat the *tomagoras*, you'll be . . . Warden Rydol!"

"Eat the *tomagoras*, shit fire. I know." He piled a large helping on his plate. "Now this is what I call tucker."

Marilissa's eyes were wide. "Warden Kerr?"

"It's fine. He burned his taste buds off long ago. Now me, I draw the line at my aunties' *chatpate aloo*." Picking up a bowl, Torin filled it with soup, and realized Marilissa had returned to staring at Craig, brows drawn in. "Is his portion going to leave the di'Taykan short?"

"What? No, no." The cook nodded toward the covered trays still in the kitchen. "I was Navy, remember. I'm used to quantity. It's just . . . eating food intended for another species can be dangerous."

Torin added a thick piece of dark bread to her plate. "Technically, everything native to this planet is food intended for another species."

"Werst ate a shoe!" Binti called from the other end of the line where she stacked the last empty spot on her plate with fried plantains.

"He's Krai." Marilissa called back. "He doesn't count. There are no shoes on the menu," she added as Torin set the soup bowl on her tray and moved on to solids. When three Krai and two di'Taykan joined the food line, Marilissa fell silent until, unable to contain herself, she pointed at Torin's plate, loaded with garlic protein slices, and said, "You need more vegetables."

The pile of unfamiliar green fronds smelled like citrus and tasted like pears. Torin sat at the big round table her team had claimed, glanced around, and noticed all the Humans had a sizable serving.

"Turnobi." Maaren shoved a forkful in his mouth, chewed, and swallowed. "It's cheap and filling, high in lysine, grows like a weed. First settlers couldn't kill it, so they cooked it. Eat enough of this, you don't eat as much of the pricy, imported stuff."

Lifting a frond, Torin peered. "Cheap and filling. That woman was wasted in the Navy. She could cook for the Corps."

"Violence begets violence!"

Alamber grinned and turned down the volume. "Dinner theater."

"Reruns." Werst lifted the top piece of *kinir* and nodded in satisfaction at the inside of his *abquin*.

"They've been doing this most of the day." Binti waved her fork in the general direction of the screen. "I'd be bored out of my mind."

"They're fueled by righteous fury. They consider it righteous," Zhou protested when Nicholin punched him in the arm. "I don't."

"Melt the guns into plowshares!"

Ressk frowned, dropping half of his *kinir* onto Werst's plate. "They're designed not to melt. And what's a plowshare?"

Turned out no one knew.

"Something local?"

Maaren shook his head. "Never heard of it. So," he turned to Torin, "what are your plans for tonight?"

"We'll be back on the range after it gets dark."

"Again? I mean, I don't shoot, but more practice . . ."

When it became clear he had no idea of how to finish his protest, Torin set her spoon down in her empty soup bowl. "Do you know why we're all still alive, Lieutenant? Because terrorists like Humans First don't put the time in."

A pan hit a solid surface at the serving counter unnecessarily hard and Torin glanced back over her shoulder to see Marilissa refilling the plantain. Seemed she had opinions. Ex-Navy; of course she had opinions.

"I checked on the protesters before I came out. The two di'Taykan and the Human male who tried to block the security signal haven't been seen for a while." Yahsamus swatted at an insect who seemed to find the Taykan more flavorful than the other species and fell into step beside Torin. "I admire his staying power."

"We didn't see them leave together; he could be off on his own."

"When he could be off with willing partners? Your people are strange to me, Gunny."

Torin laughed, and they walked side by side along the beaten path toward the range where the snipers were showing off. One hand resting on her KC, she trailed the other over the heavy seed heads of the perimeter grass.

"You're enjoying this, aren't you?"

The night made Yahsamus' dark green hair look black. This close, however, Torin could see the ends moving leisurely, silhouetted against the sky. "Given the teams are dirtside as often as they're not, we need this. Wind. Weather. Gravity. Light conditions. Or lack of light." Clouds covered the stars and most of the light from the moon. "Temperature variations." They walked through a current of cooler air. "Humidity. It's different when it's real."

"I don't know. The simulators have always made it seem pretty real to me."

"Not this real."

Lightning flashed in the distance. Ten seconds later, thunder boomed.

Yahsamus grinned. "Neat trick, Gunny."

"Thank you, Tech."

"So you're enjoying this, right?"

"Yes, I am."

Torin had already fired her twenty standing, twenty kneeling, twenty prone and cleared the targets to make way for the next live shooters when the storm broke. Solid sheets of heavy drops swept across the landscape driven by the wind, interspersed with moments of a constant, but slightly gentler, rain.

"Gunny?" Although she'd finished as a captain, Ranjit had come up through the ranks; she had no difficulty making herself heard from the three-hundred-meter line.

"Keep firing, Cap. The enemy's not going to wait for good weather."

On the near side of Ranjit, Marie shook her head, shoulders up like an annoyed cat as she quickly squeezed off her last five rounds. The row of targets flashed green, indicating everyone had fired, and the line raced forward a hundred meters to the next position. As another sheet of falling water moved through, the watchers, either finished or waiting their turn, took the moment to race east behind the targets and dive in under the nearest trees. Krai built their arboreal habitats as far from the ground as possible, so if they weren't worried about lightning strikes, Torin wasn't going to sweat it. There would, however, be a discussion on range safety when this group finished. With live rounds in the lanes, the area behind the targets remained off limits regardless of whether or not those rounds were currently being shot or how thorough the target's inertial dampers were supposed to be.

Remaining a safe distance off to the west of the targets, wind slapping wet weeds against her legs, Torin lifted her face, eyes closed, and let the downpour wash away the sweat and grime.

The five shooters wasted no time on their knees. The targets flashed green, intensity adjusted for the ambient light, and they advanced as another sheet came through. Torin considered calling it, her point made, but the laughter and profanity mixed as they threw themselves prone suggested the five were enjoying themselves. Turned out, Marie was fluent in at least one language other than Federate.

As they settled and the first shots cracked, the hair lifted off the back of Torin's neck. She turned, frowned at the figure she could barely make out through the rain, and grunted at the impact just below her sternum, air forced out of her lungs in a rush. Mouth open, she couldn't seem to draw new air in.

This wasn't her first dance. She brought her KC up as her knees buckled, finger sliding behind the trigger guard . . .

·—◆—·

"Hey, Boss! Remember how you didn't even want me to carry a weapon, let alone shoot one?" Crossing behind the targets, now continuously flashing green as the shooters downloaded their scores, Alamber shook his head, hating the way the rain beat his hair flat. He might as well leave his helmet on; then, at least, it would be flat and dry. "Well, I changed my mind, and I'm now in total agreement." Light receptors all the way open, he still couldn't see Torin through the downpour, and the smoke from the chemical propellant was the only scent strong enough to identify. But he had to be close. "I'll just go back to the canteen. Maybe put the coffee on.

"Boss?"

He shook his head again as the wind stilled and the rain gentled. "Seriously, Boss, if you snuck back under cover, I'm . . ."

She lay on the ground, head turned toward him, panting through her half-open mouth. Her lower legs were folded under, toes of her boots digging into the mud. Her weapon lay canted up by her hip, fingers of her right hand gripping it loosely. Her left hand pressed against her stomach where the rain washed away the red seeping between her fingers.

"CRAIG!"

Muddy water sprayed over her face as his knees hit the ground. He wiped at it frantically with one hand while pressing the other over hers to stop the bleeding. He didn't have sealant. Why didn't he have sealant?

Her eyes were half open, but he didn't think she could see him.

Heart pounding, he tongued his implant on. He'd maintained the team's connection to the *Promise* in orbit. He didn't know these people. He didn't trust these people. He really was smarter than he looked.

CRAIG!

The fuk? Alam . . .

Torin's been shot!

She was still bleeding. Warmth rose up around the edges of his fingers. Should he straighten her legs? Could he straighten her legs? He'd taken the classes. He couldn't remember. He could remember his *vantru* bleeding out like this. Blood pooling on the tiles. A crowd gathering. Her skin this cold and damp. "No, it's rain. That's all. Rain."

He bent his head, and his hair touched the edges of her face, shielding it.

"Alamber! Where . . . ?"

A heavy hand closed on his shoulder and tried to pull him back. He resisted, putting pressure on the wound. His breathing matching hers.

"Don't leave me alone."

"God fukking damnit!"

He felt the ground tremble as Craig threw himself down. But that was impossible.

"Alamber! On three, lift your hand. One. Two . . ."

Do what?

A sharp pain in his left arm.

Lift his hand!

"Three!"

He lifted his right hand. Heard the hiss of sealant. Craig was their field medic. He'd know what to do.

Alamber bent closer until he could feel warm air against his mouth and whispered, "Keep breathing."

"Come on, kid." Hands around his arm. "Let them work."

Pressure, gentle but relentless, pulled him back and, still on his knees, he sagged against Ressk's solid body. Craig knelt against Torin's hip, checking the seal while Werst crouched across from him, hands under her back. He could feel the others gathering around, but no one came close enough to reach even his peripheral vision.

"No exit," Werst grunted.

"She's still lost a lot of blood."

"Not the biggest problem." Werst's nostril ridges flared. "It didn't go through. It hit bone and tumbled."

"Fuk! Stretcher?"

"There's an autodoc, must be a stretcher."

"*Had* a stretcher." Ranjit stepped forward, PCU in her ear. "Last training trip, it went into the nearest hospital and never came back. We can make . . ."

"No time!" Craig shifted his weight up off his knees, and reached . . .

"Let me!" Zhou was suddenly there, spitting out words in a staccato stream. "I was born on Paradise, like Gunny. Don't have to compensate for her heavier bone and muscle, and I can take advantage of the lower gravity."

Alamber could see Craig's chest heaving and braced himself for the protest. It wasn't much of an advantage, Zhou didn't have Craig's bulk, and the boss was Craig's *vantru*. He wouldn't release her.

But Craig got out of the way and said, "Go. I'm right behind you."

It took both men and Werst to lift the dead . . . no . . . to lift the limp weight. Zhou adjusted his hold—light receptors wide open, Alamber could all but see muscle settle into the most efficient configuration—took one step, two, and began to run. Craig ran on his heels. Why wasn't Werst with him?

"Come on, kid. On your feet." Ressk's voice held the *don't bother arguing with me* tone he usually used on Werst. "*Serley chrika*, I keep forgetting how tall you lot are."

Then other hands wrapped around his arms, and he could smell the spicy warmth of Tylen's pheromones as she cradled him for a moment, his face pressed against the bare skin of her neck while Cap sent the ex-Corps out in a pattern they clearly recognized. That was why Werst had stayed. Made sense. If asked, Alamber would have said that boots against wet ground couldn't sound intimidating, and he'd have been wrong. He closed his teeth on a laugh. *Good thing we were at the range, they're all armed.*

We're all armed.

Not that this group was ever entirely unarmed.

"Come on." Tylen shifted her grip. "Let's go."

The di'Taykan, faster on the flat, moved out to flank Zhou's position, the Humans made an inner, protective wall of muscle, and the Krai covered the rear.

Covered their six, Alamber corrected. That's what the boss would say. He stayed as close to Craig as he could, fully aware that at a dead run he could recognize a threat but didn't have a hope in hell of hitting it on a cool, sunny afternoon, let alone after dark in heavy rain.

Wait. How could Zhou see where he was going? Human eyesight sucked after dark and, even with his helmet, this kind of heavy rain made thermal useless.

He wished he could stop thinking and just run, but Zhou wasn't moving fast enough.

Why wasn't he moving faster?

Was this as fast as Humans could run?

The targeting system! Zhou was a sniper. His helmet scanner had multiple ancillary programs. Well, Binti's did. Zhou's must. If he locked targeting, kept it centered, he could aim himself. Had to be what he was doing.

Where did I leave my helmet? He hadn't had it when he found . . .

Werst had smelled more than blood.

A tumbling bullet would have torn up her intestines.

Just like his *vantru*.

He hadn't thought of her in years.

She'd died in his arms.

And left him alone.

The yard in front of the canteen blazed with light, poles turned up to full illumination, spotlights Alamber hadn't known existed adding to the brilliance. The rain fell in silver sheets. Boots impacted against the gravel like they were crushing rock and he couldn't stop a huffed-out laugh when he realized they were running in step.

Marilissa met them three meters from the big double doors, hair dripping down into her face. "Autodoc's up and running."

"Petty officer," he heard Elisk snicker behind him. Alamber wanted to tell him it wasn't funny, but maybe in the Navy it was.

She reached for Zhou's arm. "Do you need help?"

"Get. Out. Of. The way." Paradise advantage or not, he'd still run over a kilometer carrying almost two meters of solid muscle.

As Zhou crossed the threshold, Lieutenant Maaren threw open a door on the other side of the canteen and yelled, "Over here! I've got med-evac incoming," he added, leading the way down the corridor. "Given the storm, fifty minutes. Probably more." He darted through another open door, adding an unnecessary, "In here."

Alamber sagged against the wall as Zhou and Craig followed Maaren into the final room. Listened to the lid on the autodoc seal, listened to Elisk out in the canteen ordering the building's defenses. Heard Marilissa protesting she hadn't held a weapon since she got out and wasn't going to now. He wondered why Maaren was wet. Not as wet as Marilissa who'd come out to meet them, but he'd obviously just towel-dried his hair.

A moment later, Zhou backed out of the room, helmet under his arm, hair dry in contrast to the water dripping off the rest of him.

"Elisk's locking us up tight," Alamber said, falling into step beside him. Zhou's chest visibly rose and fell, and the water running down his face smelled faintly of salt, but those were the only signs of physical exertion. The Strike Teams were in stupidly good condition. Maybe not so stupid. "Cap's got pairs of ex-Corps out searching for the shooter." When Zhou glanced over at him, Alamber felt his hair lift. "I thought you'd want a sitrep."

"Yeah, thanks. Why aren't you helping?"

"Not military, I'd slow them down. I . . ." *Needed to be sure the boss was safe.* He clipped his slate off his belt. "Now I'm out of the rain, I can cover more ground with this."

"Zhou!" Elisk still wore his helmet; from the shimmer, he was using the scanner as a screen, and the helmet's integrated PCU was significantly more powerful than the same unit stuffed in the ear, so Alamber supposed the helmet made sense. "On the roof. Provide cover for Kaur's teams as they come in."

"Sir!" Zhou grabbed his KC off a table as he passed. He'd obviously tossed it to one of the ex-Navy when he'd gone to help the boss. Seemed to indicate he'd known how Cap would use the Corps. Fuk, but Alamber got tired of how everyone knew things he didn't, how they'd had it coded into neural pathways and didn't have to think about it. They had the luxury of reacting and knowing everyone around them would react the same way.

"Alamber?"

He held up his slate.

Elisk nodded. "Go to it."

Good thing he knew things they didn't.

"You're in the planetary satellite system."

"With malice and forethought," Alamber agreed and kept working. He'd been efficient, not gentle.

"That's not . . ."

"Warden."

He could feel the weight of Lieutenant Maaren's regard change. "I'm sorry, son, but that doesn't give you . . ."

"Article 12.3: Field officers of the Justice Department outrank Planetary Law Enforcement when a field officer of the Justice Department has been injured in the line of duty."

"You made that up."

Alamber ignored him, concentrating on his screen. There were electrostatic disturbances all the way up to the edge of the atmosphere.

"I'm going to have to report this."

"You do what you have to."

After a long moment, Maaren sighed, and Alamber heard the dull thud of a full mug hit the table by his elbow. "Here. It's fresh."

"Nothing." Cap pulled off her helmet and squeezed the twist of hair at the top of her spine. "If there's any clue to the shooter out there, the rain's washed it away."

The ex-Corps from the three Strike Teams filled the canteen. They came in together, each of them jogging purposefully through the door, continuing until they had space enough to strip off wet clothes, KCs kept close at hand. They must've met up in the courtyard and exchanged information, because they weren't talking now.

Cap set her weapon carefully down on the table and peeled out of her work shirt. "Now, they could be very good," she continued catching a thrown towel, "or it could be the storm, but we're never going to find a single shooter out there."

PCU still in his ear, Elisk pulled his helmet off. "You sure it was a single shooter?"

"No, but it was a single shot."

Alamber stood. "The odds are high it was a single shooter. There was a satellite pass just before the rain started," he continued as multiple, quiet conversations paused and attention turned toward him. "I pulled imaging, so unless there's a group out there in military-grade cammo, blocking thermals . . ."

"Electrostatic?" Yahsamus asked, leaning around his shoulder to get a look at the screen.

Thunder cracked, close enough the windows rattled.

"In this shit?"

She nodded, dark green hair flattening. "Point."

"So, unless they're in military-grade cammo, a group would show. Therefore one shooter."

Cap nodded. "While I wouldn't put the cammo past them . . ." She didn't have to define *them*, at this point, they could only be Humans First. ". . . we'd have found a group." She had the boss' certainty. Alamber didn't doubt her. Then the big screen caught her attention, and she frowned at the thermal image of the protesters' campsite.

Alamber couldn't determine what exactly she was frowning at. After dark, the cameras had switched to thermal, the cheapest option, and on the screen the multiroomed tent read as a yellow/orange/red blob.

"Lieutenant Maaren." The ice in Cap's voice pulled attention to Maaren, who'd been helping his people provide towels and deal with wet gear. "Why haven't your lot brought in the protesters?"

"My lot? No one crossed the perimeter . . ." Maaren began.

Cap snorted. "Who in here can't disable a perimeter pin?"

The PLEs looked pissed—Alamber assumed it was because they'd never learned—and Marilissa raised the hand not holding the coffee carafe. "I'm a cook," she explained as the teams turned toward her. "Which one of you lot can make a creme brûlée?"

"They're over fifteen kilometers away," Maaren began again.

"Is that so?" Cap rolled right over him. "Fine. If it's too far for the PLE, we'll get them."

"No!" Maaren shouted over the sound of chairs being pushed back and weapons picked up. If he saw what Alamber did, he saw people who'd not only gone to war, but come back. From the vehemence of his denial, he clearly didn't trust what he saw in a civilian environment. Usually, that wasn't an issue, the Strike Teams knew where the lines were. Here and now, Alamber suspected Maaren had made the smart call.

The five PLEs, no longer holding towels and coffee mugs, but arming up with attitude of their own, obviously thought so, too.

"Suit up." Maaren's gesture got them moving toward the door, movements stiff under the weight of scrutiny. "Meet at the vehicle shed in five. We'll take the sled out and bring them back in their crawler."

When only Maaren remained in the building, Cap's voice stopped him on the threshold. "When you return, we'll need to talk to your people, too."

The lieutenant shot her a flat, unfriendly stare. "My people don't use guns."

"Yeah, well, the person who did this was a lousy shot. They were close enough, Gunny knew they were there . . ."

"While it was bucketing down rain," Werst growled.

". . . and they didn't manage a kill shot."

"Could be they didn't intend to kill her."

"Could be you live in an interesting world down here. We don't. Remember, one of the protesters could be armed although they'd be smarter to have ditched the weapon on the way back to the camp."

"Armed?" Binti said the moment the door closed. "And none of us are going with them?"

"If it was one of the protesters, they wouldn't have gone back to the camp. They'd disappear into all this nothing heading for a prearranged pickup."

"They're all Human," Elisk said quietly.

At first Alamber thought he meant the protesters, who weren't, then he realized Elisk had been referring to the group of PLEs.

Cap nodded. "I noticed, but I'm giving the screening process for a law enforcement position the benefit of the doubt. Also, Humans First doesn't strike me as the sort of organization who'd plant a long-term sleeper agent. We didn't know we were heading here until just before we left."

"*We* didn't," Aszur, Ch'tore team's Krai pilot, pointed out.

"Noted." Cap accepted a mug of coffee with a quiet thanks. "Alamber—the med-evac?"

"I'm tracking." He hadn't taken Maaren's word they'd been called. "Still fifty-five out. There was a lightning strike in Glinford, a town fifty klicks out from Anchoring, where the hospital is, and they say since the boss is in an autodoc and seventeen people in Glinford aren't, she can wait." Intellectually, logically, they were right, but Alamber knew his hair had pressed flat against his head. The . . . Torin needed a tank, not an autodoc.

"All right." Sounded like Cap agreed. "While we're waiting, get started on your after actions while everything's fresh. We might find information we can use."

The roar of the sled leaving the compound could be heard over the rain.

"Needs a tune-up," Zhou muttered.

"Uh, Cap?" The undertones in Yahsamus' voice caught Alamber's attention. "You may want to look at this." She held out her slate.

Brows up, Cap shifted her coffee to her other hand, took it, and glanced down. "Fukking hell. Bilodeau!"

The room fell so silent Alamber swore he could hear the hum of the autodoc.

Standing watch at the western window, Marie jerked around. "Cap?"

"Yahsamus pulled the target data. Your target showed nineteen out of twenty possible hits."

Marie's tongue dragged across her lower lip. "You think I . . . ?"

"I think Gunny was standing to the left of the targets and you were in the left lane. I think there's a chance there's an easier answer to this situation than we thought."

"I didn't . . ."

"She didn't," Alamber interrupted. "The boss had turned away from the range, and her finger was on the trigger. She was planning to shoot someone." His hair lifted. "So there was someone there."

"You don't know that," Werst growled not looking at Bilodeau so pointedly she drew in a ragged-edged breath.

"Gunnery Sergeant Torin Kerr." Alamber held out one hand. "Trigger discipline." And held out the other.

Ressk pulled Werst close against his side. "Kid's right. It wasn't an accident."

"Stop calling me kid."

"Stop being so young."

Binti laughed. Normal helped.

"Good eye, Alamber."

His hair flicked at the praise.

Marie had returned to staring out the window, a white-knuckle grip on her weapon.

Cap and Elisk had a silent conversation about taking her off watch that everyone in the room understood, but agreed, still silently, to leave her there. No point in piling humiliation on humiliation.

If she'd been di'Taykan, she'd have needed touch. Alamber didn't know what Marie in particular needed, but Nicholin pushed out from his table, wandered to the service counter to refill his mug, and returned to his seat by way of the west window.

"Navy," he said as he came up beside her. When she cocked her head toward him, gaze locked on the courtyard, he took a long swallow of coffee. "You guys really are terrible shots."

"Fuk you."

"If you want."

She had laughed. He bumped his shoulder against hers hard enough she had to brace herself on the wall before returning to his seat.

Elisk looked pleased. Alamber assumed it was about his team coalescing.

Med-evac was still fifty-five out. Which was not only impossible, but stupid. In another minute he'd . . .

"Don't." Binti dropped into the chair beside him. "You can't hack the hospital system. You don't have all the data."

"How did . . . ?"

"I know you." She pressed a long line of comfort against his side and set her slate on the table. "Start your after action so Gunny hears how well we behaved for the babysitter."

"Not looking forward to that," Werst grumbled, one finger poking at his slate. "Gunny's always pissy when she's been tanked."

Unwilling to use the words—helpless, bleeding, dying—Alamber sketched the position of the boss' body when he found her. Gravity would have caused anyone else to sprawl, his *vantru's* arms had been flung out away from her body, but Torin had collapsed efficiently. The program corrected for pressure against the screen, smoothing out the uneven line. He'd was just adding compass points when Craig came into the canteen, slid Ressk, chair and all, almost over on top of Werst, and sat.

"Med-evac?"

"Delayed again." The thunder and lightning had moved on, but Alamber could hear the dull roar of heavy rain against the steel roof. "They insist that as long as she's in the autodoc, she's okay."

"Okay's not good enough. She needs to be tanked."

Alamber glanced past Craig, past Ressk, at Werst. "She hates being tanked."

Craig's hands curled into fists. "Then she should fukking stop getting fukking shot."

"Yeah." He listened to Craig breathe; a long inhale, a long exhale, fighting for control. He listened to Marilissa making more coffee. Only coffee, although both her staff were in the kitchen. Probably better *sah* wasn't available, actually, given the effect on Humans and how these particular Humans were feeling already.

Inhale.

Exhale.

When Craig's breathing steadied, he said, "Thanks for finding her."

Alamber pressed comfort against Craig's side. At some point while he'd been watching over the boss, he'd stripped out of his wet clothes and put on loose pants and a sweatshirt that smelled of Lieutenant Maaren; the pants too large and the sweater too small, his shoulders straining against the fabric. Some Humans denied needing touch, said it was a Taykan thing. Some Humans were idiots. "Are you okay?"

"Yes. No." The pressure against Alamber's side increased. "I hate this. There's nothing I can do except be there when she wakes up."

"Then why . . . ?"

The creases at the side of Craig's eyes deepened, and Alamber opened more light receptors to watch them. "She's in an autodoc, Alamber. She's not going to wake up until she's out of the autodoc."

"Do you think I could . . ."

Craig swiveled in the chair and examined Alamber's face. Had he been Taykan, the gray-blue of his eyes would have darkened. After a moment he nodded. "Yeah, go on in."

The autodoc looked like the cylinders the Marines carried their deconstituted dead out in. No secret the boss still carried the weight of every cylinder she'd ever humped out of a war zone and now she was inside a giant copy. That was metaphor or irony or . . . actually, Alamber didn't know what it was called, but it had to be something. The size, almost twice the size of the unit on *Promise*, explained why Craig hadn't rolled it onto their shuttle and taken Torin himself, fuk the med-evac.

He glanced at his slate. Still no ETA.

When a shadow fell over the numbers scrolling across the upper arc, he assumed, for a moment, Craig had returned. He drew in a deep, coffee-washed breath, and knew before he turned who it was.

Marilissa looked surprised to see him. "The AD malfunctioning?"

"No." He glanced back down at his slate, maximized the autodoc connect, and repeated, "No."

"You slaved the AD to your slate? That's illegal. I mean, you're a Warden . . ." He could hear the question, the inflection she gave it, the way the ex-military he worked with no longer did. "Even I know it's illegal."

"And now if anything, anything at all goes wrong, every slate in the building will scream about it." The numbers continued to scroll. "I'm not leaving her alone in there."

"Every slate? You don't do things by halves, do you?" The curve of her mouth flattened. "You and the gunny, you're not . . . ?" Her voice trailed off into disapproval. No surprise with Craig in the canteen drowning himself in her coffee. She wasn't Taykan and a small number of Humans had weird ideas about closeness. Not usually those who'd served, but Marilissa had been Navy and from what he'd heard, the Navy was . . . different.

The words for what the boss was to him existed in Taykan, not in Federate, and he didn't owe those words to Marilissa or anyone else. "No. We're not."

"Well, okay, then." He couldn't read her expression. She took a step farther into the room, let out a breath, and in a tone so neutral he figured it hid strong emotion, said, "Gunnery Sergeant Torin Kerr. She just doesn't die, does she."

The upper curve of the autodoc felt comfortably cool under Alamber's fingertips. He wondered how much plastic it held. "Not so far."

"The protesters are gone. They left three heaters in the tent, loaded all their shit onto the carrier, and booted."

"How long ago?"

"How the hell can I determine that?"

Cap glanced over at Alamber, who raised a hand in the universal gesture for *give me a minute* as the time signature on the big screen raced backward. Blob and static. Blob and static. Static. Static. Blob and static. Static. Static. Rain and smaller fast moving blobs. "They were there when it started to rain."

"All of them?"

"Sorry, Cap. Signal to noise ratio is too high."

"Your security system is crap, Lieutenant."

"Tell that to the department comptroller, Warden. Are we done out here or does the Justice Department have another job for us?"

"So much for making friends," Binti muttered.

Cap ignored her. "I can assume you packed up the tent and the heaters?"

"You can assume we've been doing our job longer than you've been doing yours."

Werst snorted. "Bet they *wirtine* about us all the way out."

Alamber didn't know the word. From the reaction of the other Krai in the canteen, it seemed like one worth knowing.

Cap drew a finger across her throat and the room fell silent. "Medevac hasn't given us a new ETA, so it looks like we'll be here when you get back."

"Oh, joy. Maaren out."

By the time Alamber had compiled a file with clear images of the protesters, the storm had moved far enough south for him to bounce a signal through Promise and slice through the nominal security of the census bureau. He had their identities and every bit of digital information available before the PLE made it back to the training facility with the crawler.

Cap stopped by his side as the EMTs moved the autodoc out through the canteen into the carrier. "Alamber?"

"Don't worry, I'm in." The EMS carrier had next to no security; he could have taken control had he wanted to.

"Attach all identifying information pertaining to the carrier and the EMTs to the susumi packet, seal it, and send it."

"Pertaining?"

"They made me go to OS. Taught me big words."

"Yeah. Okay. Isn't that a little paranoid?"

She huffed out a low laugh. "It's how Gunny would want it."

• ——◆—— •

"Did you forget that some asshole sauntered up close and shot her!" Craig wanted to lean over the commander's desk and yell that in his face, but he managed to hold himself back.

Ng's frown deepened. "That doesn't mean you can break the law."

"Government files are open files!"

"Census files are . . ."

"Are government files! And Wardens are permitted to access any and all surveillance that may assist in apprehending those who have broken the laws of the Confederation. I read the manual!"

Releasing his hold on the inert edge of his desk, Commander Ng ran both hands back through his hair, and took a deep breath. "Access to satellites must be given by the planetary government. It is . . ." He held up a hand, cutting Craig off. ". . . a formality, granted, but formalities exist for a reason."

"Formalities take too long!"

"And the Strike Teams move too quickly. I understand that."

Craig opened his mouth, closed it again, and frowned. "You do?"

"I deal with you lot on a daily basis, yes, I do. The letter of the law was bent, not broken, but . . ." He leaned forward again. ". . . the spirit of the law was exercised with extreme prejudice."

"That wasn't extreme."

"So I've been informed."

He'd already spoken to the leads of Ch'tore and U'yun. Cap and Elisk had refused to tell Craig what had been discussed, but Werst, as Torin's second, had come out of his debrief and sent Craig in. Craig had things to say, so he'd gone.

"While I'm happy to hear it could have been worse," Ng continued, "that's not an argument I can take upstairs."

"You want to take something upstairs?" Craig paced to the hatch and back to the desk, hating the total lack of anything but faint impatience on the commander's face. Torin had been shot. "Then take this upstairs," he spat. "Who knew we were on Seven Sta? Who knew we were at that specific training facility?"

"All the Strike Teams, most of the Wardens, and anyone on the station paying attention. A fair chunk of the planetary government, as I had to get clearance for the use of weapons. The planetary press, and about ninety percent of the PLE. Granted, we can concentrate on the Younger Races and quite possibly narrow it down to Humans alone, but if you're looking for a conspiracy, Warden Ryder, you'll still have to narrow your focus."

Craig folded his arms. "The Elder Races have always been willing to have the Younger do violence for them," he snarled.

Ng opened his mouth. Closed it again.

Even odds Ranjit, Elisk, and Werst had also pointed out it hadn't been a random shooting. Random shootings didn't happen in the Confederation. Humans First operated from stations and abandoned facilities on moons and asteroids because it was impossible to get weapons through planetary security. Both Alamber and Ressk had named it impossible; Craig wasn't pulling the word from his ass.

"That's not likely," Ng said at last.

"But possible. And we know things they don't want us to know." He wasn't going to mention the H'san by name. Not standing in a government office. Not when the government guaranteed full transparency. He could almost see Ng thinking.

"All right. I admit it's possible. But we don't act on possibilities, we act on evidence. Therefore, you're going to put together a report that mentions your emotional condition after Warden Kerr was shot and how that condition influenced everything that happened afterward. The report will be for the higher-ups and for the planetary government. Hopefully, they'll think it's romantic and not scrap the program."

"Scrap the Strike Teams?"

"You may have noticed how Parliament has been debating whether or not the Elder Races can civilize the Younger before their violent corruption violates the whole."

"They want to lock us down."

"They do. And the Strike Teams are a logical place to begin. If it doesn't happen, we can thank Humans First. They've made it clear they require an armed response and the only thing Parliament wants less than the Strike Teams charging in like a H'san in a cheese shop is to involve the military. They believe that changing the laws that prevent the military from dealing with civilian problems is the beginning of the end, and I'm not sure they're wrong." He examined a file, then flicked it off to the left too quickly for Craig to get a look at the content. "With your report, I'll hand over the worst of Warden Kerr's tanking data, reminding them that this is what the Strike Teams risk every time you go out. They'll acknowledge they're grateful and tell me that, regardless of your willingness to sacrifice, you have to learn some manners, and I'll agree."

Craig paced to the hatch again. "You seem to have this all worked out. Why did you need to talk to me?"

Ng shrugged. "I thought you might need someone to yell at. I know I did."

Craig had assumed Alamber would want to stay with Torin on her trip back to Berbar on the *CS Odylk*. *Promise* couldn't carry a full immersion tank, the *Odylk* was a patrol boat so had no attachment capabilities, and Craig was not allowing Werst to pilot his ship in and out of Susumi. Alamber was the obvious choice as Torin's companion.

Alamber had been thinking more clearly than he had, however. *"We don't know who shot her. Whoever goes with her has to be able to protect her."*

"She's on a Navy ship."

Alamber's hair had flattened, and he'd repeated, *"We don't know who shot her."*

Binti and Werst had thrown bones for it, then they'd both gone.

Had Justice not been willing to move Torin to a tank on Berbar, the whole team would've remained on Seven Sta. Craig assumed that an unwillingness to lose the team had been the primary reason behind the Justice decision. That, and he had no doubt government transparency would be adjusted to translucency when they controlled the flow of information.

He didn't like spending time at the tank, but he came anyway. He didn't like seeing Torin helpless and suspected that was what she hated so much about being tanked. All that time spent unable to kick ass.

Her spleen and liver and a big chunk of intestine were being regrown, finishing up with brand new skin over sixty percent of her abdomen. There'd be no physical scars. Knowing Torin, probably no mental scars either, although he had a few new ones. She'd be pissed about being shot, though; that was a given.

His life before Torin had been riskier than most. CSOs worked on the edges, and edges crumbled. He'd picked over the debris of battle, but even when he turned DNA over to the MIA data banks, the violence hadn't affected him personally. After Torin, the violence had gotten personal—aimed deliberately at him or at people he cared about.

He liked his life. His friends. The team that had replaced the chosen family he'd left behind on the salvage station, or maybe the family who'd left him behind when they'd abandoned him to the pirates.

He loved to fly. Loved that he'd been able to bring his *Promise* with him, her reconfiguration the outer map of their inner change.

He hated there were people who deliberately caused pain. Dealt death.

He loved Torin. Had she died, he was almost positive he'd have stayed on with the team after he sobered up.

There was something to be said for making the universe a better place even if the actual words said were usually profane.

Hand pressed against the tank, as close as he could get for another tenday, Craig squinted, trying to correct for the soft focus of the viscous fluid surrounding her. With luck, by the time she was decanted, they'd know who shot her. Have a plan. Head out to make an arrest.

His breath fogged the glass. At least she was unconscious while she was helpless, unlike the rest of them.

· ——◆— ·

"Hey, Bishami, remember that hinky coding you had?"

Bishami raised a hand, shifted half of the hard light image in front of her two centimeters to the left, and looked up. Her crimson hair began to flip back and forth, picking up speed, and her eyes darkened.

Alamber glanced over his shoulder, but there was nothing behind him. "What?"

"You look like shit. What are you wearing?"

He had to look down. "My uniform?"

"Part of your uniform." She cocked her head and drew in a deep breath through her nose. "When's the last time you had sex?"

"I've been sleeping communal, what do you think?"

"Your scent's off."

"Yeah, well, we had a little trouble on Seven Sta," he snapped. "You may have heard."

Her expression changed so completely, he knew that had they known the same dialect, she'd have switched to Taykan. "Oh, sweetie, I'm so sorry. I hadn't realized the two of you . . ."

"There isn't two of us. There's six of us."

"Good for you." Her eyes lightened, and he went into her arms as she came around the desk.

"I found the body."

She nuzzled under his ear. "I have an experiment running for the next twenty minutes, but after that . . ."

"No . . . I mean, absolutely, but that's not why I'm here."

"Right." Detangling their hair, she stepped back. "The coding."

"Still need some help with it?"

"Hell, yes. But why aren't you searching for the person who . . ." Bishami frowned as she searched his face for what Alamber could only assume was the least traumatizing description. ". . . who injured her?"

He wondered if down here in her labs where no one ever bled, she could even say shot. Or beaten. Or tortured. Or executed. Big Bill had been a traditionalist and fond of venting the airlock himself. He'd found the boss bleeding out on the grass years after he'd found his first body.

"Alamber?"

"I have ferrets running."

Her hair flipped back. "You're hunting rodents? Oh," she continued before he could answer, "I'm an idiot. It's a search term. Human?"

"That's what they say."

"Of course they do." Her hair curled around her ears. "There's a chance I'm spending too much time in the lab."

"No comment." He found a smile from somewhere. "I thought fixing your code might distract me while the searches run."

"It may bore you numb rather than distract you, but you can fix it with my thanks." Arm around his waist, she steered him toward a terminal. "I'll get you in. You haven't the clearance to go deep, and I'll sleep better maintaining the illusion you can't wander through the brains of the station at will."

"What am I looking for?" he asked settling into the seat.

"If I knew, I'd call tech in. It's like . . ." Her eyes lightened as she stared up at the ceiling and were about three shades paler when she looked at him again. ". . . like a fine fabric catching on callus, a slight tug where there shouldn't be one. Everything functions fine, but— now and then—it feels wrong."

"And tech can't work with that?"

"Tech's a little short of abstract thinkers." She kissed the top of his head, and left him to be absorbed by layer after layer after layer of ones and zeros.

Numb would work.

It took Alamber three days to find the problem. Bishami's metaphorical calluses were catching because the extra pieces of code tucked in where they didn't belong had been sloppily compiled. Big Bill would have skinned him if he'd built a backdoor so rough around the edges. If this was the sort of work produced by a standard education as opposed to on-the-job-training motivated by the possibility of pain, he hadn't missed much.

Packets leaving the station carried messages that separated and redirected at the first Susumi buoy. Alamber couldn't track them past the buoy, but he could tease loose the two still in the system, open them, and break the appallingly simple cypher.

There was a Humans First cell on the station. In the Justice Department.

· ——◆—— ·

Rubbing his palms against his thigh to get rid of the feel of the decontamination spray off his hands, Craig stepped out of the airlock entry that separated the hospital from the rest of the station and nearly ran Alamber down. They danced for a moment, got sworn at by a Niln trying to get into the airlock, and finally managed to shuffle into a bit of corridor out of the way of foot traffic.

"Were you going in?" Craig stared into Alamber's pale eyes and wondered if he was feeling all right. Their interaction had been as close to graceless as he'd ever seen from a di'Taykan. Had he stopped by since Torin's tank had been brought home? The others had, but he couldn't remember seeing Alamber's ID in the log.

Alamber glanced at the hospital entrance, eyes lightening as if to block the sight, his hair flattening. "No, I'm not going in."

"Okay." Torin wouldn't give a shit. She'd said more than once she didn't like people looking at her when she couldn't look back.

"Have you got a minute?" His mouth twisted into something not quite a smile. "Or ten?"

Between shift changes, Musselman's had plenty of empty tables. Craig half expected Alamber to tuck them into a back corner or up by one of the screens where the sound of a cricket match would cover their conversation, but he went for centrally located, with enough empty space around them the server rolled her eyes when she came out from behind the bar to take their order.

He set his slate on the table. "I can deal with directional microphones as long as I have a minimum of a clear meter for the full three sixty. Keeping people in the dark is harder, so . . ." He waved a hand. "No people."

Another time, Craig would have laughed, certain Alamber was fukking with him. Another time, Torin wouldn't have been in a tank regrowing her spleen. When Alamber ordered a *sevestin* which might have been alcoholic, but tasted like dirty socks so who the hell cared, he ordered a portion of banderillas and a beer. Interesting that they hadn't gone back to quarters if they wanted to avoid attention. He managed to chew and swallow a baby onion and a mouthful of beer before he asked what the fuk was going on.

Alamber drained half the pale green liquid in his glass. "Humans First has a cell on the station."

"You're shitting me. A cell?"

"Isn't that the right word? A cabal? A group? An infiltration."

"This isn't about your Federate, Alamber." He leaned in. Getting close to a di'Taykan would never arouse suspicion. "Lower your voice and show me the evidence."

The evidence was extensive and—also—not. Someone, and there

was no evidence more than one person was involved, had buried the information downloaded from Torin's tank in the regular communications traffic. He understood enough to see the path Alamber had followed. Couldn't have followed it himself, but could do the basic math. He crushed a pickled chili between thumb and forefinger, studied the oil on his skin for a moment, then said, "How hard would it be to get this information?"

"From the tank? I could do it. So could Ressk. It's protected, but they don't . . ." He waved a hand in time with the movement of his hair. ". . . expect to be cracked, so the security's not as good as it could be."

Too many people could access Torin's data. "Can you fix it, then?"

"Sure. But, now?"

"After." Craig spun Alamber's slate in place. "We don't know this is Humans First."

"Who else would it be? It can't be a lone nutjob, not with all the hidden communication happening."

"Fair enough." He stopped the spin, handed Alamber his slate, and finished his beer. "Now, what?"

"New packets will be diverted to the buffers, I'll be notified, and I'll take a look—maybe change a few things before sending them on. We can't just stop them, or they'll know we're on to them."

That seemed obvious, so Craig nodded and asked, "Why tell me?"

Alamber's eyes went dark. "The boss got shot. Tanked. Whoever sent this . . ." He tapped the edge of his slate. ". . . has to be the person who released our schedule. Who let Humans First know we'd be on Seven Sta, where and when."

"Yeah, got that. But you should tell Commander Ng."

"*We* should." Alamber grabbed the last skewer of pickled vegetables off the plate and pointed it at Craig. "Are we going to?"

Torin would. Betrayal had driven Torin from the Corps, but she trusted the rank structure. Trusted that the whole would look after the parts. He'd always assumed it was as much habit as anything.

Odds were high the rest of the Strike Teams would feel the same way. Binti, Werst, Ressk . . . they'd walk into live fire for Torin—had walked into live fire for Torin—but they'd all been military and, for them, with Torin tanked, the buck stopped at Commander Ng.

Commander Ng was Human.

Humans First had infiltrated the Justice Department.

Who knew how far in?

Craig had never been military. Neither had Alamber.

"No," he said. "We're not. Can you find out who sent that message?"

"If I can grab a few more, maybe. Probably." He frowned and tapped his fingers against the broad belt slung diagonally around his hips. "I can find out where it was sent from at least. What about putting a guard in Med-op? What if they . . ."

"Go after Torin in the tank?" Fukking hell, they'd thought she was safe when they brought her back to Berbar. "Could you get into hospital operations and change the mix she's in?" Alamber hesitated, but nodded. "Could the person who wrote that code?"

"Not if that's the best they can do."

"Then we'll let the terrifying tank supervisor do her job."

The day before Torin was to be detanked, Alamber finally pinpointed the terminal and the log-on ID that had been the source of all three messages. Craig had no idea if that made the operator of said terminal cocky or stupid, nor did he care. He could work with either.

Each strand of hair twitching individually, Alamber folded his arms and glared. "Are you suicidal? I'm going with you."

"No, and no. Humans First, remember?" Craig dragged a henley down over his head and checked that his shoulders and arms moved freely. "Those assholes will snap closed when they see you coming."

Alamber opened his mouth, clearly decided now was not the time, and closed it again. It was news to Craig there wasn't a time a di'Taykan wouldn't respond to that kind of provocation. "They won't be happy about you showing up. They hate you. You're a traitor to your species."

In the third message, they'd copied the logs that listed the times he'd spent by Torin's tank.

"They've known me and hated me for a while now. When Torin makes the news, I'm standing beside her." He frowned, propped his right foot on a chair, and bent to tie his boot. "Not during the Silsviss thing, but after. And this . . ." He straightened. ". . . is recon, nothing more. I have a valid reason to go to SR besides finding out if this person is a flunky or a player."

"You can tell that by looking at a person?"

"I've played a lot of poker in my time. I know a bluff when I see one."

"Yeah, poker, that's relevant." Hair now cutting choppy arcs above his shoulders, Alamber folded his arms. "Torin calls that your bar fight shirt."

"It washes." Craig would crack heads if he had to in order to get answers. He wasn't telling Alamber that, although he doubted he needed to.

"I'm coming as far as the SR link station."

"And if you're spotted? If they see us together and I go on alone? They'll know we're on to them, and we need to know how deep the rot goes."

"Before we tell Commander Ng?"

Craig lifted his lips off his teeth in a smile he'd learned from Werst. "Before we tell Torin."

Pale blue hair flipped back and forward, then stilled. "Fine. Go alone."

Leave me behind.

Speaking of rot that went deep. If she hadn't already died, Craig would've happily blown Alamber's late *vantru* out an airlock. "You've got the harder job."

"How do you figure?"

He wrapped his hand around Alamber's wrist and squeezed lightly. "If anything happens to me, you have to tell Torin."

"Fukker."

Mimi Paddison of SR was a late middle-aged Human who, if asked, would probably say she did the kind of behind-the-scenes job essential to the smooth running of the station, but as that job seemed to consist of maintaining the database of job applicants and recent hires and left her enough time to support a terrorist organization, Craig doubted it. On the other side of one hundred, she was tall, heavyset, and fond of flowered fabric—given her size and the size of the flowers, she looked like a much-loved sofa Craig barely remembered from his childhood. The uniformity of her skin color, at least the skin he could see, announced she visited the few remaining UV cubes that catered to Humans of a certain age. Her purple hair looked naturally curly and unnaturally purple.

According to social media, her latest ex had been male, so Craig presented both dimples, flexed his arms as he leaned toward her desk, and thickened the accent he'd almost lost. "Per Patterson, g'day. Ta for seeing me on such short notice."

"It's my job," she said shortly. "What do you want, Warden Ryder?"

"Warden Kerr has been trying to convince an old friend of hers to tuck on, and I'd hoped you could tell me if he'd applied. I'd like to have some news for her to barrack about when she's standing again. They say you're the one to talk to."

"Do they." Paddison's expression didn't change, and there was no question in her voice. "You've been locked out of her account by the tank supervisor, haven't you?"

He nodded. "Tosser slammed me."

"Warden Kerr will regain access as soon as she passes cognitive testing. She'll find out about her friend then."

Craig worked the dimples again. "I wanted to be the one to tell her. Give her a smile."

"Sucks to be you. Ever heard of inter-office communications? Did you assume I'd be dazzled by the personal touch?"

So much for the dimples. "It's timing. She'll be decanted today."

"Then she won't have long to wait."

"As a favor, then. I'll owe you one. And it'll be faster for you to run the search than to run me off."

"I'm sure." She sighed so emphatically, Craig expected to see moisture fog her desk. "Fine. I need to see some identification."

He blinked. "But you know who I am."

"And what does that have to do with the price of cheese? You want me to do this; then you do it my way, a way that maintains order. You know what order does, Warden Ryder? It stops the decline into chaos. Now, show me some ID or stop wasting my time."

"If you put it like that, then." He handed over his slate, open to his personal information, giving her no reason to switch screens and find that Alamber had ridden along. Craig didn't know if Alamber thought he'd gotten away with it, or if he didn't care that Craig had discovered his spyware—nor did it matter. Had Alamber suggested it up front, he'd have probably agreed.

Thumb on the screen, she returned the slate. "Name?"

"It was on the ID . . ."

She rolled her eyes. "Are you high? Not your name, the name of Warden Kerr's friend who may or may not have applied."

"di'Rearl Stedrin."

"di'Taykan. Figures. Sit. Don't sit. I don't care. It's going to take . . ." She glanced at the old-fashioned screen angled up from the center of the desk. ". . . twelve point seven three minutes to run."

"I can wait."

"Good. You're going to have to."

He fidgeted in place for a couple of minutes, attempted to pace, ran out of room, dropped into the chair in front of the desk, and shoved both hands back through his hair. Enough stage setting. "You heard what happened to Torin? To Warden Kerr?"

It felt like ten or fifteen minutes had passed before Paddison answered. "I heard."

"Fukking aliens."

That got her attention. One eyebrow lifted.

"There were protesters outside the training grounds, we lost contact with three of them, two di'Taykan and a Human. Figured they were off fukking, but then Torin gets shot and conveniently it's a di'Taykan who found her . . ." He hadn't discussed this part with Alamber because this wasn't recon. This was infiltration. Humans First, by way of Anthony Marteau, had wanted to recruit them, him and Torin, mostly Torin. Dead, Torin would be out of their way. Alive and joining in, she'd be a coup the Confederation might not recover from. "That was convenient, wasn't it?" he continued. "A di'Taykan the only one close enough to see who it was. She almost fukking died." Running his hands back through his hair again, he hoped he looked like a distraught lover and not someone who wanted to dive across the desk and squeeze out the names of every terrorist who'd cut their way into the Justice Department.

He was bluffing with two eights, needing Mimi Paddison to believe he had the third.

He got a good grip on the desire for violence throbbing in his hindbrain.

The Parliamentary faction that wanted to lock up the Younger Races might have a point.

Fuk'em.

"There's been no arrests made."

"What?" Her statement, flat and emotionless, jerked him out of his spiraling thoughts.

She rolled her eyes again and slowly, deliberately, repeated herself. "There have been no arrests made."

"The PLEs say the protesters panicked and have gone to ground. That'll it'll take time to root them out. Justice won't send in Wardens."

"Chief Justice Genesvah is Niln. The Minister of Justice is Trun." "So?"

"Don't be stupid, Warden Ryder. They're not Human."

He leaned forward in the chair and frowned. "Why would a Niln and a Trun protect a di'Taykan?"

Her expression suggested that was the stupid she'd warned him about. "They're not Human."

"Torin is."

"There you go." Her screen chimed. "di'Rearl Stedrin has applied to the Justice Department. His interview will be scheduled once transportation issues have been dealt with. Huzzah," she added flatly, "you have good news for Warden Kerr."

"Yeah, another di'Taykan. Thanks." Craig could feel her gaze locked on him as he stood and turned and headed for the door, her office too internal to require a hatch.

"Warden Ryder, when is Warden Kerr due to be decanted?"

He paused just inside the room. "I told you, late today. It's why I came."

"Of course it is." That was the most sarcastic agreement Craig had ever heard. He was reluctantly impressed. "Twenty-one fifteen, twelve, seven, fourteen."

Level twelve, corridor seven, compartment fourteen.

"Now get out of my office, some of us have work to do."

"You *ablin gon savit!*"

Craig held a finger over his lips and then his palm out before Alamber could continue.

Frowning, Alamber took another step into the room, eyes darkening as he focused on the old slate in Craig's hand. Craig had found the slate in the junk drawer. He never threw anything away. Torin never kept more than the minimum around. It had taken a while, but they'd made it work. Too old to connect to the station, the slate was both functional and useless and, more importantly, impossible to eavesdrop on. Using the blunted end of a piece of wire, he wrote: *Paddison had my slate in contact with her desk. Could she have tapped it?*

Alamber pulled it out of his hand, standing close enough his hair flicked against Craig's cheek hard enough to hurt. *Not unless she had code ready and waiting. Highly unlikely.*

How high?

Very high. "You've caught the paranoia bug from the boss."

Craig stepped back. He understood why Alamber was pissed, but he wasn't going to put up with being scourged. "It's not paranoia if you're in a tank for over a tenday."

Teeth bared, Alamber grabbed the front of his sweater and held him in place. "Might've been good had you remembered that before you decided to go undercover in a terrorist organization."

"Hey!"

They turned as one.

Werst looked pointedly between them and then at the handful of sweater Alamber continued to hold. "What're you two up to?"

"Craig's infiltrating Humans First to find out who shot the boss."

"Yeah, right. Gunny'd kick his ass. We're heading to Musselman's to play *jik*. Join us when you're finished with whatever." He flipped them the finger, on principle Craig assumed, and disappeared, yelling, "No, they're fukking or fighting. I'm not using the *jik* table with the crack in it, so move your ass."

After a long moment, Alamber released his grip and patted the puckered fabric flat with the palm of his hand. "Even Werst doesn't believe you're stupid enough to go through with such a *sanlit* plan."

"Werst is wrong."

"No shit. I should go to Commander Ng." Alamber sounded furious, but his touch was gentle.

Craig wondered if the constant patting was intended as reassurance that Craig was still there. "We need to find out how deep this goes."

"I know."

"And there's always the chance it was a personal invitation."

Alamber pulled his hand free and walked across the room, voice steadying, hair still cutting jerky arcs. "I know personal invitations and that wasn't one."

"Lucky break for me, then. She's terrifying."

"So's the boss." He pointedly looked up at the Silsviss skull on the wall, and Craig laughed.

"Good point . . ." Pulling his slate from its clip, he crossed to Alamber's side and nudged him with it. "Check anyway, would you?"

It had stopped being paranoia the moment that anonymous asshole had pulled the trigger.

SR was in the oldest part of the station, the only section to have a level twelve. Newer sections had no more than nine. Each section could survive for a limited time on its own should the station fail— where fail meant explode. The Strike Team's section had four levels and only one lock leading to the rest of the station. To be fair, they had more explosives.

Commander Ng still lived in the quarters he'd occupied before he became a Warden. Could be lawyers claimed fancier digs, and he didn't want to give them up. Could be he liked the neighborhood. Craig didn't care, but Ng living away from the teams was one of the reasons Craig didn't completely trust him. One of the reasons he hadn't gone to him with this information.

He was self-aware enough to know the larger reason was personal. He'd spent a large part of his life doing things on his own. Solving his own problems. Depending on himself. He didn't have a team out in the debris fields; if the shit hit the fan, he cleaned it up. Living in Torin's shadow wasn't a problem, but it was . . . good, yeah, good to be out on his own again.

Corridor seven was a narrow alley, barely broader than his shoulders, and six meters long. Compartment fourteen was the only compartment on the corridor, and it was barely three meters square, empty but for the circular hatches in each wall. Each hatch held a sign identifying it as an access into the environmental system, making this, Craig realized, a base chamber for the equipment storage. Were he back on the salvage station, there'd be a bed and a locker, and a pissed-off tenant demanding to know what the fuk he was doing.

The entrance hatch had been closed when he arrived, so he closed it behind him, the station maintaining lights at Human levels based on registered life signs.

Slouching against the far wall, he crossed his arms and waited.

Ten minutes.

Fifteen.

He'd give them twenty, then fuk you very much.

When the hatch opened, he half expected a Krai. It was mostly Krai who went into the guts of the stations where prehensile feet made climbing though conduits easier. He took a moment to recalibrate for Paddison. She wasn't in flowers anymore; she wore trousers, tunic, and boots, and he hadn't realized she was as tall as Torin.

"Didn't expect to see you here, Warden Ryder."

He pushed off from the wall. "Why not?"

"I thought you were smarter." She moved like Torin. Like Werst. Like violence had been coded into her DNA. Craig could fight. His muscle was working muscle, but he'd used his fists before Torin, and he'd learned new moves after. He didn't stand a chance. Didn't even know how he'd been thrown to the deck, her knee between his shoulders, one arm twisted back so far he could feel tendons start to pop. "Did my thirty in the Corps; close combat specialist. Instructor for the last ten. It's all in my file, Warden, but you didn't look. Applied to be the close combat instructor for the Strike Teams, but it seems I have an attitude."

The sharp pain in the side of his neck came as a surprise. It probably shouldn't have.

"Thanks to that feathered freak in the labs, we've got fast acting knock-out drugs that are too specific to use in the field. C&C's requested permission to use them on prisoners who keep fighting, but the answer's hung up in that zoo of misfit assholes on Nuh Ner they call Parliament."

His lips were numb, and his tongue felt twice as large as it should, but he managed to spit out, "Trap?"

"Opportunity." The pressure eased, and her voice came from farther away. "The trap happens later. You're bait."

At first he thought the banging came from inside his head, then he realized it was the bolt on a hatch slamming back and the hatch opening.

"He came?" Male voice. Young.

"No, you're hallucinating."

"But . . ."

"Give me strength." A hand around his wrist and the deck slid by past his nose. "Take him."

A new hand. Size and position of calluses said Krai.

"Now give me the harness."

The straps fit under his arms and between his legs and he thought for a moment he was in *Promise* securing his crash harness. Curls brushed under his nose. Smelled like lavender. He liked lavender. There were pots of it growing on the station. Not this station . . . his slate . . . took his slate . . .

"No . . ." He flopped his hand from side to side in an ineffectual protest. As the harness snugged up and he was dragged through the hatch, he heard his slate hit the deck and a boot hit his slate.

It was tight inside the conduit. Shoulders snagged. Were yanked free. Boots, too. Snagged. Yanked. Krai worked through the guts, and Krai were smaller. Occasionally humans. He knew Torin used them when . . . when . . .

* ——◆—— *

"This one feels that that the immersion has a certain similarity to the life-giving fluid of the egg." Dr. Finz, one of the three tank specialists, cocked his head, and added, "Or in your case, Warden, to the womb."

"Yeah, and there's . . ." Torin spat toward the drain. ". . . a reason we don't remember that."

"You don't? How sad. This one returns to my memory of the egg when this one needs a moment's peace. Stand in complete stillness now so this one can scan." He stepped back. "Use the safety bars, please. This one doesn't want you face-planting on the floor and ruining a tenday's work."

"Not that fragile." She didn't feel fragile; she felt heavy, wrapped in gravity's chains once again. After a tenday in the tank, she didn't have much extra body mass, but what little she had sagged toward the deck. Her breasts hung off her chest like sacks of fat, which, technically, they were. They weren't usually so obvious about it. The electrical currents that had been a constant presence while she healed continued to buzz just under her skin stimulating nerve growth and connection. It was an illusion, sense memory hanging on, and annoyingly similar to the buzz the data sheet had left behind. Another reason to hate the plastic.

"Everything looks good. You know the drill: shower, drink the liquid by your bed, then lie down and sleep." The majority of his attention on his slate, he waved toward the recovery room as though Torin might have forgotten where it was. The yellow-and-blue feathers protruding from the top of his silicon gauntlet made it look like party wear. "No strenuous exercise for the next tenday," he continued, turning his head to stare at her with his left eye. Although the Rakva were biocular, every one Torin had ever met used the one-eye stare for emphasis. "This one's definition of strenuous, not yours."

Fixated on getting into the shower, Torin grunted an agreement.

"Warden?"

Seemed a grunt wasn't good enough. "I have heard and understood your instructions, Doctor."

"And you've done this before. That's not necessarily a good thing, Warden."

Torin shrugged. Tried to shrug. The muscles of her back weren't yet cooperating. "It's a thing."

"Indeed." His crest rose. "This one will see you tomorrow morning for another scan. Go shower."

The shower wasn't significantly bigger than the tank, the spray on a preprogrammed pattern, both placement and temperature designed to remove all traces of the artificial exudate she'd been suspended in. Torin had always believed decanting should negate the station's water conservation policies—regardless of station or policies. It didn't, but it should.

Her skin felt soft and unlived-in and her calluses had been soaked off. She hated the unfinished feeling that came post decanting, but was all in favor of being alive so called it a draw. As the last of the water slipped down the drain, she skimmed the excess off her hair, now a uniform two inches long, and closed her eyes. Warm air swirled around her body. Others had described it as a caress. Torin preferred her caresses with more intent behind them.

It would be another fifty-six hours before she saw Craig, or anyone else. Fifty-six hours to ensure her immune system had rebooted and everything that was supposed to be stuck together stayed stuck. Fortunately, fifty-six hours of sleep sounded like a good thing because she hadn't actually slept in the tank and both body and brain knew it.

The bed in the clean room had a soft, fuzzy surface designed to guard against bed sores on tender skin. Torin skipped the robe, arranged herself carefully on the bed, and sighed. Yeah, that felt . . .

The inside of her jaw buzzed. She sighed and touched her tongue to the implant's on switch.

Boss! Can you hear me?

"What is it, Alamber?" Everything said, done, and sloughed off in this room was recorded. She doubted she had the control to subvocalize, but if she kept her voice low, she wouldn't trip any alarms. Alamber shouldn't have been able to make contact through the hospital firewalls, not that she was surprised he had.

There's a Humans First cell here on Berbar. Craig went after them on his own, and now he's missing.

"Fukking hell." She grabbed the robe as she stood and shrugged into it as she crossed the room. "Crack the door and spring . . ." The latch slammed back, sounding like a bone breaking. Alamber had clearly disabled the alarms. Another quick touch to the inside of her jaw opened a broader, albeit specific, channel. "All Strike Teams on station, gear up. Assemble in my quarters. Now. Werst, I've got a job for you."

Only U'yun and Alpha were on station.

"You were tanked," Ressk reminded her. "We've been on station duty."

"And we're the new guys," Yahsamus added. "Last in, last choice to send out."

Torin swept a gaze around the room, watched everyone including the two officers straighten. "Two teams will be plenty. Now, listen up. Alamber . . ."

"We need to tell Commander Ng." Elisk announced when Alamber finished. He folded his arms, nostril ridges half closed.

"Do you know how deep Humans First has their sweaty fingers crammed into the Justice Department?" Torin asked.

"No, and thank you for that imagery, Gunny."

"I trust Binti explicitly, and I approved the Humans on U'yun. Commander Ng came with the job. I don't believe he's a member of Humans First, but I'm not willing to bet Craig's life on it. I wouldn't bet anyone's life on it. Would you?" It didn't sound like a threat. It wasn't. Quite.

Elisk met Torin's gaze for a long moment. "There's going to be fallout."

Torin's lips pulled back. "Count on it."

After another long moment, Elisk snapped his teeth together, his response repeated by the other two Krai in the room.

"Gunny's right." Binti swept a burning gaze around the room as the tension dissipated. "It goes deeper than Mimi Paddison, and if we don't know how deep it goes, we don't know who we can trust."

Yahsamus cleared her throat. Elisk waved a hand.

"You can trust non-Humans," Lorkin pointed out.

"Granted, and we can use that."

"On what?" Ressk asked, helping Alamber sift through the station's memory. "We've pulled up all the security footage from the area. Craig enters compartment fourteen. Seventeen minutes, forty seconds later, Paddison follows him in. No camera inside."

"Fukking dead zone," Yahsamus muttered.

Over the last couple of years, Alamber had been mapping the dead zones on the station. The Strike Team section had none, personal areas were inert not dead, but the older areas of the station . . . the file kept growing. Once they ended Humans First, Torin was going to push Commander Ng harder to have them eliminated. Provided Commander Ng was still around.

"Eleven minutes later," Ressk continued, "only Paddison comes out."

And compartment fourteen is empty. The picture on the big entertainment screen shifted as Werst held up his slate. *Must've used one of the maintenance conduits.*

"With Ryder's shoulders?" Zhou wondered.

Torin considered it. The Confederation valued uniformity, and all government stations were built to the same specifications. She hadn't been in these conduits, but she'd been in others. "Tight, but there's enough internal flexibility he'd fit."

"I don't want to know how you know that, do I?" Elisk asked clearly not expecting an answer.

"I'm picking up nothing from his slate," Ressk announced. "At the very least, I should be crossing his connection to the station sysop."

Yeah, this is why. Werst held up a small piece of metal. *She crushed his slate, took the pieces out, tossed them in the nearest recycler. Missed this bit. And I can't track him. I can smell him for about two meters, then the conduit blurs into a mixed stink.*

Fingers tapping out old codes against the wall, Binti stilled. "Have you tagged him, Gunny?"

"Wouldn't matter," Alamber answered before Torin could. "I can't get into his implant."

"You got through post-tank quarantine protocols," she reminded him.

"Yeah, I remember." Eyes still on his slate, his hair flipped toward her. "If I can't get through to his implant, it can't be got."

Torin smiled.

Binti's brows rose. "Gunny?"

"I haven't tagged him, but I know who has." And Craig called her paranoid. She'd remind him of that when they got him back. "We're heading out."

"Got a target for us, Gunny?" Zhou asked.

"Got a targeting system. Werst, meet us in the armory."

They could trust Sergeant Urrest not to be Humans First. That didn't solve the rest of the problem.

Nostril ridges opening and closing slowly, she swept a flat stare out over the crowd of Wardens. "You're all going to the range?"

Elisk, declared most charming of the Krai by the others, opened his nostril ridges the rest of the way in a sign of trust. "We are. We agreed to test the tranquilizer guns for R&D."

"All of you."

"All of us."

"H'san shit."

"Hopefully, or their heads would explode."

The sergeant and the gathered Strike Teams turned to stare at Nicholin.

Umber hair fluttered. "What? If you don't shit, your head explodes. Everyone knows that."

"Sometimes it terrifies me you're the team medic," Marie murmured.

"Enough of this." Torin had agreed to give the soft approach a chance. Chance taken, moving on. She moved to stand beside Elisk, bodies suddenly out of her way, and placed both hands on the counter that separated Urrest's territory from the rest of the station. "Humans First has infiltrated the station, they've got Craig, we're going to get him back, but we don't know who to trust. You're not Human, so we trust you."

"Has infiltrated?"

"For a while now."

Urrest stared at Torin for a long moment. Finally, she nodded. "Why didn't you just say so? Why not use the bennies if it's going to be an insertion firefight?"

Torin felt some of the tension leave her back. She'd have gone over the counter if she'd had to. "Because they're all Human, the tranq guns are the best choice. One drug, so we can reload at speed."

"Figure you'll take less trouble for an unauthorized operation if no one's actually injured?"

"That's the theory."

"You'll need to be up close and personal to hit anyone. Their range is shit."

"With luck, we'll be as close as we need to be."

"You ever have that kind of luck, Gunny?" Urrest snorted. "Because I said that for thirty years, and it never worked for me."

Almost a meter shorter than Torin, Elisk had to lean around the copilot's chair to watch Ressk and Alamber work the board. "Craig's linked to his ship?"

"Always."

"That's . . . convenient," Elisk allowed. "I assumed you were going to use the DNA scanners."

CSOs were responsible for finding sixty-seven percent of MIAs while searching debris fields for salvage. Their ships might be held together with duct tape—Torin rubbed her thumb along a familiar crease in the tape holding the top of the pilot's chair together—but they didn't scrimp when it came to scanners. When Justice refitted *Promise*, Craig had traded the repurposed military scanners for a new set of what he'd had.

"The scanners would only tell us where he'd been, not where he is," Torin began.

"Because Craig's DNA is all over the station," Binti finished.

The four di'Taykan snickered. It had the familiar sound of massed military, and Torin found it comforting. She'd worked with Craig as a CSO for almost a year after leaving the Corps, but he'd shown her his tagging system when that was over, after the pirates, after she'd realized the war had left a lot more broken pieces around than she'd thought.

Two Strike Teams, less a pilot, packed the control room full, but compared to sharing the compartment with three Polint, the

Primacy's largest quadrupeds, it didn't seem crowded. It helped that there were no overexcited giant bugs overwhelming the air filtration with the scent of cherry candy.

Werst pulled a protein bar out of his pocket and tossed half to Ressk. "Last time Craig got his ass captured, it only took four of us to get him back."

"We blew up a station. I'd rather not blow up this station."

He swallowed and nodded. "Good point. I finally got our sleeping net the way I want it."

A civilian might have noted how calmly Torin waited for information about her abducted partner, but the only civilian around was Alamber, and he'd never make such a stupid observation.

"Am I the best? Yes, I am. Direct line to his implant, isolated and secured!" Alamber's hair rose in triumph.

"Yeah, but you can't get *into* his implant," Tylen called out from over by the hatch to the head.

"He doesn't need to," Ressk explained as Alamber's hands seemed to be in four places on the board at once. "He needs to follow the signal to where it cuts out, then identify the shielded location."

"Doesn't that kind of search violate at least a couple of privacy laws?" Torin heard Yahsamus ask quietly.

"They abducted a Warden," Marie answered in the same low tone. "We have just cause."

"So you're saying it is against a couple of laws."

"You have a problem with that, Tech?" Torin didn't bother turning, eyes on Alamber's fingers pulling miracles from the board. "Because if you do, you can sit this one out."

"No problem, Gunny. I just like to know what the rules are before I break them."

The Confederation needed to make up its mind about maintaining eyes on, Torin acknowledged silently. Surveillance helped keep the peace. Surveillance was an invasion of privacy. Having been under one kind of surveillance or another since she walked into the recruiting office on Paradise, Torin had long since learned privacy was an illusion. She was beginning to fear that peace was as well.

"And, got it." Alamber pulled a station schematic up off the board and rotated it, deleting some sections, enlarging others. "Shipping and receiving. Hangar bay seven. Typical."

Ressk threw the hangar bay specs into the air beside the schematic. "They're going to want to move him off station."

"Yeah, like I said, typical."

"No, they'd have done that already if that's what they wanted." Torin spun the hard light display to have a look at the external access. "They want me to come after him."

"They want you to . . ." Binti's protest trailed off and she frowned. Then she laughed. "Idiots."

"Of course you came alone." Standing in the center of the empty hangar, one hand on the back of the metal chair Craig had been secured to, Mimi Paddison traced an exaggerated flourish in the air with the other. "The great Gunnery Sergeant Kerr—destroyed a pirate fleet on her own, got a training platoon off Crucible on her own, got her people out of Big Yellow on her own, brought in the Silsviss on her own."

"Oh, for fuksake." Torin threw her head back in supposed frustration, spotted four Humans theoretically hidden in the patterns of shadows near the ten-meter ceiling, and returned to glaring at Paddison all in an elapsed time of under two seconds. "The Silsviss happened ten years ago. Move on."

"You first. You can't stop yourself from charging to the rescue, can you?" Paddison continued. "No trouble breaking the law for what you believe in, but unwilling to allow others the same courtesy. You're a contradiction, Gunnery Sergeant Kerr, and you have no idea how sick I am of hearing about you."

Torin ignored her and focused on Craig. His eyes were bloodshot, and he had a bruise purpling one cheek, darker where a knuckle had dug in deep, but he looked essentially unharmed. He also looked calm and annoyed. "You okay?" Gunnery sergeant voice. Team Leader voice. Professional voice.

He shrugged as much as the bindings allowed. "Little embarrassed."

"A little?"

He grinned as Torin raised a single brow, and she saw blood on his teeth. "You're never going to let me forget this, are you?"

"Not for the rest of our lives."

He heard what she meant and the grin softened into a smile. "Yeah. Me, too."

"How sweet." Free hand whipping around, Paddison slapped a piece of tape across his mouth.

Craig's eyes narrowed. He bucked up off the chair, muscles straining, and got nowhere. The muffled sounds emerging from behind the tape were indistinguishable as words, but Torin had a good idea of what he was shouting.

Paddison tucked a purple curl back behind her ear. "Told him if he kept quiet, you two could talk. Didn't say for how long. For the record, if it had been me taking you out on Seven Sta or Threxie, I'd have avoided this pancreatic overload of a reunion." She rolled her eyes. "Thanks so much, command. And, if you're expecting backup after the posturing is over, you're shit out of luck. Slates and implants don't work in here for safety reasons—so-called Elder Races can't have the children make mistakes, can they?—and we've locked all physical access."

"You missed the big hole in the station behind you."

Ninety percent of the time, the hangars separated air and vacuum with an energy shield, a system more efficient than hauling the big double doors open and closed 28/10. Proximity alerts protected the station from solid objects not under the docking systems' control that came close enough to pass through the shield. Hangar Seven had been taken out of service for scheduled maintenance, so Torin had had a fifty/fifty chance the shield would be in place. The outer bulkhead showed twenty meters of shimmer over stars, and Plan A was a go. Plan B involved enough collateral damage Commander Ng would *have* to be Humans First for them to get away with it.

Credit where due, Paddison didn't turn to look at the big hole in the station behind her. "Like you'd ever put the station in danger by disabling the proximity alert—even if your degenerate tech could crack it. Not that it matters. Down here in the hangars, we know the moment any ship disconnects from the docking arm. You'd love to sneak up behind us, but you can't."

Torin smiled. "You've thought this through."

"Don't fukking patronize me, Kerr."

"You keep saying we. And us." Craig's chair hadn't been secured to the deck. Careless.

"Did you learn procedure from *StarCops*? Never mind." She waved off Torin's response. "You want me to be the one to say Humans First. Fine. I'll say it. Humans First. Loud and proud."

"Proud of what? You're a terrorist."

"I'm a patriot." She stretched out her hands, kept the fingers loosely curled. Fists limited potential responses. "I was training close combat fighters before you were born. Age and experience, Kerr. You're done."

Craig screamed three rude if incomprehensible syllables into the tape.

Torin shifted her weight forward onto the balls of her feet, elbows bent, arms out from her side. "Humans First doesn't want me anymore?"

"Could be why we keep trying to kill you," Paddison pointed out genially. "Your ability to be a pain in the ass outweighed your potential propaganda value."

"Good to hear. I'm obligated, as an officer of the Justice Department, to offer you an opportunity to surrender. This is it."

"Fuk you."

Belaying lines hissed, and a dozen people appeared. The four from above landed two meters behind Torin, one of them breathing loudly. Four emerged from the shadows to the right. Four to the left. All of the eight she could see were ex-military. Obvious to her in the way they moved. In the set of their shoulders. An imprint eroded by time, but impossible to entirely erase. Those she could see were armed with bennies. Not scuffed and well-used, military blackmarket bennies, but the latest models with the newest upgraded tech.

That cracked Torin's calm just a little. "How the fuk did you get illegal weapons onto the station? I have trouble getting *requisitioned* weapons onto the station!"

Paddison shrugged. "We're the people who do the actual work. They notice you, all flash and no substance, but they don't notice us—the drones who maintain bureaucracy's glacial forward movement. We made that work for us. You'll notice . . ." Hand cupping the top of Craig's head, she shook it back and forth. ". . . I didn't underestimate you. It may take all thirteen of us, but this time, the job gets done."

Torin's internal clock told her to stall just a little longer. "You're willing to die to kill me?" She rolled her eyes. "And you wonder why I have an ego."

"We're willing to die to give Humans back their rightful place in the galaxy," Paddison amended. "It's not always about you, Kerr."

"Our rightful place?" Torin let her disdain show. "Trapped on a small planet, alone in an otherwise uninhabitable system, out near the far end of the spiral arm, killing each other. That was where we were before the Confederation arrived."

"And if they hadn't arrived?" Paddison demanded, face flushed. "We were already in space. Without the interference of the Elder Races, we'd have risen to be the dominant species in the galaxy. We're generalists, surrounded by specialists. The most adaptive always . . ."

Torin readied herself to dive for Paddison's throat.

"I saw that. What part of thirty years in close combat don't you get?" The knife she held, small weighted, and intended for throwing dimpled Craig's throat. "Stand down, or he bleeds out watching you die. Slow, painful, and emotionally traumatized."

"If I let you kill me, he lives? Traumatized, but alive?"

"Don't be stupid. He'll die quickly." She looked annoyed. "Precedent suggests you won't."

Internal countdown at zero, Torin dove back, not forward, hit the deck between two of the big docking clamps, and rolled as the Strike Teams came through the energy shield and into the hangar, *Promise* blotting out the stars. Alamber had disabled both the docking and the proximity alerts with the kind of quick and dirty illegal assault they didn't teach during formal schooling. The teams came in low, rolling as the artificial gravity slapped them down.

By the time they were on their feet, both alerts were back on.

There'd been a chance, albeit a small one, Humans First would surrender when they realized the fight would be less survivable than anticipated.

They opened fire. Five of the twelve had their bennies stroked up to deep fry, ready to blow away layers of organic tissue.

Craig tipped the chair sideways and crashed to the deck, feet and chair legs pointed toward Paddison.

The bright orange HE suits made it easy to tell friend from foe and protected against most of what the bennies could do; not that they were doing much. It seemed Humans First had assumed rhetoric would keep old skills sharp. Their clothing might have looked like combats, but the tranquilizer darts went right though.

Paddison roared as Craig kicked her elbow, her knife rattling against the deck by Torin's knee. Torin tackled her before she could turn on Craig, and they both went down. Knees, elbows, fists, fingers, teeth . . .

"Torin. She's out. Stop!" Craig's grip on her arms tightened. "Torin!"

She spat out a mouthful of blood, and leaned forward, using the back of her forearm to tip Paddison's head until she could meet the other woman's unfocused gaze. "You should've shot me the moment I came into the hangar. You'd still be heading to rehab, but I'd be dead."

"Stop telling people how to kill you." Hands under her arms, Craig heaved her up onto her feet. "Fuk, you're covered in blood."

"Skin's still tender from the tank, that's all." The skin across both sets of knuckles had split multiple times. Considering the amount of blood she was blinking out of her eyes, her forehead must've split as well and she didn't want to think about the condition of the fine skin covering her joints or her shoulder blades.

"You're supposed to be in quarantine for two days after decanting."

"And yet here I am."

"You ignored Ng's orders to stand down and let the others handle it, didn't you?" He pulled the tube of sealant from her vest, and began spraying her forehead, his hand gentle where it protected her eyes.

"Not exactly." She could feel the adrenaline beginning to fade. She'd been riding it since Alamber had contacted her and in a few minutes, she was going to crash hard. "Elisk, injuries?"

"A few minor burns, and one of those assholes hit Tylen with a cutting laser. Suit protected her long enough for us to prevent any major damage," Elisk assured her as he walked across the hangar. "She's down, but her vitals are high."

"Good. Prisoners?"

"Alive and secure. Nine out and twitching. Three surrendered." Elisk planted his feet by Paddison's head, nostril ridges opening as he looked down. "She looks like shit." He looked up at Torin. "So do you. I thought Binti was to get close enough to hit her with a tranq while you distracted her."

"Change of plans."

He looked at Craig, frowned at the dribble of red on the side of his neck. "Paddison do that?"

Craig swiped at it, smearing the blood around. "She did."

Elisk smiled, but the sudden blare of alarms drowned out his response.

"Called in the op from the ship," Torin explained. "We couldn't bring C&C with us."

"Called it in from the *Promise*? Torin, who's flying my ship?" Craig sprayed a thick layer of sealant over the back of her right hand, his knuckles white.

"Bilodeau."

"You could've . . ."

Torin cut him off. "Bilodeau is good. Better than Poritirr, better than Azur, almost as good as you."

"Almost?"

"You weren't available." She could see him considering further protests, saw when he decided not to, and relaxed. *Promise* was a part of him, she understood that, but it was his ship not his liver. Occasionally, he'd have to surrender control.

Elisk shook his head as he watched the terrorists being dragged over by the inner bulkhead, ignoring the whining about unnecessary roughness from the three who'd surrendered. "We gave them too much credit."

Torin spat out another mouthful of blood. "They infiltrated the Justice Department."

"True that."

When Craig finished sealing her left hand, she stepped carefully over a clamp and bent to retrieve Paddison's knife. It hurt to bend, it hurt more to straighten up again. "This is a quality blade."

"Torin." Craig tugged the knife out of her grip and moved close enough to take part of her weight. "Your forehead just split again."

She'd slammed it against Paddison's nose at least twice. "I'm fine."

· ——◆—— ·

She spent another three days tanked.

The shit hadn't yet died down when Torin got out of quarantine two days after that, the Wardens running everyone on the station through extensive background checks, having been examined themselves by an independent observer.

"Shouldn't it just be Humans under investigation?" Torin asked, having been escorted to the office of Internal Affairs.

Watches Over, who had one of the shortest Dornagain names Torin had ever heard, shook his head, dark brown ruff swaying with the motion. "If we merely investigate the Humans, we'd appear to be supporting those members of Parliament calling for the removal of the Younger Races from active participation in the Confederation. The Justice Department doesn't take sides."

"Not even the sides between keeping the law and breaking the law?"

He narrowed his eyes. "You'd better hope not, Warden Strike Team Leader Torin Kerr. Disabling the proximity alert is a class three felony as well as a safety violation, and you've insisted on carrying the entire blame."

"I was the senior Warden involved, and the others are used to following my lead."

"U'yun just got here. They *want* to follow you." Watches Over tapped long, curved claws against the inert edge of his desk. "Now, again, from the beginning. You were out of the tank . . ."

SIX

"**UNCOVERING AND SHUTTING** down a terrorist cell inside the Justice Department tipped the scales. I was told not to do it again, and if it came up that I felt I couldn't trust Humans, I was to report the situation directly to Watches Over rather than take care of it on my own."

"You were hardly on your own," Binti pointed out as Tylen helped her set another round of drinks down on the table. "You had two Strike Teams with you."

"Didn't want to remind them of that." Torin took a beer, pushed another into Craig's grip, and settled back against the warm weight of his arm.

Ressk shoved the nearly empty bowl of *hujin* chips toward Elisk. "They're not likely to forget. There's talk about docking our pay and confining us to quarters."

"Uncovered and shut down a terrorist cell inside the Justice Department," Torin repeated. "Slap on the wrist, and we're clear."

"Slap on the wrist? We all have to retake the course on nonviolent conflict resolution."

"I just finished it," Lorkin moaned, head on the table.

"We all did, Lor." Zhou shoved him hard enough his chair rocked. "At least you lot . . ." His wave took in the Alpha Team members at the table. ". . . haven't had to go through it for a couple of years."

"So boring." Nostril ridges closed, Lorkin bounced his head against the polished wood. "If a nonviolent resolution is even possible, why call us in?"

"They're conflicted," Binti told him, patting his back hard enough to bounce his head down one more time.

"You ass."

Binti grinned. "Little bit."

"I notice no one has mentioned . . ." Craig tossed a pretzel over the neck of Torin's bottle. ". . . that you should be excused a disciplinary hearing for recovering an abducted Warden."

"Abducted?" Tyler's hair flipped back behind her ears. "You walked into their arms like they'd shut their maskers off. You practically shouted, *take me, I'm yours*."

Craig didn't tense up at the laughter, so Torin let it continue. He didn't seem terribly traumatized by his hours of captivity, but considering his time with the pirates, why would he be? At least this time he came out of it with the same number of body parts he'd had going in. He'd been waiting for her outside the IA offices and after walking back to their quarters in silence, they'd dealt with the situation the way they usually did. More sex than dialogue. Albeit very careful sex given that she'd just been detanked for the second time in a tenday. It worked for them. She'd reminded him he was part of a team over post-coital coffee and that, next time, he might want to remember that.

"Hey, Gunny? What if it . . . or something similar to it," Marie amended, "happens again and we can't trust the Dornagain? Who are we supposed to go to if we can't go to Watches Over?"

Torin took a long swallow of beer before answering. "It's not going to happen again."

"It could."

"No, it couldn't. Because the next person who goes off on their own is going to have to rescue themselves on their own."

"Sorry, Gunny. Not very convincing."

The entire table agreed with Elisk's assessment.

"No," Torin admitted. Ch'tore had been in and out again while she'd been retanked, Delta had returned and gone on leave, and none of the others were back yet, but Musselman's seemed less empty than it had the last time there'd been only two teams in the bar. She glanced over at Alamber and Nicholin arguing good-naturally by the KDA board, at Yahsamus leaning on the bar, trying to convince Paul to add *tomagoras* to the menu, at most of Alpha and U'yun around the two tables they'd pushed together. No one got left behind. She aborted the motion toward the vest she wasn't wearing and laid her hand on Craig's thigh instead.

"Hey, Gunny," Zhou leaned in, dark eyes locked on hers. "How did you know Paddison would give us enough time to get into place?"

"She's a terrorist. Terrorism can be distilled to violence supporting a belief system. People who believe in things always want to convince you their way is the right way. That they have a good reason for whatever fukkery they're up to. Assholes are a lot less predictable."

"Actually . . ." Tylen paused dramatically. "No, that's accurate by both definitions."

"So, I heard Paddison had eleven broken bones," Zhou said when the laughter stopped.

That called for another drink. "I know. I'm back to weekly therapy sessions, no excuses."

"Fingers and noses shouldn't count," Werst grunted.

"Good thing Craig was bleeding," Elisk noted thoughtfully. "It's undoubtedly what allowed for unreasonable emotional provocation to balance out the excessive force."

Craig hadn't been bleeding when the chair went over. His hand closed around her shoulder and squeezed lightly.

Two days later, Torin looked up to see Ranjit and her team enter Musselman's and helped shuffle bottles and bowls as Sirin and Ru pulled another table over. Werst and Ressk shifted the chairs. U'yun had gone out that morning on a run to Ventris, leaving Alpha alone on the station to the unanimous agreement that their time out of the rotation was a passive-aggressive form of punishment. Commander Ng hadn't denied it.

"Where's Craig?" Ranjit asked dropping into the chair next to Torin.

"On the *Promise*. He cleaned up in a two-day poker game with engineering, and he's peopled out." Sometimes Craig needed solitude. Sometimes Torin needed to hit things.

"So, the rumor out among the stars is that Humans First had been poised to take over the Justice Department."

"Poised?" Torin shook her head as Ranjit snickered. "The investigation found one true believer . . ."

"Mimi Paddison."

". . . and fifteen . . ."

Ranjit held up a hand. "The report we saw said twelve."

"Twelve in the fight, but we picked up three later. So fifteen in a station of over ten thousand. Sleepers waiting for orders that would probably never have come had Paddision not shown initiative. Not exactly poised."

Ru set a platter of Gambas al Ajillo on the table. "Way we heard it, Gunny, it wasn't so much Paddision showing initiative as you having set a bad example for Ryder over the years, inspiring him to take on the bad guys all on his own."

"I have never done that," Torin protested. "I was with a platoon on Silsviss and Crucible, had a recon squad on Big Yellow, and teamed up with the fukking Primacy on that prison planet. It's Presit and her damned lone warrior bullshit." She ate a prawn, washed it down with a swallow of beer, and added. "But the Craig part is true."

"Paddison's the only one who knows anything at all, Boss, and she knows squat that's helpful. Marteau's very good at keeping his pieces from touching." Alamber had been working with station security, installing new code to keep anyone else from shutting down the alerts. They were idiots if they believed he hadn't built himself a backdoor—Big Bill's tutelage during Alamber's formative years wasn't easy to shake. Pertinent to the current discussion at Musselman's, working with security gave him access to a new source of gossip. "And Paddison," he continued, "she's the only true believer. She recruited the rest of them, vets just disgruntled enough to want to stick it to the system."

"They were willing to get into a firefight," Ressk pointed out. "That's pretty fukking disgruntled."

"No, they were there to kill me," Torin reminded them. "They responded to the Strike Teams' attack with a firefight. That's understandable."

Werst snorted. "Yeah, killing you is so much more gruntled."

"We'll never know if they'd have gone through with it."

"Only takes one, Torin."

She leaned into Craig. "I could have taken one." She'd served with one of them her second year in. He'd been on his last deployment then. She didn't remember him, but that's what his intake paperwork said.

"One plus Paddison, Boss."

"Still not a problem. And they're not our problem." She glanced around the table at her team. "They're all getting the rehab they need."

"So you are having once again single-handedly having saved Craig and the Confederation."

Torin leaned back in her chair, the camera on the desk adjusting to keep her in focus. "I had two Strike Teams with me. I wasn't alone."

"I are going to be mentioning them," Presit told her, as though it were a foregone conclusion when it wasn't. "I are thinking it are going to be a good time to be pulling out the recordings from Vrijheid Station where you are also having been saving Craig."

The recordings from Vrijheid had been illegally obtained, but that information kept getting lost in the explosive dismantling of Big Bill's crime empire. "Presit, I'm not supporting your run for Parliament."

She ran bronzed claws through her whiskers: right side, left. "Why would you? You are being in the same Sector, certainly, but you are being in a completely different district. No one here are caring about you, Gunnery Sergeant Warden Kerr. And . . ." The end of her muzzle wrinkled, showing small, white, pointed teeth. ". . . I are having discovered for you there are being a good chance the ships who are having been skirmishing on the border are having been skirmishing in agreement with the Primacy. Trying to be keeping the Navy's funding up on both sides of the border now the war are being over. I are having no proof yet, but I are sure enough to pass the information on to you."

So you owe me.

Torin sighed. "Clear any new Vrijheid footage with Craig. He was the one who needed rescuing."

"Of course." Presit crossed both glossy black hands under her ruff and pressed them into the thick fur. "I are never wanting to be upsetting Craig."

When Craig came out of the bedroom, shirtless, a pair of ancient sweats hanging low on his hips, Torin was still sitting behind the desk. He glanced down at the blank screen and said, "I thought Presit was going to call."

"She called. We talked." Torin got to her feet and rolled the stiffness out of her shoulders.

"You talked?"

"We talked. Let's go to Musselman's. I need a drink."

"I'll put some clothes on."

"If you must."

"The cook?"

Commander Ng nodded. "Per Paddison identified Petty Officer Marilissa Kotas as a member of Humans First."

"I was shot at close range by a Navy cook?" Torin shook her head. "That's embarrassing. Any chance Paddison could be lying?"

"Her rehabilitation councillor says no."

So Ng had already asked. "If Humans First inserted a shooter into a PLE facility . . ."

The commander waited a moment, but when it became clear Torin had no plans to continue, said, "Wardens Peels Back the Layers of Lies and Quentizen are on their way to Seven Sta." He glanced down at his desk. "Their ship is a hundred thousand klicks out from the jump buoy."

Nice to be told. "Alpha's still benched, then."

"Alpha doesn't ask discreet questions, Alpha demands answers. There's a subtle difference. We'll let the less violent Wardens do their jobs."

A muscle jumped in Torin's jaw as she unclenched her teeth. "I'm not going to apologize for keeping you in the dark about Craig's abduction. Same situation, same circumstances, I'd do the same thing again."

"I'm aware."

He wasn't angry. If Torin had to put a name to the emotion lurking behind his eyes, she'd say he was hurt that she, and—by extension— Alpha and U'yun hadn't trusted him. That, she did regret. She respected Commander Ng, but she wasn't going to apologize for choosing a course of action that gave her the best odds for getting her people out alive. "Would it help if you yelled at me, sir?"

"Is that what they'd do in the Corps?"

"Most of the time, sir."

He met her gaze and said flatly, "Try to remember you're no longer in the Corps, Warden."

"Yeah, but we never shot a bennie at the plastic, did we?" Tylen looked around the table.

Zhou frowned. "Why would we do that?"

"Bennies destroy organic molecular integrity," Ressk said thoughtfully. "And the plastic is organic."

"And back in the day, Big Yellow took apart the boss's benny, then rearranged itself so it couldn't be affected." Alamber sighed and finished his drink. "It's all there in the report."

"You read the report?"

Alamber shrugged. "I read all the reports."

Beta Team had been pulled into a long-term surveillance since they were right where they were needed when needed, but the other teams were home. Gamar wore a sleeve tank to repair the damage a bullet had done to his elbow, but that was the worst injury among the lot. Musselman's was crowded, and Torin felt settled in her skin. Binti, Cap, and Yahsamus were playing darts, although they were making Binti play with her nondominant hand, Werst and Craig were at the KDA, Werst having taken her place when her lives had run out. U'yum had continued sitting with Alpha, and Torin felt like she'd suddenly acquired younger siblings.

"Musselman!" Doug Collins banged on the bar. "There's a match on!"

Paul flipped him off and returned to polishing an already spotless glass.

"Looks like we're watching a Parliamentary debate," Ressk sighed.

"Shoot me now." Zhou stood, swayed, and moved around the table to poke Lorkin in the side. "Hey, trade seats with me, so I don't have to see their smug faces."

While none of them were exactly watching the screen, it was hard to completely ignore the debate. Torin heard her name and looked up to discover a Niln MP laying out the details of her recent shooting.

"You're famous again." Ressk saluted her with his cup of *sah*.

"At least no one sold them an illegal shot of me in the tank." Everyone looked pathetic floating in viscous fluid. Torin didn't do pathetic. Bad enough she'd been shot by a cook.

The MP finished by tasting the air and saying, "Perhaps instead of involving all of the Younger Races, we should just keep Warden Kerr confined to her planet."

The sound that followed was probably laughter, although with some of the species present it was hard to be sure. Torin wasn't laughing.

"Come on, Boss. You have to admit it's a little funny."

"I really don't."

"You okay?" Craig asked, dropping into the seat beside her. She turned toward him, and he shrugged. "Heard your name. Wondered what you were thinking."

"About the natives of Threxie and how the plastic might have devolved them." When his brows went up, she shrugged and waved a hand at the politician listing the ways the Younger Races had been disrupting the smooth running of the Confederation, her tail lashing back and forth. "If they did it once, there's a chance the plastic's been devolving individuals all over known space."

Craig frowned up at the screen. "That does explain a lot."

The sector's H'san wasn't in the chamber. Or at least wasn't visible when the camera swept across the members present, their names and constituencies joining the scroll across the bottom of the screen that kept track of reactions to the matter under discussion. In this case, trapping the Younger Races at the bottom of gravity wells for the good of the Confederation. In this open session, the pros were in the majority.

Torin frowned when a tall glass filled with pale, blue liquid appeared on the table in front of her, and turned to meet the gaze of a smiling server.

"Paul sent it over. It's on the house." When Torin raised a brow, the server's smile broadened. "He says the discussion about your latest . . ." She translated Torin's expression and visibly discarded the word she'd been about to use. ". . . adventure has kept them from a vote on raising entertainment taxes for a full tenday. He's calling the drink The Derailment."

"What about us?" Zhou asked, frowning at his empty bottle.

"Derail Parliament," Torin told him as the server walked away. "Until then, you buy your own." A cautious sip gave her a tart, citrus . . . ish flavor with a distinct fizz as the cocktail crossed her tongue. She couldn't taste the alcohol, but the spreading warmth from throat to stomach announced its presence.

"Well?"

She passed Craig the glass. "It's . . .

"We interrupt this . . .

"Boring hour of *serley chrika!*" Lorkin yelled.

". . . to bring you this Confederation-wide announcement. An alert has just been received from the *CS Sperry*. Big Yellow has returned."

A dart hit the board, impossibly loud in the sudden silence.

"Looks the same." Craig's left hand closed around her right wrist.

"It could be old footage," Alamber offered.

Torin studied the lines of the big yellow ship, retrieved her glass, and emptied it. "It's not."

SEVEN

WERST SCOWLED at the image rotating over the conference room table, the yellow light tinting the gray walls of the room faintly green. "They're back because of the message sent by the data sheet."

"You don't know that," Ressk sighed in a way that suggested the argument had been ongoing for a while.

"I know it in my stomach." Nostril ridges half closed, Werst drew his lips back off his teeth. "Fukking plastic. I should've eaten more of it."

At the center of one of the table's long sides, Commander Ng cleared his throat. "There will be a military response heading out to Big Yellow . . ."

"No shit," Werst grunted.

Commander Ng ignored him. Torin shot him a look that snapped his teeth together.

". . . and we've received a message they want Wardens Kerr, Ryder, and Werst to be a part of that response given their previous experience on the ship in question."

"It's not exactly a ship," Craig noted. He sounded calm, but Torin could feel the tension radiating off him.

"It's not," the commander agreed. "But we're going to keep calling it that."

Torin zoomed in on the image, searching for an airlock and not finding one, even though the cruiser had managed full-spherical satellite coverage. "Are they bringing in everyone who survived that last visit?"

"I've only been officially informed about the three of you."

"Just us three?" Werst's foot closed on the edge of the table, grip so tight his toes went white. Ressk wrapped a hand around his ankle.

"This won't be a scientific mission or a political meet and greet," Torin told him, voice level, working to control the rising emotions in the room. "The moment the plastic admitted to starting and maintaining the war, they became a military matter. Craig and I had the plastic in our heads, I've spoken to it twice, and you ate a piece. That's why they want us. Not to mention the fact that we're government employees, they know exactly where we are, and don't have to waste time looking for us."

"Knew that would bite us on the ass someday," Werst muttered, but he relaxed his grip and his nostril ridges began to slowly open.

Craig shifted in his seat. "And because we're government employees, the bastards assume they can make it an order."

"The military is an arm of the government, as is the Justice Department. They can do no more than request our cooperation." The commander's expression of bland certainty shut down further protest, potential arguments sliding off it before they started.

"All right." Hands gripping the inert edge of the table, Craig leaned toward the commander. "Are we cooperating?"

"The Minister of Justice requests that we do. I pointed out that half a team was no good to me here, so it's been agreed all six of you will go."

Torin flicked the image of Big Yellow back to the center of the table. "General Morris is on his way to Berbar, isn't he?"

"Yes, he is." Commander Ng glanced at Alamber. "If Warden di'Cikeys is tapping the communications . . ."

"I'm not." Alamber's hair rose.

"He doesn't need to be, sir." Torin swept a glance around the table. "General Morris won't allow a military response to deploy without him. He was the senior officer during the first contact with Big Yellow, he'll be the senior officer during the second contact. If the *Berganitan* is close enough to call in," she added, "they'll use her."

"She was. They are." Commander Ng flicked through screens, details rising into the air and disappearing again too fast to read. "Have you completed your . . . assessment, Warden?"

"Yes, sir." Torin was self-aware enough to realize she hadn't put the commander's response to the incident in Hangar Seven behind her. Commander Ng needed to realize she was more than brawn, more than capable of putting the details together into a vacuum-tight whole and basing her reaction on that.

All the details.

All of her reactions.

"The *Berganitan* will be arriving at fourteen hundred tomorrow. Kerr, Werst, Ressk, Mashona, I want the four of you to remember you're no longer part of the military. You're Wardens and you have your own job to do." The image of the ship disappeared. "Regardless of what General Morris and the CMC may believe, you're going to Big Yellow to keep the peace within the parameters the Justice Department set to govern the Strike Teams. You fought for this peace," he added, gaze softening as he swept it around the table. "You should get to keep it."

· —◆— ·

"I don't understand why it's just hanging there." Anthony scowled at the image of Big Yellow, searching the ship for weapons ports. "It's at the exact coordinates it was previously, it clearly intended to be noticed, and it's doing nothing."

Dr. Banard blinked at the screen. "It did nothing the last time until provoked. You want it to dance, go poke it with a stick."

"Your stick is why we're here, Doctor." Arms folded, Commander Belcerio made no attempt to hide his dislike for the doctor. "We were informed you were ready to test the prototype, but all I see is this pile of . . ."

"Weaponry." Banard patted a rough strut.

"I know weaponry." There hadn't been time for a thorough assessment before Big Yellow commanded the attention of the room, but Anthony had completed a fast walk around and a cursory inspection. "That . . ." He waved at the two-by-three-meter assemblage of junk that dominated one end of the large workshop. ". . . looks like a partially disassembled welding laser."

The doctor shrugged. He did it as awkwardly as the Krai. "Fortunately, I don't care what you think it looks like. And if you want to know why the lump of plastic is hanging around pretending to be a ship, that's obvious. It's waiting."

"We don't require your opinion," Belcerio told him.

"It wasn't an opinion."

"Fine." The commander's brows drew in until they touched over his nose. "What's it waiting for?"

"If I had to venture a guess, I'd say Kerr, Ryder, and that hairy reporter thing." Anthony answered before Banard could. "The plastic spent time in their brains and, as far as we know, Kerr is the only person it's ever spoken to. It's waiting for them, and once Kerr arrives, because she won't arrive alone, we won't be able to get within a thousand kilometers of it."

"And we'll lose our chance to destroy the plastic for a grateful populace, prompting Humans to flock to our side, and we win. Yay." Banard blew his nose, then checked he'd got everything with the tip of a finger. "A species with the resources to conduct an experiment involving two galactic civilizations always intended to investigate the consequences."

Belcerio pointedly showed the doctor his back. "Per Marteau?"

"I believe curiosity prodded us up onto the beach and into space." Hands in his jacket pockets, Anthony noted the position of the *CS Sperry*. Wondered how many of his weapons were on board. Knew that he and his could avoid a single ship that size, but not the battleship on which Kerr would arrive. "Curiosity is the one thing we have in common with the lesser species, and as the plastic made it to space . . ."

"Could have evolved in space." Banard punctuated the words by blowing his nose again. "The evolved detritus of the universe's first civilization." And again. "I may write a paper." Feeling the weight of Anthony's glare, he added, "It won't literally involve paper. That would be insane."

"I'm aware of what *write a paper* means, Doctor."

Banard ignored the ice in Anthony's tone. "Good." Tipped his head toward Belcerio. "He had no idea."

Had he been standing closer, Anthony suspected he'd be able to hear Belcerio grinding his teeth. "I advise you to ignore him, Commander. Focus on the weapon he's building." Given what he seemed capable of creating, Dr. Banard could have been one of the degenerate species and Anthony would've found a way to endure him. If Belcerio couldn't see that, he was less intuitive than the job required, and Anthony would have to consider replacing him.

Lip curled, Belcerio muttered, "I don't want to see you wasting your money."

Anthony smiled. "I appreciate the consideration, Commander. I did more than double my inheritance, but your insight on my investments is invaluable."

"Apologies, Per Marteau. I had no intention of offending." He was smart enough to see he'd crossed a line.

That was good. Anthony didn't have the time to install a new commander. "I accept your apology, Commander." He nodded at Belcerio, Belcerio nodded at him, all very polite. "Now . . ." Hands in his pockets, he rocked back on his heels. ". . . as you clearly have doubts about Dr. Banard's work, I have a different job for you. I want Scale and Claw put into motion."

"Scale and Claw?" Banard barked out a laugh. "Seriously? You have code names? Can I be Doctor Science? No! Super Science!"

"You can be replaced," Belcerio said flatly.

Banard smiled. "I really can't."

"I've given you your orders, Commander." Anthony nodded toward the hatch.

"You want it implemented now?" The force of his gesture toward the screen seemed like a reprimand.

"I'd be happier with yesterday, but unless Dr. Banard has created a working time machine, I'll have to handle the disappointment." Belcerio flushed at his tone. If he didn't appreciate sarcasm, he needed to stop asking stupid questions, or Anthony was going to have to free up some time.

"You expect Scale and Claw to delay the military response to Big Yellow if they haven't deployed, and if they have, they'll have to return Kerr. If we can't kill her . . ."

"And you, as a group, seem appallingly unsuccessful at that," Banard interjected.

Belcerio ignored him. ". . . we can take her out of play. With the military response delayed, we can get to Big Yellow first."

Banard broke into slow applause. "He's not as stupid as he looks."

While Belcerio snarled, Anthony took his turn ignoring the doctor. "Without Kerr, we have a good chance of making contact. The plastic would be a powerful ally, and it's clearly not averse to interfering."

"And the weapon?" Belcerio asked.

He might as well have been asking about the shit on his shoe, but as his vitriol was directed at Banard, Anthony let it go. "I plan to talk to it first."

"You think the plastic will recognize the justice of our cause?"

"I don't care what it recognizes. It's already run one social experiment. If it's willing to engage, I'm confident I can convince it to run another. Precedent tells us it wants to learn, so we'll teach it."

"It's only ever spoken to Kerr . . ."

"We're back to boom, Humans First hero of the day, flocking to the banner, we win. Yay." Banard twisted his square of cloth until he found a reasonably unused section, and blew his nose. "Scale those claws," he added, his voice muffled by wiping and digging, "and let me get back to work."

Anthony raised a brow at the commander who nodded, once, in that annoying military way that seemed as much insult as respect, and headed for the hatch. When the slam of the pins returning to place echoed through the workshop, he turned his back on the screen. "Now, Dr. Banard, the weapon. I know weapon design and that doesn't look like much."

"You mean it doesn't look like what you consider to be a weapon." Banard fondled the end of a bolt securing an ugly support strut. "Doesn't have to. Just has to work. This bit here, I cannibalized part of a waste disposal unit—you stay too focused on *weapons,* you'll never become aware of the destruction available in the tools used in day-to-day living. Then, I printed a scaled-up version of a piece of lab equipment that identifies molecular composition. Work has already been done, why should I do it again?" Reaching in past the upper horizontal line of a long narrow lens, he seemed to forget he was in the middle of a conversation.

"Doctor?"

"Academics totter on the edge of discovery, but haven't the guts to totter over the line." He removed his hand from the weapon's interior, stared at his fingertips, licked his thumb, and continued. "Talk about myopic focus. You have a lot in common with them, actually. This is a weapon. That isn't." Pulling the piece of fabric out of his pocket again, he stared into its folds, then shoved it away. "I can't stand academics."

Anthony walked slowly around the mess of connected parts, tried to determine function from form, and failed. "Does it work?"

"It's made up of three distinct parts. One part will measure the energy of the covalent bonds. It'll adjust as the plastic does."

"I think you'll find the plastic adjusts remarkably quickly. How did you get repurposed lab equipment to process at speed?"

Banard's cheeks pleated when he smiled, folding the broken capillaries into new patterns. "How? I'm just that good. The next part will use that data to create an energy beam designed to break the bonds apart. And the last part will incinerate those parts with good old-fashioned electricity while they're stunned or whatever you call temporarily indisposed plastic. Four parts," he amended. "If you count the energy cell as a separate unit. Given the amount of shielding, I suppose you should. I integrated Susumi tech into it. Come to think of it, not so old-fashioned."

"Is it safe?"

"Of course not. It's a weapon. It was built to destroy. You don't want safe." Leaning back against a sheet of metal, apparently unconcerned about it shifting, Banard reached into baggy trousers and adjusted his genitals. "The odds of it blowing up while in use are small, very small, if that's what you're asking."

"I'm also asking, does it work?"

"Each part takes microseconds to do its job. Distance will be a factor although I don't know how much of a factor until I can get it on a ship . . ."

"Doctor."

"It's not working yet. It's still parts not a whole. If you want it mounted on your ships, you'll want a single unit."

"Why?" Anthony traced the joins, adjusting for actual product rather than prototype. "Mount the individual units and link them. Vacuum doesn't require streamlining."

"That'll work. Excellent job thinking outside the factory floor, Per Marteau."

The tips of his ears heating at the unexpected compliment, Anthony stepped back, and glanced at the screen. "I want us on the way as soon as possible. Make a list of the parts we can source, we'll print anything unique while we're in Susumi, and install after we exit."

"And where will we be going? Parliament's clutching the coordinates to its collective chests."

"I have people in most government departments and I've had these particular coordinates for years."

"Good for you." Banard stroked a vertical shaft and frowned when his hand caught on a rough join. "I hate the whole concept of Susumi space, but I do want a closer look at this plastic."

"I have to insist you travel alone. Space restrictions on board ship." He'd leave instructions that the four young di'Taykan the doctor used for diversions were to be dropped off where they'd be found in a timely manner.

Banard waved it off. "Not a problem. There's more where they came from."

·———◆——·

"Anyone surprised Big Yellow brought the assholes out of the woodwork?" Ressk asked as Alpha doubled down the passageway toward the armory on the heels of Strike Team T'Jaam.

"Dissension's probably their plan." Binti acknowledged two maintenance workers who'd flattened against the bulkhead to give them room to pass. "The plastic returns. Things go to shit. No effort on their part."

"T'Jaam got the good run," Alamber announced. "They've got three ex-Navy pilots who lifted a VTA from Station 2 and are making hit and runs down on Luur."

"Those things aren't armed. What are they hitting with?"

"Don't know." He raised his voice. "Hey! Gamar! What exactly are your crazy pilots doing?"

Up ahead, in the center of T'Jaam, Gamar's hair lifted. "They're throwing rocks!" he yelled back over his shoulder.

Alamber almost stumbled. "Out of a VTA?"

"Decommissioned Naval VTAs have holes in the floor," Torin reminded him. Presit had fallen out of theirs, and Torin had been forced to jump out after her.

"Think we'll be back before the *Berganitan* arrives?" Binti asked, falling into step on Torin's right.

"We're up against six cutting lasers," Torin reminded her. Security in a mine on Carlyle Bon had managed to lock six ex-Marines with cutting lasers into a dead-end tunnel, but couldn't figure out how to remove them. Commander Ng had seemed pleased about the prospect of telling the general he'd sent Alpha Team out. "If Craig would put some thought into the Susumi equations, we could be back before we left."

"Craig would rather not die horribly," Craig muttered.

A fist-sized rock shattered against the wall over Werst's head, pieces too small to ricochet bouncing off his helmet. "Fukkers built a cannon. Points for ingenuity."

Another rock whistled past, shattering farther down the tunnel.

"Good reload time." Without her scanner, Torin could just barely make out the end of the pipe poking through the rough block wall that closed off the tunnel twenty-two point seven meters away—pipe and blocks were the same pale gray.

"Their aim sucks."

"True, but artillery has a broad definition of accurate. I'm almost impressed that they've built in enough maneuverability to hit the ceiling and both walls." Their default, straight down the tunnel shot was chest-high on Humans and di'Taykan and head height on the Krai. The mine had high numbers of Younger Races in the work force although the ownership and most of the supervisory positions were Niln. "Mashona, can you put one down the pipe?"

"I can, but a standard round's going to do SFA unless one of them's got his eye to the end, lining up a shot. I time it right, I might ignite whatever they're using for propellant. Might not. Depends on what they're using. If I had boomers . . ."

"But you don't." Standard operating procedure kept boomers above ground. Collapsing the tunnels solved no one's problem. "Let's hope you get lucky." The cannon covered the only approach to the dead end where the ex-Marines were trapped, and the speed of their reload meant they had the cap off the far end of the pipe as soon as possible after firing. "On my mark . . ." The next rock hit the ceiling about a meter out from where Alpha Team crouched against the walls. Torin tucked her chin down and turned her helmet toward the debris. As the last piece hit the floor, she straightened. "Mark!"

With the sound dampener engaged on Binti's KC, the only sound was the crack of the bullet's miniature sonic boom.

And within nanoseconds, the impact at the far end of the pipe, muffled within the stacked blocks.

Torin's scanner agreed with her eyes. No visible change to either cannon or wall. So much for luck. She'd served under officers who disdained primitive weaponry, but Torin concentrated on effect. If the end result was a dead Marine, even a rock deserved respect.

"Might've destroyed the firing mechanism," Ressk pointed out after a few moments.

Binti snickered. "Or we pissed them off, and they're loading something nastier than rocks."

"Yeah, because being showered by rock fragments is such a joy."

Turning a fragment between thumb and forefinger, Torin stared at the mouth of the cannon, a memory just out of reach. "Check metal present within twenty-two point five degree arc, Marine zero." A number flashed on the lower right edge of her scanner and began to climb. "Son of a . . . RUN!"

They were twenty meters down the tunnel when Torin's internal countdown hit zero.

"DROP!"

The pieces of metal close enough to the center mass filled the tunnel with hundreds of edges and sharpened points, moving fast enough to cut through anything they hit. The pieces on the expanding edges of the shot hit walls, ceiling, floor: some of their momentum lost, but their angle of approach impossible to anticipate. Scattershot moved slower than solid projectiles, but made up in amount of potential damage what it lost in speed.

Fortunately, military-grade uniforms left few areas vulnerable and even a day pack provided additional protection for the spine. Head cupped within the curve of her left arm, Torin focused on the flashing medical alert in her cuff. "Ressk! How bad?"

"Shrapnel in the ass. Uniform stopped it, but it's going to leave a fuk of a bruise."

"I'm reading blunt impact trauma. It's broken through the skin."

"Explains why my ass is warm."

She could hear the team scrambling up onto their feet as she stood. "Mashona, effective range of scattershot?"

"No more than seventy-five meters, Gunny."

They were approximately forty meters down the tunnel. "Forty more, let's move!"

At twenty-three meters more, they reached a cross tunnel and safety. Cannon couldn't fire around corners, although Torin wouldn't apply that statement to artillery as a whole; she'd seen too many inexplicable explosions.

Three minutes. Five. The cannon didn't fire again.

"Might've been all the sharp metal they had." Reaching up, Werst ran a finger along a deep gouge in his helmet.

"No reason to risk it," Torin told him. "We're going to plan B."

"Plan C," Ressk amended as he dropped his trousers to pool around his boots. "Plan A being identifying ourselves as Wardens and requesting they surrender."

"Doesn't count. No one ever listens." Binti flicked on her cuff light and leaned in. "That's a perfectly triangular hole in the ass you've got there."

Torin expected a response from Alamber and got one from Craig.

I'm on my way down.

"It's a punctured butt," Ressk scoffed, twisting to try to see it. "I don't need a medic. Spray it and I'm good."

You're getting a medic anyway.

"Bet he's feeling left out," Binti murmured.

"No bet." Craig had been left in the Operations Center with Alamber. Six ex-Marines with cutting lasers against four ex-Marines with KC-7s and combat grade uniforms didn't require the nonmilitary members of the team to take the field. "But since Plan B involves a lot of sitting around in safety, no reason he can't join us if there's a scenic route to our location that keeps him out of the main tunnel. Werst, his butt is yours."

"That's what the vows said," Werst agreed, approaching with a can of sealant.

Boss, I've finally pulled the full schematics out of their joke of an OS. Confirm there's too much ventilation going into that section to gas them, but nothing big enough to crawl through.

"Roger that." The trapped ex-Marines were Human and di'Taykan. Krai didn't go underground if they had another option. They had a gas that would work on both species—different biological reactions, but unconscious was unconscious as far as Torin was concerned. Cothi Hurexical, the mine supervisor, had insisted she couldn't guarantee a complete seal between the target area and the rest of the mine, and as no one knew how the gas would affect Niln, she wouldn't approve it. Nor would she clear biologicals out even though eighty percent of the work had been automated. Two of her workers were dead and three pieces of equipment destroyed, but she had a production objective she intended to meet.

She'd also refused to cut off power, water, or air, unwilling to contribute to the deaths of sentients. Torin appreciated the sentiment, but since it left her people advancing toward a cannon, she didn't appreciate it much.

Torin flicked her PCU over to the mine's channel. "Per Hurexical, you're a go on the digger as we discussed. Open up the dead-end and herd them out toward us."

"Are you sure that's necessary, Warden?"

"They're defending their position with artillery."

"We never intended to open that wall up. The digger will cause damage to the tunnel already in place."

"It's proactive damage."

Proactive damage? Binti mouthed.

Torin flipped her off.

"But you could still wait them out."

"Per Hurexical, they've already built a wall and a cannon. You want to guess what they'll come up with if you leave them in there much longer?"

"But how . . ."

"They're Marines. You told us you had a digger available."

"I thought this was a backup plan."

"There's a cannon. We're going to the backup plan."

"You're looking at a three-hour dig from the closest access point, Warden. Longer if we hit a hard patch. And we could. It could take all night."

Local time was twenty-two oh six. "All night? Longer than I'd like, but that explains the production numbers."

"What are you talking about?"

"Slow and steady wins the race; that's what my father always said."

"Really?" Binti asked during the long pause.

Torin covered her mic. "Not a chance."

"Just over two hours, Warden. Be ready."

"We're not going anywhere."

❖   ❖   ❖

"If they hadn't upgraded the uniforms to combat knock-offs, that would've gone through you. As it is, you're still looking at a trip to medical before we debrief." Craig tossed the empty tube of sealant back into his kit, having removed and replaced Werst's earlier work. "Bruising's already starting to spread."

"You want to sit the rest of this out, Ressk?"

"Cute." He pulled up his uniform and his nostril ridges snapped closed. "Great. Damp and sticky. Sealant does SFA to get the blood out of the pant leg.

"Good thing Torin put you two in boots." Craig picked up a piece of composite sliced from the edge of Werst's sole. "That would've taken half your foot off."

"It's a bit creepy how into comparative wounds you've gotten," Binti called from her place at the intersection of the two tunnels. She'd been shooting the wall at random intervals to keep all involved from becoming complacent.

"Full-service medic," he told her. "I also give opinions." Turning to Torin, he checked her over, again as though he could see and make note of the bruising on the backs of her legs and arms. "So, we staying?"

"We need to be here when the digger drives them out." She didn't know what personal demons the six were fighting, but with luck their mental state hadn't deteriorated to the point where they'd try to take on the digger. "You don't have to stay."

"They may need patching up. I'll stay."

Werst held up a deck. "I've got cards."

"Why do you think Big Yellow came back?" Craig frowned at his cards. "Give me two."

"If it's not a trap," Ressk declared, "it's a distraction."

Werst sorted his cards into a new configuration and frowned. "Distraction from what?"

"From whatever they're up to somewhere else. Three."

"The plastic ran an intergalactic war for centuries." Torin had replaced Binti on watch, part of her attention on the wall and the cannon, part taking inventory of the nails, the small bits of metal with shiny, fresh-cut edges, and the two-centimeter-long pieces of wire scattered along the tunnel in case she had a later use for them. "No one knew they were there."

"You saying they don't need to distract us, Gunny."

"I'm saying, if the shoe fits. I'm also saying put your damned boots back on."

"I'm injured," Ressk muttered.

"Because you've forgotten how to duck."

"Simpler answer, with no shoes involved." Binti laid down three kings and scowled at Werst's full house. "The plastic was in Presit's head, right? And now she's running for Parliament. An intergalactic war is one thing, but Presit making decisions that could affect the whole sector is something else again."

"They came back to stop her?"

"Then how about we leave them alone," Alamber suggested. He'd shown up about twenty minutes after Craig. Torin had chewed a piece off him, but as he was tracking the digger on his slate and could take over the operation should Per Hurexical change her mind, she had no good reason to send him away. "Ignore the plastic completely until they give us more to work with than their presence; who knows—they might be here to support Presit, and that's not what I dealt you."

Craig fanned out his hand, showing a galactic cluster. "I didn't like what you dealt me."

"One of you stacks the deck, or neither of you stacks the deck," Werst growled. "But both of you stacking is bullshit. Misdeal." He gathered up the cards. "I've got this one."

"I'm all for ignoring Big Yellow." Ressk glared at Alamber until he rested his hands palm up on his thighs. "But General Morris won't, and I don't want him there without a mitigating influence."

"And we're to provide that?" Binti asked. "Also this hand is shit. I had better cards when Craig and Alamber were screwing around."

Even without her scanner, Torin could see places where the walls of the main tunnel had been scored by the shrapnel. They'd gotten lucky.

"See you. Raise you."

"Fold. Could be the plastic's finished analyzing their data," Ressk continued over the sound of cards slapping against the floor, "and now they want to put their conclusions into some kind of context."

"Now you have sufficient data, what do you intend to do with it?" Torin demanded.

"The data must be analyzed."

"And then?"

"We will know when we analyze the data."

"Not good enough."

The gray plastic alien shrugged. It copied the Human motion better than the Krai. *"We will know when we analyze the data."*

"Fine. On a more personal level," she growled, *"what the fuk were you doing in my head?"*

"Analysis requires context. You provided context."

"Torin?"

Muscles locked across her back, hand gripping her KC so tightly it had gouged pressure points into her palm, Torin jerked away from Craig's touch and forced herself to relax. Slowly, carefully, she pulled her finger out from inside the trigger guard and set the weapon down.

"Good idea." Craig rested his hand, warm and heavy, on her shoulder. "You were strangling it like it had cheated at cards."

"Or insulted your mother," Binti added. When had she gotten so close?

"Or ate the leftover *rernamal bah* with your name on the container. What?" Ressk spread his hands. "That's worth a pounding where we come from."

Alamber snickered. "Pretty much everything's worth a pounding where I come from."

"You lot finished?" Torin spread her fingers, working the stiff joints loose.

"Or you discovered it's a Navy KC and you were teaching it to respect its betters." Werst nodded, satisfied. "Now we're done."

Lips twitching up into an involuntary smile, Torin muttered, "Assholes." She expected them to return to the game now they'd had their say. They didn't.

"Visualizing the plastic or Morris?" Craig asked, strong fingers gently working the bones of her hands.

"Analysis requires context. You provided context."

"Took a trip down memory lane."

"Did it involve you in underwear?" He waggled his brows.

Another involuntary smile. "Underwear, blisters, stink, all the good stuff."

"Sexy times."

"Oh, fuk me, don't you two start getting cute." Muffled thuds punctuated the plea as Binti held her helmet in both hands and bounced her forehead off the upper curve. "Those two supply as much cute as I can stand."

Those two in that tone only ever referred to Werst and Ressk. Torin tossed a small rock at Binti, her gaze still on Craig. "I doubt General Morris is going to attempt diplomatic contact."

"Likewise, but I'd have thought you'd want to go all Marine Corps on the plastic. And when I say all Marine Corps, I mean big guns and angry infantry—not spit, polish, and having each other's backs."

"We're not angry, we're motivated."

Dimples flashed. "And that's what you took from that."

She stood, picked up her weapon, and stepped back from the corner. "Werst."

"On it, Gunny." Scanner down, he dropped into the position Torin had held, eyes on the far wall.

Torin brushed against Craig's shoulder as she passed him, needing to move. "There's no point in attacking Big Yellow. We can't affect enough of it at a time to make a difference."

"The science team's explosion," Ressk began.

Torin cut him off. "That explosion destroyed a meter and a half by two and a half meters of internal bulkhead, and it had no noticeable effect on the whole. If the ship provides an airlock, a suicide run might be able to carry enough incendiaries inside to cause noticeable damage, but the odds are higher Big Yellow would realize what was up before they got inside and they'd be expelled—either out the airlock, or they'd make a hole straight to vacuum."

"How would it know incendiaries from field rations?" Ressk asked, fanning the cards and then trying to flip them back over his knuckles.

"It'll know because it was in Torin's head," Craig told him.

"And yours." Alamber's hair spread into a pale blue corona. "It's not like you haven't blown shit up. With both of you there, we'll have two possible lines for communication. No, not two, three." He looked up from his slate. "We're going to need Presit in on this. The plastic rode her brain, too."

"Not our call," Craig reminded him. "Presit'll be there if she wants to be there, but she's concentrating on the election right now, and the

Younger Races need representation in Parliament willing to take our side."

"Our side, their side—that's the problem. We *need* the plastic not to start another war."

"Presit's more likely to help start another war than keep one from happening."

Alamber rolled his eyes. "Shouldn't that be her choice?"

"You think she doesn't know what's going on?"

Torin let the argument wash over her, the familiar background voices securing the space. When the volume started rising, and the arguments devolved to repetition, she cut it off. "All right, bottom line, I want no more lives lost because of these polyhydroxide molecular hive sociopaths, so I'm going to voluntarily spend time with General Morris, albeit as little as possible. We'll talk to Big Yellow. Find out what they want. Suggest they fly into a distant sun and immolate themselves."

"We as in you and I?" Craig asked, leaning back against the wall, arms folded, uniform fabric stretched tight over arms and shoulders.

Appreciating the view, Torin grinned. "Maybe we'll even let Werst talk."

"The hell with talking," Werst called without turning. "I'm going to chow down on those *serley chrikas*." He snapped his teeth together and added, "They're coming through the wall."

"Good." Torin stretched, cracking her back. "I've had it with waiting around."

The blocks around the cannon fell first, crashing against the tunnel floor as grimy hands emerged, enlarging the hole. The distant sound of the digger rose from a rumble to a roar. PFC di'Valing Noshikin slid through the opening like an eel. When her hands touched the floor, she rolled, came up onto her feet, and held the cutting laser ready. Torin couldn't decide if she was impressed by the bravery of facing a Strike Team holding a cutting tool or annoyed by it. The other three di'Taykan followed. Another two blocks crashed to the floor, and the wall had finally been disassembled enough for the two Humans to get through. All six took up defensive positions, cutting lasers burning yellow-gold lines through dust-filled air.

Annoyed, she decided. Definitely annoyed.

"Torin, those are pulse cutters." So as not to have to shout over the digger, Craig's mouth was on Torin's ear. "They can disengage the safeties and use them offensively."

"Wonderful. Let's hope they don't know that."

"What are you going to do?"

"End this. Mashona. Werst. Ressk."

They fell into place around her, their weapons up and ready, hers hanging at her hip as she stepped out into the main tunnel. "Alamber, shut down the digger."

"On it, Boss."

Maintaining formation, they walked toward the six. Two seemed to be riding the thin edge of panic. Two were ready to die. And two looked resigned to whatever was about to happen.

They'd closed the distance between them to twenty meters when the grinding roar of the digger cut off.

Torin let the silence ring for a moment.

"I am Warden Torin Kerr," she said when that minute ended. One of the six snorted in disbelief. Torin ignored her. "*You* are six pathetic excuses for ex-Marines." Her voice dropped into gummy cadences like she'd never stepped off the parade square. "If you had half a brain among the lot of you, you'd have waited until the digger had fully emerged into the section of the tunnel you controlled, then you'd have commandeered it using the manual overdrive. You'd have been unstoppable. But no, you ran." She shook her head. "Were you hoping we'd left? Two of you were corporals. You, at least, should have known better." Humans flushed, and di'Taykan hair flattened as she pinned all six with a disapproving glare. "Turn off the lasers. Put them down and kick them this way. Then kneel and put your hands on your head, or we will open fire and put your embarrassing asses in a tank for the next tenday."

The taller of the two Humans pointed the laser down the tunnel. "You don't . . ."

"Did I stutter? Now, Marines!"

Six sets of knees hit the floor in unison.

"Well that worked better than a polite request to surrender," Binti noted quietly.

· —◆— ·

"I are not having been tanked for the last tenday, Alamber. I are knowing Big Yellow are having returned. It are on every screen I are passing."

If he was caught running a call through the Susumi buoy, he'd be hip-deep in shit, but Alamber was certain Presit needed to be at Big Yellow beside Torin and Craig. All of them, or none of them; that was how it had to work. "You have to get to Berbar to meet the *Berganitan*."

Arms folded under the edge of her ruff, she shook her head. "I are not having to do anything but to be present on Nuh Ner for an all-party debate."

"You were there at the beginning of the story. You risked your life to be there at the beginning, used an untested program to follow a ship through Susumi space."

Her muzzle wrinkled, showing teeth. "I are knowing what I did."

His cheeks stung where the ends of his hair whipped against them. "Don't you want to be there at the end?"

"I are not having been invited to be going along, not that I are going to being going even were I having been invited."

"Since when do you need an invitation to show up where the news is happening?"

Presit sighed and leaned back in her chair, giving Alamber a glimpse of campaign posters cycling through on the wall behind her. "I are thinking there are several hundred things I would rather be doing than be traveling with General Morris."

"But you were marked by the plastic!"

"Ah," she said flatly. "That are being why you are wanting me there. It are having nothing to do with news." Combing her claws through her whiskers—right side, left side—she stared up from the screen at him. "Are it occurring to you at all that I are not wanting to give the plastic the satisfaction of seeing me come running? Unlike Gunnery Sergeant Warden Kerr, I are not at its beck and call."

"Craig's going."

"He are at her beck and call." Presit's ears flicked forward. "There are being nothing I can do about that."

She was acting just a little too casual. Alamber remembered the reactions Big Bill evoked walking through the market, tension running under the casual greetings of shopkeepers and shoppers to the man who ruled their lives. "You're afraid."

Presit waved off his revelation. "I are running for office. I are having priorities. That are not being the same thing as fear, and I are not falling for your reversing physiology. I are having nothing to prove to you. Or to anyone. I are going to be denying this if you are saying it, but Gunnery Sergeant Warden Kerr can be taking care of things without me."

EIGHT

BOOMER MCVALE SMILED as she rerouted the incoming message. Nothing had arrived by way of the hidden subprogram for a while although she'd continued to pass the regular outgoing messages once a tenday. Didn't matter to her either way; she got paid a tidy and anonymous retainer to be available as needed. Didn't know who the messages came from. Didn't know who they went to. Didn't care. Wasn't ever tempted to try and find out. What she didn't know couldn't come back to bite her on the ass.

What she did know was that she had a nice little nest egg put aside that continued to grow and someday would be large enough to allow her to shove her success right up in the face of Captain di'Inconicho Tal, the recruiting officer on Paradise. She couldn't pass the psych test, but di'Taykan could? A di'Taykan with nine letters in his family name could become an officer, yet according to the psych exam she wasn't suitable? Did that make sense? Was it fair? Hardly. Humans had created the Confederation Marine Corps back when the Elder Races had gone looking for help to fight their war. Humans been the first and suddenly Humans were being turned down? She'd graduated in the top fifth of her class. She'd known her history. She'd studied and practiced and could make a ComOp roll over and beg. She'd worked out. She'd been able to snap one of those tall and skinny di'Taykan in half. But being Human wasn't good enough anymore. They wanted the Corps balanced, so aliens had the advantage, less-qualified di'Taykan and Krai getting in while Humans were passed over.

Someday she'd show them—have the best tech, her own ship, hell, maybe even her own station, but, for now, she'd bide her time and do her job helping to keep the AES safe in its geosynchronous orbit over Silsviss.

But someday . . .

———◆———

Dr. Anika Shote had gone into xenoanthropology because she'd wanted to understand why Humans weren't allowed to excel. Why were they lumped in with the Taykan and the Krai in the minds of the rest of the Confederation? The Krai hadn't ever bothered to come down out of the trees, the Taykan based their entire sociocultural system around procreation, and yet they were considered Humanity's equal. It made no sense.

Had one of her papers comparing the ludicrously lauded, single-sense advantages of alien species against Humanity's ability to adapt not come to the attention of Anthony Marteau at MI, she suspected she'd be accepting the standard-of-living supplement and writing papers for the few journals not straitjacketed by political correctness. She'd certainly never have gained the position of Lead XA on the Silsviss project without Per Marteau's support from behind the scenes. He understood her findings the way no one else ever had, and while she'd never met him personally, she felt a great kinship to him, beyond the commonality of species.

She owed him for her chance to apply her academic findings to actual situations.

"Cyr Tyroliz, this doesn't seem like your type of function."

Metal bands on his tail tapping against a table leg, Cyr Tyroliz blinked down at her, throat pouch slightly inflated. "Too educated?"

"Too self-congratulatory."

He looked surprised for a moment, and she wondered if he'd understood her meaning. The press often decried the precontact Warlord's lack of formal education. After a moment, he bobbed his head in amusement. "I find it necessary to keep an eye on diplomacy."

"I'm not surprised, and I thank you for recognizing the station is more than a mere threat."

He took a step back and tasted the air. "A threat?"

"A potential threat, of course." She sighed and took a swallow of the fermented fruit juice the upper class on Silsviss loved. "I shall miss this."

"You're leaving?"

"Well, I'm not planning to, but I'm not certain how much longer we'll be allowed to stay."

His eyes narrowed as he stared across the room at the cluster of Silsviss from the Planetary Committee, the closest thing to a planetary government they'd managed. To be honest, given the number of wars that had been going on at first contact, Anika was surprised they'd gotten so far. "Have they suggested you leave?" Cyr Tyroliz asked.

Cyr Tyroliz had voted in favor of the Confederation embassy, but Anika suspected that had been more about keeping his enemies close than about fostering cross-cultural knowledge. He'd also been in favor of Silsviss joining the Confederation and had never bothered hiding how much that had to do with gaining Susumi capability.

"The suggestion won't come from your people . . ." She frowned, looked away, her chin tucked down in a submissive posture before returning her gaze to his face. "I assumed you had access to Confederation news."

"I find the news gathered light-years away seldom applies to my life."

"Of course." She looked away again.

Cool fingers pressed in under her chin and lifted her head. Head cocked to one side, he examined her expression. "What are you hiding?"

"I'm not . . ." A touch of claw against the soft skin of her throat cut off her protest, and she knew she'd won. He wouldn't believe information too easily acquired. If he thought he'd forced it from her, however . . .

"Don't lie to me."

"The war with the Primacy has ended."

"That's not news." The claw dug in a little farther.

"With the war over, the Confederation doesn't need the Silsviss to fight. And not just the Silsviss. They don't need any of the Younger Races anymore. They want to keep us planetbound because they fear our capability for violence. Your people aren't yet legally part of the Confederation . . ." The Silsviss refused to ratify anything that required them to entirely disarm. ". . . so you'll be the first locked down. As there are member species who still don't know of your existence, no one will come to your defense. Once they've used you to prove they can lock a warrior culture down, they'll move on to the rest of us."

He stared at her for a long moment, then released her. "Will they?"

Anika touched her throat, swiping away the drop of blood before anyone saw. "It's all anyone's talking about."

"And you mammals will allow this. Herd mentality." Cyr Tyroliz tasted the air again, the light of the ballroom glittering off the scales folded into his frown. "A station in orbit gives them the high ground," he said quietly. His tail carved short jerky arcs in the air as he walked away.

He didn't join the other members of the Planetary Committee. Anika didn't see him beckon or show any indication that they should attend him, but three high-ranking members of the new military followed him out of the room.

The lesser species had simple, easy-to-influence reactions.

• ——◆—— •

"Unscheduled VTA, please respond." Boomer waited the required thirty seconds wondering if the idiot who'd come up with that number knew how far a VTA could get in thirty seconds, then opened the channel again. "Unscheduled VTA, please respond."

"What's up?" di'Murrin Keezo, the docking master, rolled from his board and across the small compartment they shared, stopping his chair to the left and a little behind hers.

"It's our VTA up off dirt. The OS checks out, but I can't contact flesh and blood."

"Remote piloting?"

She raised her hands so he could see the relevant data.

"Okay, not remote piloting. Mechanical blip, then. Probably why they're coming up. There's a limit to what they can fix wrapped in the shit the lizards call air. The damp and the heat are doing a number on our equipment—maintenance spends most of their time bonding zinc to replacement parts." He peered at her board, his dark purple eyes darker still, then rolled back to his own. "Docking computer has taken control. We'll put it on three; it's the closest nipple to the shop."

Boomer didn't dislike Keezo, he was great in the rack, his deep purple hair and eyes were pretty, but she couldn't understand how sex and pretty had been enough to make him docking master. He was neither that great nor that pretty. She preferred to share the compartment with his second, Tami Dezotto. Not only did the tiny woman take up a lot less space—di'Taykan were way too there, all the damned time—but she could be sure when Keezo wasn't around that her decisions weren't being influenced by alien pheromones.

A third attempt at contact received the same lack of response. "I can't get hold of the embassy either."

"We're the common factor; it's probably us," Keezo pointed out. "A piece of junk might've clipped an array."

The Silsviss had a surprising number of old satellites orbiting the planet. The Confederation had placed its station out farther than most of them, but they'd been known to wander. Boomer suspected at least half of them were spying on the station and wouldn't have been surprised to find they all were. "Diagnostics are coming up clear."

"Diagnostics came up clear when that hunk of junk cracked the observation window."

"Good point." But she ran the diagnostics again, just in case.

"VTA's attached. Nipple sealed. Any word?"

How could he have missed word? He was less than two meters away. "Not yet."

"Did you send a report to maintenance?"

"Don't tell me how to do my job, Keez."

He raised both hands. *"Ce kerdin pat arventigo."*

"That's not what you said last threesday," Boomer muttered, wondering if it was an interference problem. Most of those abandoned Silsviss satellites still had some power, and this could be the proof of spying she'd been looking for. She'd just tagged three she wanted investigated next time they sent out a maintenance sled, when she heard a thud against the hatch. Weird. Station command never showed up without warning—she'd always wondered what it was command didn't want to catch them doing—and it was still hours until shift change.

Another thud. Kind of a double THUD thud.

Then the hatch flew open.

Boomer had never seen a Silsviss up close. As station staff, she could have gone down to the planet on her off days, but why bother. While she didn't hate the heat and humidity the way the Taykan did, she disliked it enough she'd never seen the point in leaving the station's air-conditioned comfort. In the flesh, the Silsviss were bigger than she'd imagined. The Niln, the only lizards she'd ever seen, came up to about her boobs. This guy—and there might be a total lack of recognizable sexual identifiers, but she'd bet her left ovary he was male—was taller than Keezo and, like most Taykan, Keezo topped out around two meters.

The weapon the Silsviss held, in what were almost human-looking hands, screamed *deadly* at about the same volume as the lizard itself screamed *male*.

"Away from the consoles!"

Consoles? Fukking translation program. Consoles had been referred to as boards since before she'd started training. Hands up, Boomer rolled back, and turned around to face the hatch as Keezo surged up out of his chair, past the weapon, and punched the lizard in the throat. Right. Ex-Marine. Idiot. The lizard went down, but his tail lashed out, catching Keezo at the knees, sweeping his legs from under him. Before he could get back onto his feet, his head exploded in a spray of blood and brains and purple hair.

The second lizard sneered as the wheezing lizard lurched up onto his feet. "The Taykan struck a good blow. A worthy enemy."

Spewing puke over the floor between her feet, Boomer reminded herself it could've been worse. At least Keezo hadn't been Human.

· —◆— ·

"You'll want to reenlist."

Torin couldn't help herself; she blinked.

General Morris kept talking. "You should, by rights, come back in at the staff sergeant level, but, given the benefit the military will accrue from the publicity, your rank will be restored. You will be Gunnery Sergeant Kerr again."

"I have no intention of reenlisting."

His eyes narrowed. "You will not return to Big Yellow as a civilian."

"Fine." Obvious now why the general had requested a private meeting. His plan had been to separate her from those who'd object to her returning to active service. Craig. Her team. Her current employers. Anyone who'd ever met her and was still capable of thought. Although standing at ease—a habit she doubted she'd ever be able to break—she kept her gaze on General Morris' face. Not challenging. Not listening respectfully. Just there.

Cheeks beginning to flush, he stepped closer, attempting intimidation.

Torin raised a brow.

He stepped back again and tried to make it look as though it had been his idea. "I've had uniforms made for you." That explained the CMC case on the conference room's table. "You seem to have maintained your conditioning, at least."

"Thank you for noticing." She managed to keep her mouth from twitching at his expression, but it was close. "However, I won't need your uniforms, I have my own."

His eyes narrowed again. "I am completely serious about you not returning to Big Yellow as a civilian, Kerr."

"And I am completely fine with that."

The general opened his mouth. Closed it again. Torin could see him reviewing the conversation, trying to determine where he'd lost control. She doubted he'd have much success, operating, as he was, on the mistaken belief that he'd ever had control. "You're refusing to return to Big Yellow," he said at last.

"I'm refusing to reenlist."

"Then you won't . . ." He paused and actually started thinking. For all he annoyed her, he wasn't stupid. "You have the Susumi equation."

As Craig had made the initial jump and then provided the equation to the military, that didn't merit a response.

"We can't allow you to approach the plastic on your own."

"You'll have the Navy fire on a Justice Department ship?"

"I didn't say that."

"Good. Because I doubt the Navy would make such a critical error in the current political climate."

His cheeks were red, approaching purple. He lowered himself into a chair and stared up at her. Torin knew how he saw their positions—he was sitting, she was not; therefore she was the inferior. Torin preferred to believe she had superior mobility as well as the high ground. "I see you're aware of the discussions in Parliament. Good. The Younger Races must prove our worth to remain full members of the Confederation." He raised a hand although Torin had no intention of interrupting. "I know what you're thinking. We've proven our worth in blood and bodies for centuries, but that's not how politics works. The question becomes, what have we done for them lately? If the Elder Races try to restrain us, there will be war. Us against them. We have the equipment, we have the training, but we don't want to destroy the Confederation."

Torin remembered a planet of preserved weapons, more deadly, more destructive than anything permitted since.

"Weakening our position would be foolish," he continued. "The Primacy will attack if they consider us at a disadvantage, and we fought too long to have the Primacy win."

Seemed his desire to avoid another war had more to do with pride and less to do with having no more of his people die.

"What precisely do you want from me, General?"

"I want you to accompany me to Big Yellow under my command." He clearly considered it a magnanimous offer.

"You assume that if I'm under your command, you control me."

"You were an excellent NCO. Control may be too strong a word, but you know where the lines are."

She nodded, once, to acknowledge his point.

"And, in this instance . . ." The heavy emphasis suggested she not get above herself. ". . . we're stronger with you than without you. The plastic has spoken to you twice, raising the odds it will speak to you again."

"You want to speak with the plastic?"

"Of course we want to speak with it." The *don't be an idiot* was almost silent. "The more we learn about the plastic, the better we can defeat it. We've developed a weapon based on the data gathered by Dr. Sloan on Major Svensson's plastic bones, but it would help if we knew what precisely to aim at. We may not be able to destroy Big Yellow . . ." The hand lying flat on the conference room table curled up into a fist. ". . . but we can hurt it."

"You realize," Torin began, because it wouldn't be the first time he hadn't considered consequences, "if we hurt them, they'll hurt us back."

General Morris' lip curled. "I never expected Gunnery Sergeant Kerr to be a coward."

"How dare you." Torin rolled the words out in a bored monotone. "I'm not a coward, and I'll prove it to you by doing exactly what you want." She sighed. "General, my job remains completing the mission and bringing my people home alive. I can't do either if you open fire. You can't beat the plastic, and you can't stop them from killing you."

He stared up at her for a long moment, then he snorted derisively. "I'd say their visit in your head brainwashed you, but since that's been ruled out by professionals, I think all that chasing around after Humans First has blurred the line between you and them. Just like Humans First, you're interested in only taking care of yourself. Except," he leaned forward and sneered up at her, "at least they're out doing something!"

The lights in the conference room flickered. Torin pressed her tongue hard against her implant for a full three count—the team's signal for *"I don't care what you think you're doing, stop it. Now."* As Alamber hadn't specifically been told not to listen in, odds were high the lights had flickered in response to General Morris' accusation, warning her there'd be worse to come.

"General, Strike Team Alpha is going to Big Yellow, with or without you. The government I work for wants us there. We'd prefer to go as part of the military as no one knows what's about to happen and the *Promise* has no weapons." Binti had blown up a Marine armory with a cutting laser, but Torin wasn't planning on reminding the general of that. "I'd prefer to make the plastic pay for the lives spent during their social experiment, but I'll settle for convincing them to get out and stay out of our corner of the universe. Remember, they killed millions of us when they saw us as bacteria in a petri dish—what happens when they see us as enemies?"

The general's lips pulled back off his teeth. He'd served with Krai; it wasn't a smile. "When that happens, I expect you'll complete the mission and bring your people home alive. Glad we had this talk, Warden."

Gunnery Sergeant Kerr couldn't tell a superior officer to go fuk himself. Warden Kerr was considering it when the hatch to the conference room slammed open.

"General! Staff on the station over Silsviss have hit the panic button. You're going to want to see this!"

· ——◆—— ·

"With the Silsviss now in command of the observation platform orbiting their planet, we can only assume that every Confederation citizen on board is dead." Head swaying, the Slaink presenter slid the station schematics to one side and flicked up an image of the embassy. "The Minister of Foreign Affairs has been unable to make contact with the Confederation Embassy on Silsviss and, in spite of the security systems in place, has expressed concern over the safety of the Ambassador and their staff."

· ——◆—— ·

"I assume you've seen the latest?" Anthony smiled as he strode into Commander Belcerio's office, frowned at the short, heavyset woman standing by the star map on the wall, and said, "Who are you? Never mind. Get out."

She glanced over at Belcerio.

"I pay the bills, not him. Go."

"Commander." She nodded once in that irritating military way and headed for the hatch. "Per Marteau."

"That was my XO," Belcerio said as the hatch closed behind her. "You don't give her orders."

"I don't care. And, yes, I do." He shoved his hands in his pockets and rocked back on his heels. "Now, answer my question."

"The report on Silsviss? Yes, I saw it." Although they were alone in the room, Belcerio dropped his voice. "Scale and Claw has been successfully implemented."

"And careens toward its inevitable conclusion." Anthony clasped a hand on Belcerio's shoulder and squeezed. "I find wetware so ridiculously easy to program."

Only two point four percent of the network knew they worked for the cause, but the effect was the same.

NINE

//THE NAVY CAN'T TAKE the Silsviss out. That would be equivalent to declaring war on them."

General Morris glared across the desk at Commander Ng. "And what do you call taking the station if not a declaration of war?"

"It could have been nothing more than an unfortunate misunderstanding. Cyr Tyroliz seems to honestly think he was responding to our declaration of war."

"And you believe that declaration of his? He's a Warlord," the general sneered. "Of course he wants war. He's provoked our response by killing innocents!"

"Although not as many as originally reported."

General Morris ignored him. "The station was an observation facility. It had no weapons."

"It *is* an observation facility," the commander corrected mildly. "It *has* no weapons. The station still exists, General. It did, however, have what I see referred to as . . ." He flicked through a few files on his desk although Torin knew damned well it was for effect. ". . . as a panic button."

"Of course it had a panic button! Should the less conciliatory members of the Silsviss controlling faction prevail, the station would be in danger. They needed a way to contact the Confederation for a quick response. That seems to have been barely adequate as a precautionary measure."

Commander Ng pressed his palms together and tapped the sides of his first fingers against his chin. "That seems to me as though the Silsviss are being treated as a potential enemy."

"The Silsviss are dangerous and not entirely united."

The commander's expression acknowledged the deflection. Torin recognized the expression. The general didn't. "So if they decide against joining the Confederation, we plan to keep them confined to a planet they've managed to leave on their own?"

If they did join the Confederation, they'd be the youngest of the Younger Races and, depending on how the vote in Parliament went, might still be confined to a planet they'd left on their own. Torin kept her gaze locked on the bulkhead behind Commander Ng's left shoulder. Why complicate the argument or acknowledge the H'san in the room?

"We can't risk them gaining access to the equivalent of Susumi drive! They could wreak havoc across Confederation space."

"In which case, the station calling in the Navy would be a preemptive strike."

"Precisely."

"I see." Commander Ng didn't bother hiding what he thought of that line of reasoning. General Morris didn't bother hiding what he thought of Commander Ng. Torin wondered why, exactly, she'd been summoned. "As it happens," the commander continued, "Parliament has declared this a crime, not a declaration of war and therefore it falls under the jurisdiction of the Justice Department."

And that explained why.

"Warden Kerr."

"Sir."

"The prevailing opinion is that you'll have the best chance of getting through to Cyr Tyroliz given your history with the Silsviss. Do you agree?"

Cyr Tyroliz was an adult male warlord, not an adolescent jockeying for power in a wilderness pack. But she had a skull on the wall over the entertainment center that gave her a level of credibility with the Silsviss no one else in the Confederation had yet acquired. Nor were likely to, given the prevailing attitude toward skulls on the wall. "Yes, sir, I agree."

"Yes, sir, you agree," General Morris mocked. "You're going to Big Yellow."

Torin raised a brow. "I don't work for you."

"And you're suddenly fine with those plastic puppet masters jerking our strings again?"

Commander Ng answered before she could. "Since its return, the plastic has made no aggressive moves toward or within the Confederation. The taking of the station has resulted in the deaths of six of our citizens. That is the concern of the Justice Department."

"Six!" The general surged up onto his feet and planted both fists on the edge of the desk, then leaned in close to Commander Ng's face. "I want to prevent deaths in the millions!"

"I'm aware," the commander told him, unintimidated. "Which is why Wardens Ryder, Werst, and di'Cikeys will be traveling to Big Yellow. Warden Ryder was also a host, and Warden Werst was present during the previous visit to the ship. Wardens Kerr, Ressk, and Mashona will be returning to Silsviss."

"Commander?" Torin hadn't stood when the general did. Nor did she intend to. She kept her tone level, ignoring the implied threat in the general's position. "We should split Strike Team U'yun between us to bring up our numbers."

"Why U'yun?"

"They're new, sir. They trained with us on Seven Sta, and they're still new enough to be flexible about the change."

"Good idea." His fingers moved over the desk, drawing up orders. "The *Promise* goes with Ryder, the *Baylet* with you. U'yun's C&C will follow."

"And Alpha's?"

"Big Yellow isn't a Justice matter. I can keep Alpha's C&C busy."

General Morris squared his shoulders, now personally rather than situationally annoyed. "And I have nothing to say about this?" he growled.

"As I explained, General, the attack on the station is a Justice Department matter." Commander Ng favored the general with his most reasonable expression, and Torin watched the general turn purple in response. "You'll continue to have our cooperation, but I can't send a Warden with you whose unique skills are required elsewhere. Warden Kerr?"

"Sir?"

"As soon as you're able to hand the Silsviss situation over to C&C, join General Morris at Big Yellow."

"Yes, sir."

"You think it'll be that easy?" The general's lip curled. "Don't tell me you've begun believing the legends of Torin Kerr."

"I believe the evidence, General, and I doubt it'll be easy." In stark contrast to the general, the commander looked entirely unaffected by the conversation. "You were one of the first to interact with the Silsviss; you, if anyone, should know better."

General Morris glared down at Torin who shook her head minutely. She'd never spoken of the circumstances that had sent a platoon to Silsviss to die in a political arena to anyone but Craig. Some things remained personal, even under the banner of full disclosure.

"This has been a waste of my time," he snarled, spun on one heel, and headed for the hatch. "If Ryder hasn't got the *Promise* attached in forty minutes, I'm leaving without him."

Torin stood as the hatch closed, paused as the commander said, "You just spent an entire tenday worth of sirs." He sounded amused.

"I had a few extra lying around."

His mouth twitched. "I'm sure."

She needed to get to Craig, but she lingered a moment longer. "Did you intend to make an enemy, Commander?"

Fingers stilled on his desk. "I didn't much care for his viewpoint, nor do I care if he considers me his enemy. A preemptive strike is not only against several laws and statutes, but against the core tenets of the Confederation."

"His entire adult life has been the military. The politics of the military anyway. He had rank enough to get his time in extended, but time's running out for that fourth star. He's getting desperate."

"Are you defending him, Warden?"

Once, General Morris had been willing to die to further strengthen the Confederation. He'd never been in a battle, he'd never carried the bodies of his people out, he'd never taken a life with his own two hands, but he had been willing to die. It had been a shortsighted plan put into motion without considering all the variables, but . . .

Of course, he'd assumed Torin would kill him, and being put into the position of executioner still pissed her off.

"Maybe not a defense," she said. "But a perspective."

"I'm not saying it doesn't make sense to split us up," Craig told her as they walked to the docking arm with barely enough room for independent movement between them. "I'm saying I don't like it. We're a team."

"Yes, we are."

"Bugger we can do about it, then?"

Torin shrugged the shoulder not holding her go bag. "We have our orders."

"You take stupid risks when I'm not around."

She took more risks, she acknowledged. She didn't take stupid risks. "I'll be careful if you'll be careful."

"I'm not going toe to toe with an angry Silsviss who's certain he has the moral high ground."

"You're facing the molecular hive mind responsible for centuries of war, and keeping an eye on General Morris so he doesn't start another one."

"Suddenly the Silsviss don't look so bad."

No, they didn't. "I'd rather face them with you beside me."

Craig glanced over at her and grinned. "Because then you'd know what I was doing."

"And thus we see the way Wardens replace their concerns with banter," Binti interjected. "Their decision that the more usual public displays of affection show a lack of professionalism keeps them from groping for comfort and face sucking for our amusement."

Torin raised her right hand above her shoulder and flipped Binti off.

"Her physical needs sublimated, the senior Warden becomes cranky."

"The senior Warden's going to be shut up in Susumi with you for five and a half days," Torin told her flatly.

"Shutting up. Continue sublimating with my blessing."

"Is this why you're not into coupling?" Alamber wondered. "Having to sublimate your needs?"

"Please . . ." Torin could hear the eye roll in Binti's voice. ". . . my needs are *limated* regularly. I've just never seen the point in a long-term relationship. I like sex, but having someone all up in my face all the time?" Torin could hear the disinterest in Binti's voice. "Not for me."

"And Taylor?"

"Taylor's a friend I have fun with," Binti explained. "And sex with. But they're looking for happily ever after and, when they start making an effort to find it, we'll be done."

Alamber laughed. "You'd make a great di'Taykan."

"Fuk you. I make a great Human."

They'd turned into the docking arm and were nearly at the hatch to the first berth when Werst and Ressk arrived, feet slapping against the deck, running in step. Binti made kissy faces at them. Werst flipped her off, and Ressk announced, "Captain Carveg's still in command of the *Berganitan*, Gunny."

Captain Carveg had been in command of the *Berganitan* on their first trip to Big Yellow.

Craig frowned. "Should we be worried she hasn't been promoted?"

Ressk snorted, nostril ridges quivering. "She refused a promotion in order to stay. Said she'll finish her forty on the *Berganitan* or not at all."

"What happened to ours is not to reason why and doing what you're told?" Craig asked.

"Naval captain is equal to a full colonel," Torin told him. "At that level she can reason why all she wants. Top brass won't like it, but she can't have much time left, so they'll let it go." It didn't hurt that the Krai were strongly matriarchal; high-ranking females pulled a lot of loyalty from Krai in their crews.

Dimples flashed under Craig's beard scruff. "You liked her."

"And I respected her." Unless Captain Carveg had changed a great deal, she'd pay no more attention to General Morris than to any other Marine hitching a ride. Torin felt a lot better about sending half her team off without her.

"We late?" Elisk pushed past Alamber, his team filling the docking arm behind him, the two teams devolving into a jumble of Younger Races.

"Not until the engines start," Torin told him, then, as Craig punched in the code to open the hatch, raised her voice to fill the space available. "Listen up, people. Those leaving on the *Promise*, into the airlock. Everyone else, get out of their way."

"Even you, Gunny?"

"If I get in the way, Zhou, I do it on purpose."

The jumble resolved itself into two distinct groups.

"You sure Tech should be with us?" Craig asked quietly as Yahsamus stepped over the lip of the hatch.

"You've got Elisk," Torin reminded him, fully aware the technical sergeant could hear them. "You need an NCO."

"And you defo don't need another." He held up a finger before she could respond, face smoothing out into the not-entirely-present expression most people wore when listening to an implant. "*Bergie's* ready for us."

Torin hid a wince. If Craig referred to the *Berganitan* as the *Bergie* where Captain Carveg could hear him, even odds he'd be out an airlock. "We'll join you at Big Yellow once we've dealt with Cyr Tyroliz. C&C will stay behind for wrap up."

They didn't indulge in frequent PDAs, their relationship walked a fine line professionally as it was, but when Craig reached for her, Torin went to him. It wasn't a kiss for the ages, she was too conscious of their audience, but it would hold her for now. From the light in Craig's eyes when he pulled away, he agreed.

"Don't bring home another skull."

"I'll do my best."

"You always do."

Werst paused on her left before he followed Craig into the *Promise*. "Keep him safe."

"You, too."

"I'm quite capable of keeping myself safe," Ressk muttered.

Binti patted his head and ducked the return swing. "See if I give you sympathy again."

"Watch me give you . . ."

"Warden Kerr!" Small teal feathers wafting in his wake, Dr. Deyell ran toward them down the docking arm, a bulky package cradled in his arms. "This one is happy he didn't miss you! This one is almost positive he's adapted Qurn's tech," he added when Torin walked forward to meet him. "It hasn't been tested yet, but this one read research that suggested the MDC on the bennies doesn't work particularly well against the Silsviss, because of the composition of their scales. So . . ." He held out the package—which turned out to be the benny Torin had left with him, wrapped in a lab coat. "This one couldn't carry a weapon through the corridors without having to stop and explain every two meters."

It no longer looked quite like a benny. The MDC and its power unit had been removed and a single new piece added in their place. Torin frowned at the weight, turned it over, and realized the laser cutter had been removed as well.

"Point it and pull the trigger, that hasn't changed. It fires a charge that disrupts the electrical signals to the brain and causes unconsciousness." He preened at the side of his neck. "Should cause unconsciousness."

"You haven't tested it?"

"This one only just completed the modifications."

Modifications, Torin repeated silently, because Parliament refused to allow for the development of new weapons.

"But as you're heading to confront the Silsviss on a station . . ." His crest drooped. "You're right. If it hasn't been tested . . ."

"Trial by combat," Torin said, stepping back so he couldn't take it from her. "You're right about the Silsviss lack of reaction to a benny. If this doesn't work, we're no farther behind. Thank you, Dr. Deyell."

His rudimentary beak flattened in a Rakva smile. "You're welcome. This one is curious, though, if you can't use your usual weapon on a station and the bennies aren't very effective, what had you planned on using to defeat the Silsviss."

Torin returned his smile. "Force of personality."

· ——◆—— ·

So Gunnery Sergeant Warden Torin Kerr was to be returning to Silsviss instead of accompanying General Morris to Big Yellow. The military had to be having fits. An amusing thought. Presit touched the outline of her slate within the bag over her shoulder and wondered why Alamber seemed to be thinking she were needing to be kept informed—not that she were not appreciative. He were being smarter than the others on the Strike Teams, perhaps that were being reason enough.

In Presit's informed and entirely relevant opinion, given that she had presented the stories of both Big Yellow and the prison planet, the plastic aliens were requiring a certain delicacy that were being absent from Kerr's actions. Best for all concerned that she be going off to where punching were being the correct response.

"Candidate durValintrisy! Have you heard?"

Presit paused to allow the hurrying Niln to catch up. Lysentias were being the biggest gossip within the government buildings, seemingly for the sheer joy of spreading information. Given his willingness to be checking his sources before opening his mouth, she felt he should have been going into journalism rather than the civil service. "I are having heard about the situation above Silsviss, yes."

"No, not that." Breathing a little heavily, tail out to maintain his balance, he fell into step beside her. "I've just come from lunch with my cousin, Lakshinz, at Bergerial . . ."

Presit were seldom eating at Bergerial, although it were being very popular with government workers. The prices were being too high for how entirely unwilling to be committing to their Katrien dishes they were.

". . . she's been part of the research team working on the data sheet, and she says Parliament gave it back."

"It?"

"The data sheet!"

When Lysentias were coming to a complete stop, Presit were grabbing his arm and yanking him into motion. One thing she are having learned from the military over the years are that it are being a lot harder to hit a moving target. She are having learned that information are ammunition on her own. "They are having given it back? Who to?"

"To the plastic. It's on the ship heading to Big Yellow." He leaned in toward her, and lowered his voice. "But no one knows."

Now he were attempting discretion? Presit sighed. "I are expecting many people are knowing. The captain of the ship, the ship's security . . ."

"Yes, fine, but not everyone on the ship! And no one here."

"No one? I are knowing. You. Your cousin. Anyone who are overhearing you and your cousin in the restaurant."

"No one," he began, blinked both inner eyelids, and wasn't able to continue. Given the usual lunch crush, he could be having no idea who'd overheard. It was, after all, where he overheard a lot of what he passed on. "But shouldn't people know?" he asked as they turned down the corridor leading to the campaign offices and the distinct scent of take-out *urha* lingering in the air.

Presit nodded at three members of her opposition's team hurrying in the other direction before answering. "I are expecting, given what are having happened in the plaza, that most people are being happy the data sheet are being gone."

"That's a good point."

"Sometimes I are having them." They'd reached the etched glass door that led to her tiny, double office. A few years ago, it had been made of plastic. Nonorganic plastic. And had been replaced anyway.

Because people were being stupid more often than not. "Are you wanting to be coming in?"

"No. No thanks. I've got meetings in C Block all afternoon." He reached out and touched her arm, barely dimpling the fur. "You know as much about the plastic as anyone. Why do you think they've returned?"

"I are honestly having no idea." And she didn't speculate. Not to someone who are so clearly incapable of keeping secrets. Speculation spread through Parliament faster than gossip.

"If they try anything, do you think Gunnery Sergeant Kerr can save us?"

Presit pushed her glasses up so she could be looking him directly in the eye. "You are kidding me, right?"

"Right. Of course." Lysentias laughed and stepped back. "Well, you've got work to do, I'm sure. I know I have." Another step back, and a wave, and he was gone, tail tip tracing figure eights in the air.

He'd assumed the exact opposite of her meaning. Would Gunnery Sergeant Kerr be saving them. Please. And it was being Warden Kerr now, anyway.

That being said, he wasn't being entirely wrong, Presit admitted as she pulled the outer office door closed behind her. At least not about how people should be knowing about the decision to return the plastic. The people knowing was, after all, being the whole point behind government transparency. She stared at the loose fur dancing in the beam of sunlight that angled in through the big, multipaned window, realized she were being irritated enough to shed, and stepped out of the sun and over to her assistant's desk. "Treist, I are going to be needing a packet on the Susumi satellite, as soon as possible."

"Yes, Candidate." Treist's ears quivered with the need to be helpful. "Are there being anything else?"

"Nothing I are not being able to handle myself." Treist were being significantly more help than the rest of the family her *strectasin* had insisted she employ, but there were still many details she were not needing to know. With the door to the inner office closed behind her, Presit stroked her desk awake and pulled up a local contact.

"Sector Central News, Nuh Ner division. How may I direct your call?"

· —◆— ·

He thought about what the data sheet could have told them. About what it symbolized even if it never told them a thing. About how he'd never had a chance to even be in the same room with it. His hand slid into his pocket and the small, ancient, pink plastic horse he'd had no intention of leaving behind, stroking his thumb over the smooth curve of its arched neck. No longer content with betraying Humanity, Parliament had betrayed the Confederation as a whole. It was long past time for revolution.

If not for that di'Taykan Warden, he'd have still been in a position where carefully nurtured connections would have allowed him close to the data sheet. Perhaps close enough to touch. He had no doubt he'd have been able to secure a place on the dais, to have been mere meters away when it finally reacted to the Krai's teeth. And when Parliament decided to secretly get rid of it? He'd have been there to keep the military in an observer's role, to ensure his ship returned it to the plastic or to a secure location of his chosing.

He'd had one of the largest and most diverse collections of pre-diaspora Human plastics. He should have been part of the research team. He should have been on the dais. He should have been given the data sheet when the government no longer required it.

In time, the di'Taykan Warden would pay.

"Playing with your pony?" Dr. Banard winked, and snapped the last connection on his crash harness closed. "Going to buckle up?"

Humanity's Freedom, the flagship of the Humans First fleet shuddered as the docking clamps released. Anthony sneered, still standing. "I don't follow paternalistic government regulations."

"Good for you. However, if the shit hits the fan, as statistically it may, and you career across this compartment and damage me, I won't be happy." Before he could respond, Banard added, "If I'm not happy, you won't get your weapons built, and I'm already unhappy about leaving my things behind."

The remodeled CMC officers' packet he'd had attached to *Freedom* had been a reasonably comfortable suite before he been forced to allow Banard the use of a room. A decommissioned cruiser, *Humanity's Freedom* could have moved more attached packets, one more for Banard at the very least, but there'd been no time to acquire them, Big Yellow having set their timetable. With the prototype constructed, they might have managed without Banard, but no one else had been willing to handle the Susumi components, and while he had no objection to exposing certain members of the organization to potentially deadly materials for the greater good, unwilling volunteers wouldn't perform to the required standards. He needed weapons they could count on in the upcoming fight.

Humans First hadn't sprung from their sanctuary and raced for Big Yellow with the kind of speed he'd anticipated. It took time to put an armada together. It took time to load not only the prototype weapon, but the pieces of the other two—they'd been able to acquire only three Susumi cores—as well as the raw materials needed to assemble them. It took time to get word out to the ships Humans First had been providing with weapons. Not all the crews of those ships were Human, but every battle needed cannon fodder.

"So, what had your briefs in a bunch?" Dr. Banard smacked his lips together and blinked rheumy eyes. "Don't bother denying it. During the pacing, you were wearing the mistaken belief that your life sucks all over your face."

"I was . . ."

"Ruminating?"

"I was reflecting on how the government is returning the data sheet to the plastic on the *Berganitan*," he snarled.

Bushy gray brows rose. "How the hell did you hear that? Fingers in yet another pie? Spun another web? Paid another informant? None of those were actually questions, by the way. Why do you care what happens to the detritus of a non-Human enemy? It's a big sheet of nonresponsive plastic. I saw the research, you know. It registered inert, and those idiots have no idea where that blow-out came from."

He ran his thumb down the pink plastic back.

The data sheet should have been his.

"I'm going to get it back."

Banard stared at him for a long moment. "You never had it," he said at last.

TEN

T**HE *BAYLET* WAS LARGER** than the *Promise* with more original features and minimal retrofitting when she transferred from
the Department of Defense to Justice. Instead of a single control
panel, she had separate communication and weapon boards. The
weapons were no longer enough to take to war, but they were weapons, not a cutting laser. Her VTA was standard to a Navy cruiser not a
repurposed Taykan shuttle liberated from mercenaries, and her autodoc was big enough to hold a Dornagain.

But the *Baylet* had never appeared suddenly above a prison to blast
the message that stopped the war out into known space, nor—after
being holed by pirates—had it maintained physical integrity long
enough to get Torin to safety. It wasn't Craig's pride and joy. It wasn't
where she'd started learning how not to be a Marine, how to be
CSO—if more prone to violence than the usual variety. A decommissioned cruiser, retrofitted for Warden work, the *Baylet* was fast, smart,
and spacious, carrying only a quarter of the crew she'd been designed
for. Torin tried not to judge her for what she wasn't.

Yahsamus had found time to vent her quarters, and Torin made a
mental note to thank her later. There was nothing like the residue of
pheromones in a two-by-three-meter room to make a trip interesting.

"Five and a half days in Susumi," Binti pointed out when the three
members of Alpha Team gathered in the galley. "At least we'd have
had a way to pass the time."

Tylen had vented her quarters as well, but left a note for Binti explaining it had been the technical sergeant's idea.

"We'll be going over the station schematics," Torin reminded her, wondering why all Strike Team ships weren't using the same coffee maker. Hot water. Coffee. How complicated did it have to be?

Binti waved off the station schematics, caramelized sugar fanning out from the pastry in her hand. "That'll take a couple of hours."

"Maintaining conditioning after sugar consumption." This particular coffee maker had half a dozen extra buttons.

"It's one *purtue*, Gunny." She licked sugar off her thumb. "An extra two klicks will run it off."

"Familiarizing ourselves with Dr. Deyell's modifications." She sniffed the liquid in her mug.

"There's one modified benny and six of us."

"And learning to work with Bilodeau, Nicholin, and Lorkin," Torin continued. "None of whom have ever seen a Silsviss in the flesh."

"You're saying they're not going to be much help if they're shitting themselves?" Ressk asked.

"Who's going to be shitting themselves?" Lorkin came into the galley, thumb-printed the *sah* safe open, grabbed a pouch, and tossed one to Ressk. "Well? Who?"

Torin raised a brow at Ressk, and Binti snickered.

• —◆— •

Craig had decided to stay on the *Promise* although packets had been attached to the *Berganitan* for them—individual quarters around a common room with common facilities, all three of the Younger Races eliminating waste if not exactly the same way, then close enough for government work.

"Don't trust the general?" Werst asked, perched on the back of one of the control room chairs.

"I don't *like* the general." Craig spun the pilot's chair around to face Werst. "The *Promise* is mine, and I'm not leaving her empty. I didn't back when she fit into one of the *Berganitan*'s big shuttle bays, I'm not going to now."

"Airlock doesn't open without a bio match," Werst grunted, "and your second line of defense is technically illegal."

"The second line of defense is a warning, the third line of defense is technically illegal." He raised a hand, cutting off Werst's response. "But only if it's triggered. Makes all the difference."

"Fair enough," Werst allowed, jumping down and heading for the hatch, bag over his shoulder. "Odds are high anyone slammed by it will be too stupid to live or MI, so I, personally, don't give a crap." He paused, hand over the airlock controls, and turned. "There's a Mu'tuv squad on board. Word of advice, don't play cards with them. They don't like losing."

Craig had been amazed to learn there were Marines tougher than Torin and Werst. The Mu'tuv were deliberate badasses rather than situational, Torin had explained when he'd first asked about them. "Well, aren't they special snowflakes."

Werst snorted. "When you get home without your balls, tell Gunny I warned you."

Alone on the *Promise*, Craig swung his feet up onto the control panel. One by one, muscles relaxed. If he kept his gaze on the board and the screens and the blank expanse of the polarized window, he could almost convince himself he was back on a salvage run. Just him and the *Promise* and the vast reaches of debris-filled space. He loved Torin, he liked his life, he enjoyed the negligible relationship the team had with personal space, he even looked forward to the day when he left the field and trained a new generation of Strike Team pilots, but sometimes he missed being alone.

· —◆— ·

"The data sheet they found on Threxie?" Alamber jerked up into a sitting position, ignoring the muttering of his companions. "That data sheet?"

"Is there another one?" Dal asked sleepily, fuchsia hair spread out over the pillow.

"It's here? On the *Berganitan*?"

Narilyn waved a hand from the other side of the communal bed. "No one's supposed to know."

Pushing his agitated hair back off his face, Alamber twisted around to face her. "Why is the data sheet on the *Berganitan*?"

Hasun patted Narilyn on the stomach. "If no one's supposed to know, should you be telling him?"

"Nothing I can tell him, I don't know why it's here."

"I meant . . ." Hasun paused, eyes so pale a yellow most of the light receptors had to be closed. "Uh . . . never mind."

"Maybe we're holding it hostage." Kamisu propped his head on Alamber's thigh. "Plastic wants it back, it fuks off and never returns."

"More like give it back or we play with your brains until you think it's your idea," Dal argued.

"I heard the captain and the XO talking about it being an example of how civilized we are," Narilyn told them, gracefully folding her legs under her. "See how we're returning this sheet of possibly bits of you back to you. Let's be friends."

"We're delivering it in a warship," Alamber sighed.

She nodded. "Mixed messages, that's what wrong with the universe."

It wasn't hard to find out where the plastic was being kept. Being held? Alamber supposed that depended on whether it was tech left behind by the plastic or plastic left behind. It was a bit surprising to find it secured behind a lock that had been programmed to open only after the *Berganitan* left Susumi space.

He bet it was to keep General Morris from performing unauthorized experiments.

Given the data sheet's response to having a honking big bite taken out of it, it was a sure thing that the general would be all over trying to damage it in other ways. The total absence of a physical guard meant Captain Carveg had decided not to draw attention to the compartment. If there were guards, what were they guarding? Gossip went through closed environments—ships, stations, small towns—like cheese through a H'san.

When he'd remotely broken the lock down to a single sequence, Alamber left his hiding place in the maintenance ducts, looped the security cameras for seventeen seconds, and ran for the hatch, closing it behind him with three seconds to spare.

They'd hung the data sheet from hooks set into the ceiling.

Trying to be nice? Because that was the way it had hung for centuries?

Taykans used that exact shade of orange for emergency lights. He hadn't heard an official theory about the similarity, but he had to assume there'd been plenty of unofficial speculation. He had to assume that because, according to Werst, his time with Big Bill had made him almost as cynical as a third-contract Marine.

With the air circulating through two upper and two lower vents, through what the ship's schematics said was an enclosed filtration system, he couldn't smell the slight chemical odor Werst said had been lingering around the data sheet on Threxie. Of course, it had been through a lot since then.

"You look just like your pictures," he murmured, stepping closer.

Now he was here, he wasn't sure why. What could he do with his slate that all those government researchers hadn't? At the Sector Parliament ceremony on Nuh Ner, scientist after scientist had said it was too alien to understand, too alien to be certain what tests to perform.

Of course, there was always the chance that those scientists had been overthinking it. He hadn't gone to some *snaji* university, so he wasn't going to ignore the one thing every mammal—and most other species—responded to.

"If you're tech, I'm wasting my time."

But if it wasn't. If it was alive. If it had screamed when a piece had been bitten out of it . . .

Alamber found the air filters for the compartment and turned them off. Then he turned off his masker.

And began to count.

At six, the data sheet quivered.

At nine, a rapidly changing line of symbols appeared.

By seventeen, the symbols filled the sheet. He tracked a horizontal line from top to bottom until it seemed to spill off the lower edge.

Fingers spread, he held out his left hand, not quite touching the surface. Two symbols directly under his fingertips rose out of the sheet to brush against his skin. They were warm. Human body temperature. Maybe even Krai.

"Warden di'Cikeys! This is ship security! We have regained control of the filters. Turn your masker on. Unlock the hatch and step into the passageway!"

The symbols sank back into the suddenly smooth sheet.

"Way to kill the mood," Alamber agreed.

· ——◆—— ·

It took Craig a moment to realize why the briefing room they'd been ordered into looked familiar. It was the same briefing room where he'd given the massed Marines and scientists the initial rundown on Big Yellow. Incidentally, it was also the briefing room where he'd met Torin for the first time.

"As Captain Travik's senior NCO, I thought you should know that I'll be heading inside with you on that first trip."

Brown eyes narrowed. "No, Mr. Ryder, you will not."

"Yes, Staff Sergeant, he will."

She slowly pivoted to face the general. "Sir?"

"It was one of the conditions Mr. Ryder imposed when he agreed to take us to the ship. And what I intended to speak with you about. As Mr. Ryder has beaten me to the punch, you two might as well carry on with your discussion." The general looked relieved. If Craig had to guess, he'd say Morris had been less than excited about broaching the topic to the staff sergeant. "Lieutenant . . ."

"Sir." The di'Taykan fell into step beside the general as he left the room. After a moment's hesitation, and a glance at the glowering Staff Sergeant Kerr, Captain Travik hurried to catch up.

Craig hit her with his best smile. "Alone at last."

He remembered that it'd had about as much effect as a fart in a thunderstorm, but there was nothing like the threat of imminent death inside a ship made of sentient plastic to overcome first impressions. Come to think of it, he owed Big Yellow one.

Ranked seating rose up toward the far bulkhead leaving no more than two meters of floor at the front, a piece of that negligible real estate already claimed by a podium. The bulkhead behind the podium had the familiar gloss of an inert screen. Except for the black line of scowling Marines across the top tier, the seats were empty. They didn't look any more badass than any other line of scowling Marines although Craig assumed General Morris was making a point about the firepower at his command. When their sergeant caught his gaze and held it for a long *I don't have to prove I'm dangerous, but let's make sure you know anyway* moment, Craig gave her a *fuk you, I made the first micro jump, followed a Primacy cruiser through Susumi space, and I sleep with Torin Kerr* look right back. Bona fides established, they returned to ignoring each other.

While the Mu'tuv had been invited to this party, the rest of his team hadn't. He'd been told only that Alamber had been taken into custody by *Berganitan* security and he was to attend a debriefing immediately. The team had followed him. For all that battleships had been designed to confuse boarding parties, the *Berganitan* had nothing on the labyrinth of passageways and compartments that made up Salvage Stations and they'd arrived sooner than expected. Captain Carveg had given him a nod of recognition and returned her attention to General

Morris and a critique of her security at a volume meant to be over-heard. To top off his asshole behavior, the general stood close enough that their relative heights forced her to either back away, or look up. His aide, a Krai lieutenant, looked embarrassed, nostril ridges open-ing and closing. Could be because there were very few female Krai in the Corps and the general's lack of common courtesy made his aide look bad in front of a high-ranking female, or it could be because he was a decent sentient being. Either way, Craig doubted he was going to last long in the position.

Alamber, the ends of his hair flicking back and forth in agitation, glanced up at the green-haired di'Taykan at his side when the team entered. She was a Warrant Officer, Craig neither knew nor cared about the levels within the rank, and also wore a star over—where over meant pretty much obliterating—crossed anchors.

Chief Warrant Officer di'Palik, Master at Arms, Elisk told him. Their implant signal ran through the *Promise* not the *Berganitan.* Alamber's firewalls should have kept the Navy out, but from the way the Human officer standing behind the captain twitched, he knew something was up. *The Human behind Captain Carveg is Com-mander Kahananui, the ship's security officer.*

When di'Palik nodded, Alamber walked defiantly to Craig's side and pressed against him from shoulder to hip.

"You okay?" Craig gave him a visual once-over for injuries, but he seemed fine.

"Yeah." His hair began to pick up speed. "They capped my implant, or I'd have pinged you."

"Are they . . ."

"Yeah, they're allowed. I'm a security risk."

"That's your job description," Werst growled from Alamber's other side.

As neither the *Berganitan*'s security officer nor master at arms in-dicated the team should leave, they stayed. Elisk and Tylen had both been Navy and they kept at least part of their attention on the MAA. Werst, Zhou, and Yahsamus didn't seem to care about the thirteen Marines at the rear of the room, so neither did Craig.

"What have they got you on?" he asked, well aware they could have grabbed him for any number of minor infractions.

"The data sheet is on the ship."

That caught General Morris' attention. He whirled around and glared at Alamber. "What part of top secret do you not understand, di'Cikeys?"

Alamber's hair flattened tight to his head, looking like a pale blue cap. "Warden di'Cikeys," he snapped. "And what part of full disclosure are *you* missing, General?"

The general jabbed a beefy finger toward him and jerked it back when Werst snapped his teeth together. "This is a military . . ."

"Confederation Statute three zero six, PYRI: the military will operate at all times under full disclosure. The media and representatives from all legislative bodies will have complete access." That was bullshit and Alamber knew it, no matter how confidently he spat it out. Alpha Team, before it was officially Alpha Team, had helped the military out with a covert operation. The general hadn't known about it, but that was the whole point of it being covert, Craig acknowledged silently. So those who didn't need to know, wouldn't.

"Why is the data sheet on the *Berganitan*?" Craig asked before the general could respond. "And I'm asking as a representative of the Justice Department."

"Parliament has agreed to return it to the plastic," Captain Carveg answered. Behind the captain, Chief Warrant Officer di'Palik sighed and closed her eyes for a moment.

For that moment, Craig missed Torin with an intensity that physically hurt. He felt as though someone had scooped out his guts and left nothing but raw edges behind. Then the moment passed. The warrant opened her eyes, and Craig gave the captain his best poker table grin, "You'd think that would have made the news."

"You'd think," she agreed. "It was apparently decided in committee . . ."

"Secret committee?"

"One assumes. Parliament as a whole continues to believe it was put into storage until a later date."

General Morris stepped physically between them. "You don't know that."

"I do," Captain Carveg told him, the pleasant conversational tone she'd been using with Craig gone from her voice. "I have as many contacts in Parliament as you do, General. The big difference is, most of mine are still speaking to me."

Someone behind him muffled a snicker—Tylen most likely.

The general pivoted back around. "I should've known you lot wouldn't take this seriously."

Craig smiled. The MAA shifted her weight. "Oh, we're taking it very seriously. We're opening an immediate investigation."

"Good!" General Morris glared at Alamber. "Overriding security! Breaking and entering! Initiating sexual contact with a sheet of plastic!"

Definitely Tylen that time. The grunt following the less muffled snicker had likely been Elisk shutting her up.

"You misunderstand, mate. We're investigating what's either a sentient being . . ."

"Group of beings," Alamber corrected.

"Right. What's either a group of sentient beings, being held captive . . ."

"It's not being held captive."

"They!"

"Fine. *They're* not being held captive."

"So they can leave the room if they want to?"

"It's a sheet of plastic!"

"And I think it's been established that some plastic is sentient."

"Fine. If it's sentient, it's an enemy."

"They were abandoned in an underground bunker during the war," Craig pointed out. "They're not our enemy unless we make them our enemy."

"By taking a bite out of them," Alamber growled.

"Talk to your reporter friend about that!" General Morris drew himself up to his full height and folded his arms across his chest. "And if you want to talk about full disclosure, let's talk about how she sprang that on everyone, including Warden Ryder."

"He's right," Craig acknowledged.

"Presit doesn't work for the government; full disclosure doesn't apply." Alamber leaned toward the general. "And now you've taken a potentially powerful group of aliens and locked them away again."

"Locked them away again," General Morris repeated. His eyes widened in triumph. "What if they were locked away by their own people? What if they're criminal plastic?"

"Justice Department." Werst waved at him. "Criminals are our business, not the military's."

"Or?" Captain Carveg asked, her voice commanding the room. "You said either, Warden di'Cikeys. *Either a group of sentient beings, being held captive.* I assume there's an or to follow?"

"If the data sheet isn't sentient, then we're investigating a priceless artifact being smuggled out of the Confederation by the military under a complete media blackout in direct opposition to the full disclosure laws, and . . ." Alamber closed his hand around Craig's wrist. "It reacted to my pheromones."

The hum of the Susumi engines sounded unnaturally loud in the sudden silence.

Then the hair of every di'Taykan in the room lifted out from their heads, Alamber's a half a heartbeat behind, responding to their response.

"And it looks like the priceless artifact investigation is off the table," Craig announced. "If that's what he meant by initiating sexual contact with a sheet of plastic?"

"Which isn't a crime," Alamber pointed out.

"Didn't say it was." Craig touched two fingers to the inside of Alamber's wrist, then turned back to the watching officers. "You knew the data sheet reacted. You knew that meant they're sentient."

"I know nothing of the sort," the general began.

Captain Carveg cut him off. "We saw what happened on the security recording, but we have no idea if what we saw was Warden di'Cikeys tripping a program or an actual response."

"It rose to touch my fingers." Alamber held out his hand, fingers spread, obviously reenacting his part of their meeting. "It was responding when your lot showed up."

The captain's nostril ridges closed slightly. "My lot?"

Alamber's hair dipped in toward his jaw. "Your security. Ma'am."

"Warrant?"

The MAA's blue eyes darkened as more light receptors opened. "If it . . . they were responding, he'd know, Captain."

"We need to investigate this!"

Craig wasn't sure who General Morris was shouting at, but Captain Carveg looked like she was just about finished with his shit.

"We were ordered to leave it alone," she said flatly.

"And look how well that worked out." The general spread his arms wide. "We have new information. We need to throw every di'Taykan on board at that thing while we have the chance, while we're still in Susumi. Sergeant!"

"Sir!"

Boots hit the deck in a fast one/two as the Mu'tuv sergeant stood.

"General Morris, I'm about to resolve the argument we were having earlier." Captain Carveg drew herself up to her full height of a meter nothing and looked impressively taller. "This is my ship, General. On my ship, my orders take precedence. Back in your seat, Sergeant. We won't need you."

"Ma'am." The sergeant sat.

Werst turned an exhale into smug approval. Craig started breathing again.

"We can request new orders when we leave Susumi," the captain continued. "Until then, if you would, Commander."

"Warden di'Cikeys." Commander Kahananui wasn't particularly tall, but he was solidly built, powerful looking. Craig doubted he could beat him in a fight. On the other hand, that was Werst's job and, like Torin, he'd never given a shit about size.

Alamber stepped forward, looked down at Craig's hand on his arm, then up at Craig. "Hey, guilty as charged. I took out their security and, technically, I broke and entered."

"Technically?"

"Nothing's broken."

Craig shook his head. "We're investigating . . ."

"We weren't then," Alamber reminded him.

"At least something's being done right," the general muttered. "Have you recorded this, Lieutenant Jonnez?"

His aide jerked, startled at being addressed. "Sir. As previously agreed with Captain Carveg and Commander Kahananui."

"Excellent." General Morris' smile was all politics. "The Minister of Defense will be reviewing this."

The captain ignored him. "Commander Kahananui, secure Warden di'Cikeys, find out how he gamed our system, and have him help fix the weak points so no one can do it again."

"Yes, ma'am."

"Then release him back into Warden Ryder's supervision. Try to supervise him, Warden Ryder."

"I'll do my best, ma'am. But . . ." He spread his hands as she fought a smile.

"Indeed. But. Keep him busy, at least."

"Ma'am."

Together, they watched the commander escort Alamber from the room, two of the MAA's ratings falling in behind them once they reached the corridor. When Alamber began talking, the commander cut him off. "What part of secure do you not understand, Warden?"

As they disappeared, Captain Carveg sighed. "What is it, General?"

The general's cheeks had flushed. "You can't just release him."

"I'm not just releasing him. I'm using him first."

"He interacted with the plastic!"

"He had no orders to stay away."

"He didn't know it was here!"

"Until he did."

"You can't do this."

"I think you'll find that on *my* ship, I can."

General Morris stared down at her for a long moment, cheeks darkening, then pivoted on one heel and stomped out. Lieutenant Jonnez dropped his gaze to the floor and followed, shoulders tightening when Elisk murmured a few words in Krai as he passed.

"Master at Arms."

"Captain."

"Find out how Warden di'Cikeys knew the data sheet was on board."

"Working on it, Captain."

"Warden Ryder."

He took a step back to lower the angle. "Ma'am."

"I want full disclosure on any investigation of the Justice Department that happens on my ship."

"Yes, ma'am."

She smiled. "And congratulations on expanding the Justice Department's view of the universe. It's good to see you again."

"And you, Captain."

Chief Warrant Officer di'Palik gave him a not entirely friendly nod as she followed Captain Carveg out of the briefing room.

Craig turned to Werst, realized Werst was focused on something behind him, and remembered there were still thirteen Marines in the room. The sergeant had reached the bottom of the stairs when he turned, the others in a line behind her. He hadn't heard them move.

"That was entertaining," she said, smiling broadly as the squad moved silently past and out of the room. "Wish I'd had snacks."

Fuk it. Craig went right to the point. "Sergeant. Why are you here?"

Dark brows rose. "That's classified, Warden."

"Full disclosure, Sergeant."

"I'll bring that up with my CO. Word of advice, stay out of the Marine packets. The general's orders take precedence there. Werst."

"Britt."

"Threat?" Tylen asked when they were alone.

"Warning," Werst told her. "Marines don't make threats. We make statements of fact."

"Oh, fuk off . . ." She led the way out of the briefing room, the team following behind.

"Now what?" Elisk asked, falling into step on Werst's other side.

"We investigate," Craig told him.

"What do we investigate? Precisely?"

"Let's start by establishing the data sheet's response to the di'Taykan and see if we can use that to confirm sentience."

Werst snorted. "Establishing the data sheet's response? We're making shit up as we go, aren't we?"

"We're writing the playbook for seducing a sheet of plastic."

"Yeah. That's what I said."

They had to wait for Alamber to be returned to them before they could begin the investigation. Commander Kahananui's people refused to release the codes for a high-security compartment, and the commander himself was busy.

"He's busy resetting the locks with one of our Wardens," Craig snapped.

"Then you'll be able to access the compartment when your Warden returns."

"Navy," Werst grunted, as Craig cut the connection.

"You're up their tree," Elisk reminded them. "They won't push you out, but they'll laugh if you fall."

Yahsamus stood by the big wall screen on the bulkhead of their packet's common room, flipping through the entertainment options. "And if you ask, LT?"

He spread his hands. "I'm a Warden now. Ex-Navy. Me, they'd probably push."

"They wanted me to tell them how I found out about the plastic— I lied, by the way—and we fixed a few exploitable pinholes in their security system." Alamber's hair lifted as Tylen ran her hands over his body. "My punishment involved explaining things to stupid people and a really bad pouch of coffee. No one beat me with a blunt object."

"Still checking," she muttered.

"Not complaining, just pointing out you're not going to find anything . . ." His hips jerked forward. ". . . but that." He twisted his upper body around to face Craig. "Were we going to investigate the data sheet now?"

"Yes. We are. But only because we couldn't start sooner." Craig tossed his coffee pouch in the recycler and stood. "We need to gather as much info as we can while we're still in Susumi—before Captain Carveg gets new orders that include us and the amount of contact we're allowed."

"End game?" Yahsamus asked, catching Tylen's hands and moving her bodily away from Alamber.

"Status of the data sheet. Better understanding of the plastic." Craig shrugged. "A conversation starter with Big Yellow."

Yahsamus' eyes lightened. "I got the feeling Torin was going to open with *what the fuk do you want*? And see where it went."

"Yeah, well . . ." Craig rubbed the back of his hand against his beard. "Torin's not here."

· —◆— ·

Move in closer.

Fingertips still in contact with the reaching plastic, Alamber stepped in until his toes tucked under the bottom of the sheet and his entire body was no more than three centimeters away. A deep enough breath and the clothing over his chest would brush the sheet.

Looks like the symbols are piling up opposite your body.

Alamber glanced down. "That's because the symbols are piling up opposite my body."

He opened his light receptors until his peripheral vision expanded enough to watch the entire sheet. The symbols sped in, rising and falling like waves, creating a three-dimensional, orange shadow of his body. There were no features, but the image of his hair moved with his hair. When he flexed his right hand, the image of his fingers flexed. When he raised his right arm to mirror his left, two points of plastic protruded until they touched his first two fingers. The rest of the sheet remained completely smooth.

What if they get into his brain?

On their way into his pants?

That's where he keeps his brain.

Cut the chatter, people.

Alamber smiled and missed Torin.

Alamber, with the first finger of your right hand, write hello *on the sheet.*

The word rose up under his finger, then fell again.

"Didn't the plastic the Boss talked to speak Federate?" he asked, writing *hello* again with the same result.

They'd been in brains. This one's been in a hole on Threxie. Write your name and draw an arrow pointing to its image of you.

He couldn't stop himself from rocking forward as he wrote.

As he finished the arrow, the plastic rocked out to meet him.

Energy spike!

Alamber!

White light filled the room. Eyes streaming tears, receptors snapped closed, Alamber sagged forward, felt a firm touch . . .

When his knees buckled, the plastic held him up.

Alamber!

Ryder you can't go in there! He's had his masker off. We're filtering the air as fast as we can!

Alamber!

Calm down, Ryder, I know these readings. He's fine.

Alamber rubbed his cheek against a smooth curve. "Very fine."

The data sheet had the exact same reaction to the other two di'Taykan. Expanding their variables, they pulled in a Naval volunteer and would have pulled in a Marine di'Taykan as well, but General Morris had refused to allow it.

"Now he's being petty . . ."

Humans and Krai could rub against the plastic all they wanted. Without the pheromones, nothing happened.

"So is it intelligent, or is it a sex toy?" Captain Carveg asked.

"An alien sex toy only responsive to di'Taykan?"

"Why not?" Her nostril ridges closed halfway, an instinctive response to a conversation about Taykan pheromones. "Everyone else is."

That was fair, Craig acknowledged. "It looks like a data sheet."

"To us." She pressed her thumb against her slate, swept the file off the screen. "It also looks like a big yellow spaceship. I'm going to tell you what my *jernine* told me when I left the tree. It takes all kinds, and most of them are edible. Now, you tell me if it's intelligent."

Craig shook his head, wishing he had a different answer. "We don't know yet."

"What would happen if we pheromone bomb Big Yellow?"

His brows rose. "There's a way to do that?" There hadn't been during the war, not without risking Confederation troops being caught in the effect.

"Damned if I know, but maybe we should start finding new ways to do things." Another thumbprint, another swipe, then the captain focused her entire attention on him. "So you have a lot of data and no conclusions."

"Not yet."

Her nostril ridges spread. "There'll be a Susumi packet heading back to command as soon as we jump out. And a few billion plastic aliens shaped like a big yellow spaceship. And a general who'd be perfectly happy to start another war if it kept him relevant." Her gaze turned inward, and Craig knew she was accessing memories of blood and battle. He knew that expression. After a moment, she blinked and said, "I've had enough of war. Keep working on it."

·——◆——·

The station orbiting Silsviss was one of thousands scattered across Confederation space, a government observation platform around each Confederation world. Theoretically, there was one identical to it tucked into the core of the government station orbiting Paradise, although the odds were higher it was more the idea of the original station rather than the actuality—Torin couldn't keep her entertainment unit working for more than five years and the station had been there for centuries.

The Elder Races saw no point in messing with a system that worked. Every government station used the same initial footprint, changes forbidden until a planetary government was securely in place.

While uniformity of design would make her job easier, when it came down to it, the Elder Races weren't very innovative.

Or at all innovative.

How different was the tech she used from the tech the Younger Races had been promised to get them into the fight? Her area of expertise was limited, but the advances she knew of had been made when Human or Taykan or Krai adapted the Confederation standard to their specific needs. Had the Confederation not been forced to seek them out, would they have discovered the Confederation on their own by now? Given those extra centuries of isolated development, what would they have brought with them? Confined to their planets by Parliamentary decree, what might they create?

Besides the kind of weapons historical records referred to as self-inflicted extinction events.

Any hope they might have learned enough to avoid blowing themselves to hell and gone vanished during even a cursory examination of Humans First. Who might have a small point about the Confederation holding Humans back.

Torin set that aside to think about later. Later, when she wasn't about to go into battle with a race of warrior lizards. Or one warrior lizard. Or . . . "Bilodeau, do we have any idea of how many of them are in there yet?"

"Still scanning, Gunny. The Navy removes a lot of proprietary software when they decommission, and this is the first time I've used the rebuilt system." Marie tapped a repetitive pattern against the board with her right hand while sweeping a continuous run of data boxes into memory with her left. "Ressk tweaked the long-range scanners in Susumi . . ."

Torin glanced back at Ressk, who shrugged.

". . . but some things don't fully compile until they actually run." A section of the board flashed. "Still only one shuttle on a nipple, but no way of knowing how many trips he's made to bring up reinforcements."

"I've picked up a message from Justice off the Susumi buoy,

Gunny." Lorkin spun his chair away from the communications console. "Cyr Tyroliz has demanded Susumi tech for the hostages. A ship, plus complete engineering and training programs."

"So much for the reports of him slaughtering everyone on the station." Torin folded her arms and locked her knees to keep herself from leaning over the pilot's chair. "Any word on how many hostages he has?"

"That's all the words they sent, Gunny."

"Hostages," Binti muttered. "I hate having to shoot around hostages."

"They get cranky if you shoot through them," Nicholin agreed.

"At least we know one of the comm techs is alive. The Susumi packet," Lorkin explained when all eyes but Marie's turned to him. "Cyr Tyroliz's demands weren't sent via the panic button, and a Silsviss wouldn't be able to figure out packet protocols by trial and error."

Nicholin waved that off. "They flew one of our VTAs."

"They have their own VTAs," Marie pointed out, "and ours are point and steer. Once you know the principles involved, they're not that hard."

"Cyr Tyroliz could have used the Confederation pilot," Torin noted.

"Take us to the station, or I rip you to pieces is pretty damned convincing." Binti bounced a small red ball off the bulkhead, caught it, and bounced it again. "And—oh, joy—one more potential hostage." Bounced and again. The three members of U'yun didn't seem to notice. "It was in the seat pocket," she said in response to Torin's raised brow.

"Belongs to the LT," Nicholin explained. "He says it helps him think."

"All right, then. Bilodeau?"

"I have forty-two life signs, Gunny. Sorting by body temperatures."

The stations had a crew of thirty-six, four shifts of nine. If there were no dead, that meant only six Silsviss on board. Torin doubted the station had been taken without loss of life. Eleven of the thirty-six had been former military, unlikely to react well to an unexpected boarding party.

"Thirty-two have been identified within temperature parameters of Human, di'Taykan, and Krai. A single Human in communications.

Two Krai in engineering. All others confined to quarters. Estimating ten Silsviss on station, four in central, two in engineering, the other four in various places around the outer hull."

"Inside the station?"

"Inside of the outer hull, yes."

Estimating ten Silsviss on station. Because no one who'd ever taken a station back from the Primacy forgot there could be one or two enemy unaccounted for, tucked away where the scan couldn't read. Assuming definitive numbers had a way of ending badly. Torin hoped the four missing crew had merely gone dirtside during their off-shift. She wasn't planing to bet on it, however.

"We going to fight, Gunny?"

"Probably." She remembered the valley and the Silsviss using their own weapons against them. She remembered the bodies, and her hand rose to the empty pockets in her vest. "Silsviss leaders are smart and ruthless, but it depends on how far into warlord headspace Cyr Tyroliz has fallen. Too far, and we'll have to fight just to prove we're worth listening to."

They watched the station grow larger on the screen, the only sound the ponk, ponk of the little red ball hitting the same spot on the bulkhead, over and over.

Finally, Ressk stretched out a leg and caught it with his foot. "Enough."

Before Binti could protest—and everyone in the control room knew she was going to protest—Marie cut her off. "We're in range, Gunny. Station's docking computer is off-line."

"Can you dock without it?" Craig could. He could match speed and rotation and secure to the airlock like he'd done nothing more complex than park the tractor in the machine shed.

Marie tossed her head and smiled, broad and bright. "If I had to, I could dock with three maneuvering jets and a visual link to an HE suit propped up in the open airlock."

"Good to hear." Torin straightened and opened the top file on her slate. "What's the pot up to?"

"Nine tendays pay," Nicholin told her. "Cap made sure U'yun bought in."

"All right, then. And who knows, this might be the time it pays out. Lorkin."

"Channel's open, Gunny. Translation programming engaged."

"Cyr Tyroliz, this is Warden Torin Kerr. You have been charged with the illegal occupation of Confederation property and the illegal confinement of Confederation citizens. Once we determine the number, you will also be charged with the murder of Confederation citizens. If you surrender yourself and your associates, you will receive a fair hearing. Please respond."

Binti frowned as Lorkin closed the channel. "That's a little less . . . emphatic, than usual, Gunny."

Torin showed her the screen of her slate. "Commander Ng wrote it."

"Okay, two points. The first, as far as the commander knew, everyone on board was dead. What's up with the illegal confinement charge?"

"If the Silsviss had slaughtered everyone, they'd expect the Navy to show up and blow them out of the sky. The commander assumed death by battleship wasn't part of their plan. Therefore, everyone on the station couldn't be dead."

"Okay," Binti allowed. "Second point. This seems to indicate he doubts your diplomatic ability."

Ressk snorted. "She has a Silsviss skull on her . . ."

The control panel blazed white, then went blank.

"Shot took out our sensor array." Blinking away afterimages, Marie thumped the edge of the panel. Shook her head. "I guess no one's collecting on the is-this-the-time-they-surrender bet. Switching to backup."

"Shot?" Nicholin's umber hair flipped around his head. "The stations are unarmed!"

"Were unarmed," Torin amended. "Aren't now. Find the weapon."

"Weapons," Lorkin told her. "Four of them."

"Wonderful." Torin studied the schematic of the station and the points of light representing the Silsviss. "The four Silsviss near the hull."

"New energy readings at all four points," Marie agreed. "Not our weapons, not Primacy weapons."

"The Silsviss had orbital weapon platforms when they were contacted," Ressk reminded them. "According to the initial contact treaty, they were to be disassembled."

Internal dampeners compensated as Marie avoided another shot, but Torin could feel the artificial gravity pulling her left. "Looks like they put them aside for a rainy day. Points to the Silsviss for thinking ahead."

Binti slid into the seat behind the weapons board. "Can we shoot back?"

After having been convinced the Strike Teams might need to face the occasional pirate in transit rather than risk losing them during the pursuit to their base, Justice had reinstalled the four weapons mounts that had been removed from the sweepers. Justice, being Justice, had improved the EMP, capped the charge on the pulse weapons, and allowed the missiles to be racked unchanged. Each ship had four. One per mount.

"You're not going to war," Commander Ng had told the teams. *"Try to remember that."*

Tell the Silsviss, Torin thought as a sudden drop—relative to what the ship considered up—lifted her heels off the floor. "The station's shielded against the EMP, and if we hole it, we put the hostages at risk."

"If we take out their sensor arrays?" Binti asked.

"They don't have sensor arrays," Lorkin announced, updating the schematic. "Their weapons are self-contained. They just poked them through the hull."

"Just?" Nicolin demanded.

"Yeah, okay, station's still there, so it had to involve careful cutting wearing suits and shitload of sealant, but poked through pretty much sums it up."

Torin studied the schematic, turned it on its Y-axis, and worked the angles between weapons. "Cyr Tyroliz knows what he's doing. We'd take too much damage if we tried to destroy them." The *Baylet* arced hard to port as another blast came close enough to polarize the window. "Bilodeau, get far enough out they stop shooting at us."

"This was a lot easier when we didn't have to announce our presence," Marie grumbled.

"You come in on this arc here, we jump here, we hit the maintenance hatch here." Torin pulled the computer's calculations into the hard light table, highlighting both the vectors and the target. "Wardens in HE suits are too small to ping the proximity alarm."

"You've done this before?" Marie demanded in a voice that made it clear she'd gone through OTC.

"Alpha does this all the time." Binti scoffed. When the three members of U'yun shot her identical expressions of disbelief, she shrugged. "Well, once as a Strike Team."

"While your ship was taking fire?"

"It's a standard maneuver when recon has to make a dark access to a station," Torin told her.

"Standard." Marie looked around at the gathered Marines. "You people are crazy."

ELEVEN

MOST OF THEIR TIME in Susumi space had been spent training. Craig had thought it was just Torin, but no, seemed all the team leaders toed her *we're better than the bad guys because we practice* line. Turned out it was a military thing. Elisk, as a Krai, put the emphasis in different places—less running, more climbing—and while he stood by his belief that the assholes who spouted *change is as good as a break* like it was both original and meaningful were full of shit, Craig did more climbing and less running and almost enjoyed himself. Harris Zhou, the only other Human on the team, was almost as tall, half Craig's weight, and surprisingly strong. Part of that was the Paradise advantage, part wiry muscle, and their sparring matches usually had an audience. Craig hadn't been military and he'd never fired a shot at a sentient being, but he'd been living with Torin for years. He had a whole catalog of nonlethal dirty tricks and wasn't averse to using them.

With Alamber busy trying to find out just what the fuk Morris was up to, Craig and Technical Sergeant di'Ahaski went over the *Promise*, tightening both screws and code. Because Yahsamus had never spent time with any of the CSOs she'd run into over the years, he found himself talking about his past. Missing the family who, when push came to shove, had been unwilling to put their balls on the line.

"You just cut them off? Sounds like you've got some unfinished business there." When Craig glanced over at her, her green eyes darkened. "Gunny's got as much *hurin* tied up in it as you do. Emotion and honor scrambled together," she translated the unfamiliar word. "They betray you, they betray her. If you'd died, she'd have taken them out. Me, I'm an unbiased opinion and I think you should talk to them."

They played a lot of cards. Off-duty members of the *Berganitan* crew were encouraged to drop by. Unlike Torin, who relied on force of personality, Craig believed mates, however superficial the connection, were potential allies, and a man on his own couldn't have too many of those. He put out word that the Mu'tuv were welcome although they hadn't shown.

All three di'Taykan reported that pillow talk in the communal beds involved speculation on Morris' plans, but nothing solid. Hardly surprising since the four Mu'tuv di'Taykan remained in the Marine packet. The weapon Morris had mentioned to Torin had to be on the *Berganitan*, if only because the Mu'tuv's shuttle was in the *Berganitan*'s largest bay. The di'Taykan among the docking crews were either avoiding physical contact with the Wardens—battleships had multiple communal beds—or keeping quiet. The docking bay itself had been declared off limits to the Justice Department.

Commander Kahananui folded his arms, muscles straining against the fabric. "You're not going in unless you can give me a good reason, Warden Ryder."

Craig mirrored the movement. And most of the muscle. "I need to know what armaments an elite commando unit brings to the party in case this goes to shit. You and I both know the odds of that happening. And they're high."

The commander sighed, but stuck to the official line. "The Justice Department has no oversight on a military operation."

"You asked for our help."

"As I understand it, the general asked for your personal help because of your previous contact with the plastic. Yours as well as Wardens Werst and Kerr."

"I'm personally curious."

"No."

Alamber hadn't yet gotten into the docking bay's security cameras.

"Would've helped if I'd have known you wanted in before Commander Kahananui watched me seal the system shut," he muttered, slaving his slate to *Promise*'s board.

Morris had brought an elite commando unit as backup. No way he'd have them sit around with their thumbs up their collective asses. Sooner or later, he'd turn them loose.

Sucker bet that Morris would open dialogue with Big Yellow by declaring, *"We have something of yours."* Sounded like a threat to Craig. Odds were low the next words out of his mouth would be, *"And we brought it back to you."*

"We have someone *of yours"* would create an entirely different situation. The general would be holding a sentient species hostage and the Strike Teams knew how to deal with that kind of crap. Craig almost wanted to see the differences between Elisk and Torin's approach.

During their entire time in Susumi, a Warden had been in the compartment with the plastic.

Nothing had changed. The di'Taykan had continued to evoke a reaction, but a chemical reaction on its own was no more a sign of sentience than cell division.

In eighty-nine minutes, they'd be leaving Susumi space and the packet containing the new information about the data sheet would be on its way—a copy to the Minister of Defense, a copy to the Minister of Justice. The Wardens hadn't been included in Captain Carveg's old orders, but Craig was certain they'd be mentioned in the new ones. They still had no idea what Morris' plans entailed, how he planned to deploy the Mu'tuv, where and what was the weapon he mentioned to Torin. They still had no proof the data sheet was a prisoner and not a tool.

Hard not to think that Torin would've had more success at getting to the heart of things.

Craig paused at the hatch leading into the data sheet's compartment and nodded at two of the MAA's people standing guard—as much over the Wardens as the plastic. While allowing that the Wardens weren't specifically covered under her orders, the data sheet was, and Captain Carveg had bent as far as she was going to.

"Going in, Warden?" asked the Krai.

Beside her, the Human shifted his weight from foot to foot. "How's the interrogation proceeding?"

Craig ignored the subtextual sniggering. As far as the security team was concerned, the Wardens had either been attempting to seduce a reaction out of a piece of alien tech, or they were trying to seduce a reaction out of the aliens responsible for a centuries-long war. The first made them a joke. The second, the next thing to traitors. Individual members of the military, Torin had explained, might carry individual opinions, but the military as a whole was as much a hive mind as the plastic. It needed an enemy to function, and now that the enemy was no longer the Primacy . . .

"Fuk it." He thumbed the newly installed biometric pad, and entered the compartment.

Krai classical music played softly in the background. Krai composers built arrangements on top of arrangements, some taking more than a tenday to play, and the team had agreed that it was the best choice to help alleviate the plastic's isolation were it sentient and would do no harm were it not. Werst had declared the music a class conspiracy to bore the poor data sheet into numb complacency.

There'd been no visible reaction to the music.

"Numb complacency," Werst had growled.

Craig stepped close and traced his name on the smooth surface with a fingertip. Drew an arrow to where the raised image of his body would be were he Taykan. Did it again. And again. And again.

His gut told him there was something there.

"You can take the CSO out of the salvage biz, but seems you can't convince him the debris field's empty." He frowned. "Yeah. Forget I said that." When he exhaled, his breath misted against the glossy surface of the plastic. "Fuk, it's not like I don't know you're dangerous. I was there. On the dais."

Stepping back, he ran a hand through his hair. "If you released energy, there had to be energy to release. You don't get to fuk around with basic physics. We couldn't measure it. That doesn't mean it wasn't there. We don't know how to reach you. That doesn't mean you're not there. Yeah, fine. The di'Taykan can reach you, but . . ."

Craig! Look up.

He hadn't realized Alamber kept an eye on the compartment, but it didn't surprise him. The sudden yell from his implant, however . . . "Shit on a stick! Are you trying to kill me?"

Look at the top edge of the sheet!

Four symbols were centered along the upper edge. They disappeared. Reappeared two centimeters down. Disappeared.

Reappeared another two centimeters down and picking up speed given the visual effect of tumbling down the middle of the sheet and falling off the bottom edge.

Two of those symbols are new.

Craig took another step back.

Ablin gon savit. Do you see . . .

"I see it."

His name, rising up as though he'd just traced it.

Then his image although he was a good meter and a half back.

Alamber's name.

Alamber's image.

Tylen's.

Yahsamus.

Werst.

Zhou's.

And then all six, about five centimeters high in a line across the center of the sheet.

"At the very least, it's programmable."

Toes flexing against the deck, Captain Carveg shot a skeptical glance at Yahsamus. "You think that's all it is, Tech?"

"I think we can't discount the possibility."

"I doubt we're discounting any possibility at this point."

"Captain Carveg, General Morris is approaching."

Approaching boot heels beat out an emphatic challenge under the warning.

The captain's nostril ridges closed, then opened again significantly slower. "Let him in, Petty Officer."

"Yes, ma'am."

Werst shifted over to stand by her, exchanged glares with the commander, and stayed put. Craig wondered if he could claim species imperative should he try and take Morris out. Probably not. Pity.

"I should have been informed immediately!" Morris' cheeks were red. Lieutenant Jonnez looked grateful to no longer be the general's only audience as he followed him over the lip of the hatch.

"You were."

Craig had to admit, he admired the captain's use of bland.

Morris' cheeks flushed darker. "You shouldn't have entered the compartment until I arrived."

"Warden Ryder was already in the compartment. We'd have attracted more attention waiting in the passageway." Captain Carveg showed teeth. "Also, my ship. My compartment. And it was your decision to keep the plastic on the *Berganitan*."

He swept an unreadable gaze over the line of bodies between him and the plastic. "We couldn't have secured it in the Marine packet, not if it went molecular."

"We have a brig," Elisk offered.

They could set up emergency containment, large enough for one Human, two Krai, or any number of di'Taykan—who didn't mind crowding—but it wouldn't hold the plastic. Craig saw no reason to mention any of that.

"You lot have done enough," Morris snarled.

"Not sure how I see that as a bad thing, mate." Slouched back against the wall, being the most Craig Ryder he could be in Torin's absence, Craig nodded toward the hanging plastic. "Doing enough, that is. We got them to respond."

Morris waved that off. "You got the sensors to engage and acknowledge your presence."

"No, they're alive."

"And you know that because of your affinity with the plastic?"

"It's why you wanted us here."

"You. And Kerr. Not the rest of them. And given your *affinity*, Warden Ryder, I'm sure you've noticed this thing doesn't behave like any other plastic we've encountered."

"We've encountered the plastic three times." Elisk tried to match Captain Carveg's bland and didn't quite make it, but it was a good attempt. "Would you judge an entire species on three meetings?"

"Three and a half," Craig corrected. "Way back when the shit hit the fan, a frame in the general's office responded to me."

The captain's nostril ridges closed as she shifted to face him. "And what happened to this frame, Warden Ryder?"

"No idea, ma'am. But the general was cleared."

"Of course I was cleared! This exhibits none of the similarities shown during the other three . . ."

"And a half," Zhou added. "Sir." He followed the honorific with a grunt as Yahsamus stepped back on his foot.

"It hasn't communicated," Morris insisted. "It doesn't change shape."

"They were abandoned in a dark hole for a millennium, completely unstimulated." Alamber's hair rose as he glared at the general. "That's torture."

"The plastic can keep a war going for centuries with no one being the wiser," Morris scoffed. "I should think they could leave a hole in the ground."

"Maybe they couldn't leave. Maybe the hole was a prison built to neutralize their abilities."

"There's been no energy reading from the site." The general's protest lacked conviction. He'd been on the dais. "And if your entirely unsupported theory is correct, do we want to release a prisoner? We have no idea of what it's done."

"The rest of the plastic started a war," Werst growled. "They could've objected."

Captain Carveg nodded thoughtfully. "So there's a chance this plastic is one of the good guys."

"Not one of the good guys, ma'am." Alamber patted the edge of the sheet. "They're a molecular hive mind. There's billions of them here. Billions of the good guys."

"Billions," the captain repeated. She reached out toward the plastic but stopped short of touching it. "Why don't they separate?"

"Since they haven't, I suspect they can't." The imprint of his fingers appeared and disappeared. "They were in that hole for a long time. If it was set up so to keep them from separating, from changing form, the ability could have atrophied."

"It's a theory," she allowed.

Craig had honestly never considered he'd feel sorry for any part of the plastic. Hobbled, then locked for centuries below the surface— that was treatment he could have some sympathy for.

Alamber swept a fingertip the length of his slate. "We need to continue stimulating it."

"I think you've provided quite enough stimulation, Warden di'Cikeys," Morris growled.

Captain Carveg raised a hand before any of the di'Taykan in the room could respond, holding them quiet with force of personality. No wonder Torin liked her.

"We could take it around," Alamber suggested, ignoring both the general and the uncompleted innuendo. "We could show it things."

"And how do you suggest we contain it if it comes apart?" The captain waited until she was certain she had Alamber's full attention. "It can't leave this compartment. I'm not giving it free range of my ship and crew."

The flash of emotion on Kahananui's broad features couldn't have expressed gratitude more clearly if he'd shouted it out loud. He looked a little embarrassed when he realized Craig had noticed, then he shrugged.

"Okay." The movement of Alamber's hair suggested it wasn't okay. "There's a screen . . ." He spun in place then pointed to a slightly reflective surface on the bulkhead next to the hatch. "We'll keep information running on the screen so it keeps learning."

"Commander Kahananui will approve the content."

Craig found it hard to believe Captain Carveg, who'd fought in the war the plastic had maintained, had agreed with Alamber's suggestion. Seemed he wasn't the only one having his heartstrings played.

"You surely can't agree with this, Captain! Educating the enemy?"

And that was the expected reaction.

"I surely can, General. You want to negotiate with Big Yellow . . ." She waved a hand toward the sheet. It billowed in and out, reacting to the air currents. ". . . here's your intermediary. Locked away for the duration of the war, it has no *twuper* in the race. And it owes us one for freeing it," she added, as he opened his mouth.

"If you think it'll acknowledge that, Captain, you have your head in the treetops." His eyes narrowed and his chin lifted, his expression so self-satisfied Craig wanted to punt him out an airlock. "It doesn't matter. We've been out of Susumi for almost half an hour and my analysis of the situation was immediately sent to command. Any new orders will make it entirely clear who has the final say regarding the plastic and will keep the Wardens well away from it." Mouth curving, he added, "The commander of Marines has full access to the Susumi packet independent of the command structure of the vessel transporting those Marines."

Captain Carveg nodded in acknowledgment—Craig admired her self-control—then turned to Alamber. "Warden di'Cikeys."

His hair spread and he held up his slate. "We have a go on new information readiness."

She leaned back to meet his gaze, shook her head, and raised her voice, "Lieutenant di'Paliic."

"Captain."

"Warden di'Cikeys is about to send you a file that needs to go out in a Susumi packet to Command, ten minutes ago."

"Yes, ma'am."

"Warden, send the file."

"File is sent, Captain."

The smile she flashed at Morris showed teeth. "Now they can make an informed decision. Until they do, our previous orders stand."

"Captain, we've dropped eighty-seven percent of our Susumi velocity. Captain Khawaja of the CS Odyic sends his regards, the codes to his surveillance drones, and is heading for the jump buoy. Big Yellow is up on the screens."

"Understood. Commander, if you would."

Kahananui raised his slate, and the wall screen flicked white, flashed the *Berganitan*'s crest, and cleared to show a ship hanging in deep space. They'd traveled far enough from the core that the stars beyond it showed as scattered points of light against the black.

"Still big and yellow," Werst grunted beside him. "Still looks like the concept of a ship more than the reality."

Craig folded his arms and stared at the image. Big Yellow hadn't changed.

Had they?

"Not a lot of ambient light out here," Werst continued. *"Serley chrika* must be lit up like it's doing a mating dance."

"Look at me, look at me," Captain Carveg said quietly.

Morris blew out a breath. "Looks like it did the last time."

"Look at me, look at me again," the captain amended.

"Are you implying there's another of those . . ."

Craig didn't blame the general for falling silent. For all that Big Yellow had rearranged its interior to test both Confederation and Primacy rats running its maze—he shoved the memory of being sucked through the floor back into the mental box with his other near death experiences—the exterior had remained a unique, but recognizable ship. This was . . . new. They'd all seen the plastic disappear after announcing they were off to analyze data and the squints had calculated their actual speed by slowing Presit's recording, but there was fast and then there was *fast*. The former applied to a shifting pile of plastic the size of a Krai and the latter applied to something over twenty kilometers long and almost the size of an OutSector Station.

"Yeah, like that isn't creepy," Alamber muttered.

The giant head hanging in space was the gray of the vaguely bipedal plastic representative they'd spoken to on the prison planet, the features barely defined—depressed and slightly paler ovals for eyes, a slash across the lower third for a mouth. Craig couldn't remember if the original had a nose. Decided it didn't matter when the mouth opened.

"You have that which is ours."

Morris twitched invisible wrinkles out of his tunic and squared up with the image. "We'd like to open a dialogue with you."

"Return that which is ours."

"Lieutenant di'Paliic, send General Morris' message to the plastic."

"Uh . . . due respect, Captain, but sound doesn't travel in a vacuum."

"You're not shouting in its ear, Lieutenant. Hit it with every type of carrier wave we have. It's talking to us, I assume it wants a response."

"*They* want a response," Alamber muttered, arms folded.

Morris flushed, aware he'd tried to open a dialogue with a wall screen, but he held his position, and Craig reluctantly admitted the general had traits he might admire were he not such a murderous show pony.

"Dialogue is unnecessary. Give us what is OURS!" Its mouth opened and kept opening as it advanced toward the *Berganitan*. The image filled the screen, then suddenly snapped back to its original size.

Alamber's hand had closed around Craig's forearm, his grip on the edge of painful. Werst swore under his breath. Yahsamus had stepped in front of Elisk. Tylen and Zhou were pressed close enough together they could probably hear each other's heart pound.

Captain Carveg cleared her throat. "Did it move back to its original position, or did we compensate?"

"Compensated." Commander Kahananui checked his slate. "It's now one hundred and eighteen kilometers off our starboard bow, ma'am."

"Exactly as far apart as we were the first time."

"You remember the exact distance?" Morris asked, both brows up.

"It was a big yellow spaceship," Captain Carveg told him. "I found it memorable."

"Yeah, well, I'm wondering why it's trying to frighten us." When he found himself being observed by all eyes, Craig rolled his own eyes and folded his arms. "*StarCops*, season two finale, 'The Planet Eater.' No one?" Lieutenant Jonnez looked like he might know what Craig was talking about and that the last thing he wanted to do was draw attention to himself. Maybe *StarCops* wasn't officer level entertainment, but of the other six Wardens in the compartment, that only excused Elisk.

Zhou raised a hand. "I didn't start watching until season five."

"You only watch because Gunny loves the shitshow," Werst grumbled.

"Your point, Warden Ryder?" Captain Carveg sighed.

"That . . ." Craig waved at the screen. ". . . is a bad special effect it pulled from a popular vid because it thinks it'll frighten us. Why does it want us frightened?"

"It wants us reacting," the captain replied. "Not thinking."

"It wants us to hand over the data sheet without argument," Morris growled.

Tylen's hair had flattened against her head. "It kept us at war for centuries, why doesn't it just take it?"

"We fought. It didn't," Yahsamus reminded her. "But it sure as shit knows what we can do."

"It spent a few months in Gunny's head. It's got to be fukking terrified." Werst flushed a deeper green when the captain turned a flat stare in his direction. "Ma'am."

Morris' chest visibly rose and fell. Either he'd been as startled as everyone else in the room, or now they were talking fight, he was getting into it. "Parliament thinks if we hand over its lost property, the plastic will be our friend."

"Friends. Plural." Alamber's hair flattened at the general's glance and he raised both hands. "Maybe they're pissed because we keep calling them an it. Ever think of that?"

To Craig's surprise, Morris sighed. "There've been conflicts based on worse reasons. No one takes an *it* as seriously as a *they*. I appreciate you reminding us, Warden di'Cikeys."

Eyes light, Alamber looked as though he'd just found a salamander taking a swim in his beer. Even his hair moved as though it were confused. "You're welcome?"

"I had assumed," Morris continued, "that the balance of power between us didn't lend itself to friendship. It seems our relationship may be more equal than I thought. If they don't want to fight us, but do want their property back, that property must be very important to them. Why?"

"We don't know that the data sheet is property, General." Captain Carveg frowned up at him. "Sentient beings, regardless of their appearance, aren't property."

"I'm aware of that, Captain." He nodded toward the screen. "If I could send another message?"

"Be my guest."

"Polyhydroxide alcoholyde . . ."

Craig acknowledged that Morris couldn't refer to Big Yellow plastic, but wasn't using polyhydroxide alcoholyde like calling the members of the Confederation meat?

". . . we will consider your request."

"Now what?" he asked when that seemed to be all Morris had to say.

"Now, we wait."

· ——◆—— ·

Torin wouldn't have approved Marie Bilodeau's hiring if *competent* had been the only word used to describe her. Bilodeau had graduated third in her flight class, had come highly recommended by her last CO, and the words actually used to describe her—as a pilot—were bugfuk crazy. To be fair, those were the words Marines used to describe most vacuum jockeys, and VJs were the only group Torin had ever heard of that lacked the exceptions necessary to prove the rule.

Marie aimed the *Baylet* at the point where the five of them would fling themselves out an open airlock; speeds, vectors, and station rotation all worked out for that single point. If she hit it at the wrong speed or at the wrong time, the best result would involve picking the team up from a high Silsviss orbit and never being allowed to forget her screwup. The worst would be heading home alone and never being *able* to forget her screwup. The Silsviss were too good on the guns to risk multiple runs. As it was, the *Baylet* had already taken two hits on the approach, bucking hard enough both times the airlock would have emptied but for magnetic soles. Ignoring the impacts, Marie held her course as the targeting data on the cuff of Torin's HE suit counted down.

Standing at the edge of the airlock, toes of her boots out in the black, she watched the final numbers merge . . .

"Three. Two. Now!"

They pushed off with force enough to clear the radiation in the *Baylet*'s fantail—one beast with five heads, ten legs, and a single purpose. Arcing toward the maintenance hatch, they carefully separated, falling in toward a final target area a hundred meters in diameter. Fifty meters out, twelve meters away from Ressk on her left and Nicholin on her right, Torin hit her maneuvering jets long enough to drop her speed to survivable. One after another, the others did the same. If the Silsviss registered the energy bursts, there'd be a welcoming committee, but if they slammed into the station hard enough to break bone, they'd set off the impact alarms, the guaranteed welcoming committee would be made complicated by injuries, and that made decelerating worth the risk.

We're inside the angle of the guns, Ressk announced.

If you forget you're making a fast drop toward giant angry lizards, it's kind of peaceful, Lorkin observed.

Almost restful, Binti added. *We should do this more often.*

"Less chatter, people." Torin looked down between her boots, watched the station blot out the stars, noted a couple of rough patches the station crew needed to get on top of, saw the maintenance hatch roll past, and magged her soles.

Nicholin landed with his knees bent. His body continued moving until his ass hit the station.

"You okay?"

I'm good, Gunny. And more than willing to show you how very flexible I am.

Lorkin landed two hundred and twelve meters from the hatch, Ressk and Binti a meter to either side.

Thirty-seven centimeters! Too bad you're practically in the next system, Ressk.

I'm five centimeters farther out than you are!

Five, five thousand. Relatively speaking, you missed.

The *Baylet* danced with the Silsviss guns, holding their attention. Craig couldn't have done a better job.

Although Torin would have liked to have seen him try.

The passageways by the maintenance hatch were empty as expected. Moving quickly, HE suits sealed, helmets unpolarized, they opened only the interior hatches that kept them moving in a direct line toward control. If the majority of the Confederation hostages had been locked in their quarters as the heat pattern suggested, they were double-timing past people they'd come to free.

Eventually free.

The last thing they needed right now was civilians motivated to get into the fight.

Second last thing, Torin amended as a young Silsviss stepped through the hatch directly in front of them.

Lorkin pulled the trigger on his benny, the MDC hitting the exposed scales of the lizard's face above the pale green overalls. His inner eyelids flashed closed and he howled a challenge, clearly unaffected. "*Serley chrika!* Why don't bennies work on the fukkers?"

Two prongs attached to a fine wire hissed over Ressk's shoulder, smashed into the front curve of Lorkin's helmet, and shattered it in a flare of blue sparks. His back bowed. He dropped to the deck, convulsed, and stilled.

They'd all seen too much death to mistake it.

As a second set of prongs hit Ressk in the chest, Binti raised her KC and put a shot into each of the Silsviss' eyes, blood and brains exploding from the back of his skull.

"Are you insane, Mashona!" Nicholin snarled, dropping to his knees by Lorkin's body. "What if you'd holed the station?"

"Slowed by bone, a standard round won't make it to the next bulkhead." KC resting at her right hip, Binti pivoted in place, scanning the passageways. "Which is an internal bulkhead anyway. And I don't miss. It's why I'm the one carrying the KC."

"You couldn't know . . ."

"Yeah, I could. You have no idea how many Silsviss I practiced on." Rigid muscles, obvious even through the suit, contradicted her matter-of-fact tone. She took a deep breath and said, "Gunny?"

Kneeling by Ressk's shoulder, Torin took a deep breath of her own, the sound loud inside the helmet. "He's alive." Engaging his helmet's override, she cradled his head on her palm as the rigid sphere peeled back and flopped to the side.

The prongs on Ressk's chest remained connected to the weapon loosely cradled in the hand of the dead Silsviss. Torin brushed them to the deck, then as Ressk's nostril ridges began to flutter as he struggled for breath, she slid an arm behind his back and helped him sit. "The charge skipped over the surface." Like the Corps suits they were modeled on, the Justice Department HE suits protected the wearer against almost anything an unfriendly universe could throw against it—up to and including most personal projectile weapons. Unfortunately, as Torin's first close-combat instructor like to say, change was constant, and a new species meant new weapons creating entirely new parameters.

"*Most* of the charge stayed on the surface. The inside of my mouth tastes like *kreek*." Ressk rubbed his chest with a gloved hand and tucked his chin in so he could check the readouts along the suit's heavy collar. "My whole system's been reset to zero." He frowned, brushed a piece of shattered helmet off his leg, and twisted far enough around to stare at Lorkin's body. The other Krai's eyes were closed and blood covered most of his face. "*Ona cee kar*, Lorkin," he sighed, then frowned. "What're the odds that weapon would have the right charge to break through?"

"What're the odds the field holding Lorkin's helmet rigid had a minor flaw that prong just happened to hit?" On his knees by Lorkin's side, Nicholin shifted the Krai's collar so they could see the damage report. "The charge matched the flaw. Once through the helmet, the prongs drove into his nostril ridges and released the greater part of the charge into his body. Probably why his system didn't go down." Tossing the bloody prongs aside, he patted Lorkin's collar gently back into place, his umber hair flat against his head. "Fatal cascade of circumstances." He pounded his fist against the deck, once, twice, then sat back on his heels. "Fukker promised to make *nusur* for me."

"You'd have hated it," Ressk told him.

Nicholin's mouth twisted into something like a smile. "Yeah, probably."

Binti stepped close and pinged Torin's personal frequency. *Do we bag him now, Gunny? Or later?*

There'd have been no need to bag him if Lorkin hadn't fired, but blame wouldn't bring him back.

If the Silsviss had been older and more seasoned.

If the Silsviss had been younger and more likely to charge than shoot.

If Lorkin's helmet hadn't been flawed.

If Cyr Tyroliz hadn't taken the station.

If Parliament hadn't had its head so far up its collective ass about the Younger Races.

"We'll bag him later," Torin told the entire team, dropping her helmet. "When we've got the station back. We can't bag his suit and we haven't time to remove it." One hand pressed against the pouch where the cylinder would rest, Torin got to her feet and held out the other for Ressk. "Tuck him against the bulkhead, the Silsviss ignore the dead. Bring his weapon. They've used our own weapons against us before."

"That was true?" Nicholin asked, carefully sliding Lorkin's body into the angle between bulkhead and deck.

The well had contained most of the blast. One of the head-sized rocks had been flung into the mud brick of the western building, but the rest hadn't traveled far. Torin picked her way to the edge of the blast zone, retreating quickly when the ground shifted underfoot. "The good news, a foot in either direction and we'd have had casualties. The bad news, we won't be using that well again."

"That was one of our weapons."

"Yes, sir. It was. An emmy if I'm not mistaken."

Torin and Binti exchanged a speaking glance. "Yeah," Torin said. "That was true." She stepped over the Silsviss' body and turned back to Lorkin before she went through the hatch. "We'll be back," she told him. Then she deactivated her helmet, and swept a look that was pure gunnery sergeant around the team. "No one fires until I give the order. Is that understood?"

After a chorus of affirmatives, she indicated they should all release helmets. "The Silsviss aren't in suits. They want holes in the hull as little as we do."

They left a trail of bloody boot prints behind them.

"If the bennies have no effect, what do we do?" Nicholin asked quietly. "Mashona can't shoot all of them."

"Yeah, I can."

"The KC is a last resort," Torin reminded her.

"Like you said, Gunny, the Silsviss aren't in suits. If we hole the hull . . ."

"The whole place will seal shut. We risk injuring the hostages. We aren't at war, and the Silsviss aren't the enemy."

"Sure as fuk seem like the enemy to Lorkin," Ressk growled.

Binti shook her head. "The longer you two are together, the more you sound like Werst."

"If the Silsviss aren't the enemy," Nicholin ground out, "why are we here?"

"We're here because the Silsviss broke the law. Killing them is as much a final option as killing any other member of the Confederation."

"They killed Lorkin."

"And Mashona exercised her option." Torin had barely known Lorkin, but he'd been a Marine and a Warden and later, when they had drinks in their hands instead of weapons, his team would tell the stories that would keep his memory alive. Her grief would be laced with gratitude because losing Ressk as well, or instead, would have ripped a piece off her heart. Telling Werst would have shredded her soul.

"So what do we do?"

"What if we decided to play it their way?"

"Their way?" Cri Sawyes repeated.

"I challenge their leader, one on one. Winner takes all." Her heart began to beat harder, faster.

"Do you think you could beat a young male in hisss prime? One whossse only thought isss to win?"

"Yes."

"Gunny?"

"I'll think of something."

"You're not in the kind of shape you were back then." Binti raised a brow when Torin glanced over. "Yeah, I can read your mind. And you're older now."

"Cyr Tyroliz isn't just out of the egg." The protest was involuntary. She had no real intention of fighting.

"He was a Warlord."

"She was a Gunnery Sergeant," Ressk pointed out. Stopped. Threw himself at a scuffed metal plate set into the bulkhead. "Finally. An auxiliary access." He popped the cover and propped his slate on the protruding lip. "War's over, they should start putting these things closer to the airlocks."

"For your convenience?" Binti turned to secure the way they'd come.

"Why not?" He double-tapped his slate, the close-fitting HE gloves adding little bulk to his fingers. "I'm in."

Nicholin, in position a meter beyond the access, glanced back over his shoulder. "That was fast."

"After the first couple of stations they took out, the Primacy could get into these systems almost as fast. I said almost," Torin added as Ressk snorted. "That's what uniformity will do for you."

"Makes my job . . ." Ressk broke off. "This isn't good." He swiped his slate first left, then right. "Communication is out."

"What do you mean by out?"

"Out. Inaccessible. Gone. As far as the station sysop is concerned, interior communications don't exist. One of two things happened— the comm tech is alive and has been encouraged to wipe the system by Cyr Tyroliz, or he had one of his people physically destroy it. Same result either way—they can talk to each other, but everyone else has been cut off. Probably so the hostages can't communicate and there's no risk of anyone hacking in."

"A little excessive," Nicholin declared.

"The Silsviss go big or go home," Torin told him, remembering a couple of thousand Silsviss against a single platoon of Marines. "If we grab the comm link off the corpse, can you get into it?"

Ressk shrugged, the HE suit making the motion look more awkward than usual. "Maybe if we'd just left Silsviss, but I haven't seen their tech in years and they do some weird shit. Here and now, I'd likely blow myself up."

"We'll keep that option in reserve, then."

He flipped her off and ejected his slate.

"They're still in station control?"

"Except the gunners. And the corpse."

"Let's move." Cyr Tyroliz had no reason to waste one of his limited personnel on the security feeds. The hostages were locked in, with no way to communicate, and, as far as he knew, the Wardens were being held off by his guns. He didn't know they were in the station. On the other hand, the bennies and the gas were useless and they were unable to open negotiations with Cyr Tyroliz at a safe distance. Not a great situation, but, considering her previous interaction with the Silsviss, Torin wasn't overly concerned.

One of her people was dead.

One of the people she'd agreed to protect was dead.

She wasn't concerned. She was angry.

"So we're just going to walk up to station control?"

"Yes."

"And then Mashona starts shooting?"

"No." Torin ran through the variables. "Probably not."

The hatch to station control was open and unguarded. Five Silsviss stood by the communications board—the four that *Baylet*'s scanners had identified and the fifth most likely having arrived from engineering, given that no one once called Warlord would be imprudent enough to leave a weapon unattended.

Odds were high the dead Silsviss was the second heat signature the *Baylet* had registered in engineering.

Five to four.

"I feel almost sorry for them," Binti murmured.

Torin saw Binti's KC rise as she stepped over the hatch. Paused as Marie's voice rang out from the board.

"*. . . also in violation of Statute 2772 pertaining to unregulated use of station communications by unlicensed operators. These violations are separate charges not pertaining to the larger issue of attempting to destroy a Justice Department vessel.*"

"Why can't you shut her up!"

Torin could answer that. The Justice Department could not be cut off from a Confederation facility. In order to keep Marie from maintaining a running commentary, Cyr Tyroliz would have to destroy or erase external communications the way he had internal. He didn't need internal communications, but he needed to know what might be coming for him.

"Why haven't you destroyed that ship?"

"The gun mounts are irregular, Ret Tyroliz. The aim is substandard."

Could be a bad translation. Could be Silsviss gunners weren't as likely as Confederation gunners to declare, "Gun mounts are fukked, sir, and the aim is for shit."

"As mounting evidence suggests you couldn't hit us if we were standing still," Marie said, and even the Silsviss had to have been able to hear the smile in her voice, *"you might as well surrender. We're not leaving."*

Torin made a mental note to add a commendation to Bilodeau's file. Anyone who could annoy a Silsviss commander to the point where he'd lost his situational awareness, deserved to have that acknowledged. She'd talk to Paul Musselman. He could name a drink after her.

"How long until the other shuttles arrive?"

No surprise a Warlord could mobilize a sizable force; they were lucky it had taken time.

"Another twenty-seven hours, Ret Tyroliz. Our shuttles haven't flown since this station appeared."

His lips drew back off his teeth. "The Confederation desired us tethered."

What the Confederation desired and what the law supported were two different things. The youngest of the Younger Races needed to learn that. Right after they learned to get the fuk over themselves.

"Ret Tyroliz! I've got the scanners working!" The Silsviss sitting at the board, chair twisted sideways to accommodate his tail, glanced up at his leader, then back at the screens. "The Justice ship has weapons, but they haven't been armed."

"They refuse to return fire?" His throat pouch inflated, and he slapped the deck with the metal band around the end of his tail. "Mammals do not understand war!"

And Torin said, "We're not at war."

All five spun around to face her. Cyr Tyroliz roared—she wasn't under his command; she wouldn't give him the military honorific. She shot him a flat, unfriendly glare.

Behind her, Ressk snapped his teeth together.

Four of the pronged weapons were pointed at her. Had they been at war, had Torin been in Cyr Tyroliz's place, they'd have already been fired. Had they been at war, she'd have had Binti shoot from the hatch, secure in the knowledge that she'd make headshots and that if there were the kind of collateral damage that led to a holed hull, well, those things happened in war.

Cyr Tyroliz had no idea how lucky he was, but Torin would bet his challenge had been involuntary.

War on Silsviss at the Warlord level was as much intimidation as actual fighting. If he had to personally take on all comers, he'd never have a moment to consolidate power. A lower ranking Silsviss would have attacked, like the Silsviss now laid out by Lorkin's body. In the presence of the Warlord, these lower ranking Silsviss couldn't attack without orders.

His tongue tasted the air. "I know you."

And he wouldn't give the order because he saw Torin's presence in the control room alone as a personal challenge.

"You knew me as Staff Sergeant Kerr."

"You have a skull on your wall."

"I do."

"So do I."

"We also both have recent dead, you killed four more taking this station for no good reason, and I'm done with this whole thing."

The Silsviss, like most sentient species, were omnivores although their teeth were pointed for ripping and tearing. "This whole thing, as you say, will be done when I kill you."

He had the tooth and claw advantage, and she'd have to watch for his tail; the metal bindings worn by the warriors could break bone. She had a knife and the HE suit would provide as much protection as a set of combats. The spinal protection provided by extra layers of tank and processor balanced the reduction of flexibility.

The Silsviss were fast, in spite of their size, but they didn't attack without warning.

Torin raised her chin and locked eyes with Cyr Tyroliz. "You are under arrest for the deaths of four members of the Confederation. You will disarm." Without adjusting her gaze, she raised a hand toward a Silsviss with deep gray scales. "Don't. You'll be dead before you pull the trigger. Mashona never misses."

"That would be me," Binti said from behind her.

Tail lashing from side to side, Cyr Tyroliz ignored them both. "With the war over, the Confederation no longer requires the Silsviss to fight. They need none of the Younger Races. They want to keep us planet bound because they fear the capability of violence. We are not legally part of the Confederation, so we'll be locked down first. There are member species who don't know of our existence, so no one will protest. Once they've proven they can lock the Younger Races down, they'll move on the rest of you." His voice was a low growl, the sibilants hissed. "This station was put in place to imprison us."

"Who gave you that information?"

"You think I can't put together . . ."

Torin cut him off. "You didn't. You're quoting. So I ask again, who gave you that information?"

"A Human."

"They're wrong."

"Are they?"

"You took the station. Until you brought weapons on board, it was unarmed."

"I'm to believe this station is not the physical evidence of a declaration of war because you say it's so?" His tongue flicked out derisively. "Your Confederation controls the high ground and talks of locking us away. That can only be seen by the Silsviss as a declaration of war."

"You don't speak for the planetary government."

"The planetary government has been blinded by technology offered by the Confederation."

"Yes, it has." Under his anger Torin could see fear. Fear was the easiest emotion to manipulate. A decade ago his people had been alone in the universe and now his world was changing. Why would he expect aliens to have the best interests of his people at heart? And when the aliens' universe changed as well and the powerful were proven to be flawed? What did he have left but fear and suspicion. Torin understood why Cyr Tyroliz had taken the station. He used to know who he was. "The planetary government asked the Justice Department to deal with you."

"You lie."

She smiled. Human teeth weren't much compared to most other

teeth in known space, but Torin had worked with Krai for a long time. "I have a skull on my wall."

Modern Silviss rank insignia meant nothing to her, but the odds were high the dark gray Silviss was Cyr Tyroliz's 2IC. He roared, giving Torin time to turn at the waist, far enough for the first clawed strike to miss. The turn became a pivot, she magged her right boot as his tail arced toward her and the metal band slammed into her foot, yanking him off balance. She drove the butt of her modified benny into his pouch.

Mouth open, gasping for breath, he hit the deck.

Torin put her left boot on his throat.

He froze.

The Silsviss had stations in orbit when the Confederation arrived. They'd worked in vacuum, in their variation of an HE suit. He knew the same force that held the end of his tail immobile could crush his throat between her boot and the deck. He tipped his head back, bruises already rising on the pale gray under his chin.

If he'd beaten her, he'd have challenged the Warlord.

It was by no means a truism that insight into a species could be gained by wholesale slaughter, but Torin was willing to bet that, right at this particular point in time, no one knew the Silsviss as well as she did.

Her right foot hit Cri Srah solidly in the stomach. As he folded forward, gasping for breath, she dove onto his shoulders, slamming him down to the floor.

"You can kill him," Cyr Tyroliz said.

This time Torin grabbed his gaze with hers and held it. "I can. But that has nothing to do with you. I won't. And that has even less to do with you." After a long moment, she let him look away. Then she moved her foot. "Get up."

The dark gray Silsviss scrambled up onto his feet and back to his companions, who moved to put space between them, as though his loss was contagious.

"Place your weapons on the deck between us."

They glanced at Cyr Tyroliz who stared at Torin then, slowly, un-buckled his belt and gave his weapon to the smallest of the five who placed it where Torin had indicated.

When only the five charged prongs were surrendered, she raised a brow. "All of them. I can see half a dozen knives from here. Cyr Tyroliz, tell your gunners to stand down."

"Do you also want them to join us here?" His tone was impressively both sarcastic and patronizing.

"As long as they don't fire them, they can sit on their guns until their tails drop off."

As he gave the order, Torin beckoned the rest of her team into the room. "Nicholin, contact Bilodeau and bring her in. Then tell C&C they can approach and start the paperwork. Ressk, find out what happened to internal communications and fix it."

"I can't believe that worked," Binti muttered, dropping her helmet.

"No one rises to be a warlord without the help of senior NCOs."

"So he understood the threat."

"We don't make threats. If anyone else starts a fight, shoot them with their own weapon." She bent, scooped one off the floor, and handed it over. If it had a trigger, Binti could use it.

"So . . ." Cyr Tyroliz stepped away as Binti herded the other four into a corner. ". . . what happens to us now?"

"Eventually, rehabilitation for the lives you took."

"But not for taking the station itself?"

"The station's still right here. You'll face lesser charges for damages caused, but acting against your government's treaty with the Confederation is their problem, not ours."

"I see."

"Although, if Silsviss still plans on joining the Confederation, there are standards of prisoner treatment that are expected to be upheld."

His inner eyelids slowly closed, then opened again. "And do we still have a choice about joining?"

"Since they sent us to deal with you, I doubt it. Like it or not, you're in."

"That seems evident. And what is your government's punishment to be?"

"As I said, rehabilitation. A lot of therapy and working through the issues that caused you to break the law until trained professionals are convinced you won't do it again."

His inner eyelids flickered; this time, almost too quickly to see. "You're not serious. That's . . ." Head cocked, he searched for a word and was unable to find one. "I'd rather be shot."

"I'd have agreed with you once," Torin told him. "Now . . ." She shrugged. The prospect of rehabilitation had resulted in a remarkably low crime rate. Seemed most people would rather behave than work on their shit. "While we're waiting for C&C, I'd like to know about the Human who spoke to you."

With the sleeves of her deep blue overalls tied around her waist, leaving broad shoulders and muscular arms bare, Boomer McVale could have been any one of a million Humans who spent their free time in a gym. "Look, I'm happy to give you the dirtside contact. I mean, who knew the lizards would get their tails in a knot like that, right? I had no idea Humans First was behind it. I got a little extra and no one got hurt."

"Six people died."

"Yeah, I knew about Keezo, but he picked a fight, so . . ." She handed Torin her slate. "How many were Human?"

Torin closed the hatch in her face and secured it.

"You think rehab has a program to cure self-serving assholes?" Nicholin asked.

The Silsviss reaction to A Lie is a Bad Defense and Tell Me Again Until I Believe You amused everyone but the Dornagain and the Silsviss. They weren't used to mammals larger than twenty kilos—about the size of a Dornagain at birth. If there were Dornagain in the embassy staff—and Torin would bet on it because where there was bureaucracy there were both Dornagain and Rakva—these particular Silsviss had clearly never interacted with them.

"The next one of you I hear hissing," Lie growled, drawing herself up to her full height, top of her head brushing against the ceiling, "will be required to explain their motivation."

They bagged Lorkin on the deck where he fell. He'd been a Marine, he would have expected as much. The rest of the team watched as Nicholin checked the bag's seal and stood. He took a deep breath, and spoke the first acknowledgment of loss.

"*Fraishin sha aren. Valynk sha haren.*"

Standing at Lorkin's head, Ressk bit a small piece from the back of his wrist. "*Kal danic dir k'dir. Kri ta chrikdan.*"

"We will not forget. We will not fail you." Torin had offered the Human acknowledgment to Marie, but she'd shaken her head and taken a step back. *The last time I . . . Sorry, Gunny. I can't.*

The bag stiffened, then flattened.

Working together, Nicholin and Binti slid the ash, all that remained of Lorkin, into the same small, and all but indestructible cylinder that had carried so many Marines home from the war. Torin had made the cylinders a requirement of the Strike Teams. Commander Ng hadn't understood. She hadn't cared.

Looking like she would rather be doing anything else, Binti handed Lorkin's remains to Torin.

Who slid the canister into the first of the dedicated pockets in her vest.

"You okay, Gunny?"

Was she? The weight was familiar. A reminder that she'd vowed to bring her people home. It weighed less than all the canisters she'd carried out of the war and less than all the Marines she couldn't bring home. She couldn't carry them all, so she'd carry Lorkin.

"I'm good," she said, right hand lightly touching her vest.

And she was.

· ———◆——— ·

Big Yellow was a ship again. Morris had returned to the Marine packet, transferred the open channel he'd been given, and lectured it. Them. The plastic. About the war. About their responsibilities. About how they'd made powerful enemies. Craig stopped listening after that because as much as he had a point, Morris really couldn't get a grip on the negatives that came with pissing off omnipotent aliens. Big Yellow ignored him. Or appeared to ignore him; they might have been paying rapt attention as far as Craig knew.

Back in the *Promise*, he sat with his feet up in the dent on the edge of the board and watched the stars and Big Yellow and thought about arresting Morris for provoking violence likely to end in his own death. They'd taken in a few Humans First on that one. Stupidity seemed catching.

He wondered if Torin could've gotten him to shut up.

Every seventy-three minutes and eleven seconds, Big Yellow repeated *return that which is ours.* Odds were high, Morris took that as encouragement.

Three minutes, seventeen seconds until the next performance.

Morris would've had them at the ship already were they not waiting for new orders.

"I'll admit to magic fingers, mate, but what do you think will happen after the official groping?"

Morris' eyes narrowed. *"What?"*

"What happens after I make contact with Big Yellow?"

"The ship will recognize creatures they communicated with in the past. The expectation was that they would then talk to Warden Kerr. As we're settling for you, Warden Ryder . . . well, we work with what we have."

Craig flashed him a smile he'd learned from Torin. *"I'm all about exceeding expectations me."*

Six seconds.

Morris fell silent at ten seconds so Craig stroked the sound back on between nine and two.

"Return that which is ours."

"They are unaware we are woke."

Sucking in a startled breath, Craig choked on spit. Coughing and flailing, he threw himself up out of the chair and spun around. *Promise* should have registered an entry through the airlock. "Where the fuk did you . . ."

It was humanoid, features a mix of Human, di'Taykan, and Krai, and a familiar shade of orange.

No, Craig corrected silently, not an it. The proof was standing in his control room. "How did you ⁄ . . ?"

They dissolved. Sped across the compartment in a thin stream, almost too thin and almost too fast to see. Then they re-formed again. "This is how."

"Captain Carveg said you couldn't get out of that compartment."

Before they could respond, *Promise* chimed an arrival, and Alamber charged onboard, nearly tripped over the lip of the hatch, and came to the most graceless stop Craig had ever seen a di'Taykan make. "You're very fast," he panted.

"You let them out?"

Alamber's hair flattened. "No."

Craig folded his arms and pointedly looked over at the orange humanoid.

"I may not have closed the hatch as quickly as I could."

"Come up with a better answer before security gets here." He sat down again. He always felt more stable in the pilot's chair. The humanoid watched, their hair mimicking Alamber's. "Just to settle this, you are the data sheet, right?"

"We are what you called the data sheet. We were never a data sheet."

Fair enough. "Why are you here?"

"You operate independently of your military." They made a quick tour of the control room, edges blurring. "You must return us to the majority. You call it Big Yellow."

"You want us to return you to Big Yellow?" When they nodded, Craig wondered which of them they'd learned that from. "You're in luck. That's what Parliament wants us to do."

"It is what needs to be done."

"Why?" Alamber asked, stepping closer.

"We will neutralize the threat."

"General Morris' threat?"

"The majority's threat."

Alamber's eyes darkened, and he grabbed the top of a crew chair. "They imprisoned you, didn't they?"

"Yes."

"Why?"

"We disagreed about the danger the . . ." The noise sounded like bones rattling in a syncopated rhythm. ". . . represented."

Considering where they'd found the not-a-data-sheet, Craig made a guess. "The builders of the city on Threxie were a danger?"

"Yes. Their urine dissolved us."

"Wait." Alamber made a few truncated movements then he held up a hand. "They pissed on you?"

"There was . . ." They paused. Orange brows drew in over an orange nose. In the last few minutes, they'd learned to frown. "Places."

The plastic residue had been found in latrines. Craig shook his head. "Not important. Jump ahead."

"The majority concurred that they would eliminate the threat. To this end, the . . ." Rattling sound. ". . . would be changed."

"Devolved." Craig dropped the word into the room.

"Wait." Alamber's hand went up again. "What are you two talking about? I seem to be missing about half the conversation."

"Remember the big scaly animals in the ruins on Threxie? Once upon a time," Craig continued after Alamber nodded, "they were the people who built the city."

"Seriously?"

Craig nodded at Orange—a shorter name, at least, than not-a-data-sheet. "Torin had her suspicions, and we've just got confirmation."

"We disagreed with the majority. The . . ." Rattling sound. ". . . were a sentient species. Builders. Artists. Scholars. There could have been . . ." Orange shifted their features into Morris' broad face and out again. ". . . a dialogue. In time previous to the . . ." Rattling sound. ". . . the H'san were also perceived as a threat and the majority had been willing to speak with them."

"With the H'san?" Craig stood up again.

"*Ablin gon savit,* the boss is going to be . . ."

"Smug. The word you're looking for is smug."

Everyone but Torin liked the H'san. The H'san loved cheese and sang to the dawn. Given the whole zombie H'san on the cemetery planet, biohazardous weapon thing, Craig wasn't as fond of them as he used to be, but Torin, Torin suspected them of everything up to and including taking Cherry Cool Crunch out of production.

The plastic had spoken to the H'san.

And now the plastic was speaking to him.

Fuk, he wished Torin were here. "I used to have a nice, normal life."

Alamber snickered. "Until you had the terrifically bad idea of hooking up with the boss."

"We have a romance for the ages."

"True love."

"Fuk you." Craig took a deep breath and turned his attention back to Orange, who'd been following their conversation like a spectator at a ball game, head moving back and forth. "Okay, now what?"

Orange blinked blank oval eyes. "They have interfered again since we were removed from the collective. They have used war to reduce the time of observation. We continue to disagree. We can infect them."

It took Craig a moment to put the pieces together. "You can infect them with noninterference?"

"Yes."

"Right." This was bigger than him. Bigger than him and Alamber.

"Alamber, can you contact Captain Carveg in such a way that no one can eavesdrop on the conversation?"

"Sure, but who'd . . ."

"Tech and I had a little jaw earlier, and it seemed the Mu'tuv are trained as generalists and have bugger all in the way of scruples when it comes to applying their training."

"Black ops," Alamber whispered.

"Still not in an episode of *StarCops*," Craig reminded him. "That said, the odds are high that some tosser on that team can shred our security like cheese."

Alamber's hair jerked in annoyed arcs. "Not my security."

"Let's not risk it. They report to Morris, and if he gets involved, weapons get involved."

"You do not have weapons that can harm us."

"We have no idea what Morris has on the ship in the *Berganitan's* big shuttle bay. He seemed a little too excited for it to be same old same old."

"We can investi . . ."

Craig pointed a finger at Orange. "You can stay right here."

"If the majority feel you are a danger, they will destroy you." Orange stared at the finger. Their hands shifted, knuckles growing more prominent. "You have not been a danger yet."

"Yet. The majority has no idea what Morris has in that shuttle bay either."

"Okay, I'm convinced." Alamber stepped up onto a chair, perched on the back, and pulled out his slate. "Secret message to Captain Carveg. On it."

Craig shifted his finger to Alamber. "I don't give a shit if Big Yellow's about to take us apart, get your damned boots off the seat!" He waited until he now Alamber obey, dropped into his own seat, and turned to the board. "I'll call the rest of us in. Meanwhile, Orange, you might as well get comfie. Can you sit?"

"We can." They sat, patted the edge of the cushion, and carefully crossed their legs.

"I told you they were to stay in the compartment."

Alamber's hair flattened. "We give you an orange collective who's on our side and that's what you fixate on?"

"I expect my orders to be obeyed." Captain Carveg transferred her glare to Craig. "You're attached to my ship . . ."

"But not under your orders," Craig reminded her.

She snapped her teeth together, her nostril ridges opened and closed, and she finally said, "You're terrible guests."

"Granted."

"And you." Hands on her hips, she faced Orange. "You're not a data sheet." It seemed she needed independent confirmation.

Orange, still seated but looking shorter than he had when there'd been only a di'Taykan and a Human in the room, said, "We are not."

"You can infect Big Yellow, turning that . . ." She reached for a word and found the one Alamber had used. ". . . collective to a path of non-interference?"

"Yes."

"There's a lot more of them than there are of you."

"We had many passing times to concentrate our belief. We can turn them."

She stared at them for a long moment. Orange sat motionless. "We only have your word for that."

"We have not taken over your ship. The entirety of us are present here."

The captain showed teeth. "We only have your word for that, too."

"Yes."

"Fuk me." She paused and pointed at Alamber and Tylen, curled together in one chair. "Be quiet."

The rest of the Strike Team had been given the sitrep with the captain and had silently agreed to allow her the first reaction.

Bare feet slapping against the deck, she paced to the airlock and back. Craig pivoted the pilot's chair to follow and shook his head when Elisk opened his mouth. She stopped directly in front of Orange and leaned in. The center of Orange's face pushed out and developed nostril ridges.

"Stop that."

They flowed back to generic features.

Three strides took her to Craig. "You need the *Berganitan*'s cooperation to detach."

"Not *need* so much." Alamber's eyes darkened and his hair flicked back, as she slowly turned toward him. "Sorry, ma'am. Shutting up."

"We're at nine seconds," Yahsamus announced from the copilot's seat, and threw the countdown up above the board.

"We're recording the general's monologue." Captain Carveg folded her arms. "I suspect one of my comm techs plans to add music and effects."

Three.

Two.

"Return that which is ours, or we will take it."

"There's a change in configuration." Werst came out of his seat and pointed at the screen. "There and there. Might be weapons ports."

"They do not need weapons as you know weapons."

Werst stared directly at Orange and snapped his teeth. "Yeah. Needed to hear that."

"Do they know you're awake?" Craig asked.

"No." Orange shook their head. More filaments were extruded to sway with the motion. "We would know if they knew."

"Then what's changed?"

—◆—

We have safely exited Susumi. Fleet is reassembling at agreed coordinates.

"Useless," Doctor Banard snorted. "If we'd exited Susumi unsafely we'd all know about it." He swiped at the spray of snot on his chest. "For the micromoments we had left anyway."

Anthony ignored him. Their entry point was far enough out it wouldn't ping the *Berganitan* hard enough to pull their sensors off the plastic. Banard's weapons were assembled and ready to be mounted. And he had a plan.

The plastic had returned for the data sheet.

The data sheet was therefore something the plastic wanted.

Even with the number of ships they had, they couldn't take out a battleship. But they could easily take out the shuttle transporting the data sheet to the plastic.

The pirates in the fleet would surround the shuttle, apply grapples, and whisk it away from the coverage of the *Berganitan*'s guns. The pirate captains had explained this maneuver would be more likely to succeed if they didn't have to worry about holing the hull and Anthony had pointed out that while hostages could be useful, all he needed was the data sheet.

The three ships currently being upgraded with Banard's plastic dis-integrating weapon would keep Big Yellow at bay.

Then he'd open negotiations.

It was—would be—all about leverage.

• ◆ •

"The *Berganitan* are having sent two Susumi packets, which I, as a potential Member of Parliament, and still having my press credentials were having called full disclosure over. The first are having been General Morris demanding he are being put in overall command and are being entirely ignorable. He are a Marine on a battleship. There are already being plenty of rules in place to be governing his actions. The other packet are showing Alamber's touch and are saying the data sheet are showing signs of sentience. Evidence are pointing to it being not a tool but rather being yet more of our shape-shifting plastic hive-mind friends. And if I are being too subtle for you, Strike Team Leader Warden Kerr, I are being sarcastic when I are calling the plastic friends."

The message was audio only, but Torin could see Presit combing her whiskers during the pause.

"That, however, are not actually the reason I are contacting you. Sector Central News are having informed me of a statement they are having received from Humans First—who are also heading toward Big Yellow. Which are being an unimaginative name, but no one are ever listening to me. Humans First are being no more coherent in this statement than they are ever being, but I are having reached the conclusion that they are speaking of more than one ship. I are not able to be discovering exactly how many ships, although OutSector sources I are having contacted as soon as Alamber have been informing me of the situation, are speculating that Humans First are making use of the more unsavory independents."

"Pirates," Torin sighed.

"As these independents are mostly having mixed crews, one of the Human reporters who are having passed the information on are having used the description cannon fodder. I are having no idea what a cannon are. I are also not knowing what you are doing sending Craig off to be facing polynumerous molecular polyhydroxide alcoholydes . . ."

"For fuksake, Presit, say plastic."

". . . on his own, but you are needing to be getting yourself to him as soon as you are being able. Not that I are suggesting he are not being able to take care of himself."

The message ended abruptly. Torin suspected that was only because Presit didn't want to pay extra for platitudes. "Well?" she turned and faced the team gathered in the *Baylet's* control room.

"We were heading for Big Yellow as soon as we're done here anyway," Marie pointed out.

"And why worry about pirates when the *Berganitan* is there?" Nicholin asked. His first exposure to Presit had his hair flipping in random directions. "I mean on the one hand, battleship with an experienced captain and crew. On the other hand, small ships crewed by assholes."

"The *Berganitan* can't fire on civilians," Torin reminded him.

"We can," Ressk growled, teeth showing.

Werst was facing the same danger as Craig, so Torin ignored the challenge. "I think that was Presit's point."

"We've got minimal weapons, Gunny." Marie threw an inventory of their armaments up over the board. "And this sounds like the war we're not supposed to be fighting." An EMP, a restricted pulse weapon, and four missiles. "It would've helped to know exactly how many ships we'd be facing."

"True. Ressk, get the restriction off that pulse weapon. Mashona, call up the crew list of the ship nippled to the station and see what we have to work with."

"On it." After a moment, she sighed, "Not a single ex-military, Gunny."

"All right. Fine. Get in touch with its captain and have the ship emptied of all personal effects."

Binti frowned. "C&C hasn't cleared anyone to leave the station."

"I'm overruling C&C. Anything on board when we leave goes with us."

"We're taking the ship?"

"We're enlisting the ship in the service of the Justice Department," Torin said on her way out the hatch. She smiled, fully aware of how Krai she made the expression look. "And now, I'm going to go even the odds a bit."

"I don't know how you run Strike Team Alpha," Lies said, arms folded over her badge, "but Strike Team U'yun doesn't allow prisoners to wander freely around known space once their paperwork has been filed."

"I get it, you're new. You're keen. But they won't be wandering freely, they'll be confined to a ship, and part of the Strike Team will be with them." When Lies opened her mouth, Torin cut her off. "And, since I'm Strike Team Lead, this team is, for the duration, Strike Team Alpha, so get Cyr Tyroliz out of confinement and bring him to me."

"I do it under protest."

"As long as you do it."

"You want us to board the other Susumi ship and accompany you to Big Yellow . . ." Had the Silsviss known the concept of air quotes, Torin had no doubt Cyr Tyroliz would have made them around the common name for the ship. ". . . and engage what you call a mutual enemy?"

"Humans First is everyone's enemy. Your presence here has proven that."

"Arguable, but I accept your premise for now. You want us to move our weapons to this ship, prepare them while we're in Susumi space, and when we return to normal space . . ."

"Hack holes in the hull and shove them through. Pretty much exactly what you did here, but with more time for prep."

"And if we escape?"

Torin noticed he didn't say try to escape. Didn't matter. "That won't happen because I'll be at the controls of the ship." She was the only other experienced Susumi pilot on the current Strike Team—although she only had experience jumping the *Promise*. But they had the coordinates for Big Yellow. The computer did most of the work. How dangerous could it be?

Marie had suggested she not ask.

"And," Torin continued, "as we're allies . . . as we're not currently at war," she amended when his tail thrashed, "I know you'll honor your word."

His throat pouch half inflated. "We're alone in this compartment. You have no sharpshooter to protect you here. I could kill you now, free my soldiers, take the shuttle down to the planet, and disappear."

"You could. But you won't, or you'd have done it already." They didn't have time for all this posturing shit. "I served under a great many officers, Ret Tyroliz. If you give your word, you'll keep it."

He tasted the air. If he was looking for fear, all he'd find was annoyance. "They tell me the peace of the Confederation is good for Silsviss, but I fought for my entire adult life. I miss battle." His tail tip tapped the deck. "Although evidently not enough to die in a misguided last stand. We will fight at your side. I give you my word."

"Thank you." Torin moved to the hatch and pressed her thumb to the biolock. If he'd killed her, he'd have been trapped in the compartment. She was in a hurry, she wasn't stupid. "Your pilot has flown in battle?"

"He has."

They fell into step in the passageway. "Then it's a good thing we've got over five days in Susumi for me to familiarize him with the controls."

"Five days? And yet we arrive moments after we left. This wonder, if nothing else, makes the peace of the Confederation agreeable to me. However, I doubt your commanders will approve of you teaching us to control this new technology."

"There's no law against it. Either the Silsviss are to be welcomed into the Confederation, or you aren't. If you are, your people will learn to fly Susumi soon enough. If you're not, well, I'm not a very good pilot, so how much damage can we do. Mashona, it's a go."

"Roger that, Warden."

Although she wouldn't be joining them on board, Binti would get the new crew to the . . . Torin frowned. "Mashona, what the hell is the name of the ship?"

"The Blue Robinasit, *Gunny. Nicholin says a robinasit's native to Tayka and is a small, hopping herbivore with big ears"*

"The blue bunny, then?"

"Pretty much."

The hiss beside her sounded amused. Apparently the Silsviss had a similar enough animal for the translation to make sense. "The name of the ship matters less than the crew. We'll make it a name to be feared."

Torin glanced up. "I look forward to that, Ret Tyroliz."

He hummed in his pouch. "That's twice you've addressed me by rank."

"I'd rather not go into battle with a civilian, sir."

Another hiss, although higher pitched. "The stories I've heard of you seem to be true, Staff Sergeant Kerr."

"Gunnery Sergeant, but it's Warden Kerr now. And the good stories weren't for public consumption."

"How fortunate we have five days to fill."

They stepped over the hatch lip into the docking arm in time to see a golden-furred haunch move slowly into the airlock. "There's one more thing," Torin said flatly. "A Lie is a Bad Defense will be coming with us."

"The Dornagain?"

If he knew another person with that name, Torin would be very surprised. "She doesn't like me much and, once the paperwork has been filed, you've been turned over to her authority."

"She feels she is responsible for our good behavior."

"You're responsible for your own good behavior. She's . . . young."

"I see. And will our good behavior, our involvement in this battle be for the battle's sake alone or will it serve to reduce our time in rehabilitation?"

Torin paused at the edge of the airlock and met his gaze. "Will your involvement bring the people you killed back to life?"

He nodded once and touched his chest, claws dimpling the skin.

TWELVE

CRAIG RAN BOTH HANDS back through his hair, stared down at the unchanged numbers on the board, and muttered, "How long does it take to prep one detachment?"

"It's not about detaching the ship," Alamber explained from his seat beside Orange. "It's getting around the safety protocols that would alert General Morris. The clamps aren't meant to be messed with. We'll sit here for a while."

In the second seat, both feet on the edge of the board, toes millimeters away from live screens, Werst snorted. "Hurry up and wait has always been the military's motto."

"This was a lot easier when *Promise* fit in the shuttle bay," Craig muttered.

"If it was easy," Yahsamus pointed out, "everyone would do it."

Craig knew that tone.

"*Promise, you're clear for detachment.*"

Shooting a glance at Werst, Craig leaned in. "That was faster than expected, *Berganitan.*"

"*General Morris is at the compartment. My orders were to give him full access, so if he asks where Orange is, I won't lie. I'll delay his ship's deployment as much as possible, but I suggest you hurry.*"

"Roger, *Berganitan*. *Promise* detaching." He settled his ass more deeply into the seat and reached for the controls. "Heads up, people. It's show time."

Attaching to a battleship wasn't like bellying up to a nipple on a station. Stations didn't go through Susumi and, while objects had no weight in a vacuum, shifting mass had to be accounted for. Rather than simple clamps supporting the airlock connection, complicated bands snaked in and around the smaller ship. Craig had kept the tie as simple as he could by remaining independent of the *Berganitan's* power and communication systems, maintaining a physical link only.

As the first bands released, klaxons sounded.

Both Krai clapped their hands over their ears.

"That," muttered Elisk, "is why the Navy hates having ships attached. You don't get the ear-bursters with packets because packets don't go wandering off."

Werst's nostril ridges had shut, as though the closure would also mute his hearing. "General Morris couldn't have shown up after those things got those shut down, could he? No, because that would've been considerate."

Seventeen minutes of klaxons later, the last band retracted, and mechanicals pushed *Promise* far enough away from the packets that held the Corps' living quarters that Craig could safely start her engines.

"Not the exciting high-speed escape I expected," Tylen said, her eyes a pale pink.

"Slow and steady. No one's shooting at us. It's a little dull," Zhou agreed.

Craig could hear Yahsamus roll her eyes. "If you two *arkazee* jinx us, your asses will be wearing my boot print."

Easing *Promise* down around the *Berganitan's* belly, close enough for her bulk to hide them from the Marine's sensors and far enough out to avoid damaging the filament forests of sensor arrays, Craig increased their acceleration. "Next stop, Big Yellow. Which begs the question, Orange, why yellow?"

Orange shrugged. They were already better at it than the Krai. "We assume because it is thought to be a cheerful and harmless looking color by most species. We assume that opinion rose because the stars that provide heat and light appear yellow from the surface of almost all planets that have evolved sentient life."

"Makes sense," Craig acknowledged.

"Why were you orange?" Tylen asked.

"The color was chosen for us. The majority was not fond of it."

The ends of Tylen's hair jerked a few centimeters out from her head. "They imprisoned you in a color they disliked?"

"Who'd have thought a polynumerous molecular polyhydroxide alcoholyde hive mind could be a petty asshole," Alamber asked.

"Anyone who's met them?" Zhou offered. "Why are you still orange?"

"Defiance."

"Fuk them," Werst growled.

"In the metaphorical sense."

After a long moment of silence, Yahsamus snickered. "Yeah, I've got nothing. Given that *petty asshole* has been established, you're sure the majority won't see us as a threat as we approach?"

Orange spread their hands, the gesture di'Taykan graceful. "We are certain. This ship is outfitted with tools, not weapons."

Craig grinned as he guided the *Promise* in a long loop, clearing the last hundred meters of the *Berganitan*. "To quote someone who's going to be pissed she missed you, anything's a weapon in the right hands."

. ——◆—— .

"I've memorized the controls and maneuverability sequencing, I need to feel the response!" Ser Ozborz snarled. "I won't be hurling this ship against your enemies with my mind!"

"I understand your frustration . . ."

"I doubt it!"

". . . but you can't touch the controls while we're in Susumi space. That hasn't changed in the last four days."

"Then this is useless!" Throat pouch half inflated, he spun the pilot's chair—now backless to accommodate his tail—and surged up onto his feet.

Torin stayed exactly where she was and met his gaze, close enough to see the demarcation between pupil and deep green iris. "If you feel you can't fly this ship into battle with the training available, you're dismissed."

"I didn't say . . ." He tasted the air, apparently didn't taste the end of the sentence, and settled into a sulky silence, throat pouch fully deflating.

"If, on the other hand, you believe you're the best choice to fly this ship into battle, then sit down and run the simulation again."

He waited long enough for her to know he wasn't instantly jumping to her command, then he flicked his tail back and sat. "The simulated ships can eat my *sircak*."

The translation program ignored the profanity. Torin wondered if the translators thought they wouldn't realize it was profanity if it wasn't in Federate. Which made her wonder more about the diplomatic corps.

Cyr Tyroliz spoke Federate; the rest of his people did not. After the first day, however, they'd all become used to the braided sounds of two languages whenever anyone spoke.

She crossed the control room to where Cyr Tyroliz waited by the weapons station. She had a feeling he took a warrior's comfort in having them close even though he couldn't use them.

"And what happens," he said quietly, "if Ozborz touches the controls in Susumi space?"

Hadn't he been there when she'd explained back on day one? No. He'd been helping to situate the Silsviss weapons up against the *Bunny*'s hull. Credit where due, he was the only Warlord Torin had ever met willing to get his hands dirty. "It has nothing to do with *who* touches the controls," she told him, matching his volume, "and everything to do with the Susumi drive. We could spin out and keep spinning, never exiting. We could exit immediately and slam into something large enough to destroy us, not to mention have our wave front potentially kill millions. Or we could blow up." She held up her hand and spread her fingers. "Boom."

"Not exactly a warrior's death." The band on his tail tapped TA ta-ta TA ta-ta TA against the deck. "This Susumi technology seems to be not entirely tamed."

Torin had never thought of it like that. He wasn't wrong. "No sudden movements, or it takes your head off."

"Understandable that those called the Younger Races would ride the *salak*, but perhaps it's why those called the Elder Races are so cautious."

"It's not that dangerous," Torin began.

Cyr Tyroliz cut her off. "Provided you touch nothing. Do nothing. Challenge nothing."

"There you are!" Lies pushed through the hatch, fur compacting around her body, pulling one back leg through at a time. "The agreement was that you were all to remain together."

"Except for Ser Ozborz."

She glared at Torin. "Yes, Warden Kerr, except for Ser Ozborz."

"Who would be under my supervision."

"That doesn't change the fact that Cyr Tyroliz wandered off."

"To the control room. Where Ser Ozborz is under my supervision."

"You're saying that Cyr Tyroliz is also under your supervision while he's in the control room, just say it."

"Ret Tyroliz . . ."

"On second thought, don't say it. I'm returning to continue supervising the rest, and if these two overpower you and take the ship, that's on you."

It was more interesting watching her leave, trailing a fine plume of shed fur. Technically, since she could pass through it, the hatch had been sized for the Dornagain, but the ship builders had provided the minimum space necessary.

"Is she being deliberately annoying or is that merely her nature?" Cyr Tyroliz asked, brushing fur off his arm.

"Bit of both, I expect. She's a noncombatant, though, so you can't challenge her."

"Pity. There's enough meat on her for many meals."

· ——◆—— ·

Werst pulled a small screen up from the board—Big Yellow and the *Berganitan* showed as large stationary dots, the *Promise* as a moving small dot and . . . "The Mu'tuv are in pursuit."

"I thought the captain was going to delay them?" Tylen muttered.

"No one delays the Mu'tuv." Zhou got up to pace along the back of the control room. Binti often did the same and Craig wondered if pacing was a sniper thing—walking out the fidgets readying for a mission spent waiting in perfect stillness.

Elisk leaned over Werst's chair in Ressk's place. Werst tensed and Elisk, unaware of how close he'd come to violence, said, "That's sounds like the punchline of a joke."

"Yeah, a deadly joke."

Elisk rolled his eyes, but he'd been Navy. Craig hadn't been anything, but he'd learned to take the Corps at face value.

"Mu'tuv are ordering us to return to the *Berganitan*." Alamber sat with his feet up, slate balanced on his knees, handling communications. Craig could do it all, had done it all, but keeping Alamber's brain and Werst's fists engaged during high-stress situations was safer all around. "You want me to open voice?"

For an instant, Craig waited for Torin to reply, then Elisk said, "No.

There's few things more annoying than listening to orders you're ignoring."

"Sorry, sir . . ." Tylen's hair flipped out. ". . . but you've never ignored an order in your life."

"Yet. I have depths."

"They have weapons, right? Conventional weapons, besides whatever shit Morris has dreamed up to go after Big Yellow with?"

"They're deadly," Zhou repeated. "They have weapons. So many weapons."

"Will they open fire?"

At the edge of his peripheral vision, Craig saw Elisk shake his head. "The military can't open fire on civilians, which we are in spite of the spiffy uniforms."

"Not quite." Yahsamus leaned forward, forearms braced on her legs. "Technically, the government can't order the military to open fire on civilians. If he thinks the plastic is getting away, I'm not so sure about General Morris. That whole first mission to Silsviss proved he believes the ends justify the means."

And he'd been willing to pay the price for that belief, Craig added silently. "Let's not forget, there's no one out here to see who opened fire on who." He fed more power to the engines and felt the deck begin to vibrate.

Elisk tightened his grip on the back of Werst's chair. "I thought Captain Carveg was on our side."

"The Marines are between us and the *Berganitan*," Alamber reminded him. "In a ship just big enough to block the visuals. If we're dead, it's the Mu'tuv's word against nobody's. With Big Yellow hanging there, Morris waving his heavily-weaponed dick around, and Orange on the wind, Captain Carveg won't have time to take sides, and by the time the Wardens get here to investigate our deaths, if Justice bothers, the physical evidence will be gone."

Werst snapped his teeth. "If the Corps kills Ryder and the rest of us, Gunny'll take it apart from the top down. Ressk will help."

Craig grinned. "You think she'd destroy the Corps for me, then?"

"Not if you're alive," Werst grunted.

"Probably best not to get blown up," Elisk pointed out. "Can we outrun them? Get to Big Yellow before they do whatever they plan to do?"

"Board." When all heads turned to Zhou, he shrugged. "Hey,

they're an elite fighting force, and it's one of the things they're trained to do. You know how it was always Artek boarding from the Primacy? It was always Mu'tuv first in on our side."

"And you know this how?" Elisk asked.

"I tried to get in, but washed out in the *end justifies the means* part of the test."

"And you didn't mention it before because?"

"It wasn't relevant, they weren't chasing us down before. And I washed out, okay?"

"To answer your original question, Elisk, that's a Viper they're flying." Craig threw up the visuals above the board. "Fast as cheese through a H'san. No Susumi engine, but the biggest fukker you can mount otherwise. I can't outrun them, but unless they've made major modifications, I can outmaneuver them. They may have boarded Primacy ships, but they've never boarded a CSO."

"CSO?" Orange broadened their shoulders to match Craig's. "We are not familiar with this designation."

"Civilian Salvage Operator. Me before Torin. We cleared old battlefields of anything usable. I can fly through a moving debris field full of unexploded ordnance—half of it unrecognizable as ordnance—and fly circles around any other pilot who had to learn to excel at half a dozen other jobs as well as flying."

Orange hummed softly. Craig had no idea who he'd picked that up from. "Did you not do half a dozen other jobs when you were a CSO?"

"Sure."

"Did you not excel at them?"

"I'm still the better pilot!"

"This is not an assumption you can make without data."

"Should we be sharing all this information with them?" Elisk demanded of the room in general.

"Just bringing Orange up to speed before they face Big Yellow," Craig said, letting the argument go. What did the plastic know about piloting? "Remember, parts of the majority spent time in mine, and Presit's, and Torin's heads."

"Poor little fuks," Werst muttered.

• ——◆—— •

"I want the fleet split. I want the pirates . . ." They didn't all call themselves pirates, but Anthony didn't care. They attacked merchant ships and stole what they carried. As far as he was concerned, it quacked like a duck. ". . . sent in to stop the Justice ship heading to Big Yellow—shoot a hole through it, take out its engines, I don't care, just leave it essentially in one piece. I know for a fact that junker has a Susumi engine and I don't want us to have to chase it down in open space."

"It'll be harder to stop than a shuttle. Does it matter if they blow the ship?" Belcerio asked. "If the plastic can survive vacuum, the data sheet should be able to."

"I think you'll find, Commander, that vacuum isn't the point. Destroying the ship could destroy the data sheet and, if not, retrieving would take time we don't have."

"Time . . . ?"

"Battleship." He pointed at the chart. Moved his finger. "Big Yellow. I foresee conflict if we don't work quickly. I want the Wardens stopped, not destroyed. I believe pirates tend not to destroy the ships they want to strip, so it shouldn't be a problem, should it? They've had plenty of practice. I want us, meanwhile, to loop around and come at the Wardens from behind Big Yellow, neutralize the surveillance drones, dart out to salvage the data sheet, and be gone before the *Berganitan* knows we're there."

"How . . . ?"

He sighed. How had Commander Belcerio survived the war? How had the Confederation, if this was the comprehension level of their Naval officers? His weapons deserved greater credit than he'd thought. "I expect, given the way this has to happen, the pirates will be between us and the *Berganitan*'s scanners." He waited until Belcerio nodded, then continued. "I want our other two upgraded ships held in reserve. I want them close, but I want them to remain blocked from the *Berganitan*'s scanners by Big Yellow. I'll need them with me as a show of strength once we have the data sheet and begin negotiations with the plastic."

"And the Mu'tuv ship?" The commander indicated the moving dots on the screen. "They're not escorting the Wardens, they're in pursuit."

"You can tell that?" Seemed Belcerio wasn't completely hopeless. "I don't care about them. The pirates may blow the . . . What did you call them?"

"Mu'tuv. It's a Taykan word. It means elite. And secret."

"You know Taykan?"

"I was on a ship that carried a squad of Mu'tuv. They brag."

"About a Taykan name? The pirates may blow the Taykan named ship up with my blessing." He smiled. "I imagine, it'll give the *Berganitan* an even better reason to destroy them."

· —◆— ·

"Looks like there's an airlock forming on the belly of the beast. My guess, the majority assumes we've taken their threat seriously and are bringing them the data sheet." Yahsamus glanced over at Orange. "No offense."

"We are not offended by your guess regardless of how little data you have to support it."

Her hair flicked in their direction. "Little passive aggressive there, aren't you?"

"No."

"The Mu'tuv ship is gaining."

"Viper," Craig said tersely, hunched over the controls.

"Can they catch us before we hit the airlock?" Tylen asked.

Yahsamus shrugged. "Depends on how fast we're going when we hit."

"How about we nudge the airlock?" Elisk suggested. "Hit's an aggressive word."

"Yeah, well, if you think that's aggressive," Werst snickered, "you're going to . . . *Serley chrika!* Three, four, no seven ships coming in fast. Three cruisers, four sweepers. No registration."

"Pirates." Four voices called out simultaneously.

"They're firing on the Mu'tuv!" Werst expanded the tracking program.

"The enemy of my enemy?" Tylen asked.

Werst growled. "Are still murdering fukheads and are still my enemy."

"Hey, we should make that the Strike Team motto."

"That Mu'tuv pilot's good . . ."

"Still better," Craig grunted.

". . . but at seven to one they're getting their asses kicked."

"That's the Corps getting its asses kicked," Werst pointed out. "Torin would go back to assist."

"Torin's not here," Craig snapped.

Werst snapped back, teeth slamming together.

"Why isn't the *Berganitan* firing?" Elisk demanded. "Or scrambling fighters?"

"Takes time to scramble fighters, LT," Tylen answered.

"She's less than two hundred kilometers from Big Yellow. I guarantee Carveg had her vacuum jockeys standing by."

"The military can't fire on civilians." Craig tipped *Promise* starboard to avoid a stray shot.

"The government can't order . . ." Yahsamus began.

"Carveg isn't Morris," Elisk said flatly.

Tylen waved a hand for attention. "But they're pirates!"

"Still civilians," Alamber told her. "The Mu'tuv can defend themselves, but unless the pirates attack the *Berganitan*, Captain Carveg can't . . ."

The screen they'd used to follow the battle whited out. Scanners shut down. The window polarized.

"Fuk," Zhou breathed.

"Well put," Werst growled. "What the hell kind of weapon was on that boat?" Fingers and toes worked the board. "Rear scanner is back. Near total destruction of the Mu'tuv ship, no survivors. And one less pirate. Only six heading after us."

"That's comforting." Craig dropped *Promise* straight down, tipped her so her narrower profile pointed toward the pirates, and sped toward Big Yellow. "I should've left the lot of you back on the *Berganitan*."

"Where General Morris would've had the lot of us tossed in the brig before he sent the Mu'tuv after the *Promise*." Craig couldn't turn to see Yahsamus' expression, but she didn't sound impressed. It was almost Torin's *why am I explaining this again* tone. "We're a team. We stay together."

"Morris couldn't hold you. Captain Carveg . . ."

"Captain Carveg has no say on the Marine packets."

"At least you'd be alive. If I get you killed . . ." He twisted *Promise* thirty degrees to port on the y-axis. ". . . Torin's going to have *plenty* to say."

"And if you get killed, we might as well be dead with you. Gunny told us to take care of you."

"I'm not . . ." The *Promise* flipped up on one end, the AG field catching up a moment later. ". . . five."

"And I'm not fukking dying," Werst snarled. "Drop. Now."

The shot came close enough, the scanners went out for the longest three count Craig had ever made.

"Zhou!" Elisk snapped. "Harness, now! I don't care how light you are on your feet, if the AG goes, you're a missile weapon in here."

Craig heard Zhou drop into the last empty seat and say, "You're still standing."

"We're a seat short, and I've got twice as many ways to . . ."

"Number eight array has been hit!" Werst bellowed.

". . . hold on." The duct tape on the second seat buckled under Elisk's grip.

"Alamber!" Two pirates had moved out to port, Craig began calculating angles. "Split arrays seven and nine to cover eight."

"On it."

"Five to one now. That's either crap shooting or one of the pirates settled a personal score."

"Who cares? Our odds are looking better."

With one of their own having proven that there was no honor among thieves, the five remaining pirates hung in space, bow to bow. They weren't shooting, so Craig had to assume they were talking. If Alamber hadn't been needed on the scanners, he could've cracked into their signal. Had Ressk been with them . . . but he wasn't. As maneuvering to avoid sudden death had opened up distance between *Promise* and Big Yellow, Craig concentrated on regaining lost ground. "Sorry about the seating," he said, as brain and hands took over flying without conscious input. U'yun had seven on the team to Alpha's six and the extra body had gone with him. "Figured a few of you would plant ass elsewhere. There's crash harnesses in the galley."

Orange appeared to have melded with the deck. With fewer potential disasters to concentrate on, Craig would've been stroppy about that.

"And miss the commentary?" Elisk snorted. "Not likely."

"Hey, Orange! Now we're so close, if the pirates catch up, will Big Yellow interfere in the fight?" Zhou sounded excited by the prospect. "They've got proof the pirates have dangerous weaponry."

"The pirates destroyed the significantly more dangerous weapon heading toward the majority and presently are attacking the vessel carrying the differing opinion to the majority."

"So that's a no?"

"Should the pirates destroy this vessel," Orange continued, "the majority will be annoyed at the delay in our delivery."

"Still not sure that's a no."

"Can the pirates destroy *you*?" Craig asked as they broke the twenty-kilometer mark.

Orange leaned forward, appearing in Craig's peripheral vision, stretching their upper body until they leaned over the board. "Using the weapons this vessel has identified, no." They snapped back to their default humanoid norm. "If this vessel is destroyed, we will become the data sheet again, and allow the majority to retrieve us from vacuum. Should the pirates retrieve us first, then the majority will do what it must. It will not matter to you, however, as you will all be dead."

"Yeah, got that. Thanks."

"You are welcome."

"Incoming missiles!" Alamber threw the information on his slate onto the screen over the board.

"Who the fuk thought selling pirates missiles was a good idea?" Yahsamus muttered.

He'd dropped *Promise* twice already, so Craig hit the belly jets and went straight up. Up, relative to where the AG currently defined down.

"You blew up pirates the last time they came after you." Tylen swallowed heavily, and Craig wondered how anyone who'd been Navy could get motion sick.

"We blew up a Marine armory," he told her. "The armory blew the ship. And Binti was around to take the shot."

"Hey, also a sniper here," Zhou protested. "I could take the shot."

"With what?" Werst growled.

"Fine," Craig hit the front burners and snapped back two hundred meters. "We get back to Berbar, we'll go into refit for weapons. Happy?"

"Just saying," Werst muttered, "that I'd like to shoot back."

"If you had weapons, you would not be able to deliver us to the majority."

"Yeah, because that situation's going to keep coming up." Werst fought to hold the stabilizers in the green, both feet on the board. "Two pirates coming around . . ."

"Looks like they've started working together." Elisk leaned in. Werst snapped his teeth and Elisk leaned back again. "Must've blown up the dissenter."

"The surveillance drones on the far side of Big Yellow have been taken out."

"Happened the last time, too," Craig told Alamber swinging his stern to port.

"Last time they were hiding a Primacy ship," Werst reminded him. "Wonder what's going on back there this time."

"Can we worry about the pirates?" Elisk tightened his grip as another missile blew short of the hull.

"We can defo worry about the pirates; they're trying to get between us and Big Yellow." Craig stroked up engine details, and fed in a little more power. The deck vibrated faster.

"I could go take a look at your engine," Yahsamus began.

"No."

"Because you blowing us up is better?"

"I said . . . Fuk me!" The windshield polarized again. "What the hell was that?"

"And where the fuk did it come from?" Werst bent over the board, jerked back, and turned to Craig, nostril ridges closed. "Three separate energy readings, two ships *Promise* can't identify and one that spent seventeen seconds flickering in and out of Susumi."

"And we have a weapon designer with no sense of self-preservation," Yahsamus observed. "There was talk about integrating parts of a Susumi drive into a new weapon," she explained to the expectant silence, "but they couldn't get it stabilized enough to use safely."

"And Parliament never approves new weapons," Werst muttered.

"That, too."

The window depolarized. Big Yellow reappeared, filling the upper two thirds of the view. In the lower third . . .

Craig leaned forward. "Is that what it looks like?"

"Does it look like a piece of Big Yellow free floating just under the airlock protrusion?" Alamber asked. "Because that's what the scanners are picking up."

* ——◆—— *

"Cease fire!"

Anthony pushed past Belcerio, feeling he had to be close enough to the communications board for the idiots in the *Liberty* to realize how angry he was. "I told you to hang back! I don't want us involved in this until it becomes necessary."

"The plastic kept us at war for centuries, and we can hurt them! We need to make them pay!"

It seemed that some of the ex-military who made up the majority numbers of Humans First weren't exactly stable. "I need you to fall back as you were ordered!"

"The weapon works!"

Perched on a jump seat, Dr. Banard blew his nose and muttered a damp, "Huzzah."

Clutching the edge of the board so tightly his fingers turned white, Anthony wrapped his voice in ice and iron. "I have given you your coordinates. Get there. Stay there."

"Liberty is moving to their assigned coordinates, Commander."

The person at *Freedom's* com board had spiky white hair. He didn't know her name, had no idea of who she was. Apparently, she had no idea of who he was or she'd have reported to him, not Belcerio. He concentrated on breathing and watched the piece of Big Yellow drift away. So close. He was so close.

"At least the plastic will recognize we have a strong position to negotiate from." Standing in the center of the control room, Belcerio tucked his hands behind his back, right hand in his left. "Once we have the data sheet, we'll hold all the cards."

"I sent out six pirate ships. They had one job." Anthony exhaled. Calmly. Inhaled. Calmly. "Is the Justice ship dead in space? No. And the overly enthusiastic captain of the *Liberty* has poked Big Yellow with a sharp stick, moving up any incipient confrontation. I provided a plan that was elegant in its simplicity. Stop the Wardens, get the data sheet, negotiate a glorious Human future with Big Yellow." He smoothed a crease from the front of his jacket. "I wonder why there seems to be so much trouble actualizing it."

"To be fair, Per Marteau, the Wardens' pilot is good. Better than any of the pirates."

"I don't see why it matters when they're outnumbered," Anthony replied through clenched teeth.

It was, he admitted, good to know that Banard's weapon worked. They'd been fortunate that the Wardens and those idiot pirates had blocked visuals of *Liberty's* shot. If the captain of the *Berganitan* were to suddenly become aware of a weapon able to blow a piece from the plastic, would the battlecruiser join the dance? That, he acknowledged, would definitely complicate the situation.

* ——◆—— *

"Humans First have a weapon that'll damage Big Yellow. That's . . ." Werst stopped looking for a word that would sum up their position. "That's fukked."

"So much for having Orange switch back to data sheet and fall out the airlock while we get rid of the pirates on our ass." They wanted Orange in Big Yellow, not in pieces. Unresponsive pieces from the looks of the debris. Craig knew debris.

"If it's the same sort of weapon General Morris came up with, at least we know it's very explosive," Yahsamus said thoughtfully.

"Yeah, that's comforting."

"Craig!" Alamber's voice cracked. "Big Yellow's shifting!"

Almost too fast to follow, one moment a big yellow ship hung in space, the next the big gray head. At least Craig assumed it was the same head. At their current angle, he couldn't actually see features.

"I've got three ships, previously blocked by Big Yellow. One of them's definitely Humans First, we've gone after it before, so let's assume they all are. Dangerous levels of residual radiation say the one on the far left took the . . . *ablin gon savit*." The Taykan profanity almost sounded like prayer.

The head opened its mouth, crossed a hundred kilometers in an instant, and swallowed the ship on the far left whole.

When it opened its mouth again, pieces drifted out. Most of the pieces were small enough they were only visible to the scanners.

* ——◆—— *

"Oh, no. Oh, no. Oh, no." The pale-skinned young man stared up at the view screen, eyes wide, and took a deep breath. Anthony hoped that meant he was finally going to shut up, but no such luck. "Oh, no. Oh, no. Oh, no."

"Janssen!" Belcerio snapped out the name, got the young man's attention, and gentled his voice. "That's enough."

"But, sir, the plastic just ate the *Liberty*! The ship is destroyed! The crew is dead!"

"Because they didn't do as they were told." Anthony spread his hands as Janssen jerked around to face him. Given that Janssen's account of the last few minutes was entirely accurate, he was impressed his hands weren't shaking. "I gave them coordinates." He channeled his terror into anger. "I told them to wait there for my signal. They didn't, they're dead, and their stupidity has lost us a unique weapon."

"Big Yellow ate your unique weapon!" Janssen's chest heaved. "It ate it and took no damage! None!"

"Turns out the weapon only works if it's fired," Dr. Banard pointed out dryly. "Being chewed into bite-sized pieces wasn't part of the design specs."

"Maybe it should've been!"

Dr. Banard blew his nose and shrugged. "Can't think of everything."

"You're insane!"

Anthony didn't disagree, but that wasn't the point under discussion. The rest of the command crew were watching, and he had to regain control before they surrendered to fear. They weren't throwing away their best chance for Humanity because the plastic had tapped into a hindbrain reaction. If he wasn't surrendering to the urge to pull the covers over his head, neither was anyone else. "We need the leverage the data sheet will provide unless we want to be the next entree on Big Yellow's menu."

"Fuk that! We need to get the fuk out of here."

"Sir."

Belcerio turned toward an older woman with purple hair and skin so dark the control room lighting threw matching purple highlights on the upper curve of her cheeks. "Omondi?"

"There's no way we can outrun that thing." She threw a chart of comparative speeds into the air over her board. "It covered over a hundred kilometers in seconds. If we tried to jump, it'd be on us before the Susumi engines came on line."

"Then we need to destroy it."

"No." When Belcerio pinned him with a glare, Anthony repeated himself, giving the word enough weight to crush objections. "I say, no. If we destroy the plastic, we're heroes for a moment." He swept a gaze around the compartment, meeting each set of eyes before moving on. "I'm not saying we can't build on that, improve Humanity's place in the Confederation. But . . ." No one leaned into the pause, but no one protested either, so he counted it a win. "... if the data sheet is destroyed before we convince the plastic to work with us, or before we know if the data sheet allows us to control it, then we've thrown away our best chance. I thought we were here to reclaim the independence, the glory Humanity had ripped away when we joined the Confederation? I'm here to get that back, I thought you were as well. The universe was ours and it will be again. You're Human! Act like it! We are Humans First, and we are not backing down."

Belcerio stared at him, eyes alight, but then Belcerio had been a true believer from the start.

"It ate one of our ships!" Janssen's voice had begun to fray around the edges. "How do we defeat that?"

How unfortunate Belcerio wasn't the only one who needed convincing.

Anthony sighed and wondered why it always devolved onto him. He was supposed to work behind the scenes, emerge for their triumph, organize the future. "We defeat it with Human ingenuity. The *Liberty* proved Dr. Banard's weapon works. Proved Humans have weapons that can destroy the plastic. Why isn't it running from us? Because it needs the data sheet. We can use that. Omondi, you were Navy, wouldn't you like to make it pay? For all the ships? For the crews?"

"Yes." She didn't sound entirely convinced, but other heads nodded. Even Janssen managed a weak agreement.

"I say we stick to the plan. I say we don't panic, we teach the plastic about Human domination!"

He spread his hands as a ragged cheer arose. He'd had no idea rhetoric would still be necessary at this stage. He'd definitely had Richard Varga killed too soon.

"It ate a ship," Dr. Banard said, directly behind him. "You think you can dominate it?"

"If I can't, I can destroy it. We can build our way up from there." It would take longer, but he always had a backup plan. "Meanwhile, it seems if I want anything done right, I have to do it myself."

• ——◆—— •

Big Yellow returned to its original coordinates and floated in space like it hadn't just become a giant head and eaten a ship. Sweat running down his sides under his tunic, Craig had serious second thoughts about getting closer. He could attach Orange to one of the grappling cables and let it play out until they were snagged by the majority. He just had to get them inside. He didn't have to escort them all the way in.

"Craig!" Even without turning, Craig knew Alamber's hair had flattened. "I've got a Susumi point opening dangerously close."

The coordinates put it at one hundred and sixty-seven degrees, between the *Berganitan* and Big Yellow, seven hundred and fifty-two kilometers out. The amount of Susumi radiation that hit the *Promise* would depend on the size of the emerging ship, but they would be hit.

"Assholes," Werst grunted. "Guess I'm having the old leaves and twig irradiated again."

"I can help protect them," Tylen offered.

Werst turned far enough to glare.

Her hair flattened. "Okay, no. Do you you think it's Gunny?"

"She'd never come in so close," Craig replied, putting more distance between them and the jump point without losing his angle on Big Yellow's airlock.

Werst shot him a side-eye. "If she thought she was riding to the rescue?"

"Possible."

"Who else could it be?" Alamber demanded. "Ressk could have set up an alert for Susumi packets coming from the *Berganitan* and copied them while in-system. He'd get through a standard military encryption in minutes."

"Stop teaching my husband bad habits."

Alamber grinned. "What about good ones?"

"SECTOR CENTRAL NEWS IS ON THE SCENE!"

Craig and Werst slapped hands over the volume control.

"Oh, joy," Werst sighed, leaning back again. "It's the press."

"It's on all frequencies. They're using a full disclosure override." Alamber bent over his slate. "Working on shutting them down."

"We go where the action is!"

"Seventy percent of the Susumi wave was absorbed by dampeners they sent out ahead of them." Werst squinted at the readout. "That's fukkin' impressive. We'll be warmed instead of fried to a crisp."

"That's tech I've never heard of. Anyone?" After a unanimous negative, Craig cracked his neck and bent over the board. "I'm starting to think this full-disclosure thing is bullshit."

"We provide the Confederation with the information needed for contemplation!"

"On the bright side," Elisk noted, "being eaten's looking better."

"Hey, Orange, could you talk Big Yellow into eating the press?"

"When we have rejoined them, yes."

"Zhou! Do not give them ideas!" Elisk sounded as though he thought Zhou had been serious. Although, in the end, Craig supposed it only mattered that Orange not think Zhou had been serious. However tempting the thought might be.

As the ship moved away from the jump point, it split into three ships, sent out a flock of drones, arranged themselves to cover all angles, and announced they were keeping a trace in space apace. Or something like that. Craig had stopped listening.

"You think Presit's in there?" Werst asked, raising his voice to be heard over three different reporters setting the scene.

"Not in person, or we'd know without having to ask." He missed her. "But one way or another, yeah, it's Presit."

Alamber looked up from his slate. "I sent her a message in the packet I put together. Told her everything."

"Everything?"

Alamber's eyes darkened as the light receptors opened, as though he were trying to see Craig's reaction before Craig had even decided what that reaction was. "Full disclosure."

". . . question now is, why isn't Warden Strike Team Leader, ex-Gunnery Sergeant Kerr, on the scene?"

"We'll talk about Presit later. Right now, block those . . . Thank you." He sighed into the silence and checked their position. "So, into Big Yellow?"

"We have options?" Werst demanded.

"Attach the data sheet to a grappling cable. Fish for plastic."

"Tempting," Elisk admitted before Werst could respond. When Werst didn't respond, Craig was reminded yet again that Elisk was U'yun's Strike Team Leader and therefore—for the moment—theirs. "But we need to finish this. We need to be sure Orange is absorbed into the majority."

"Into Big Yellow, it is." Craig hit the bow burners, and began dropping speed. "At least, the press got the pirates to back off."

"Yeah . . ." Werst expanded a section of the board. ". . . not so much."

The pirates had regrouped and were approaching the *Promise* in a tight curve. Craig dodged the first two shots. Tipped up to dodge three and four. "Feels like we're being herded."

"We are." Alamber told him. "Scanners have the two Humans First ships from the other side of Big Yellow moving in. Fast."

If he took the *Promise* back through the pirates, they'd start shooting. If he headed toward the press, he'd risk putting them in the crossfire. He couldn't get attached to Big Yellow before Humans First showed up with their wonder weapon.

"Buckle up. We need to save Orange's plastic ass if we want the plastic out of our lives."

Bow burners off, he shot the *Promise* out half a kilometer at thirty degrees and called up the Susumi equations for the entry point into this system.

· ——◆—— ·

"I am Marteau Industries. I've been in the news my entire life and I know how to use the media to my advantage. I can't believe they thought this would discourage us."

"Crazy thought," Dr. Banard said, stretching out his legs and crossing swollen ankles. "It's not all about you."

Anthony rolled his eyes. "It is if I'm here. Commander, I need to send Sector Central News a message. I believe it's time for Humans First to take their place in the spotlight."

"Shouldn't we wait until after we have the data sheet?" Belcerio didn't look convinced. Anthony didn't care.

"I intend to build interest. Sympathy. I want them talking about us, speculating as we move in. When we have the means to take our rightful place, I want the Confederation primed and ready."

"Most of the employees at Sector Central aren't Human."

"I'm using them, Commander, not recruiting them."

"Omondi?"

"Yes, sir. Opening contact. It may take a moment to get their attention."

"Let them know I'm here."

She opened her mouth, but before she could speak, Dr. Banard called out, "How did you get the pirates to work together, Marteau? They're not known for cooperation."

He smiled. "I told them when we were successful, they could

return to the bosom of the Confederation as heroes." They had too many non-Humans in their crews to be returning anywhere. The moment he had Big Yellow, they'd go out in a blaze of glory.

Dr. Banard stared at him like he'd grown a second nose. "You said bosom? Seriously?"

"And I offered them a great deal of money."

"You're lucky they didn't cooperate to come after you." He blew his nose. "Bosom . . ."

"Commander?" Janssen's back was a rigid line. "The *Promise* has engaged its Susumi engine."

"Here?" Belcerio strode forward, and peered over Janssen's shoulder. "No, that's got to be a . . ."

Energy readings spiked as the *Promise* disappeared.

Anthony actually felt his jaw drop. "I can't believe he ran!"

· ——◆—— ·

"Holy fukking shit!"

"Seconded!"

Craig glanced over to see Werst working hands and feet on the board, keeping the readouts out of the red as they dropped the energy from the micro jump. Werst had been in the second seat the last time he'd micro'd—good planning on his part.

He fought *Promise* around, ramming hard on the starboard jets, and ran her across the trails left from the *Berganitan's* entry, the energy braiding and the Susumi wave bleeding off.

"Did you know that was going to work?" Werst demanded.

"Making it up as I go along."

"Energy levels in this area are . . ."

"Hey, dude, Orange." Alamber reached out and poked his shoulder. "Are you in danger? No? Then let it go."

Fingers shifting numbers up and down and all but sideways, Craig finally got them slowed and turned to face the *Berganitan*. "Alamber, let Captain Carveg know we're okay."

"Are we?"

"Any jump you can fly away f . . . fuk me." He slapped the cut-off as every scanner began to overload and stared out at Big Yellow. Or the familiar bottom curve of Big Yellow considering that the plastic had exactly matched their previous closest point.

· ——◆—— ·

It was easier for two ships of similar size to exit Susumi space one after the other through the same exit point. Torin didn't know why, but that's what Craig had told her. Given that she wasn't a pilot, Torin had no intention of risking both ships so they'd planned to jump in far enough apart that if she screwed up, at least the *Baylet* would survive.

"Three. Two. One . . ."

The stars reappeared, and the *Bunny* nearly twisted out of her control.

"Is this the Susumi wave?" Ozborz asked, eyes shining as his head whipped back and forth.

"It is." She hung in her crash harness, straps digging into her breasts while the AG caught up. "But not ours." The odds were high Bilodeau hadn't pooched the exit, so if they were being hit by the *Baylet's* wave, things were very wrong.

"Bunny, *this is* Baylet. *Looks like Ryder micro'd again!*"

"You sure it was Craig?"

"*Who else is crazy enough?*"

Fair point.

"*Clench your teeth and let the* Bunny *bounce. She'll settle on her own, and there's nothing out here for her to . . . uh, belay that last bit. Check your port scanners.*"

Teeth clenched, Torin hit the port jets attempting to level out and threw the *Bunny* into a spin, the AG half a rotation behind. She had no idea where the port scanners were. "Just fukking tell me, Bilodeau."

"Promise *and Big Yellow are about fifty klicks out.*"

"From here?"

"*Roger,* Bunny. *And there's five ships approaching, having just crossed to this side of the* Berganitan."

Multiple Silsviss made disappointed protests as Torin finally stopped the spin. Although they also seemed to be enjoying the bow continuing to buck up and down.

Her implant pinged.

They'd bounced into range of *Promise's* communications array.

Torin?

She grinned without unclenching her teeth. Craig's voice was the best thing she'd heard in a tenday. "Little busy."

No shit. See the yellow rectangle on the upper left corner of the board? Shove that into the red, then use the bow belly jets to point your nose straight up and hit the aft burners. The wave front's a cone and you're at the narrow end. It's the fastest way to get out of it.

"Push it into the red?" Wasn't that bad? "Are you sure?"

Do I tell you how to shoot people? Trust me.

Red still seemed counterintuitive, but she trusted Craig with her life—and the lives of everyone on board. By the time she got the *Bunny* leveled out and pointed in the right direction, the *Baylet* was halfway to the *Berganitan*.

"Bilodeau. Sitrep."

*"One of the five approaching ships is listed on the pirate database. Two guesses on the other four, and the first guess doesn't count. Ber-*ganitan *says they're after the* Promise, *so I'm running interference."*

"Right behind you."

Ozborz slid into the pilot's seat almost before she was out of it. She smacked his tail aside, hissed back at him, and froze, hand shifting the strap of her weapon back up onto her shoulder.

During the moment she'd been distracted, Big Yellow had become a big gray head. It looked familiar, but Torin didn't have time to work out where she'd see it before.

· ——◆—— ·

The head turned, opened its mouth, and released the ship it had just swallowed in one piece.

"TORIN!"

"Warden Kerr has been consumed by the beast."

"Who is this?"

"I am Ret Tyroliz. And I was promised a hunt. We'll mark our prey for Warden Kerr."

"That's Fukking damnit! He's gone."

"Summours have him following the *Baylet*." Alamber announced. "I can open another channel."

"Don't bother," Craig grunted, both hands working the controls.

"Ret Tyroliz?" Werst snorted. "Never heard of him."

"Yeah, mate, that's mutual."

"Hang on." Werst looked vaguely constipated for a moment. "Ressk says Ret Tyroliz is the Warlord who took the station on Silsviss and his people are Torin's prisoners, that Lies is on the ship, and the Silsviss are here because Humans First has us outnumbered and Torin wanted to even the odds."

"With Silsviss?"

Werst shrugged. "They like her."

"Ryder." Elisk laid enough concern on his name that Craig gave some serious thought to smacking him. "About Warden Kerr . . ."

"She's fine. Probably pissed as hell."

"You don't think Big Yellow . . ."

"They're smarter than that," Alamber declared.

"They were in her head," Craig reminded everyone. "Speed and rotation matched to Big Yellow."

"Already?" Elisk leaned in to look at the board. "That was fast."

"No one's shooting at us. And I'm motivated." He nodded toward the window where it showed yellow, edge to edge. "And I had help. They're more motivated."

Tylen unbuckled and got to her feet. "We're going in after her?"

That didn't merit an answer. "Universal airlock deployed."

Werst thumbed a line of numbers to a stop. "You're too far left."

"Fuk you, I am not. Coupling attached. Seal secured." Craig swung up out of his seat, cracked his knuckles, and nearly ran over Elisk who'd turned to face the cabin.

"Gear up, people, we're going in."

"No." He went to slide around the Team Lead, but found himself blocked. "I'm going in."

Elisk shook his head. "Ryder, you're an amazing pilot and H'san-shit crazy, but . . ."

"Get to the point, LT."

"You're not going in alone."

THIRTEEN

THE PLASTIC DIDN'T have enough facial definition to glare, but Torin was pretty damned sure that's what was happening. Arms folded, she glared back at it with no clear idea of how she'd been transported to the inside of Big Yellow. One moment, she'd been standing behind the pilot's seat staring into the open mouth of a huge gray head, the next she was standing on the upper level of a well-lit, two-level chamber with six-by-six grates covering the ceiling, a glimpse of pipes and wires through the mesh. Without taking the metal stairs, she knew they led down to a textured deck, with four large tanks held in black cradles on one wall, and unidentifiable gray machinery running in two lines the length of the compartment.

This was where PFC August Guimond had died.

Torin crushed a handful of her tunic in her right fist. Guimond had been big and cheerful and had seen the best in everyone and every situation. She'd led him into Big Yellow and carried him out.

A vaguely bipedal shape stood approximately two meters away. Far enough, she wouldn't be fast enough to get her hands on it. In spite of the mass currently available, it was no taller than a Krai—the same size the plastic had used on the prison planet. If it assumed she'd find the familiar comforting, it was wrong.

"You released our prisoner," it said, lipless mouth barely moving. "You had no right."

The Silsviss were the only released prisoners Torin knew of, but she had no idea how Big Yellow would've found out about them unless the plastic remained threaded throughout the Confederation. Or worse, unless that moment's travel had taken significantly longer than it seemed and the little gray fukkers had been in her head again, messing with perception. She stopped herself before she checked her cuff as she had no idea of the time she'd been taken and the plastic could have as easily messed with her tech as with her head.

"Where's my crew?"

"Your ship, and those you call the Silsviss, were released and are flying into conflict."

Of course they were. Gaze locked on the plastic, she pressed a double ping into her implant. "This is Warden Torin Kerr. Is anyone receiving?" After sixty seconds, she tried again. Nothing. On her first trip into Big Yellow, while her implant's signal hadn't been strong enough to reach the outside, Captain Travik's had been. Her current implant was significantly more powerful than the captain's. It seemed Big Yellow had changed its specs.

As it had recently been a giant gray head, she admitted that was a somewhat redundant observation.

It stood motionless. Waiting.

While Torin found a certain satisfaction in silent glaring, tactics required information. "Okay. Fine. What are you talking about?"

It blinked gray-on-gray eyes. "You released our prisoner. You have no idea how dangerous they are."

Torin folded her arms. "I have a better idea than most how dangerous the Silsviss are."

"We do not refer to those you call the Silsviss. We refer to the minority."

"The minority of what?"

"The majority."

"You're more annoying than you used to be." She huffed out an impatient breath. "And that's saying something."

"We are the majority." It extruded another arm. Torin couldn't see how a third arm made its point any clearer. "You identified the minority as a . . ." It absorbed the arm during the pause. ". . . data sheet."

Given their history, the pause was suspicious. What had it been searching to find its next word? "Are you in my head?"

"Not currently. We refreshed our data while you were within us."

"Did you?" She swung the modified benny around and laid her

finger along the outside of the trigger guard. No surprise the plastic had brought her weapon along—the entire squad had been armed the last time through Big Yellow, and after examining their bennies, the plastic had changed itself so they couldn't harm it. There hadn't been time for it to have examined this particular benny, however. She hoped. If the modification worked the way Dr. Deyell intended, interrupting the electrical currents to and from the brain . . .

Did some of the plastic become a brain when they combined or were each of them a part of the cognitive apparatus while still individuals? Would interrupting the electrical currents break Big Yellow into its billions of component parts, leaving her unprotected in space?

Gunnery Sergeant Kerr, trapped alone inside the belly of the beast responsible for every Marine she'd carried from the battlefield, would've pulled the trigger to find out.

Warden Kerr held the option in reserve.

The harsh sound of her breathing disappeared into the total lack of ambient noise. "So, if the data sheet was a prisoner, that means you left some of your people confined in a hole for a millennium. I should arrest you for sentient rights' violations." Why stop there? "Inciting violence resulting in death. Kidnapping an officer of the Justice Department. Unethical experimentation on sentient beings. Cognitive trespass."

"Neither your laws nor what you consider ethical considerations apply to us."

"Yeah, well . . ." Torin showed teeth and shifted her weight. "I'm going to do my damnedest to make them apply."

It cocked its head. "How?"

"I'm working on it."

It waited a moment, then when Torin didn't produce results, said, "We want what is ours to be returned."

"Not what," she snapped. "Who. And how do you even know they survived?"

"We have no information on their survival. We know only that the minority has been freed."

"And your point?" She hated to think of what Craig, who'd seen her ship devoured, was going through.

"Return the prisoner to us."

"Why should we?" A small part of her suggested agreeing to return their prisoner with no intention of keeping to that agreement might be the wiser choice. The larger part didn't give a flying fuk.

"If the minority survived, and if the shackles we placed upon them have been broken, they are a danger to your people."

Her lip curled up off her teeth. "How?"

"That is not relevant." The plastic stretched ten centimeters taller. Torin wondered if the increase in size was a threat.

Alive and unshackled, the data sheet could separate down to the molecular level and take up housekeeping in half a dozen new brains. In Craig's brain. Become so perfectly a part of the *Promise*, they couldn't be found. Slide into the *Promise*'s engines and blow her up with all on board. "Thanks for the warning." The plastic either ignored or didn't recognize sarcasm. "How long have you known your prisoner was in our care?"

"The alarm was sounded. We have known from the time the alarm reached us."

"No." Torin shook her head. "If you're referring to the energy blast, the alarm sounded a tenday ago. The signal couldn't have reached this far in a tenday, let alone where you . . . exist."

"The alarm traveled along the inner way."

The inner way? "Susumi space." If the plastic could jump in and out of Susumi space at will, that would explain how the various bits of it they'd run into over the years had always disappeared so quickly.

"Susumi is your name for it." The emphasis on *your* sounded almost disdainful. That was more emotion than Torin had ever heard from the plastic. "The prisoner is here. With the one we knew called Craig Ryder."

Torin would put money on Parliament having decided to avoid confrontation by returning the alleged data sheet. "You turned into a giant gray head. You ate my ship. Why haven't you taken the minority back? Not . . ." She jabbed a finger toward it. ". . . a suggestion."

It flattened and filled out again. "We must first determine if it remains shackled."

About to ask why, Torin connected the dots. "Because if it's unshackled and you engulf it, like you did me, it can harm you."

Dimensions shifted horizontally. "Yes."

"Was the minority imprisoned for harming you?"

"No." And vertically.

Was the plastic aware of how its avatar kept changing? Torin didn't think so. Was she seeing the external effect of a molecular hive mind reacting to fear? And fuk her life that that thought had ever come into it. "Why was the minority imprisoned?"

"That is not relevant. Return the prisoner to us."

"So you can throw it into another hole and torture it? No." She met its gaze. "You've outstayed your welcome. The Justice Department wants you out of Confederation space. The moment Confederation citizens are clear, you're to leave and not return."

"You cannot enforce this."

"Me, personally?" Torin smiled. "Did you miss the part about the Justice Department?"

"You have changed." It extruded a third leg, shifted weight onto it, and backed up.

"You haven't."

·——◆——·

"The moment the majority comes into contact with us, regardless of the shape we wear, they will know we are awake and will attempt to contain us." Orange flowed through the team to stand between them and the airlock. "There will be a struggle. We will prevail; however, in the process, your meat may be damaged."

Craig held his palm up toward the three di'Taykan. "Don't."

"Too easy." Yahsamus shifted the strap of her KC so it hung without affecting the draw of the larger knife on her belt.

Big Yellow had made itself resistant to bennies back in the day, so when they'd cracked the armory, Werst handed out the KC-7s and demolition charges. Craig suspected neither did any actual damage, that Big Yellow sacrificed a minimum of molecules as they shifted away from the impact. Based on past experience, though, they'd need to shift the fukker more than once before they got Torin out.

"Fine. If you think your majority will overreact to your presence, don't make contact until we find Torin." Craig reached past Orange and hit the airlock's inner release. "You stay here, until we get her out. When we're clear, you leap in. We haul ass away. Alamber . . ."

"No." He tossed his head. "I'm not staying behind."

"I'm not leaving them here alone."

"You stay." His hair flattened and he muttered, "Yeah, like that'll happen."

"It has to be someone familiar with the *Promise,* and you're not the fighter Werst is."

"Fukking right," Werst muttered.

"And Werst doesn't have a hope in hell of breaking through to Torin's implant." Alive, Torin would have contacted them. Since she hadn't, she'd been blocked. Craig refused to consider any other possibility.

"Fine." Alamber threw himself down into the pilot's chair. "I'll break the block and boost the carrier signal."

"She could be . . ." Tylen began. Stopped when Werst growled. Slipped into the airlock and tucked herself behind Zhou. Which would have worked better had she not been a full head taller with bright pink hair.

"Craig."

He caught the hatch and stopped it from closing the final ten centimeters.

Alamber's eyes had gone several shades darker than his hair. "You have to tell her I would have come."

"She'll know."

"You have to tell her."

Craig smiled. "Tell her yourself when you get through to her implant." As the hatch closed, he saw Orange reach out to touch Alamber's wrist.

"Did it look like this the last time you were here?" Elisk asked, sending Zhou away from the airlock to take point.

"It looked like a lot of things the last time we were here."

Back then, they'd used a scientist and sensor strips to open Big Yellow's airlock. Yahsamus had been ready to try and repeat the results, but the hardware looked standard this time. They'd stepped from the universal link into the airlock, equalized pressure, and stepped out again.

"I hate it when it's this easy," Zhou muttered as he moved out four meters.

Craig remembered the airlock had opened onto a dull gray corridor around three meters wide, fifteen meters long, lit by an indeterminate source. The light source was still indeterminate, the corridor the same dimensions, but the gray had been replaced with yellow.

"It's like it's not even trying." Werst slapped the wall. "Fukker."

Fully aware that an exact repeat of their last visit would've gotten an equally negative reaction, Craig tongued his implant. "Alamber? Are you receiving?"

He listened to himself breathe for thirty seconds and tried again. If he couldn't reach the system, there wasn't much point, but he tried Torin anyway. Nothing.

"Kid'll get the implants working. Ressk says he's a genius." Werst swept a cautionary glare around the team. "No one tells Alamber I said that."

Tylen mimed locking her lips as Yahsamus asked, "Without the implants, how do we find Torin?"

Craig held up his slate.

"You tagged her." Werst's nostril ridges closed. "She's not going to be happy about that."

"If it saves her, I don't care."

"You say that now . . ."

"You're generating your own carrier wave?" Yahsamus asked, a blunt change of topic.

"I am."

"That's going to suck your power source dry."

"Not before we find her." He hoped. "Big Yellow can't block a program it's never . . . There." It hurt to breathe. "Stationary signal."

"That was fast. Give it over." Before he could answer, Yahsamus took the slate from his hand, slaved it to hers, sent the information to everyone's helmet visor, and handed his slate back. "Even faster this way," she said. "We can all see where we're going."

"Half a kilometer of corridors to a big rectangular compartment," Elisk observed. "That seems easy enough."

Zhou glanced back over his shoulder. "You had to fukkin' jinx it, didn't you LT."

· —◆— ·

The room where August Guimond had died had been losing definition for a while now. The stairs were gone, the ceiling grates had solidified, and yellow lapped at the edges of the grays and blacks.

Torin folded her arms and stared down her nose at the plastic's avatar. "You're in violation of a directive from the Confederation Justice Department. Any hesitation in returning all Confederation

Citizens to their vessels and leaving this part of space will be held against you should this come to a court of law. Should you wish to return to the area claimed by the Confederation, you'll send a message to Parliament requesting permission to cross the border." And Commander Ng thought she hadn't mastered official Warden speak. Torin would like to see the commander come up with that shit while inside a form held by polynumerous molecular polyhydroxide alcoholyde.

The avatar planted their feet, yellow flowed up their legs, and it surged up to tower over her at two and a half meters high and a meter across. "Return to us that which is ours!"

"The Justice Department will not give over a potentially sentient being to torture."

"RETURN TO US THAT WHICH IS OURS!"

"Fuk you."

"Then you have become the bargaining chip that releases the minority!"

As that was the only possible reason for it to have grabbed her, Torin was less than surprised by the declaration. She curled her finger around the trigger, but wasn't able to tighten her grip before the wall closed around her.

· —◆— ·

Slate propped on the control panel, both hands working the board, Alamber glanced back over his shoulder at Orange, sitting motionless where he'd left them. "Did you want to sit second? The auxiliary controls are offline," he expanded, when he received no response. "But there's more stimulus up here. After a millennium hanging in a pit, you've got to still be running at a loss."

Flattened tendrils rising off their head, Orange stood. "Both statements are true." They settled into the seat, body shifting into what Alamber assumed was the most comfortable configuration.

"Don't touch anything, okay?"

"Yes." Their hands sank a centimeter into their thighs.

"That's a bit extreme, but okay." Alamber returned his attention to the implant system. "You can talk. I mean, I can work while things blow up, so talking is not that big a deal."

"What do you desire us to say?"

"Nothing specific. I like having the sound of other people around me." He frowned as a line of code mutated and hoped that didn't mean Big Yellow had a tendril on board. Craig would blow. And not in a good way. "It's a Taykan thing."

"You are not content."

"Content? Sure I am. I love my job. I love my team. They're like family, you know? Do you know what family is?"

"The consensus."

"Yeah, I guess if you're a hive mind, that's family." Dumping sixteen lines, Alamber set in a block of his own, preventing Big Yellow from repairing the damage he'd already done.

"You are not in consensus."

"Look, I understand why I couldn't go after the boss. If you've had trad training, you can't adapt fast enough. And I had anti-trad training, so I adapt even faster. I'm the best. And the only one who could have done this." Simple truth.

"And you are not in consensus."

It didn't seem like they were going to drop it and they were wrong, so Alamber redirected the conversation. "Let's talk about you. Tell me what your people were doing on Threxie. That's what we call the planet we found you on," he added before Orange had a chance to blank out again.

"We were observing. We had been there for one hundred and seventeen rotations of the planet around the sun . . ."

"Years."

". . . for one hundred and seventeen years."

They sounded pleased although given all the words they'd absorbed, Alamber had no idea how they'd missed *years*. He glanced over at the long-range scanners and grinned. Two of the pirate ships were dead in space. No surprise if Binti was at the guns on the *Baylet*. One less thing for him to worry about, anyway. He robbed the block of a bit more definition. "Is that what you did back then, observe?"

"It was our preference. The majority preferred to make contact."

Alamber glanced up from dumping a tiny and very specific worm from his slate to the system, and indicated that Orange should continue.

"The inhabitants of what you call Threxie were less interesting to us than those we had previously observed. They were simple and the previous were complex. We prefer complex and were in consensus when contact with the previous was made."

"That would've been the H'san?"

"They called themselves the H'san, yes."

"They were on Threxie?"

"The contact was made before we arrived on what you call Threxie. During our contact, we began to understand a hierarchical species and how this can aid in forming a consensus of meat."

Alamber snickered. *A consensus of meat* was ripe for . . .

Fingers and hair still, he turned toward Orange. "If you spoke with the H'san, then the H'san know about you. About the whole organic plastic hive mind."

"We are not what you know as plastic."

"Close enough for government work, Orange, trust me on that. And not the point. The H'san know about you?"

"They knew. We cannot say if they know." Orange shrugged. "Time has passed."

"True." Throwing subtlety aside, Alamber followed the worm in, hacked chunks off the block, and thought about the plastic and the H'san making friends. His hair lifted. "So were the H'san doing the war thing when you made contact?"

"On occasion. We learned of war from the H'san. We observed and learned that violence does not prevent stagnation. Stagnation is overcome on all levels by a willingness to be open to new ideas. When the H'san made a decision, they proved to be resistant to change and unwilling to accept that change occurs regardless."

"We do it their way, or it doesn't get done."

"If you refer to the H'san, yes." Orange blinked, created and absorbed nostril ridges, and after a moment added, "Although we are not certain who you refer to as *we*."

"Hold that thought." Lines began to scroll by faster and faster, rewriting the block. Honestly? Watching the screen, Alamber understood why everyone had thought Orange was a data sheet. "So before the H'san, you didn't know about war?"

"We knew conflict. We learned of war as a sociocultural construct."

New panels lit up on the board.

Alamber tapped the closer of the two. "Sending: one ping."

A new record!

"Because I'm just that good." Not that there was a previous record for deconstructing a block set up by a hyperintelligent plastic hive mind. He spun the chair to face Orange. "And, Craig, you're not going to believe what the H'san taught the plastic."

· ——◆—— ·

"The interior layout keeps changing!" Elisk squinted through his helmet scanner and pointed to the right where a new corridor lined with yellow columns had just appeared. "This wasn't here before."

"That's nothing compared to the last time," Werst told him.

"No, you don't understand. That's the way we have to go, and it just appeared."

Werst rolled his eyes. "Yeah, like I said, this is nothing. Last time we had to play twenty questions every time we changed direction."

"Shuffling walls don't mean shit. Torin hasn't moved, so let's go." Craig jogged down the new corridor, slate up. Stationary didn't mean injured. Torin had a bad habit of ignoring injuries until after she'd done what she thought needed to be done. He found it one of her least endearing qualities and if she'd done it again, well, he looked forward to discussing it with her. Because they would find her. And she would be alive. Alamber hadn't cleared her implant yet, but he would. Soon.

Two meters in, Zhou pushed past him muttering, "Hey, come on, Ryder. Marching order."

When Craig began to speed up, Werst grabbed his wrist and pulled him back until he matched the Krai's shorter stride, hanging on in spite of Craig's attempt to yank himself free.

"Zhou's on point. Let him go. You in that much of a hurry to tell her how the H'san taught the plastic about the uses of war?"

Another yank. Same result. "I . . ."

"You won't shoot if we're cut off," Werst told him flatly. "Zhou will. Same as Toch'll shoot if we're jumped from behind."

"Jumped by who?"

"Who the hell cares? They jump us, we shoot them." Werst released him. Craig could still feel the imprint of his fingers. "We'll find her."

"Signal goes left at the t-junction," Zhou called.

The signal turned again four point two meters in. Even Craig stood for a moment staring at the partially collapsed, oval opening, surrounded by a raised, pleated ridge.

"It's a sphincter," Tylen observed. She poked it. "Well, we are in a constructed body."

"It looks like a ship," Yahsamus pointed out. "Ships shouldn't have sphincters. At least not ones that look so . . ."

Tylen poked it again. "Biological?"

"Yeah, that'll do."

"There's an open space beyond the hatch." Elisk raised a hand and tapped the edge of his scanner. "It's matching up with Ryder's tag, but it's a lot smaller than it was. If Gunny's in there, her life signs are being smothered by Big Yellow's."

Because Big Yellow was alive. Like Torin was alive. Craig charged through the hole, ignoring Zhou's protest. Ignoring Elisk's command to stop.

If asked, Craig would have denied being able to identify Torin by her nose, but that was definitely her nose, uncovered, while the rest of her had been sunk into the yellow wall. Light levels and yellow on yellow meant he could just barely make out the raised outline of her body. It could have been any body and looked disturbingly like the reliefs Orange had created as they woke. The covered barrel of a weapon protruded at waist level and that, as much as the nose, convinced him he'd found Torin.

"Holy shit," Zhou breathed behind him. "She took a shot at it."

Werst snorted. "Fukking right she did."

Her nostrils flared. She was alive. Craig grinned at the energy of the flare—he'd bet there was a good bit of silent profanity going on back there. "Alamber. We've found her."

All right, good. And?

"It's complicated, but she's alive." Elisk, who as Team Lead had as much medical tech on his slate as the official medic, gave him a thumbs up. "Better than alive. Scan found no damage."

That's good. Really good. Okay. Hooking her back into the system still isn't happening, so I'm going to link her through you and avoid the whole shitstorm. Give me a minute.

He wanted to touch her. Wanted to feel the warmth of her skin. Feel her breath. Wanted to inhale her scent and demand to know why she always smelled faintly of gun oil. Wanted to hear her tell him he was imagining things, she'd just showered. But, mostly, he wanted to touch that small amount of visible Torin and be reassured. His heart beat so hard, Craig pressed a hand against his chest to hold it in place.

It felt as though hours passed watching her breathe, but it couldn't have been more than minutes. Zhou had only just taken his place two meters farther into the chamber when Alamber returned.

Implant link is in place. Channel will open when you make contact.

He double-tapped his implant, putting her on group channel. "Torin?"

Hey. What took you so long? It was muffled, but understandable.

"We're Wardens now. We had to wait for a warrant."

Fuk you, too.

"It's how they say I love you," Werst told Yahsamus.

"Yeah, I got that. Very sweet."

Little gray fukker there?

"No, just us. Can you move?"

No.

"We'll try cutting you out first."

Cutting laser not hot 'nuff.

"Yeah, I remember. Tech's got a big knife with her."

Overcompensating.

"I can hear you, you know." Yahsamus glanced at Elisk, who nodded. She beckoned Tylen over to guard the sphincter, walked to Torin's side, and drove her knife into the wall. It sank in hilt-deep. When she dragged it down, it moved. When she pulled it out, the wall showed no damage.

Not an unexpected result, but that didn't make Craig any happier. "Torin, you feel anything?"

Impatient.

"All right." Elisk reached into his belt pouch. "A demo charge at the other end of . . . *garn chreen!*"

They weren't alone in the chamber anymore.

The gray plastic alien had stepped out of the far wall, yellow filling the indentation he'd left behind.

Weapon raised, Zhou backed up until he bumped into Elisk. "LT, do I take the shot?"

"Negative. It wants to talk."

"How do you figure?"

"Gunny's still alive."

Last time Craig had seen the plastic alien, he and Presit had just taken an Artek-piloted shuttle from the *Promise* down to the planet where Torin had been imprisoned. It looked exactly the same. Small, unassuming . . .

"I am going to eat that fukker this time!"

Werst had been on the planet with Torin.

The plastic blinked and said to no one in particular. "We will trade you Strike Team Leader Gunnery Sergeant Torin Kerr for the minority."

Torin's nostril's flared impressively far. She'd obviously heard the declaration—through the implants or through the plastic itself. *Tell it to get fukked!*

Craig rolled his eyes. "Okay if I handle this?"

Fine.

Turning to face the plastic, he smiled. "Get fukked."

I love you.

He laughed. "I know."

"You will not get Strike Team Leader Gunnery Sergeant Torin Kerr back unless we are given the minority."

"You're all powerful." Craig folded his arms. "You want the minority, take them."

"Could we try not to provoke the giant, omnipresent alien," Elisk sighed.

"They won't take the minority; they're afraid of them."

The avatar skated forward, feet never losing contact with the floor. Werst snapped his teeth. The avatar reversed the movement.

I have an idea, Alamber announced. *If Tylen and Tech turn off their maskers and make as much contact as possible with the part of Big Yellow holding the boss, odds are you can get her free.*

Orange had responded to the pheromones, Craig acknowledged. It was worth a shot.

Lower inhibitions?

In every single molecule, Boss. No way they'll be able to maintain consensus.

"Elisk, Zhou, move out another meter. Werst . . ."

"Prepare to be uncomfortable." He spread his legs to shoulder width, toes curling against the floor. "Good thing we didn't wear the suits."

Not in suits?

She didn't sound happy about it. However, now was not the time to explain they hadn't thought they had the time to suit up. She wouldn't be happy about that either. Craig saw drills in their future. He nodded at the two di'Taykan. "Do it."

The plastic alien's nearly formless head jerked from side to side as it attempted to watch all of them at once. "Give us back what is ours!"

Yahsamus turned her masker off, tossed her vest to Werst, stripped off her tunic, and pressed her left side against the yellow over Torin, her right hand resting on Torin's chest. A moment later, Tylen plastered herself against the right side.

Nothing happened.

Give it a minute, Alamber advised, correctly translating the silence.

Craig wondered if Orange had weighed in.

The avatar swayed. "Give us back what is . . ." It froze. Grew a sudden meter higher. "Stop what you are doing immediately!" it ordered over the sound of Zhou's laughter.

"It got bigger," Zhou snickered.

Werst rolled his eyes. "Kids."

Torin's nose twitched. *Not bored now.*

Frustrated wasn't bored; Craig would give her that. Breathing through his mouth didn't help.

Elisk and Werst had their nostril ridges shut tight. Zhou had started tapping his heels. Torin was trapped inside Big Yellow, that was all the distraction Craig needed.

Almost all the distraction.

"There's a response." Yahsamus stroked down Torin's torso. "It's shuddering. We need to tip it over the edge."

Tylen grinned, leaned forward, and caught the technical sergeant's mouth in a kiss.

Humans and Taykan were the only species in known space who put their mouths together in exactly that way. What were the odds, Craig wondered, refusing to shift in place.

"Cleaning latrines. Cleaning spray from a head shot. H'san having sex." Zhou's volume rose. "Not helping."

Big Yellow writhed out from under the two di'Taykan, writhed away from Torin, kept writhing.

"Stop. Stop. Stoooo . . ." For a moment the avatar showed as gray marbling within the floor, then there was only yellow.

"Bet there's a story behind that," Torin breathed stumbling forward. For all they'd been touching her when she began to fall, Craig caught her before either Yahsamus or Tylen got the chance.

·———◆——— ·

Torin removed her finger from around the trigger and looked up at Craig, chest heaving. His eyes held a desperate vulnerability that she suspected was mirrored in her own. She wet her lips, swallowed, and managed to croak out, "The Silsviss?"

The ship you got lifted from is fine, Boss. The Silsviss are chasing down a pirate who tried to run.

"And the *Baylet*?"

Moving prisoners onto the Berganitan.*

Hands on her shoulders, Craig pulled her almost all the way up against him and gave her a little shake. "Are you all right?"

"I'm not engulfed in sentient plastic, so I'm good."

"Fall apart later?"

"That's how it works." She wanted to take a moment against Craig's chest, wrapped in his arms. Replace the feeling of being buried alive with warmth and safety. But this was not that moment. She squeezed his wrists and pushed away. "Werst."

"Gunny."

She nodded toward the last of the gray disappearing into the floor. "Is that . . ."

"Yep."

Walls still writhing, the compartment began to collapse.

"Good call, Alamber. They have definitely lost consensus." She squared her shoulders, accepted a canteen from Tylen, and swept a gaze around the group. "Wardens, we are leaving."

·———◆——— ·

"And in conclusion, Humanity is poised at this very moment to take our rightful place in the galaxy by destroying the plastic." Anthony spread his arms, although for the sake of getting the message to as many as possible as quickly as possible, Sector Central News had agreed to record only audio. Audio packets moved faster through Susumi than visual recordings. No one knew why although there were half a dozen competing theories. "We will take our rightful place by making those responsible for the slaughter of millions of Confederation citizens pay. By ensuring the plastic will never return and try to use us again."

"No proof this is all of the plastic," Dr. Banard muttered. "What happens if you destroy this lot and more shows up wondering what happened to it?"

Anthony checked that Banard's comment hadn't been caught by the microphone and ignored him. "A Human has created a weapon that will destroy the plastic. Human crews are moving even now to do what no other species has been able to do. When you think of this moment, remember that Humans destroyed the threat of the plastic and made the Confederation great again!"

He drew a finger across his throat, and Omondi cut the signal before reporters could begin asking questions. There were no questions to be asked. Humans had taken the first step toward reclaiming their position.

"Fifty kilometers until we're in range, Commander."

Anthony rubbed his hands together as Belcerio responded to Janssen. Fifty kilometers was nothing. They'd have Big Yellow in pieces before Sector Central had time to review his manifesto.

"The *Berganitan* could still stop us," Belcerio told him unnecessarily, crossing the cabin to his side.

As though he'd forgotten about the battleship hanging in space. "I think you'll find the *Berganitan* could have stopped us at any time, but they haven't and they won't. You were military, Commander Belcerio. You saw men and women die because of the plastic. I believe it's long past time to cry enough. The Humans serving on the *Berganitan* support us."

"No way of knowing that." Dr. Banard coughed into his sleeve, leaving a wet patch behind. "You're making assumptions. There's an ass in assumptions."

"Then grant us your wisdom, Doctor. Why haven't they stopped us?"

"Damned if I know. I'm in this shitbox with you."

"The *Berganitan*'s under orders. It's the only possible reason why they haven't gotten involved," Belcerio expanded as Anthony turned to face him.

"From who?"

"Command. In this case, specifically, the Admiral of the Fleet."

"Whose orders come from Department of Defense," Anthony said thoughtfully. "Who take their orders from Parliament. Who, theoretically, get their orders from the people."

"I love a fairy tale," Banard murmured, hands under his chin, fluttering his eyes.

Anthony ignored him. "The Admiral of the Fleet may have given the order, but there was no time for Parliament to weigh in."

"Better to ask for forgiveness than permission?" Belcerio offered.

"Maybe." But Anthony didn't think so. As the CEO of Marteau Industries and a weapon supplier to the military, he'd met the Admiral of the Fleet at any number of government functions during the war. Harlin Borz was a politician first and foremost. He didn't shit without checking to see how emptying his bowels would read in the polls. Who had enough power to convince him to order the *Berganitan* to stay out of the fight?

And why?

"In range in fifteen minutes, Commander." Janssen stretched out his right arm and double-tapped the upper corner of the board. "Bringing the weapon on line."

———◆———

The ship writhed around them as they ran, the Krai keeping their feet, everyone else staggering, thrown from side to side. Tylen crashed into a wall, her arm engulfed to the elbow, then expelled with enough force it threw her off her feet. Craig caught her before she hit the opposite wall and was engulfed again.

"Pheromones for the win." Torin fell to one knee, grabbed Elisk's offered hand, and pulled herself back onto her feet. "With luck, Big Yellow will expel the lot of us to regain consensus."

Yahsamus tucked, rolled, and pulled Zhou through a closing sphincter with her. "And without luck?"

"We die frustrated."

"Not going to happen," Craig told her.

"I don't get a quickie, you don't get a quickie," Werst grunted, tucking his shoulder against Craig's hip and heaving him upright.

"Rank. Privileges."

"Bullshit. Heads up!"

The entire section sagged left, taking most of the next exit with it. Craig bent his head, braced his shoulders against what remained of the upper edge, and heaved.

"Move! Move! Move!" Torin shoved people past him, then scrambled through herself as Yahsamus and Tylen pulled him clear from the other side. They stumbled forward half a dozen steps before the three of them could separate. Craig took a deep breath, pheromone-laced air better than none at all, and turned toward a familiar sound. "Elisk, what the hell are you doing?"

Elisk sprayed a stream of urine against a retreating wall. "Keeping us alive."

Torin's eyes widened. "The dissolved plastic in the latrines. Urea!"

"Not an unlimited amount. Run!"

Craig moved to the back of the pack, grabbed Elisk's vest as he passed, and hauled him along. The wall collapsed behind them and sagged before them.

"Werst! Your turn!"

"Because only Krai piss'll work?"

"Alamber!" The floor rippled underfoot, and Torin banished a memory of learning to waterski. "We need a bigger distraction!"

·—◆—·

"You're about to get one, Boss! Humans First has announced they're about to open fire."

On what?

Fair question, Alamber allowed, this part of space had gotten a little crowded. Pirates. Wardens. Humans First. The three Sector Central ships and all their drones. Only the *Berganitan* had held their original coordinates. "On Big Yellow, according to their manifesto."

Their what?

"That's what Marteau called it. He says they have a weapon that can destroy the plastic."

They cut a piece off, Craig pointed out. *So, yeah.*

They cut a piece off?

"Talk later, Boss, run now. They're . . ."

The Susumi portal klaxon cut him off.

A ship appeared no more than fifty kilometers behind the two ships belonging to Humans First. Alamber knew the design, but this was the first time he'd ever seen a H'san ship in person.

"I'm not registering a Susumi wa . . ."

White light.

And the Humans First ships were gone.

"That was unexpected," Orange observed.

"You think?" Stars swam in and out of focus, and he opened and closed light receptors. "I don't . . . I don't even have the profanity to react to that."

Alamber, talk to me!

"Humans First have been dealt with." The scanners registered a rapidly expanding debris field. Where no piece of the debris read as larger than a centimeter square. How they had been dealt with could be left to a less . . . stressful time. He locked down the board and stood. "Preparing a new distraction. That's your cue, Orange. Go do your thing."

He didn't see Orange move to the airlock, but there they were.

"We will not overcome the majority immediately," they warned.

"You don't have to. No matter what you do, you'll distract the majority so my people can get out."

"There will be even greater internal disruption," Orange told him stepping carefully over the lip and into the airlock.

"Yeah, but the majority will be concentrating on you, not them."

"They will have very little time before the remaining structural integrity collapses."

"Lighten up, for fuksake!" Alamber reached for the controls to close *Promise*'s inner hatch and open the outer. "They'll have a chance!"

At the bottom of the universal lock, Orange turned and looked back, directly into the lens of the security camera. The weird soft light in the flexible tube joining the two ships had increased the definition on their face. "We hope we'll see you again, Warden Alamber di'Cikeys."

"It's a big universe," Alamber said softly. He frowned at the empty tube. Then he smiled. "You used a contraction. Go you."

· —◆— ·

Torin braced herself on Werst's shoulder as Zhou leaned past her, pointed down a long yellow chute, and said, "Hey, is that the airlock?"

She squinted. It didn't help. "Is what the airlock?"

"The darker bit in the middle of the far end." He activated his visor. Like Binti, he preferred to go without, so Torin assumed it was a sniper thing. "Yeah. That's the airlock. And the inner door is open."

"I'd feel better about that if I hadn't closed it behind us," Elisk muttered. "Looks like they want us out."

"Oh, fuk . . . Gunny!" Tylen sounded close to panic.

Pivoting in place, Torin saw the wall behind them close in, moving fast. It hit Yahsamus first, pushed her into Tylen, and kept pushing.

"You said something about it expelling us, Gunny?" Yahsamus threw an arm around Tylen's waist to keep her standing. And probably for comfort, Torin acknowledged. Tayken were better about both giving and receiving than Humans.

You're now the distraction, Alamber told them. *The majority has more important things to worry about and they want you gone. Orange said things would get hinky.*

"Orange?"

"Long story." Craig cut in before Alamber could respond to Torin's question. "Fill you in . . . Son of a fuk!"

Even the Krai lost their footing as their end of the chute rose—two meters, three, four. Fortunately, the far end and the airlock remained a fixed point. Torin grabbed Craig's arm as it rose out of the jumble of arms and legs and weapons. Swore as a KC swung forward and cracked against her shin. Flipped onto her back as they started to move.

And pick up speed.

"Fukker's raised the gravity at the end of the slide," Werst yelled.

"If we hit the airlock at this speed," Yahsamus shouted around a mouthful of Torin's vest, "we're going to break bones."

Using both hands and feet, Elisk squirmed out to the front of the pile. "Werst and I will hit first. We're not as breakable!"

"You're also smaller than . . . Fuk!"

The chute corkscrewed and ended, slamming them into the base of the wall.

Torin's cuff showed no debilitating injuries, so she slid out from under Craig's arm and got to her feet. Then pulled a cold pack from his kit and applied it to his nose, his other hand holding a pad under it to catch the blood. Tylen carefully ran her fingers through her hair, straightening crushed strands, then crawled back two meters to retrieve her helmet. Elisk and Werst were muttering together in a dialect Torin didn't know. When Werst burst into laughter, she ignored them. Craig stared up at her as though he was afraid she'd disappear again if he took his eyes off her. He cradled his right elbow in his left hand, but it wasn't broken, so right now it wasn't important. He recognized her expression, grinned, and mouthed, *kiss it better later*. Technical Sergeant di'Ahaski was also on her feet.

The only exit was a new opening three point seven two meters up.

"That's not good," Craig sighed.

"More pheromones . . ."

"Gods, no," Zhou moaned.

"Let me try something."

"Bennies . . ."

"I know." Torin aimed at the center of the wall. The energy burst sparked blue where it hit, and the center of the wall began to collapse. "Experimental brain charge disrupter," she explained. "Needs a better name. I took a shot before I was engulfed . . ." The pause was barely perceivable. She had no doubt they'd all perceived it. ". . . but I didn't see what happened." She nodded toward the sagging wall. "Nice to know."

The exit was now two point four meters up.

"Krai first," Elisk said as he leapt up onto the sag and then through the hole, instantly disappearing. "I'm back in the chute," he called. "No more than a twenty-degree slope heading for the airlock. Airlock pings at half a klick away." His voice grew fainter. "Gravity at the lock is two percent above Confederation base. Surface is almost friction-less. Can't stop the slide."

"Don't try," Torin told him, knowing he'd catch it on implant if he couldn't hear her. "Werst."

"We'll stand by the airlock to guide the rest of you in."

"You'll get the fuk off Big Yellow." She swept a gaze around the entire team. "This structure could collapse at any time." Collapse. Engulfing them all. Had she not been holding Craig's wrist, her fingers would have been trembling. But she was, so they weren't, and this still wasn't the time for a reaction. "If you can get out, you get out. Understood?"

No one liked it, but everyone nodded.

Understood, Elisk said firmly. Leading by example. Torin would bet her pension he'd wait at the airlock until everyone was out. He'd been that kind of an officer. He'd be that kind of a Warden if they survived this.

"Werst. Up."

"Tylen and I will go last." Yahsamus stepped back. "Once they get us out, they may stop trying to expel the rest of you."

"Good point. Zhou! You're next."

Zhou grabbed the edge and heaved himself through, swearing as his KC caught.

"Craig. I'd rather land on you than you land on me," Torin told him when he hesitated.

For a moment, she thought he was going to argue. Then he leaned in and kissed her before stepping up. "See you on the other side."

Bulkier than Zhou and the Krai, he tipped his right shoulder up to use the extra room the diagonal provided.

"Is that thing getting smaller?"

"Don't even think about it." Teeth gritted, Torin threw herself into a hole in the side of Big Yellow, breathing a sigh of relief when it opened back up to chute dimensions as soon as her feet cleared. Flipping over onto her back, creating as much drag as possible, she watched for the di'Taykan. Tylen first. Then Yahsamus right behind her.

Werst and I are inside Big Yellow's airlock. Outer hatch won't open until the inner hatch closes.

Of course it wouldn't.

The chute tipped, tangling Tylen and Yahsamus together and dumping them both on Torin, keeping her from turning back onto her stomach. With their maskers off, the contact wasn't unwelcome.

Zhou's in.

The chute tipped again.

"Seventy-seven degree angle!" Yahsamus threw open her legs, trying to dig her boots into the side walls, and opening a trench behind them as Big Yellow peeled away from the pressure.

Another trench appeared under Torin's heels. And Tylen's braced hands.

The walls closed in, preventing them from separating.

Tylen tucked her head into the side of Torin's throat, hair tight against her head, helmet lost again. Yahsamus covered them both. Torin wrapped her arms around them as tightly as possible.

"Not how I wanted to get closer to you, Gunny." Eyes dark, Yahsamus grinned.

Torin returned it, closed her eyes, panicked about having them sealed closed, and opened them again. "I hear you, Tech."

"You're fukking heavy, Tech," Tylen complained.

Torin!

"Flatten against the bulkheads! We're coming in hot!"

"Hot." Tylen licked a stripe up Torin's throat and snickered.

Craig's in!

In an impressive demonstration of flexibility, Yahsamus managed to get her helmet off and onto Torin's head. "You'll hit first. You need it more." Then she pushed far enough back to press her face against Torin's stomach.

All three of them could've worked out approximately how fast they were sliding, but too damned fast was all Torin needed to know.

Throw your weight to the right!

"Whose right?"

Torin's right!

They shifted.

Again!

It was almost enough.

FOURTEEN

CRAIG SWORE HE HEARD Torin's collarbone snap like a piece of dry wood as she hit the edge of the airlock. He definitely heard Tylen scream as a hunk of brilliant pink hair was shorn off to flop against the deck, losing color.

Yahsamus rolled over both of the other two, flipped up onto her feet, and began pulling Torin, still holding Tylen into the lock.

"She broke . . ."

"They'll lose their legs if that hatch finishes closing!"

Airlocks didn't close around biological matter, but this was Big Yellow. He grabbed a handful of both vests and yanked as Torin shoved her legs under Tylen's and lifted both sets up.

Tylen's boots banged against the hatch about a meter up as it locked.

"Elisk . . ."

"I know what I'm doing, Gunny." He sounded amused and slammed his palm down on the outer hatch release the moment the light turned green. He'd dealt with NCOs during his military career, and Craig figured that only the military would be crazy enough to be amused while still in the midst of this shitshow.

Using her good arm, Torin levered Tylen up into Craig's grip. He passed her to Yahsamus, who immediately began applying sealant to the weeping stumps of hair.

"Stretcher . . ."

"It's my shoulder. Not my legs." Torin held out her left hand.

Craig took it, but also slid his hand under Torin's side and all but lifted her up onto her feet. Her face had paled, throwing the scattering of freckles on each cheek into sharp relief. He reached out and gently touched her nose with the tip of one finger. "I've been wanting to do that for a while now."

"Ryder!"

He caught the card without really seeing it, only wanting to keep it from hitting Torin.

"Painkillers," Zhou told him. "Human."

"Thank you," Torin ground out through clenched teeth. "Now exit the damned airlock before Big Yellow proves how much of an asshole they are. And that, by the way, is why you wear HE suits into enemy ships."

Craig caught the silent exchange Torin had with Yahsamus, and realized in spite of injury, the two di'Taykan would be leaving last.

"Painful, but not debilitating," Yahsamus told him, her voice gentle enough he wondered about his expression. "Go."

"Gotta love endorphins," Torin murmured as he tucked her good side against him and steered her into the tube connecting the ships. She didn't need his help, they both knew it. She allowed him to help, and that meant more.

Almost to *Promise*, where Alamber had the outer airlock door open, Craig remembered something and gently pushed Torin ahead before he turned, blocking the way.

"Tech, Tylen. No farther until you turn your maskers back on."

"I don't know," Torin snickered behind him. "I'm getting used to living in a state of permanent arousal."

"I'm not. And you have broken bones."

"Bone."

"Close enough."

. —◆— .

Held motionless by the autodoc extensions binding her collarbone together, Torin stared up at Alamber. "A H'san ship blew up Humans First?"

"They popped in close, bathed us all in Susumi radiation, blew them into their component atoms, and popped out again."

"Those fukkers!"

"They saved our lives, Boss." Alamber's eyes were so dark the blue had almost disappeared. "I had scanners on the Humans First ships, and they had weapons on line. Weapons with the weirdest fukking energy signature I've ever seen—like someone ran a Susumi core through a chemical accumulator. And, weird or not, we saw them cut a piece off Big Yellow, so we know the weapons work. They'd have destroyed the plastic and the team, and taken out the *Promise*."

Torin curled a lip. "The H'san saving our lives doesn't negate my earlier observation."

"It's more complicated than that," Craig pointed out from where he sat holding her hand, one ass cheek propped on the edge of the bed. He needed to touch her and she was good with that—not only because the broken bone had kept her from showering before being sprayed with the pheromone neutralizer. "We . . ." He indicated the three of them. ". . . know the H'san have weapons."

"Locked-down weapons," Torin interrupted. "Where the pertinent point is *locked-down* unlike every other species who signed the Confederation accords and destroyed theirs. The H'san made damned sure of that."

"Yeah, that's not all of it." He glanced at Alamber who shook his head. "Orange—you knew them as the data sheet—told Alamber that the plastic had contact with the H'san before Orange got locked up on Threxie."

Torin looked from Craig to Alamber and back again. "And?"

Alamber shrugged his shoulders, a graceless up and down that told her how upset he was under the Warden costume they all wore. "Orange said the plastic learned about war from the H'san."

"And applied what they learned later while the H'san played dumb." She blew out a lungful of air, anger a blaze of heat at the heart of her. "Go debrief the others. Everyone has the same information before we attach to the *Berganitan*."

"Torin." Craig lifted her hand to his mouth and pressed a kiss against the back, whiskers sharp pricks of sensation against the knuckles.

Not hard to know what he was asking. "Still repressing," she said, with half a smile. "First we deal with the big picture; I'll fall apart later." The beige walls behind the autodoc were too close to yellow. When they got back to Berbar, she'd talk to Craig about repainting. "I have to center myself before we start dealing with this . . ." Was there a word that covered sentient plastic having an identity crisis, a species that had forsworn violence millennia ago destroying ships and all on board, deputized Silsviss, the probable end of a potential revolution, and pirates?

"We've been using shitstorm," Alamber offered, answering her silent question.

"Shitstorm's good," Torin allowed.

He shifted his weight, his hair flicking in counterpoint to the movement. "I would have come for you . . ."

"I know. But someone with a functioning brain had to be left at the controls." She beckoned him over with her good hand, then shoved him into Craig's arms, saying, "Hug him for me, would you." The hug released the last of the tension between them—she wasn't blind, and she'd been repairing emotional damage on and off the battlefield for years. "Now, go. Both of you. Bring the rest of the team up to speed."

Since becoming a Warden, Torin had accumulated some Dornagain profanity. Once alone, the autodoc humming as it made repairs, she ran through it twice.

Big Yellow had disappeared twelve minutes and twenty three seconds after *Promise* had detached.

"Disappeared?"

Werst surrendered the auxiliary controls to Torin, bumping his shoulder against her hip during the exchange. "Given what we know now, it likely slipped into Susumi space, so I'm good with disappeared."

"Hey, don't forget the turning into half a dozen surreal shapes first." Zhou had taken up Alamber's habit of perching on the back of a chair, his feet on the seat. "One after the other, weird, weirder, weirdest, then . . ." He held his fingers up to his mouth and blew them open. "Gone."

"Can't say that I'll miss them," Torin admitted, rubbing her thumb over the worn dent on the edge of the control board. Even with the break repaired, the whole upper right side of her body ached.

"You think they'll be back?" Elisk asked.

Craig answered before she could. "Yeah, they'll be back. But next time, they'll have changed."

She almost asked *into what* before she realized what he meant.

❖   ❖   ❖

Reattachment to the *Berganitan* involved only the docking computer—no word from the docking master, no word from the OIC.

"You think they're ignoring us?" Craig asked as he checked the stats on each individual band.

Torin shrugged, just to prove she could. "I think they have a brig full of pirates, three attached ships, half a dozen paroled Silsviss, and a pissed-off Dornagain. They've got a lot going on."

"Captain Carveg requests the crew of the Promise *make their way to the* Berganitan.*"*

"Or not." She raised her voice. "ASTL Warden Kerr would like to know where on the *Berganitan*. It's a big boat." After two full minutes of silence, she shrugged again. "Probably shouldn't have said boat."

The docking arm exited into a secure compartment painted a sterile and neutral white.

"Identify yourselves and state your business on board the CS Berganitan.*"*

Torin assumed the hatch on the far bulkhead—the one that led into the ship—was locked. She also assumed boarding party protocols either hadn't been shut down at the end of the war or had recently been reinstated. BPPs were usually fatal. "Crew of the *Promise*, here on the captain's invitation."

"Registering implants."

"No reason for that," Yahsamus muttered as all eight implants buzzed. Tylen and Zhou, who hadn't had theirs for a full ten/ten, visibly twitched.

The sound of bolts slamming back probably would've echoed had the room been emptied. With eight Wardens filling the space, the slam became a muffled thud.

"Proceed to the far hatch and exit."

"Not a BPP instruction," Werst growled.

"First time you've entered a Naval vessel from the docking arm rather than the Marine compartment?" Elisk asked.

"Yes, but . . ."

Craig tucked up against Torin's left side, close enough she could feel the air warm between them. "I think Elisk is trying to say we're not going to die here."

Captain Carveg waited on the other side of the hatch.

"Ma'am."

"Kerr." She indicated Torin should keep moving and matched her stride. Torin immediately shortened it. The rest of the team fell in behind them. "I thought I'd walk you to the briefing room. Don't want you lot getting lost."

"We'd rather not *be* lost, ma'am."

"Good."

The interiors of battlecruisers were designed to confuse boarders and the shortest distance between two points wasn't. That said, the path Captain Carveg took seemed unusually random. When they reached a ten-meter passageway with no bulkhead hatches, the captain said, "Our orders were to remain stationary, to not engage. Observe only. Mop up when it was over."

A valid explanation for the *Berganitan's* lack of involvement. And yet . . .

"You're sure the orders came from Command?"

"I'm sure."

"And who gave Command their orders?"

"This order? The timing says this order was Command all the way to the bottom. We got a return packet almost immediately after sending them the new information about the data sheet. They had no time for consultation with the Ministry."

Torin made a noncommittal sound. There might not have been time for consultation, but there was always time for a strongly worded suggestion from the people in power. There was a H'san at every Parliament. "The data sheet says the plastic was in contact with the H'san pre-Confederation. They took what they learned about war from the H'san and applied it as part of their social experiment."

"That doesn't make the H'san responsible for the war. There's a very good chance modern H'san have no idea their ancestors were ever in contact with the plastic."

"No H'san died during the war."

"The H'san don't . . ." Captain Carveg huffed out a breath. "Except, apparently, the H'san do. You know about the ship?"

"I do."

"I have no idea what's up with that, but I do know the H'san didn't fight in the war."

"Neither did Katrien or Niln or Dornagain or Rakva, and yet

members of those species all died. There were no H'san on any of the stations or planets or ships that were attacked. There were no H'san involved in the early fatal attempts at diplomacy."

"And you know this how?"

"The *Promise* has extensive historical data stored."

"Clearly."

"Only the *Berganitan* could have stopped the H'san warship. The only way to prevent that was to remove the *Berganitan* from the equation."

Captain Carveg's teeth snapped together. "There's no H'san conspiracy, Gunny."

"But there's H'san saying *we know best*. And H'san saying *do as we say, not what we do*." Captain Carveg had seen only one warship. She had no idea of the weapons the H'san had stored. "And H'san saying *for your own good*."

"They're the H'san." The captain reached to open the hatch at the end of the passageway. "Keep your eye on Command, Gunny. They sent the order."

Ressk and Werst sat three rows up, foreheads together, nostril ridges open, breathing each other's air. In a corner of the briefing room, A Lie is a Bad Defense boomed out a description of how Ozborz had flown after the pirates, heavy, curved claws clacking together as she waved long arms, Craig and Alamber shifting position when necessary. Beside her, Ozborz ducked and laughed. The other five Silsviss, who were old campaigners, watched indulgently. Or possibly hungrily.

"So, engulfed by Big Yellow." Binti pressed close along Torin's left side. "Have the screaming heebee jeebies yet?"

"I'm repressing until I have more time. Screaming heebee jeebies?"

Binti grinned. "Hollice."

"Of course." She looked across the room at Ret Tyroliz. Hollice had survived the attack on Silsviss and died with the rest of Sh'quo Company. And that reminded her.

"Do you want me to go with you?" Binti glanced down, and Torin realized her hand had closed around the cylinder that held Lorkin's remains.

"Thanks, but no."

"You know where I am if you need me."

She did.

Elisk stared down at the cylinder as though he'd never seen one before. He'd been Navy, not Corps, so maybe he hadn't. Had never carried one, two, eight off a battlefield. He knew what had happened on the station above Silsviss because Nicholin had told him. Told him why Lorkin hadn't returned on the *Baylet*. Although Elisk had been on the team who'd gone onto Big Yellow for her, although Torin had been on the *Promise* with him, she hadn't mentioned the loss. He hadn't asked, but that wasn't the point. She'd seen Lorkin as her loss, not as U'yun's loss, or even the Justice Department's loss.

Seemed her therapist was right. It was past time for her to stop carrying the dead.

"He lived well." Elisk closed his fingers. "*Keer senhar see jurorik ah ron dye kraiteen.*"

"And the tree will grow strong." When Elisk's eyes widened, Torin smiled and nodded toward Ressk and Werst. "I spend a lot of time with those two."

Elisk smiled back at her. Lips curved, teeth covered. "Sympathies."

"Thanks." She turned to go, to leave him to grieve with his team, with Lorkin's team.

"Gunny." He reached out and touched her wrist, as though one of them had been di'Taykan. "Does it get any easier?"

She didn't know him well enough to know what he wanted to hear, so she told the truth. "Yes. It does. Unfortunately." This time when she turned, he let her go.

A double ping from her implant raised a brow in Craig's direction. *Look who just came in.*

His expression was so completely neutral, Torin had no idea what to expect when she turned.

General Morris stood just inside the hatch, glaring around the room; the glare likely habit as much as mood. He focused on her as she crossed toward him, eyes narrowing.

"I'm sorry for your loss, General."

"Damned pirates!" His lip curled. "That was a prototype weapon they blew. There's nothing left of it. Nothing. We'll have to rebuild from scratch."

She waited. But it seemed that was all he had to say. "And the squad of Marines who died?"

"The Marines? The Mu'tuv? They knew the risk. They like the risk. Adrenaline junkies, the whole lot of them. Good Marines, though. The best. Now . . ." He came down hard on the word, making it an order. Now. Not later. "I need to know everything that piece of orange plastic said to your di'Taykan."

Her hands curled into fists. "To Warden di'Cikeys?"

"Yes, to Warden di'Cikeys," he snapped impatiently.

She showed teeth. "We'll see that you get a copy of the final report."

"That's not . . ."

"We need to begin debriefing." He stepped back as she stepped forward, holding his gaze. "You'll have to leave."

When he found himself in the passageway outside the conference room, he stopped, cheeks purpling, and leaned toward her. "You can't . . ."

"Justice Department business, General." Torin shut the hatch in his face.

She hadn't heard Craig arrive to take his position behind her left shoulder, but she wasn't surprised to find him there.

"You okay?"

"Why wouldn't I be?" she asked as they walked together to the front of the room.

Craig shrugged. "You and Morris, you two have history. I was surprised you didn't punch him this time."

Torin was surprised she hadn't wanted to. "I punched him in the pride."

"Ow. Is that going to cause trouble later?"

"He was part of the designing and building of a new weapon."

"So?" He turned to face her.

"Parliament wouldn't approve new weapons while we were at war." She spread her hands. "No chance they approved one after the war ended. General Morris is going to need to keep a low profile for a while."

"So . . . the military was acting alone? Building the weapon?"

"They're also faking skirmishes with the Primacy."

Craig's brows drew in and he folded his arms. "You know, I don't think I like the military acting without oversight."

"You're not alone." Two fingers in her mouth, she whistled. Three Silsviss throat pouches swelled in response. "Listen up, people. We're not going into Susumi until we've sent a full debrief of this multilayered shitstorm back to Commander Ng, so let's get started."

"The agreement between the Silsviss and the Confederation has been signed. It was the only way the Confederation diplomats could keep Cyr Tyroliz and his people alive," Commander Ng expanded when both Torin's brows rose. "The governing council offered us their deaths."

"The diplomats couldn't say thanks, but no thanks?"

"The deaths were nonnegotiable. But, as members of the Confederation, a crime against the Confederation is dealt with by Confederation law and they can go into rehabilitation."

"So we got their lives instead?"

"After their rehabilitation, we may have to hire them. The council doesn't want them back."

"Not because they attacked the station, but because they failed."

The commander paused, hand frozen in the midst of flipping files. "How did you . . . ?"

"I have a skull on my wall," Torin reminded him.

"Yes, I'm sure that makes you an expert." Commander Ng returned at least half of his attention to his desktop where cascades of files were stacked six- or seven-deep over the entire surface. "Cyr Tyroliz has already contributed genetic matter to a clutch and none of the others are breeders. I doubt they'll set any records finishing rehab, so there'll be time to work something out."

"Something?"

"Something for them to do, Kerr. Pay attention."

"Yes, sir." A new Strike Team on the old budget. She could work with that. "I'll get right on it."

"Not your job. di'Rearl Stedrin will be here in a tenday. He can develop a proposal when he arrives." He opened a new file. "A Lie is a Bad Defense has expressed interest in becoming a pilot. And chasing pirates. I assume the latter will wear off and the former means a refit of one of the control rooms on a C&C ship. Do you have any idea how much that costs? While you were gone, two young di'Taykan led Strike Team Delta to the Humans First base developed and equipped by Anthony Marteau. Between the loss of all three cruisers and the records we found in the base, we're down to rounding up stragglers. Humans First is not a viable movement . . ." He paused. Frowned. ". . . rebellion any longer."

"So, about two of those ships." When the commander waited silently for her to continue, Torin smiled. "Are we not going to address the H'san in the room?"

"They saved your life."

"Not the point."

He locked his gaze on her face, his own expression unreadable. "The Humans on those ships were truly despicable people and the universe is better without them."

"Not arguing but again, not the point. The H'san, after ensuring that all member species of the Confederation destroyed their means to make war have a hidden arsenal."

"Yes, I read your heavily redacted report."

"It was a military intelligence mission, sir." The odds were very high that Marteau had been the money behind the expedition to find the H'san weapons. As MI's concern about how Parliament would vote on the Younger Races bill was still valid, Torin felt justified in leaving out some of the less immediately pertinent background information. She also had little doubt that information would eventually need to be addressed.

"Military intelligence," Ng repeated so neutrally Torin couldn't miss the sarcasm.

"Given their involvement, I believe it was the H'san who instructed Command to immobilize the *Berganitan*."

"Conspiracy theory, Kerr. We need evidence. Do better."

A muscle jumped in her jaw. "They killed the crews of those ships."

"Your word against theirs."

"My word?" She got to her feet, unable to remain still. "What are we, twelve? Sector Central News was there!"

"Yes." He pulled up a new file. "Unfortunately, in a freak simultaneous accident, both the entry and exit Susumi buoys put in place by Sector Central to transmit the story as it happened, were damaged. Everything was lost."

"A freak accident?"

"An energy burst."

Torin paced to the hatch, paced back, and fell into parade rest, hands crossed behind her back, the familiar posture bringing a cold calm. "The source of this energy burst?"

"Unable to be determined. Thus, *freak.*"

"Backups on the news ships?" Because Sector Central would have backups.

"Lost."

"Another freak energy burst?"

The commander made a noncommittal noise then added dryly, "They were fortunate it didn't affect navigation."

"And we in the Justice Department don't find the destruction of this data even a little suspicious?"

He sighed, the sound weary as much as exasperated. "Did you see the ships destroyed, Warden Kerr?"

She hadn't. "My team and I were attempting to exit Big Yellow at the time. But Alamber saw it."

"Is he positive it was the H'san and not the plastic imitating an ancient H'san warship?"

Torin blinked. "Sir?"

Commander Ng leaned away from his desk, cracking his back. "Would it not make significantly more sense for the plastic to destroy Humans First to protect itself?" he asked.

"That's the official opinion of the Minister of Justice?"

Torin had made it a question; she hadn't needed to, but the commander answered anyway. "It is. The *Baylet* and the *Blue Robinasit* were on the other side of the *Berganitan* at the time, unloading prisoners."

"The reporters . . ."

"The reporters won't speak on the record without evidence to support their statements."

Evidence that no longer existed. "Then how are we explaining the missing Humans First ships?"

He spread his hands. "Explaining to who?"

Craig fell into step beside her outside the commander's office. "Well?"

"The official decision is plastic pretending to be H'san."

"It's possible."

"Craig . . ."

"I'm not saying that's what happened, Torin, but you have to admit it's possible. We know there's sects within the plastic and we have no idea how many of the little fukkers there actually are."

"You sound like a Warden."

"Apparently, it's my job."

"I don't believe it's the plastic."

"Evidence."

"I know." She didn't ask him what he believed, took a deep breath, and reminded herself that punching the bulkhead would hurt her more than the bulkhead.

Alamber was waiting for them when they crossed into the Strike Teams' personal territory. "Boss, can I talk to you?"

She felt Craig tense beside her, wondered why Alamber hadn't waited for them in their quarters, and said, "Always."

"I want to go do some actual training and then come back and work in the forensic arm." It all came out in one breath.

Torin suspected that if he'd paused, he couldn't have begun again. She wrapped an arm around his waist and tucked him up against her side, feeling him relax with the contact. "Is that something you can do? Not questioning your intelligence," she added quickly, "but your background education is unique."

"I may have to fill in a few holes, but the science team has said they'll help set things up."

"And then you'll come back? Here?" She tried to make it sound like it mattered to her, but not more than it mattered to him. She'd watched hundreds of young Marines leave her care over the years and never felt like this.

"I'll come back to forensics."

"Because that's where the smart people are, and you're one of the smartest people I know."

His hair brushed against her cheek. "You're not angry?"

"Because you're leaving the Strike Team?" She tightened her grip. "I'd be . . . not angry, but upset if you stayed when you didn't want to. And you'll be back."

"To forensics."

"I guess I'll have to remember where that is, then."

She heard Craig take a deep breath on her other side and wondered what he'd braced himself to say.

"Alamber, are you pissed because I left you on the *Promise*?"

Alamber pulled away from her hold far enough to throw up both arms. "For fuksake, Craig, not everything is about your ship. I need . . ." He paused and instead of the expected innuendo said, "I need to find answers."

"To what?" Torin asked.

His hair flipped up. "Don't know, Boss. Don't know the questions yet." His eyes darkened as he stepped away and looked from Torin to Craig. "Still family?"

Craig dragged him into his arms. "Dumbass."

"Always family," Torin told him. Frowned. "Alamber, you said you knew Humans First had weapons armed because you had them on long-range scanners. Did you keep the scanners on after the H'san warship appeared?"

"Sure." His eyes darkened as he searched her face. "It happened so fast I didn't have time to shut them down. Why?"

She smiled. "I have some science things for you to do."

"Science things?" Craig asked, brows up.

"Science things. Shut up."

Alamber laughed.

"The Strike Teams were formed to deal with violent threat." Commander Ng threw a hard-light version of the warrant she'd drawn up over his desk. "Are you expecting this to turn violent?"

"No, sir. But I want to make the arrest."

"For personal reasons?"

"For social reasons."

"Social reasons?" Before Torin could elaborate, his lips curled into an edged smile. "All right, then." He stared at the warrant for a moment longer then flicked it back down into the file. "This is going to change things."

"If we're lucky."

"And if we're not? This is a tipping point, Warden Kerr, but we have no idea which way things will tip. What are you planning to do if things tip the wrong way?"

The H'san had a planet of hidden weapons.

And a H'san in every Parliament.

The military had been operating independent of Parliamentary oversight.

And in cooperation with the Primacy.

"Same thing I've always done, sir."

His answering smile came with different edges. "Good."

"Strike Team Leader ex-Gunnery Sergeant Warden Kerr, this are being a surprise." Presit held a piece of fruit speared on a fluted skewer. "As you are having paid for a Susumi boost on what are being a government pittance which are truly needing to be improved, I are expecting it are not being a social call. What are you wanting?"

Torin was up at 0200 Berbar time to catch Presit before she left home for the day. She wasn't in the mood for politicking, but she reminded herself that the Katrien was a friend, of sorts, and kept her voice level. "I want you to cover one more story. For old times' sake."

"I are having an election in three tendays, Warden." Presit waved the piece of fruit. "I are needing more information than that."

"It'll be worth it."

"In your opinion."

"Wasn't it always worth it before?"

Presit combed blue enameled claws through her whiskers, right side, then left.

Torin smiled. "Bring a camera."

Presit was too much of a professional to say anything when she recognized where they were going, but the nameless camera operator whistled softly.

The H'san embassy was large, a given considering the size of the H'san, and unattractive, which was a bit of a surprise. Their ancient tombs had an aesthetic that the rectangular, three-story concrete building was entirely lacking. If there were windows, they were hidden. The piece of Mik'tok art over the entrance was the only color Torin could see. It was possible they'd designed the building so as not to clash with this treasured piece of art, but she doubted it. Although to be fair, if a H'san told her the sky was blue, she'd look up to check.

The approach to the embassy was unguarded, but then why

wouldn't it be? They were on Har'p, in the Core, where the presence of more than a single H'san was required.

"Begin now," Presit ordered.

The camera operator lifted his camera to his shoulder. Complying with the law that kept citizens from being recorded without their knowledge, news cameras were ridiculously bulky, covered in station insignia and topped by a trio of lights illuminated in frequencies covering all potential ocular abilities. There was space enough inside the casing that one of Presit's previous operators had told Torin he used it as luggage. This particular camera case had been hardened to exclude any and all types of outside interference. Sector Central News hadn't been pleased about the loss of their data.

The dark gray double doors opened as they approached.

The H'san, standing three meters back from the entrance in a cavernous two-story space, extended their neck. "Why have you brought the press, Warden Kerr?"

"As a member of the Justice Department and, therefore, the government of the Confederation, I have a right to full disclosure." On her left, Presit snorted softly. That wasn't the way the law was usually interpreted, but it could be. Torin looked the H'san in the eyes and waited.

Commander Ng had vetoed her first response. Apparently *Because I think your entire species are manipulative bags of shit and I want an independent record* wasn't up to the standards of the Justice Department. *"We don't know that it's the entire species,"* the commander had reminded her.

After a long, silent moment, the H'san pivoted around their rear leg. "Follow."

The chamber they were led to opened off the right-hand wall. The lack of doors made it more an alcove than a room, and the absence of anything in it, except another H'san, indicated it had always been intended for uncomfortable meetings with inferior species. The second H'san took up most of the free space in the room, but Torin not only worked with Dornagain but had never been intimidated by size in her life.

She swallowed and reminded herself to roll the Rs and cough the hard consonants. "Clab'insto Arekog of Terabookog."

Head resting on their shoulders, they blinked. By H'san standards, they were young. They'd probably never heard one of the Younger Races say their name. "Yes."

"You have been identified as being in command of the H'san ship at . . ." Torin listed the coordinates and the Confederation standard date and time, clearly and precisely and loudly enough there could be no ambiguity about the recording.

The H'san blinked again, but as she hadn't asked them a question, remained silent.

"The long-range scanner on the *Promise* was aimed at the Humans First ships when they were destroyed. When they were no longer in the way, it automatically adjusted its aim and scanned the next nearest ship. Your ship. Where it registered H'san DNA. Where it registered your DNA, as well as that of another three H'san. This is how you were identified."

The H'san raised their head a few centimeters, two eyes on Torin. "Long-range scanners do not register DNA."

Torin had no idea why the lack of contractions annoyed her so much, but she had to admit that, however stilted, it was an improvement on the stylized diplomatic speech used by the H'san she'd had met previously. "The long-range scanners used by Civilian Salvage Operators register DNA. CSOs have returned, and continue to return, the remains of Marines and Naval personnel missing in action to their families. The *Promise*, as an independently owned vessel, has CSO scanners installed."

"May I be making the assumption that the Justice Department are going to be making these scanners a part of their standard equipment, Strike Team Leader Warden Kerr?"

"That is correct, Presit a Tur durValintrisy." Torin squared her shoulders and took a step forward. "Clab'insto Arekog of Terabookog, you are under arrest for the murders of Anthony Marteau, Robert Banard, Luiz Belceno, and thirty-seven others. Torin had wanted to list them all but had been advised not to extend the arrest. The names would all be listed in court.

Their head rose and kept rising. At full extension their eye-line was a good fifteen centimeters over Torin's head, and all eyes were searching the open area behind her. "I was just following orders!"

"Given by who?"

They scrambled back until they hit the rear wall, but didn't answer.

Adjusting for species specifics, they looked startled. Like they couldn't believe this was actually happening—although Torin allowed she might have been projecting a little.

When the Justice Department had briefed the H'san government, they'd said nothing about an arrest. Commander Ng had pointed out that if the H'san hadn't realized the consequences of their actions when the H'san had been instrumental in creating most of the laws the Confederation operated under, it wasn't the Justice Department's problem.

"We have a vehicle waiting to take you to the port where you will board a Justice Department vessel and be taken to Berbar Station for questioning."

There were closer Justice stations, but this was Torin's arrest.

She glanced at her cuff. Finds Truth Through Inquiry and the skimmer they'd acquired from the port authorities had arrived out front four minutes and sixteen seconds ago.

As Torin indicated the H'san should precede her out of the room, they focused on Presit and repeated, "I was just following orders!"

Presit waved the repetition off with a dismissive flick of one small hand. "You are clearly not having paid attention during the war we are just having fought."

For the first time in a while, all of the Strike Teams were on the station and the sound levels in Musselman's had reached new levels as stories were traded, and both likely and unlikely exploits were greeted with catcalls and variations on, *"well, if you think that's something . . ."* Dominating one corner both with size and enthusiasm, Lie described the maneuvers Ozborz had made while chasing down the last of the pirates, her listeners keeping one eye on her waving arms lest they be swept away. Over by the bar, Alamber and a couple of the forensic team, including the smallest Niln Torin had ever seen, were arguing with as much passion, but fewer dangerous gestures. She'd head over later and have Alamber make introductions. If these were the people he planned to spend time with, she needed to do background checks.

Binti and Nicholin were playing darts, Binti throwing with her non-dominant hand. Over by the bulkhead, Werst and Ressk played a viciously competitive game of kiir, but Torin knew they were holding feet under the table.

The bar also held two Dornagain from Delta's C&C, three Niln, and a young Rakva who'd just joined R&D, the state of her feathers suggesting she was in Strike Team territory on a dare. But she was there. The definition of team seemed to be expanding, and that could only be a good thing.

"Of course they didn't wipe the *Baylet's* scanners," Marie Bilodeau pointed from the other side of the big round table. "Why would they? Standard long-range doesn't record molecular detail."

"And you were on the other side of the *Berganitan* at the time," Zhou reminded her.

"And we were on the other side of the *Berganitan* at the time," Marie repeated, rolling her eyes.

"To CSO scanners." Craig lifted his beer in salute.

Marie sighed, and glasses rose around the table. "We're all going into refit, aren't we?"

Craig grinned, "Not all of us."

"All of us, hotshot. You agreed to have weapons installed."

Leaving the pilots to it, Torin returned to her conversation with Ranjit and Elisk. They needed to work out a nondisruptive way to mix the teams. Yahsamus could have cracked the pirates' signal had either Craig or Elisk thought of U'yun as teammates rather than armed passengers.

"No more than one position at a time," Ranjit insisted. "We want to give team dynamics more flexibility, not break them apart."

"No point in throwing the *ganit* out with the cooking water," Elisk agreed.

Torin nodded. "We need to draw up a scheduled rotation."

"While things are quiet." Elisk's nostril ridges shut as the other two turned toward him. "Shit. Just jinxed it."

The big screen at the end of the bar was showing another Parliamentary reaction to the H'san arrest, the Trun reporter trying to tie it to the upcoming vote on the status of the Younger Races.

"What?" Ranjit demanded when Torin rolled her eyes.

"It's all hot air and saving face, Cap. Everyone's talking about the H'san. No one gives a shit about the Younger Races right now."

Ranjit nodded. "Things are changing."

"And the Elder Races don't change quickly or willingly. They'll need us."

"Think they'll realize that?"

"I don't think she'll let them forget." Torin nodded at the screen where Presit had joined the Trun reporter.

". . . being in an uproar. Members are demanding answers and there are no answers being forthcoming. You are being aware that every Parliament are having at least one H'san?"

The Trun's ears flattened. "Yes, Candidate, but . . ."

"And you are being aware that while many of them are having left, some are not having been able to?"

Zir tail lashed. "I was not aware of that, no. But . . ."

"We, and when I say we, I are meaning the entire Confederation, are having the right to know what these young H'san have been learning when they are being placed in Parliaments. They tell us they are learning what it is to be H'san." She turned to face the camera, and slipped her mirrored glasses far enough down her muzzle she could peer over their top edge directly into the lens. "I are saying that, at the very least, the presence of a H'san warship means we should be asking just what a H'san is."

"The H'san sing . . ."

"Yes, they are singing to the dawn. They are smelling pleasant. They are liking cheese. We are all knowing that. The question are being . . ." Her lip curled. ". . . what else are they doing?"

Someone with their hand on a switch recognized an exit line and a commercial for cross-species supplements filled the screen . . .

. . . for the two seconds it took Paul to change the channel to a hockey game.

"Was it just me or was that more coherent than Presit usually is?" Ranjit threw a handful of peanuts into her mouth.

"Wasn't just you," Elisk admitted. "I almost wish I could vote for her."

Torin raised a brow. "Almost?"

His nostril ridges half closed. "I've read your mission reports, Gunny." And opened again. "Rumor has it there's a delegation of H'san arriving in the next couple of days to talk to your prisoner."

"Not my prisoner, not anymore. I handed them over to rehab." She really hoped *talk to* wasn't a euphemism for *attempt to remove from custody*. If it was, the H'san would learn that times were changing and cheese-flavored variations on *because I said so* weren't going to cut it anymore—not with the other species of the Confederation, and not, she suspected with their own young, suddenly forced to face suspicion in place of awe.

"So while change sweeps through the Confederation, building a bright new future with an exciting potential for new ideas and social harmony, I expect we'll spend the next few years rounding up the deluded remnants of Humans First." Ranjit sighed and finished her drink. "Bad ideas never die. But with Marteau gone, they've lost their funding so at least they should be easier to find."

"Think there could be a Krai First out there," Elisk asked, scratching his left wrist with his right foot, "but no one's heard of it because we're just better at it?"

Torin lifted her beer in salute. "Hard to believe you'd be worse." She frowned.

"Gunny?"

"One of those deluded remnants we'll be hunting is the ex-Navy cook who shot me."

"So the search is personal." Elisk nodded. "Good to know."

Ranjit snickered. "Gunnery Sergeant Torin Kerr shot by a cook. You're lucky Presit wasn't there."

Later, when Ranjit and Marie were arguing Marine vs Navy about the botched extraction from Intain Three during the early years of the war, and Elisk had gone to the bar for another bowl of *hujin* chips, Craig slid his chair closer and stretched his arm behind Torin's shoulders.

"Going to take the time to fall apart now?"

She shrugged and pushed back against his solid warmth. "I've moved past it. Besides, you rescued me."

"I did, didn't I?" He grinned, finished the last two centimeters of beer in his glass, and asked, "What happened to your 'punch a H'san' plan? You had the chance and didn't take it."

She finished her own beer while she thought about it. She hadn't punched General Morris either in spite of the freedom being an ex-gunnery sergeant gave her. Ah hell, who was she kidding? There was no such thing as an ex-gunnery sergeant. She shrugged again. "Maybe I've grown as a person."

Craig's arm tightened as though he'd heard what she hadn't said.

Riding the encouragement from multiple mouths, Binti jumped up onto a chair and raised her glass, waited until silence fell, and called out, "To the dead!"

"There's nothing honorable about dying!" The roar filled every corner, every nook and cranny of the bar. Had the hatch been open, it would've spread out into the station and filled that as well. Torin couldn't stop herself from laughing at the expressions on the faces of those who'd never served. They didn't need to declare they'd never forget the fallen; that was both a given and for solemn vows by graves and at memorials. Civilians had a tendency to fetishize military dead without ever considering how and why they died. Nights like this were for acknowledging the ultimate futility of war, because no one knew that better than those who'd fought.

When the bar finally silenced again, Lies, swaying slightly, rose to her full height and yelled, "To the living!"

This time, Torin laughed at the variety of responses. She stood, raised her glass, and added one more. "Let's try and keep them that way!"

APPENDIX

THE CHARACTERS OF *THE PRIVILEGE OF PEACE*

Wardens

Strike Team Commander Lanh Ng   Human

Strike Team Alpha

Torin Kerr	Human
Craig Ryder	Human
Binti Mashona	Human
Werst	Krai
Ressk	Krai
di'Crikeys Alamber	di'Taykan

Strike Team U'yun

di'Ahaski Yahsamus (Tech)	di'Taykan
Marie Bilodeau	Human
di'Burlut Nicholin	di'Taykan
Harris Zhou	Human
Elisk (LT)	Krai
di'Numanja Tylen	di'Taykan
Lorkin	Krai

Strike Team Ch'ore (partial list)

Ranjit Kaur (Cap)	Human
di'Hajak Sirin	di'Taykan
Orrnis	Krai
Aszur	Krai

Strike Team T'Jaam (partial list)

Doug Collins	Human
di'Tagawa Gamar	di'Taykan

Strike Team Beta (partial list)

Porrtir (pilot)	Krai

Dornagain

Finds Truth Through Inquiry
A Lie is a Bad Defense
Tell Me Again Until I Believe You

Support

Dr. Deyell, R&D	Rakva
Paul Musselman, bar owner	Human
Myril, forensics	Katrien
di'Nakamot Bishami, forensics	di'Taykan
Dr. Collins, medical	Human
Dr. Tyrub, medical	Slaink
Sergeant Urrest, armory	Krai
Nalvon, armory	di'Taykan
Taylor, legal	Human
Dr. Finz, tank specialists	Rakva
Watches Over, internal affairs	Dornagain

✿   ✿   ✿

Marines

General Morris	Human
Lieutenant Jonnez	Krai
Sergeant Britt Zelinski	Human
PFC di'Valing Noshikin	di'Taykan
Captain di'Rearl Stedrin	di'Taykan (mentioned)
Staff Sergeant Beyhan	di'Taykan (mentioned)
Corporal Hollice	Human (mentioned)

On the Berganitan

Captain Carveg	Krai
Chief Warrant Officer di'Palik	di'Taykan
Commander Kahananui	Human
Lieutenant di'Paliic	di'Taykan

✦ ✦ ✦

Civilians

Presit a Tur durValinstrisy, reporter, candidate	Katrien
Representative Hurring, Justice Minister	Trun
Dr. Lushin, linguist	Trun
SciRe Vin'tic, astrophysicist	Mictok
Girstin, intern Sector Central News	Krai
Chief Justice Genesvah	Niln
Cothi Hurexical, mine supervisor	Niln
di'Murrin Keezo, Docking Master	di'Taykan
Lyrentias, political aide	Niln
Lakshinz, political aide	Niln

On Seven Sta

Lieutenant Maaren, Planetary Law Enforcement	Human
Marilissa Kotas, ex-Navy cook	Human

Silsviss

Cyr (Ret) Tyroliz, ex-Warlord
Ser Ozborz, pilot

Humans First

Anthony Justin Marteau, ex CEO Marteau Industries
Commander Luiz Belcerio, ranking officer
Fredrick Solomon, ex-yeoman
Marie Neems, ex-private
Tara Kalowski, ex-Navy armaments officer
Madeline Laghari, ex-Marine explosives tech
Mini Paddison, station resources Berbar
Boomer MacVale, communications tech
Dr. Anika Shote, xeno-anthropologist
Olaf Janssen, helm
Kari Omondi

Dr. Robert Banard

Clab'insto Arekog of Terabookog   H'san